Friends, Accepting the Changes

Eileen M Shinners 2015

About the Author

Spain is where Eileen has made her home since the death of her son Brendon. Spain has given her the healing she needed and the peace inside with her grief. Working as a Consultant/Mentor and spiritually feeling that Spain has been the place she has found the energy to shine.

Her work as a Psychic Medium, Inspirational Motivational Empowerment Speaker/Teacher and the Author that she is now and succeeding in her goal of published books. Writing is her passion and her writing has now opened up for the world to see. Living the life she loves, by the sea with the mountains in view trying to find the peace in her heart.

The roads we all have to travel, to the life's purpose of our journey. Eileen's own journey has been full of learning, to that greater understanding of life. Having started her journey in Germany where she was born, living her childhood in England and a mixture of passports to be had, marrying twice with both ending in divorce.

Learning how to live her life on her own just to create that much needed security in herself and in her own love. In the past thirteen years Spain has figured twice Eileen's life where roots are concerned, now wishing to create the roots and the much needed stability in her life, even if it means that she will again move to create that stability. Eileen is on the move again and this time it's back to England.

Losing her eldest son Brendon has given Eileen the peace and freedom to pursue her life he is now at peace with his own freedom of death. So life has had its hardships but it also has its celebrations. This book makes Eileen's third to be published. Ambiance 100 Poems. Friends, The Journey, New Beginnings & Endings.

Looking forward to many more books to be written and in pursuit of bringing her children's books to be published sometime in 2015 and a move to where the universe wants her to be, her destiny, her life and her love.

There are also two children's books published. Arthur & Horace; The Magic Begins. & Arthur & Horace; Natures Magic.

Friends, Accepting the Changes

Grief

In Grief I came,

In Grief I stayed.

The Sun, the Rain,

The Sparkling wine, I played.

I worked my days so to be,

Writing, my life, I am now free.

My Son has passed and acceptance I find,

So now to leave this world behind.

Home to my family, then Italy for me,

I am now successful in all I need to be.

Exploring yet another new place.

My heart now mended, it's in my eyes,

Look always a smile on my face…

Table of Contents

Friends, Accepting the Changes

Part Three. Spiritual Journey

Part One Changing Life's

Chapter One;
Moving Forward, Angels Rejoicing.

Helen stood tall in the conference room she had being asked to give a talk on Empowerment and there were many women who had gathered to listen to her Inspirational words and all of them were looking for some guidance in the words of wisdom from the lady in front of them.

"Come on find a seat, ladies how to tackle a man that doesn't like rejection, that finds playing games fun, I have the experience of such a man, I do begin to wonder what are the motives and the so called agendas of men."

Helen then looked toward the women watching their faces as she spoke with a voice in command of the situation. "I have experienced a cold calculating man that played mind games for many years and he thought my life was in limbo, my phones were tapped.

Even my apartment bugged and my computer hacked, police running around after me, police with helicopters, the army helicopters ducking and diving, flying his missions, let me tell you he is an insecure man who screams for attention but did not get it from me, the controlling issue's he had. I did wonder why the surrounding villages, towns, Counties and yes even Country's he called for help they all played his games like sheep,

There must have been a connection to the police as they were and are a law unto themselves, my phone was a tracking device." Helen then looked around the room the women in disbelief unsure of the words that were being said, looking as though getting their heads around the mind games Helen had to endure in her years of pain.

"They thought that they were holding my life up and it continued for nearly ten years, with their games pretending to be the man I was sent to meet or is he the man I was am to meet they all made my life so confusing, if only I did not have my nails done as the manicurist decided to gossip my private info to everybody that she could.

Going to the police was not an option as their involvement made it difficult for me to start the process and they were in his pocket so to speak, in my strength I ended it all I walked forward as he followed, of course it took many years for me to gain my freedom but I did go to the police and I made sure that which police were involved were prosecuted, I also sued the main people who started the games hence me being the wealthy person I am today."

Friends, Accepting the Changes

Helen paused to take a breath. "How many of you have been bullied, intimidated and raped in any sort of way." Standing up in front of her was a lady who was beautiful Martha was her name. "I had such a man who charmed his way into my life, his name Barry he gave me all the patter, he used to pick at everything.

I was doing and everything I had getting me into the bedroom, pushing me onto the bed while he was forcing himself in me, he kept saying you are in control of this aren't you again and again you are in control, yes I was in control but also out of control of it all." Martha looked into Helen's eyes seeing the empathy she needed.

"There are many men who have an agenda, a purpose to secure, with women being pulled into their deceit, but you must learn the lesson you have been given, grow with it, forgive the situation and then move on to putting the past behind you, no forgiving is necessary for him, just forgive the situation of what happened around you while he was playing his game."

Helen spent the afternoon in the company of torn but women who were now becoming confident in themselves which was what Helen was all about, she could see the pain in their souls. Leaving this conference Helen felt she had gained a little of her life back and hoped that the ladies also had gained the knowledge and had understood how some men work.

Not all men are the same we can go from the idiot to a gentleman. Men do not change if they are of the kind of men that feel woman are there to be abused. Their only big change in life would be that of a spiritual understanding and not everybody can do that as their mechanism are not the same as the women of the world, women do have to harden up a little as they do get walked on far too much.

Helen remembered her time in Spain losing her son Mark through the demons of alcohol the days of her heart being broken into so many pieces. She knew his life was to be short but how short that she had now found out. Looking at him in the morgue she thought at last there is peace, a silence and no more trying to get through a world that he had been in trauma with. He spent most of his time in another world, he was spirit.

Walking into the morgue and being shown a small room by the matron he opened the door and waited for her to scream but Helen was totally silent in her pain she had cried the tears of love and pain for three hours and could not find the tears she just smiled at the peace within the room she felt the angels all around him, they had taken him to heaven when he was calm so he didn't know until it had happened.

"Did Mark have any illnesses that you know about it would be helpful to know at the autopsy." The matron asked Helen he was waiting for her to scream out. "Yes he had a drinking problem and his liver was failing." Helen answered looking into his eyes with a need of some love, but at this time there was none to be found. There was too much rubbish around her.

"Can I have a moment with him alone please?" Helen asked calmly. "Are you sure, I can be here for as long as you want." Helen nodded and the Matron left the room. Placing her hands on his heart she felt something was wrong and that he hadn't just died. "Mark, Mark I am so sorry, sleep soundly with no more pain and come back and speak to me when you are ready."

Helen took her hand off his heart and opened the door to the matron waiting she left her son behind for him to go through an autopsy just to confirm his death, he was found alone a friend had put him to bed to die and he wasn't found for four day, the Angels had taken him in his sleep, he walked into the arms of his grandfather and Archangel Michael guiding him to heaven yes heaven even though he had a troubled life he wouldn't hurt anyone. He communicates from heaven.

Those weeks of the funeral and her daughter-in-law were a mess so painful but still she carried on as if there wasn't a problem. To speak out now what was the purpose she would be leaving this unhealthy energy in a week. She wasn't allowed a week Helen left within a few days as the daughter-in-law from hell had thrown her out and had told her son Simon not to help in anyway Helen always knew she was this money person. Helen moved in with her daughter Harri for a few months.

Knowing her life would be drawn to Spain to get away so that she could grieve Helen started to save her pennies so she could spend some time in Spain healing her heart and soul. Her daughter gave her the chance to do that she was kind and caring. Her days of moving to Spain were creeping closer and her mind made up to where she should be.

Jerez was a place she needed to start her journey Helen had never spent any time in this part of Spain and it would give her what she needed or so she thought. In Jerez the same mind games as before even though the pain she was going through they still played, and it had followed her from Wivenhoe.

A personal vendetta against her she was beginning to feel who was this man that had so much hatred for her also his friends were no better they all followed like sheep, yet again the phones again tapped and the computer hacked everything she was doing was being given out for people to play games, word for word they played mind games of what Helen was taking about. And Helen had the trauma of her son to deal with and now this rubbish again.

Police again playing mind games. It was so boring, so mindless. The locals also had a chance to bully a chance to intimidate the lottery people played his games. This man must have so many issues it is unbelievable how he was allowed to play with her life. Jerez a town or city as the locals kept telling her, Jerez needs to visited if only for its sherry. Seven months of this Helen decided to move on down the coast to Calahonda in between Malaga and Marbella a small town mainly English people. It again was an eye opener it had its good part and the parts that Helen disliked for her own reasons.

Again the phone taps and the computer being hacked and to find out that the police knew what was going on and it seemed powerless to do anything even joining in and all they did was laugh at her. Helen was beginning to think Spain was not the place to be, she would try one more place and then it would be back to England by then she would have healed enough allow her to move on and be free of all the rubbish and pain.

So yet again she moved within Spain and to a beautiful area Mijas Golf it felt like paradise a small house with a terrace that had a view of the mountains and she felt good but there was something she was not sure of Helen had been set up yet again, coming away after viewing she did noticed her neighbours yet again playing mind games. 'Two books on the shelf in windows' they said to her in games yet again.

Should she discount it and try somewhere else. Having really by this time had enough of all these silly screwed up people, moving in and trying her luck again there was definitely two men around her both playing games, both seeking to conquer but in different ways. 'Fuck off the lot of you' she thought to herself. The estate agent had set her up for more mind games.

Would this rubbish ever go! Moving in and there was a great deal of cleaning to do and to get rid of the smell of cats was a must as her eyes were streaming Helen was allergic and really didn't need this. She left her apartment so clean and walked into dirt and smell. Two weeks of cleaning would see her through to her next move. She would decide whether Spain was worth the effort.

Helen never even got the chance to settle in and the games begun again the phone taps her computer being hacked. Pressing on with her work a distraction and to getting her books published in paperback was the next stage. Working hard and writing with every spare moment. Helen worked at her goal in life her writing she had found a publisher that would publish her books.

Friends the journey was published her greatest moment and her achievement was not felt by all, the jealous woman who tried to take her down. A woman who felt her presence threatening, but Helen held her own and she knew there and then that she didn't need to fit into her world or the people around her.

Helen smiled while looking at her and thought 'you are a life mentor and you have just tried to knock me down, what a jealous bitch you are' carrying on she had her night of fun with the women of the costa coast, and really wasn't too sure of their agenda either. Helen thought to herself, the men that play games, why would I want friends that follow like sheep, why would I want to live in a country that was neither protective of me or made my life easy and fun.

Helen loved fun and laughter in her life she had come to the end of her pain. Police included. She would be returning to England and the process of taken people to court and suing would begin. Both side of the water. England was her journey and she would take up with friends old and new. This would be the change in her life she would grow and this is where John stepped in and changed her world for the better.

The story continues to now getting herself ready to move away from more games. Back to England and if it continued she would take it to the papers, to the Home Secretary, to the Chief of Police. These games would stop as she would stop them.

Friends, Accepting the Changes

The Angels and Masters were calling she saw the visions of the heavens. Helen was summoned to the highest realms to undergo a transformation of energy she needed to be very strong.

She would astral travel to the heavens that was her mode of transport to the Angels as they stepped forward taking hold of her hand. What was it about Helen that made so many envious, what was there about Helen that made people play such nasty games, what was there around Helen that made people persecuted her like Jesus had been.

She felt that all she needed was a cross on her back, then to walk around the village so that they could taunt, whip and throw stones, would that make them feel better, would that stop the envy, would that stop the jealousy, would that stop the lies and deceit or was she the little plaything they all wanted as their own lives were so sad and unmemorable.

They all needed to know that their time was soon to be at an end, they would receive the payback from the Universe, her Psychic Mediumship Inspirational Empowerment Life Mentor helped so many but she had to work hard to help herself. The memories, the past, the hell of living in a place that hated her for the person she was, she was fun, she was light, she was love, she was laughter, and she was a dream that only a few would be able to see, all the colours of the rainbow.

They pushed her, they barricading her way to her walks of healing, gates were shut and barriers were placed across so that it would push her again another way to just get out of the way without fighting. She was not an angry person she liked to see smiles of joy, not tears of pain. What is this life that we undertake for our growth only to be slapped down by an idiot.

Divorcing years before and Helen had been single for many, many years, she was not controlling or insecure, enjoying her freedom to the full and loving life whatever was thrown at her. Would the Masters and Archangels push her man forward to stop the deceit something had to be done Helen was growing tired of where she lived and the understanding of her it now should be there, she now would be leaving it to the Universe to payback so that her life could be full once more, they would be in court, legal and universal.

Was Helen there to stop the games forever, is this the reason that the Angels and Masters had placed her in this town of Wivenhoe. Also Jerez, Calahonda and Mijas. From her daughters to Spain a tiresome journey the karma for other was on its way she was the strength of the heavens Helen could take them on and take them down to the end the death was coming, the death was here now.

"It's about time I had a good man in my life." Remarking to

Friends, Accepting the Changes

Archangel Gabriel, a man who had the qualities of an Angel but needed to be strong, he had to be her prince, no more frogs. How many boxes should he tick well in Helen's world it would be the whole page of boxes to be ticked to get into her life, also to remain there for the long term, she needed a man who understood her.

Remembering some of the disasters of sex, men that were an absolute joke she began chatting to Kate. "Well there was my husband meeting him, then of course marrying, I was pregnant with Mark, he was the first sexual experience much the same, he was controlling and boring. A young man after him gave me a great time for two weeks we were never out of bed and what great fun." Both of them began to count the men in Helen's bed. "Next please." Kate began to laugh as she made the remark to Helen.

"He was not much good either he was rough and ready, then of course my second husband who thought he was the best and all women wanted him, but again it became repetitive and boring he could not do anything at night time it always had to be the morning when he was not drunk, full or tired, he felt he performed better then." Helen head lifted she began to smile as she looked at Kate. "Men do not really think about you, they think of themselves as it is easier, I feel it has to be the right one for you to be given special attention."

"Well Helen I have had some good shags since I have been single I can recommend a few of them." Kate began with her list of men. "Lucky you, to be so empowered as taking the controlling of shagging and telling them to leave is the most empowering experience." Helen said to Kate. Not as many as some women had in their lifetime Helen was a novice, placing her fingers around the stem of the glass of Pink Champagne.

"Cheers to the lousy men and to the empowering of myself." "I'll drink to that Helen we want the next one to be brilliant in all ways." Empowerment is to be rejoiced, Helen taking control of her life for the first time ever, sex she had now gone without for many, many years, which is the most empowering place to be, as the next time she was in that place it had to be right or it would never be. And if she spent her life alone then so be it. She had enough love around her and a man had to fit her world rather than she into his, he had to be beautiful, he had to be hers alone not shared with friends or women.

Helen's knew John was her life and that she had been given her reward. As she watched John in front of her knowing that light he had around him that he was a gift from the heavens. John was on his own journey he joined Helen on her spiritual journey, he had many qualities what most women would look for in a man, kind, caring, protective, fun, he wanted a good relationship to remember, commit to what he wanted.

He was a true genuine person and a gentleman, a real gentleman. But before he was allowed into Helen's life the Angels sent him many tests to see if he could fit the bill, they would complete each other in love, in mind, body and soul. The five connections were to be Spiritually, Mentally, Emotionally, Physically and Financially. Helen too had her tests, the tests from the Angels as she thought they had left her to Mr Bolt and his games. With her tests she knew and she had passed with flying colours both in the heavenly realms and on the earth.

Helen did lose the strength, faith and trust in life, her co-workers were they looking and listening to this rubbish and Helen knew they were still around protecting her, but also watching the people around her, they were playing some nasty games. It would take her to the point of destruction, in feeling that she had been left by the Angels to fend for herself in so being vulnerable, ending with shingles that would be the last of the games as far as she was concerned, she looked back with a smile, her faith, belief, love, trust had brought great strength, it soon returned to make her a powerful woman since most people around were intimidated by her.

Helen had hardened up, she had become balanced and not the meek mild thing that everybody stood on and she had empowered herself by becoming a bitch within her Angel qualities. Just because she worked with Angels didn't mean that she was a pushover, as people seemed to think she was. Mind games bored her, who was this person hacking her computer and tapping into her calls. It was boring and there was no need for it. They were viewing her life through a two way mirror.

She could see the games that were being played she felt somebody was trying to grind her down. A man they had pushed into Helen's life his name Barry they were brought together in lies and deceit, the first time that they spoke to each other by the river, a friend beside him, Helen had also given a nickname too. Mr Handbag for reasons only she and Kate knew, she had just come back from a jog, crossing paths yet again. Both men were walking with pillows in their hands, sleeping while working Helen thought to herself.

"Pillows I see did you not get to sleep last night." "The pillows are for the roof we might need a nap." Helen began to smile and then of course conversation came to an instant connection, a gravity to what she thought, she looked at him and saw scales around him was he a snake that spirit had warned her about, they were showing her a man with snake skin around him. She looked into his eyes and beyond she knew what was there, she felt a troubled man.

A snake in which the friends or so called friends she had here in this town they were trying to push him into her life although she felt uneasy yet she still allowed him to come forward, they planned his way forward. He was not her man so why did she let him move forward into her life.

Helen watched as they all played their games, Helen watched as they all set into place the seducing of her. Slowly, slowly catchy monkey he thought, all the deceitful games, she began to think that they had nothing better to do with their time. Ridiculing her and with the intimidation and the bullying to name a few.

Friends, Accepting the Changes

She was patient, strong and caring but certainly could not understand why the Angels had brought this man to her, or did he just bring himself forward, is he for a bit of fun what did he want, she wanted to make sure she had the right man in front of her but this seemed to be a test from the Angels and what a test it was. She would be tested over the next few weeks and months.

She knew that the Angels were testing her but there also was a man that was watching her to see if she was his twin soul. Helen met her neighbour just outside her front door of her apartment 'yet another game player' she thought.

"Aren't you the lucky one is it holiday time for you?" Helen then began to wave and smile as she shouted to her. "Yes, for a week, going to spend time with family and I will be back Sunday." There was a rush in her voice as Shelly replied waving at Helen as she walked quickly away. "Ok, I am certain Sunday sounds good I will bring a bottle of wine down a birthday present we can celebrate my birthday, if that is ok with you."

Helen thinking ahead, they are not used to her a Psychic Medium, they do not understand where she is coming from and find her intimidating but perhaps Sunday would help them to see her for what she is. "That sounds good to me 3.00pm I will see you then." Disappearing around the corner and then slightly looking back at Helen as she spoke. "Ok will do have a great time with your family."

Friends, Accepting the Changes

Sunday arrived with Helen meditated before taking herself down to the river with her bottle of wine Vino Rosso a cava but good enough for a drink on a Sunday afternoon, red wine a Rioja or Champagne are the favourite tipple Helen enjoyed. Looking out of the window to see not only Shelly but also

Barry was there too, she felt uncomfortable and not too sure, but of course she still went, not even questioning why he was there and who had told him she would be there that afternoon. What! This certainly was not in her plan she thought to herself but it seemed to be part of his plan or was it their plan.

Gathering the bottle of wine she made her way to the table. "Ah, this is better more wine and good wine at that." Barry, the idiot remarked with a smirk. Helen called him an idiot as that is what he was. Shelley then began to stare momentarily over at them both and smiled.

"I know we will get this bottle open and we can have a birthday glass of wine." Again all this was planned by Barry and this group called the in crowd. Helen sensed someone else was watching but he kept himself well hidden. There seemed to be a dark energy with this man and these friends, the Champagne flowed and the world was alive but dead.

Barry was sitting opposite her as she wanted to see him, to feel him for herself not for what others were giving her, a boozy afternoon, feeling merry to say the least, she watched what was going on around her, but still could not take in the deceit that was being played, knowing she was very drunk, it was all unfolding there in front of her, they must think I am stupid all the lies, the manipulation she could see it all and had done for months, even two years on going but why didn't she listen to her gut feeling in this situation.

Barry kept going inside speaking on his phone to the man or men at the corner near the pub that someone who was dictating to him what Helen had been talking about on the phone his plan of deceit.

The next thing she noticed was Shelly handed a DVD to Helen, Barry immediately spoke. "Helen I think we should watch this DVD together what do you think Helen I am up for it if you are?" The shock of what he had just said and the champagne in her head, what would she do now he watched her every move he knew this could be sink or swim he thought to himself.

Helen had only said those exact words the day to a neighbour what was going on she had noticed Barry on the phone to someone before all the charade had happened she was so confused a trick, a test a lesson for Helen that never to trust anyone as they would try hard to discredit her, from this the hate and jealousy would come to the surface and this would be the hardest lesson for Helen to learn.

Looking at him she had not believed the words that had just past his lips, the neighbour was well not so much a friend she too was part of the games, but she can remember telling her that all she needed was this beautiful man to come in and all she wanted was to cuddle up and watch a DVD, looking to the situation of now as in front of her he had said just that, is her apartment bugged or her phone being tapped she would have to look into that, with all that was going on Helen was not too sure about anything anymore.

What was happening, what should she do her stance of no men in her apartment that would now be shattered, the question was what would that do for her, if she thought too much she would not let him in, he had planned it to the last word, well someone certainly had and Shelly had told him that Helen would be there drinking with her, so that was another one she had to clear from her life they seemed to be here there and everywhere along the front in her village, the village she loved for the healing that she got while walking through the woods and by the river.

Now they were making her feel so, so uncomfortable in her own home. "Ok, are you sure you want to do that as you are here with your friends." He followed her as she moved into the apartment, placing her keys in front of her, he kissed her forcefully she felt unsure this really didn't feel right and she knew it. Spending the night with him without really coming together, Helen had made sure that her beautiful knickers were kept firmly in place, needing time, a little time to understand him for what he was and where he was coming from.

He had come into her life pretending to be her twin soul how was she going to get rid of him, what was she bringing to her. Helen felt ill and so unsure of what was going on. Lunch was what she thought it would be in a cheap way, the plane somersaulted in the sky. "Who is that in that plane he follows me around, I just see him there, I do not feel free with him around." Helen looked high into the sky and asked the question to Barry he turned and immediately looked at her and replied. "Watch what he does."

She began to watch and to her amazement the plane formed a move and then retreated away. Her lunch finished and now they would retreat yet again to her apartment. This man now wanted a reading, what is this man all about, the lovers card came up.

Barry then pointed to the card. "Now come on tell me what is that card then Helen." Not knowing what to do or say she then answered him in a tone of laughter. "This is you trying so hard to get my knickers off." She replied with a giggle, as always quick witted was our Helen, a few more cards a few more answers there was definitely a man with money around him, the dictator that was the question. As she snuggled into the pillow Barry started again to find the spot where she would come to a closure in an orgasm.

Then she noticed him hardening standing tall and significant. "Now look at this maybe Helen you could sit on it, it wants you." He then smiled at her while he was playing with himself. "I could but I am not ready for sex, I want to make sure I have the right man in front of me before I do anything, I have waited four years, I can wait a few months more, no problem." She kept her head down and answered him, when she had finished the sentence she looked up with a beaming smile.

"I can wait, do not worry about sex, when I do take your knickers off it will be slow you will enjoy that, I will see you Thursday for lunch." He then kissed her and left, she was still not sure of this man his energy just was not right but something was keeping her there. Was he her man time would tell what he was all about.

Thursday morning came so quickly and to her surprise he cancelled, he had tried to sweep her off her feet only to dump her in a field lost to what was happening, as he hid himself so he thought Helen could not see him but she noticed him outside so he was not ill, why did he back off time will tell, was he that plant just to get her knickers off, was he all that he seemed, was he just a player who reeled others into his games and a girl of fifteen around he was a sick man.

He was very pushy and Helen did not like pushy men, she wanted to be taken care of not played with, to have someone make her life hell, she had that before and had decided now was her time it would only be the right man who would achieve the final act and this Barry kept giving Helen different signals he was so confusing.

He said he had no money or was he just a con and protecting himself again from women who wanted him for his money, he said he was broke and waiting for a deal, Helen knew her man was a gentleman not a player and that he was very wealthy, he would have to show her more than he had done so far.

He would have to put his cards on the table at some point Helen began thinking, doing this she would then know who was in front of her. What is it with men they are here and then they are gone, they chase and they conquer, life is so short and they make a big deal out of everything, she was sure life would be better without any men here at all, it certainly would not be so complicated, his agenda had not worked. Her thoughts were off shag and tell him to fuck off. In the words of a classy lady you have had an audition but you will not be getting a call back, deal with it.

Off to Kate's for the weekend dinner out have some fun and then Champagne Sunday certainly was called for. As she drove away from the town she was beginning to hate and yet again the plane that followed her everywhere seemed to make an appearance, he needed to know where she was going as Kate had moved home and nobody knew where she lived. Her first stop then was the hospital to see her son Mark he had a drink problem and now had been rushed in with liver, kidney failure and pneumonia.

He was in a bad way, walking in to find him was a shock for her, his skin so yellow, his eyes red and blood shot, tubes in his body, what was he doing to himself Helen thought to herself, in life we are but in death, he was taking life to casually and the risks he had been taking through drugs and drink were now beginning to haunt him a woman letting him down brought his final downfall just like his father did in his teens, death has no boundaries it can visit at any age, he had been given six months to live. What is six months she asked herself just a breath away, he would be gone and at peace with life.

Helen could not say a word as it was his body, his time, his life path and if he wanted to kill himself then he could, her remarks were. "Now look Mark, I am going to Creamy's and I will be having a good time, it's Champagne Sunday tomorrow please try not die as I will not be able to drive home, too drunk you see. And I did not give birth to you just for you to die early, I will be back Monday so if you need me just call." Helen then kissed his forehead hoping that he would not die without her being there.

What pain she had before her, the Angels did say she was to lose one of her children, Harri had her own problems with her health, and she had children Helen did not want her to go anywhere their connection was too strong. Mark began coughing he looked at her and then replied quickly. "Mum! I cannot believe you are standing by my bed, looking at me at deaths door and then you are telling me you are having a boozy weekend."

"Yes but Mark I will eat loads while I am drinking" Helen said smiling, gave him a kiss and said goodbye. She left him with a smile and looking to the skies the plane was still around, she was getting slightly fed up with being followed everywhere, trying to find out what she is up too and who she was with. If he wanted to be in her life then he must move forward and take her with him as his slowness was tiresome. But at the end of the day as the song goes "If you like it then you should have put a ring on it."

Barry the idiot drained Helen's energies, would he come back or would there be someone else in her life, Helen felt he would return as there was something he needed to prove sexually. Helen could not wait anymore for this man, she felt it was her time and if he was not in the same space then he was the loser.

Helen was always told she was a breath of fresh air and she had the most beautiful energy that most people found so calming. Singing all the way to Kate's, arriving with the pink Champagne in her hand this would be so good, the bags were out of the car and handing the champagne to Kate then into the house, then with two planes arriving as Helen lifted her bags into Kate's home, she did not know who was following.

He liked watching Helen have fun oh to be so interesting but such a pain to be followed and pressured that's the price of fame. Helen gave Kate a hug. "How are you doing Creams and have things is this house finished yet it is beginning to take on the look of you, where are we sleeping tonight then." Kate just laughed. "We are in the lounge on the sofa's one for you and one for me."

"What fun put the telly on not working never mind we will have to drink some more, have we a sink never mind who needs all that when we have Champagne." Helen looked around at the mess of the house but it was home and that is why Helen liked it she felt at home here it was a safe haven this is where she felt she could crash when she needed to. A night out the local Indian but this time without the dance floor, never mind we will have our own dance floor Sunday in the garden.

Looking towards Kate let's have a drink and go as I need to see what is going on in town, let's see if there is any decent talent in this god dam town. Looking to find the normal idiots yet again, where are all the decent gentlemen, all in hiding she thought, I do wish when I ask for something am given it quickly.

On returning another bottle of wine then finding the couch they were laughing, laughing and forever laughing the two of them they are the best of friends and they will be forever more then to sleep before Champagne Sunday. "I have decided Kate you can walk me down the aisle as if we make it Sunday, we can have Champagne   day as well as a wedding, rolled into one that would be great fun, at least it would not be so serious it will be fun."

Kate looking at Helen with at least one and a half bottles of Champagne in her system. "But what about your boys Helen they really should be the brides consort, it's their job to walk you even if it's only six foot." She gazed into the sky as they were now joined by planes. "It is my choice this time and I want you it will be fun, my sons would take it too serious I would have to behave and I am not too sure about that as I want to remember it as my best day ever, my Mark will not be here, he will be in heaven and Simon well let's see what pans out there."

Kate then took a sip of her Champagne and answering in the next breath. "Ok if you say so Helen, then me it is and where are we getting married." "Well I think it could be abroad, as I see me on a dock and my man coming off a boat. I would like Capri as it is more romantic, do you think I will get my own way on this but it does not matter as wherever it will be great, it will be a lifetime of waiting for something special and months or even years of stress to bring it forward.

And the patience of waiting has been hard but I will be fulfilled in the end I know I will." "Helen look just think you are off to Sicily with friends and that sounds like fun."

Moving a chair so that she could place her feet on top of the chair comfort was a must as they enjoyed their fun times. "Yes, good food in abundance, I will come back with a bit of weight, only to take it off again." Helen again placing her hand on the food Kate had placed in front of her. "But you will be rested, happy then and your life will change for the better when you come back everything will fall into place for you I know it will and you then will have happiness all around."

Kate, smiled as the cork off the next bottle of Champagne had been popped. "I do love that sound, it's music to my ears and yes I will try not to put on too much weight, but they do feel as soon as I arrive that it's their goal is to feed me up, wine I will have to be careful with as I find it hard jogging when I drink too much, planes will not find me there Creams it's a bit far to fly in a day but I do feel as though I will be watched as he will not want anybody grabbing me away, all this rubbish is stalkerish and sick."

Helen looking forward to the time away she could get on with her book and rest so that she has the energy to work when she returns, consultations in Sicily had a different feel they were not too needy like in England, people did feel as though Helen was theirs to do as they wished but it was hard enough being the Angel let alone everybody else wanting her time. She had learned the boundaries and many times people tried to cross them.

Soon there would be love, the life that had been promised and her books would take her to greater heights. Bring it on, she thought, just bring it on as it's my time to shine, bring it on Angels and Masters. Leaving Kate's to arrive home in the heat of the day. She felt she just needed to sleep as too much alcohol tire's her.

Home again to more games being played and it was now so tiresome, she was beginning to wonder if they had a life or was Helen making their life's exciting, couldn't they find something better to do, all they did was drink. Sitting in front of her was Barry she could see him from her window but Helen did not chase men, they had to want her and come forward to her as her work, her aura, her energies did not allow for that she needed a clear head to function well, she left them to it having too much to think about at this moment, he would come forward on his own.

If this was the man the Angels wanted then he would be there, but if he was just paying silly games as men do then he was not the right one and the right one will be there in the blink of an eye. And he would be taken away from her to allow the right one to progress forward into her life. Loving her weekends with Kate the laughter and the fun, throwing the washing into a pile on the floor she told herself now to meditate. How the Angels and Masters loved Helen but she hoped they were protecting her.

Archangel Michael she needed him to help her with these games. But they had stepped aside just to let Helen sort the problem out herself remaining strong she moved forward. A weekend with her son, a Sunday with a friend and her family then packing for Sicily this was fun times. If only she could transport herself with suitcases to anywhere in the world that would be fun, of course she could travel within trance but not with her suitcases and one does need clothes, wash bag and all the other items that we need.

Arriving at Sicily airport there were many Italians some looking good some just plain untidy. "Bonorgino soy qui en Areoporto Palermo Sophia." Helen trying her Italian out not many words but it was fun trying. "Helen, I will get Carlo to come and get you 10 minutos" Sophia remarked. That could be 30 to 40 minutes Helen thought to herself but I am not going anywhere. It was hot and she was tired she needed her bed. And a walk with Ben first just looking into the shops all designer but did she care.

She arrived to a world of entertainment and happiness she looked out of the window to see the mountains and they certainly looked good in the distance it was her heaven. She loved the mountains they always looked so peaceful, Helen craved for her peace and quiet. She did not mind the entertainment as long as she could have the quiet as well but life certainly was good at the moment, life was beginning to change first for the worst and then for the better. How many years for the worst time will tell!

Arriving at the apartment she heard a helicopter there it was flying above the apartment. Letting that thought of who it was go quickly Helen managed to place her case in the lift and pressing the black button for the eighth floor to the door opening, to find she was being greeted by a little white dog who made a lot of noise, he had remembered her from last year, walking into the dining room the food was already on the table, wine in her hand, she had arrived in Sicily, it was an extremely warm generous welcome.

The next morning a helicopter flying to see where Helen was, but she was quietly getting on with life in an enjoying way, leave me alone she thought. The Saturday morning was even better the helicopter flew over the apartment to see her sitting writing, looking to the sky, watching the helicopter beginning to dance, playing she watched but also she was being watched and why to torment.

The next day while she was writing a helicopter checking where she was, then to her amazement the same plane that followed her everywhere at home in England, the same dam plane with the same noise flew over the apartment she could not believe it she had been followed here, they had found her.

Not too sure that she needed that unless somebody from her home town, she knew it was not Barry he never had the money for such a venture, what was he all about he certainly did not feel or look like the man she wanted in her life and the Angels would not send such a weird man into her life. But then again most of the men were weird in her home town and where were the Angels when she needed them. Somebody was playing games but who or were there two? Planes and helicopters watching her that is a bit scary to say the least.

Mmm scary it is and I am sure you too would feel it was scary, they were controlling mind games, they were not Helen's thing. And it was something the police should have taken away from her, confusing messages that's what she was getting from everyone.

Different groups were playing mind games and trying to fathom out who was who she just gave up and allowed them all to just get on with it as it all became so boring, and so intrusive to her life, she cut them all out and remained quiet in her surroundings as she was busy writing and working and her energy had to remain focussed.

Did she really want that, would she have to have that protection factor now for the rest of her days, Helen knew she would be important but how important she has yet to find out and Helen had a lot to go through before it all was revealed and it would be soon a few years away but very close in Angel time. Her next book needed to be finished so she would spend much of her time on the balcony as that was a great place to watch and listen. Being watched from above as Angels watching was one thing, planes and Helicopters flying around that is a different ball game. They must find me so interesting to keep watching she thought.

When will the right man come into her life she was tired of waiting and tired of all the games that were being played, she deserved better than this, she deserved love, a special love but at the moment she was just getting the games. "Come on

Angels please change this for me I have waited for so long." She found her friend in Sicily controlling while she was in her company.

Helen was tense as so much was going on that she was not in control of and Helen found it hard to have her free time today she was being taken to the beach for a while then only to have Sophia ring the gentleman who had taken her. "Philippe, Helen has had enough sun so bring her back now it's her lunch time."

That was it Helen thought who does she think she is to try and control my life. While she was writing her book sitting watching the skies, hearing Sophia again telling her what to do. "You cannot stay here my servants have to put the cushions on the chairs, Helen looked around the job had already been done. "Ok that is it you cannot control me, I am a free spirit so back off."

Leaving was good, enough was enough and Helen needed some peace, but it was a hard journey back. Helen's flight was booked in on time and she took her seat. Taking off with tears in her eyes, her heavy heart, her soul so empty and looking for freedom, she was looking out of the window the flight was a bumpy one her tears began to flow, keeping it silent as not alert anybody, chatting to the Angels.

"Archangel Michael please leave me here with you, I do not

want to go back to Sicily, I do not want to be in my hometown I am so unhappy there, I want to stay up here just floating and watching, please help me, please sort it all for me, let me be happy, let me be free, as free as you, I am a free spirit but you are testing me, Masters and Angels testing me why do I have to be tested so much, please help me."

Controlling herself looking for some kind of message and seeing Stansted Airport made her heart heavy, looking at the weather they landed in cold dull miserable weather, her bus home was quiet, home again, sitting letting the tears flow, she just did not want to be there at all. Walking into her apartment Helen took herself to her room to meditate, she needed to find out what the Archangels Michael, Gabriel and Jophiel wanted her to do with the situation she was in.

Helen was told years before about the situation she was in at the moment, people would try hard to stop her man entering her life, also the Angels would try to take her back to the world of spirit, they were so worried that Helen wouldn't be strong enough to deal with everything that was going on in her life the years ahead would be one of trust and faith in the Angels and Master that in the end they would pull it all together for her and she would be the accomplished writer that she is meant to be.

So her angels they tried to take her back to spirit by a train, one minute it was not there the next minute it was, Helen had but two seconds to move herself out of the way so the heavens had now decided that she was strong enough to withstand the games, the pain, the lies and deceit the meditation Helen began, she started by calling Archangel Michael the great protector needing him at this time she felt that her life was so confusing.

Archangel Michael protecting would give her the strength, the will and the power to help her through the muddle, he would find a way of sorting what he needed to, then he would communicate to Helen with his findings he was the Archangel of truth, integrity and courage, no wonder this Archangel had chosen Helen to be his student, she felt him so close wherever she was, the sparkling colours of blue, gold and red came to her when he was around so Helen knew he was there.

Archangel Gabriel is known as the Messenger, Helen knowing that Archangel Gabriel could be known in the masculine and the feminine energy, she needed the feminine, as it was the time for guidance, vision and purification, she would give her the messages she needed now, Helen needed the path she should travel, her path clear now and Archangel Gabriel would be able to show her the way, Gabriel gave Mother Mary and Elizabeth the message that they were to give birth to their children.

Where is the love of life, the love of each-other, and the respect of fellow human beings in this world today Helen did wonder if the world would ever find that peace and not live by greed there had to be changes and soon.

Helen needed new beginnings now, Helen felt it was the right time and she knew that Gabriel would open that when she felt it was for her the right time, Helen always told her clients who were trying to become pregnant or adopting to pray to Gabriel, she would work her magic and just relax to allow Gabriel to bring you the message that you are pregnant.

Archangel Jophiel is the beauty of the Higher Spirit, he was there to give spiritual knowledge, great wisdom, with illumination and joy, Jophiel brings back the joy, Helen now back in her village of pain needed him to keep her light, happy and to find great wisdom in what was going on in her life, he would keep her light alive, that her inner child was keeping her happy she knew the worst was not over yet she needed him so much, as the village idiots are still playing their games.

Karma payback was heavy, Helen believed in what you give out, you will get back and when it comes back it will be much more powerful than what you gave out, she did not have any sympathy for these people, it was their loss, it was their karma, it will be their pain.

She needed to be free and being free was not here, she was still being told that it was not the time to move, but mixing in her village was hard work who could she trust. Hoping this man would be further out than in this small community. She now hated her life and wanted to be set free. How many times did she have to ask why were they not listening.

How and when were they going to change her life, asking her to write, orders to what they wanted, when were the books to be published, even the thought of giving her life up and not working for the Angels, they should be protecting and opening up her world, not allowing the lies and deceit that seemed to be around her at the moment..

Remembering the words that Barry said while they were talking. The first thing he said that he was her servant. "I am your servant." Barry found he could say what he wanted he said the words she had spoken only a few days before, with a view of an idiot. "Is that right, mmm sounds good to me and what do servants do." "Everything and anything I am here to satisfy your every need, what would you like me to do for you, what is your fantasy."

Helen thinking quick on a very leading question, it is too soon to reply on that one. "That is a leading question let me think about that one." No way, after two dates, well if they were dates, no way was she going to give information out that could end being the adding to the Chinese whispers that were going on all around her small town what would they all say, something small like being kissed all over could end being, tied up and whipped, Chinese whispers this town was full of it.

Friends, Accepting the Changes

Especially the ones who caused so many problems, the nail girl Tackie at the local hairdressers she would receive a heavy pay back for interfering in Helen's life and every hairdresser and nail technician after her being given information and giving out private information about Helen and her life, the gossips of the town wherever she lived.

What fun Helen thought, what fun he will be, she could play with him he would enjoy that, her thoughts were of sex but something was not right here, it felt weird unsure, unreal and she was not being true to her feelings.

She kept her curtains closed so that she could not see anybody, and they could not see her, she needed this time her energies were at their lowest and also she needed to get her book up to date and moved forward into something special life was a strange thing moments of pain and moments of joy.

Chatting with Sarah to hear about her love life what fun she was having, both sexes at her call, Sarah began in an excited tone telling her what she was getting up to. "Well I am dating Marcus who is younger and Michelle who is older." Helen smiled as she listening to Sarah after all she had been through was enlightening she was now healing and healing with fun.

"Helen, Marcus in bed well he certainly knows what to do last night as I was taken to his bedroom he had filled the room with rose petals and candles, we both had a glass of wine as we sat just looking at each other in   anticipation, then he took my glass placed it on the floor, stood me up and began to kiss me."

Helen at this point was smiling but also trying hard not to show she was enjoying what she was saying, she certainly did not want to get turned on in front of Sarah, never know what she would do. "Helen he then slowly guided his way to removing my blouse, he was sensational my breasts had never been so turned on, he sat me on the edge of the bed slowly opening me to excepting him, removing my silk panties, my skirt he pushed up as high as it could go, I felt so out of control Helen I think I must have been on the menu he then began to eat me, kissing, licking, I was on cloud nine, ten and eleven.

I had a magical orgasmic session and it was not just one but many, finding that I was ready for him, he knew I would succumb to him, I did just that, I was screaming with delight as he certainly did know what to do and what a finish to such a glorious session but when you get those sorts of sessions you want more and I most certainly did, he gave me everything I wanted and needed, what more is there in life."

Sarah then sighed with contentment she needed to find what and who she was again. Helen felt herself sigh goodness you Angels bring this man on she thought and bring him now. "Then Helen I have found that when I met Michelle I had met my mate." Goodness Helen thought to herself another sex act could she stand it she would be running for the vibrator when Sarah left.

"Michelle, well her tongue is to die for, she plays and licks, kisses, she had me screaming the other night she had bought this new vibrator and it gave us both an orgasm at the same time, but she can be a bit dirty and I really do not like that."

Both Helen and Sarah fell about laughing it was good to see Sarah laugh, it was good to see Sarah happy, it was good to see Sarah have a choice in sex not in love as she was not quite there it will take her a little while, the death of her son and father meant she would have time to explore to find herself and what she needed.

When she found it she would be happy, a solution to the end of a painful road. "Hi Helen, I want you to come over for the weekend we need to christen the hobbit house, we can have a cook on the fire if you like or do something with the fire, we will make it like Christmas." Kate laughing she knew Helen was at the end now and she was so low, being a little bit frightened of what Helen might do.

"That sounds like fun, I am feeling very low at the moment, the thoughts going through my mind were not good, I started thinking could I stand on the railway and not move an inch if a train came, as I am fed up with my life and what is going on around me it should have changed by now, the Angels are not there, my book they want they are holding onto and my man until the book or books are published he should come in and sweep me off my feet but they keep telling me clear the decks. The memories of a time she had to endure with her neighbours from hell.

I have told them they may as well take me back now as this is all too hard." Helen said in a soft voice, Kate would know how she was feeling, she would understand why she felt like this, Kate felt the people of Helen's town had no right to treat her like they were, she was angry about it all, whoever was at the end of this would have some questions to answer when Kate met them.

"Don't you dare think any of that, you cannot go anywhere, I cannot speak to Angels and if you went to heaven I would not be able to chat to you, I would miss you so much, do not forget Helen you are loved by me and many other's too and we do not want to lose you, so do not even think like that get yourself over here we can get drunk, that is unusual for us eh!"

"That to me sounds good Kate I am certainly up for that see you Saturday." Helen said. It would be freedom time for Helen just a few nights away from the lies and deceit. Kate left Helen feeling a little better, but trying to let things happen as they should is a great lesson to learn as if you push it will take longer just ask the Angels then hand it over and wait.

They will bring it all back when the time is right. She would take her book over, "Friends, The Journey, New Beginnings & Endings" Kate if she found the time could read it and see what feedback she gives. All the girls decided they would have a day in London to celebrate Helen's special birthday again any excuse for fun. And the changes in them all had begun. Never let go of special friends.

We would be starting off at Borough market for breakfast and then onto the Dorchester, for drinks, a couple of bottles of wine to then move onto Harrods this would be next for checking out the clothes for a wedding and too hats then finally they would venture to the Wolseley for tea, sounds like a fun packed day, Sunday again would be Champagne Sunday which they would spend in the Hobbit house drinking, eating and laughing, they were good at that. Work also began to be a challenge her phone calls were being listened to, all these games were boring.

Arriving at Kate's, Helen began to carefully unload her bags and that Champagne moving over to give Helen a big hug she loved their hugs full of love on a great friendly way. "Kate I got stuck in the lift and my bags outside, stuck between floors for ten minutes, I thought that I would be stuck for the night, here I am though I need a glass of wine." Helen then put her bags down and placed her arms around Kate.

"I will do that for you now Helen, stuck in the lift eh! Look at you don't you get it all, so much fun." "It would have been fun if the firemen I had asked for had been called to get me out but there was definite answer of NO to my question, I kept saying, ring the firemen I am in need of a lift but I kept getting NO we will get you out spoil sports! Anyway Kate so here I am slightly late but better late than never." Placing her bags on the floor, thy wine was being poured, she fell onto the sofa and gave a big sigh of thank you Angels for getting me here safely she could now relax, sipping her wine.

"We'll sit here and sip wine, well our Kate here's to fun and a good weekend." Helen said with a big sigh of relief she had made it a long day's work. "Yes Helen let's drink to that and a good time tomorrow." They both fell onto the couch, Kate sitting down beside Helen and answered her.

"I'll drink to anything at the moment, here's to changes, good ones, love and the book I hope you like it the Angels do, so it must go forward Kate how would you fancy becoming my agent and moving it in the right direction for me, as I was told that a lady acting on my behalf would work as an agent for me and I feel that is you my Kate." "Tell you what Kate after listening to Sarah's fun a good night of sex is needed, big time I believe." Helen sat up and laughed aloud.

"I could do that and when it is a best seller I can come with you, we can travel everywhere, with me as your agent I can be controlling you wouldn't like that but yes it would be fun I will read it to see if I like it then talk to a few people we will see what happens, I could give my job up to have fun with you, on tour Helen, on tour around the world here you come and I am coming with you."

Watching the Angels standing there smiling as Helen and Kate laughed together, Helen could hear laughter from the Universe as the Masters were clapping with glee they knew what was ahead, they had brought these two women together in a way that only the Universe could put together planning each move. Helen now knew why she had to move to this awful town, to then go to the Christmas Carol service and to then be handed a phone number for a singing group, to then joining that singing group.

To meet yet another woman named Betty who encouraged her with her books, to then be launched at a lunch party to meet the girls and this enabled her to finish her book, with the girls as part of the book this to Helen is the wonders of the Universe, the wonders of the Angels. How they worked was a master in itself, they both rejoiced with the Angels.

"I will drink to the Angels I will drink to the Universe." There in front of her was a glass of wine that would go down very well indeed Helen smiled as she raised her glass to the Angels. "Let's lift our glasses and both of us drink to that." Kate could not help herself she began laughing aloud, eh my Creamy, good on you Creams." Helen was chuckling to herself she could see her future clear and bright.

"Cheers! Here we go again I second you and will drink to that Rainbow." Both knew that their nicknames suited them completely and as their glasses came together they chinked and they were both smiling. Forever friends even if their paths took them away from each-other.

Friends, Accepting the Changes

Again this man was presented, again she was confused what was happening this was the full moon time at the end of January she knew that there was something deceitful going on. As he smiled her stomach felt unsure she still felt he was a plant, someone had sent him in to play games but she had opened the door for him to move in yet again but why, she would certainly find that out to her detriment mistakes made and major lessons to learn.

That would be good he came to the apartment and walked in as though nothing had happen. Helen now had to make some clear decision of what she wanted to do with this man, it was the full moon in Leo, her time to make a big move in her life, the Angels would take over on this and she knew it. With her work she knew that some men were hard work in that getting the right consistency with communication, they were so slow, she needed that special communication as Helen herself was that communicator, he would have to work on that one he knew he had to.

If he wanted to keep her happy as she would get fed up with no communication. One thing Helen knew she would not be on her own forever, she needed the right man, a man who can keep all of her satisfied, 100% otherwise it was a no go. Compromise, trust, love, fun were all part of the package where Helen was concerned, no relationship would work without it. Within an hour of them being in her apartment he had made a sexual approach on Helen yet again. She was so unsure of him and where this was going she left it to the Angels. The Friday night came he had made shepherd's pie a bottle of wine came with him he was just waiting for the moment to pounce, remembering his words. "I am going to make you happy."

Well he didn't it was all about him and Helen felt he was such an idiot. So sure of him-self and he was a man that liked to torment women and she was his prey. There was someone who was feeding him his information that's why he was on the phone to this person finding out what I had said so he could play that part of my life that my consultations were about. What an idiot this would come back to him at some point in his future.

Helen half fulfilled. An unsuccessful event, it was all rubbish he was not what she wanted, he was a plant, Helen let him go, but who had planted him and what were they doing to get the information that they wanted, they knew all about her, pretending to be her soul mate, he was lousy at sex. He went back and told whoever wanted to know all about her, a little bit more information for him, just what had happened that night, throughout the charade he kept saying.

"You are in control aren't you?" His words to this day are there in her head sometimes was she in control or was he some kind of rapist in his own stupid way. Weird he was a plant for what, he was definitely sick.

Helen knew she would be meeting Barry for lunch the next day but did she really want too, second thoughts why wasn't she listening to herself, why wasn't she listening to her gut feeling, it was speaking volumes to her. The car ready, Barry stepped in the   driver's seat then he took over the controls an insecure man who needed to take a deep look at himself and his motives. He was Hellen's stalker for years but now he is being prosecuted and sued with the rest of the games players.

"I'll have this one it looks big enough, many parties on here, Creamy will like this one." She smiled as they walked to the car, they had just been looking at some large boats worth millions, Helen was deciding what would suit her then moving onto the next port of call, food and wine it was a beefeater and that said it all. Two more glasses of wine, she was beginning to feel tipsy.

As Barry wanted her to tell him about his family to give him a future consultation there and then while she was out on a date, so she gave it to him. As she finished telling him about his family and what would happen, he began telling her about the women he had been playing with. Helen began to dislike this man and did she really want to know the details of his life.

Helen took one look at him as he was angry and becoming aggressive. "Are you a philanderer, you certainly sound as if you are can I just say just this you have a ok way about you, but you are shot to pieces and you have jumped into my life and I am not too sure if I want it, so if you play the games you have been playing one more time you will be taken out of my life and you will not get back in again." Arriving home she slipped into a bath and then waited for the games but his little Willy would not rise to the occasion he turned his head and said. "You're useless, I am off I will see you Monday." Barry said in a hurtful manner. "I am sorry no you will not until 7.00pm as I am working." She watched him walk away and knowing in her own intuition he would never cross her path again or to be in her life again. She would never allow him in her life again this was it he would now be gone in her head.

But that was only the beginning of his torment and the torment of others, he had given them the ammunition to torment and tease her for years to come, a stalker he became, but he was only a puppet someone was controlling him pulling his strings so to speak. Did he turn up Monday he did not, was Helen expecting him to no she knew he would not so she had drawn the line under this meeting.

He was taken off Helen car insurance, his toothbrush had gone, she had thrown it out, the roses she had been given to had been burnt so she had now set herself free from the idiot, or so she thought as waking up Valentine's day to find Barry standing against the rails near the water looking up at her apartment and laughing. Helen then decided to put curtains up, were they really that sad, to play all these games they were still bugging her in some way but not in a productive way at all she thought.

She decided to block him out of her life she knew he had been planted to have sex with her and it was listened to, she then had to face all these people here who just did not understand. He was a nasty man and who was behind him is no better than a weasel, a cauldron of lies, deceit, hatred and envy. It was in her moments of sheer quiet meditation in concentration all her memories came to her in her writing this information was so valuable and as she connected with Archangel Michael and Archangel Gabriel she wanted to make sure all women understood men who were and still are like these evil people.

She loved working with the Angels they were fun and loved the way she enjoyed life. Since she was there when they needed her then all good things would come her way, timing was the factor here, if only all people could have the patience and hand it over then wait for the right time, life would not be so stressful. But she wished they protected her better in her time of need these eight years of hell had drained her, she found to her disgust it was the police playing games with her life for their own fun and laughter. What people do to make their life's enjoyable.

Helen was chatting to Kate about colours and people and Kate was all ears. "You're a clever girl Helen ok you can be Rainbow I will keep to Cream as it makes me laugh. What shall we call Laura and Sarah any idea's mind you this lady well Joyce gave her Red I think Sarah it is because she has a lot of love to give but I do not think so." "No neither do I, I feel Red is because she is still angry about the past and has not let it go and she still feels that she should be there and that she is owed a lot more than she is getting.

So I feel that is my interpretation of Red for our Sarah. As for

Friends, Accepting the Changes

Laura I feel she should be Lemon as she does have a habit of chatting to anybody and everybody communicates very well, so she can be Limon as that has a ring to it and it sounds sexy and French that is it Creams we now all have our colours and those colours we will be." Helen wrote a poem for all of them showing their colours and their personalities.

All that thinking they were doing and with wine as well the combination made them both fall over onto the sofa beginning to laugh and it was significant roars of laughter. "Rainbow now come on I think we should drink to that." They both said together what fun I wonder if other people had the same fun, stupid fun but it is good for the soul. Helen left Kate's feeling good and more so ready for work yet again.

As Helen arrived home to her apartment not a soul did she see straight to work and that book must be picked up again the title "Friends, Accepting The Changes." It would be a story of Helen travelling to many places in the world with her books. And of course it would be fun she still felt Kate could be a great agent for her. Agent Creams or Agent Creamy that sounds better smoother rather than a bland old Creams don't you think so Bows. Creamy sounded horny well Kate thought so.

"Rainbow, I have someone who is interested in reading the book, he is very wealthy, I have asked him to see what he can do with it, he used to work with printing he could know a few people in the know. He wants a written manuscript and can I have it by Saturday, you can come over for the weekend, then I will give it to him next week." Excitement in Kate's voice she knew something big was about to happen, the phone conversation was productive, Helen beamed with happiness.

"Ok, will do I will go through it again just to make sure it's finished in a finer way for him, see you Saturday." The manuscript would be a week's work for Helen with her work load with the Angels she needed this, her curtains now being shut for two weeks, she did not want to see a soul as the games were just too much, she felt that speaking to them would upset her, her energies were still very low from the time away.

She was beginning to despair so taking her mind off that would be great and now too plodding on with her book she finished it in record time. Helen after working long hours was now definitely looking forward to a weekend of fun. Driving to Kate's Helen decided to take a detour going completely in the other direction she wanted to see who was following her and if it was the same plane she would play cat and mouse with him.

And yes that plane followed her he must have wondered what she was getting up to. Arriving at Kate's he turned away, job done Helen thought at least he knew now that she knew she was being followed, Helen thought to herself. The Angels were not telling her they were just making her feel ill and the Mediums she was speaking to were just not getting it, just not connecting to it at all.

One thing Helen did know it was that she had to stop the

readings she was having as whatever was said these people made it all happen in their own way. This was worrying to her as it was a very sick man indeed to be playing such awful games, there was nothing she could do but ride it all out however long it took, but she knew   her time would come and the readings for real would fall into place, then who would have egg on their faces. Even justice would serve and whoever played their games would be given the same.

Taking herself back to this time, the time she felt so happy being with John, they had their lives together they also had their own lives apart their independence you could see, doing what they needed John had his business, Helen was now embracing changes as she had moved out of the apartment, she also published her book. 'Friends, The Journey, New Beginnings & Endings' so she was extremely happy.

She could remember the time waiting for all this to happen, it had been a hard road to travel. Helen grabbed her phone as Kate face appeared a phone call she needed to take. "Hi can you speak, what's up what have you been up too." Helen asked as she was questioning Kate, her level of motives in her life.

"Well Helen, met this man, he was so gorgeous, I could not help myself I have found out since he has someone else in his life, I now do not want any part of it but Helen in bed my god he was a wow. I did not have to do anything he just worked on me like a dream, his hands certainly knew how to talk and he found places I did not even know I had. In twenty four hours as that was the time I was with him he had taken me to all parts of my home and outside in the garden, I even dressed for him we had great fun. But never again he has to change to want to come into my life."

Kate excitingly managed to tell Helen what she needed her to know. "Can I have the details of the sex then as it would be great to get turned on a wee bit sad little me, anyway your choice but he will change in his own time not yours, you controlling woman." Having nicknames they certainly suited their personality Creamy controlled and expected everybody to fit to her ideas and her thinking, Helen had given her the name Controlling Creams. Rainbow smiled as whatever she went through she was all the colours of the Rainbow.

Going back to the time that Helen took her book to Kate's they decided to have dinner at the local Italian. Chatting to the waiter in German, Helen knew it would be different it would have been better in Spanish but never mind all good fun. Leaving Kate with the book, Kate found that the man who wanted to read had only interests in getting Kate's knickers off and at the moment Kate was trying to be sensible, so he did not even try to read it.

What lessons you learn as life moves you forward, Kate did not see what he was trying to do, did she need his attention, Helen was annoyed at him, he was told on no uncertain terms to "Fuck off." Again to her dismay she was disappointed, always, always and forever always, when would it be her time to shine.

Come on Angels but eventually the book she published herself and its selling.

Laura had now travelled back from America she was trying to expand the business but was not sure of where and who to expand with. "I do not know Helen I am finding life with John boring and my excitement is the expanding of the business and I have met this young chap who keeps me very happy in the bedroom area but I cannot go on like this as it is too much hard work for me, either I ditch John and find someone new, this young man is not my new love he is just a shag he certainly knows how to play, I could keep him for a couple of months but after that I would be bored but there is not enough between the ears for me."

Knowing Laura as she did she spoke in a strong independent flow that was Laura so much in control of herself but not in control of others that she found hard as it was Kate's world and you had to fit. "We'll just see what happens in the next few weeks I do not suppose you are going to give me any info on his sex and the rate you give him."

Helen was finding out information for her next book, she had to ask a few dirty questions then she endeavoured to question a little more as they both were laughing at Laura. "No you naughty women not over the phone but I would say he was definitely ten out of ten. He was amazingly knew what to do he was definitely in control that's good for a young man."

It was coming up to December and the invitations were coming in thick and fast, Helen had every weekend out of her town and it felt such bliss. A helicopter telling her someone was still there or was there someone there! He could have come in for coffee the way he was flying into the French windows the first dinner and dance Helen was followed by a bike, the second dinner she was followed a close friend. The third weekend she stayed with Kate, they were followed around the town chased up the high street.

"Wait one minute girls where are you going? They did not need to ask his name just a pushy man. "You're a bit pushy aren't you mate and look you are wearing a ring I see the wife doesn't know." Walking away they both did not want to have anything to do with him. Helen moved nearer to him then took hold of his hand again. "My goodness can you see this Kate a ring he is only married."

"I want some fun, my wife is out with her friends, where are you going, where do you live? He asked excitingly what a man and what did he really think they were on. "Not telling you where I live but we will be in The Red Lion in ten minutes ok we may see you then."

Now to the turn of Kate she joked with him watching him smile as they left to turn away. As he left Kate and Helen laughed come lets hurry home, we certainly do not want to see him anymore. "It's a plant I bet what does he think he is doing again we are being followed a Kate." As they sat in the Jacuzzi laughing and wondering what the boys would do when they were not there. Sunday was a day of shopping, coffee and cake, home to Champagne and relaxing in the Jacuzzi, Monday was a day of building a snow cleaner whose name was Maria but she was soon changed to a snow wizard as she was fed up being a cleaner.

As Helen drove home she noticed a car was driving fifty miles per hour just like her as she watched him she knew he was following her, this is just too much now I have had enough. Watching him move out after twenty five minutes of their journey she moved right behind him. Now I am following you she said to her-self it would be really great to understand these games.

He moved away only for Helen to find as soon as he arrived home she was to be checked that she had arrived by a helicopter surely they know with the way I work I know what is going on. She was sure it was Police, builders and every man who decided to play the silly mind games, so many idiots out there, was Helen such a threat to them. Time will tell.

Christmas day she decided to go jogging with Brooke they were laughing and joking as they jogged, to Helen's amazement the same car that had followed her back from Kate's came out in front of them, well I now know he is definitely following me Helen thought, there is bound to be a third time. Rushing home Boxing day too work, waiting to get finished and then collecting the dinner she had left at Simon's driving back into her home town she noticed the same car and low and behold the idiots had shown her in their own way who had ordered the following a man with too much time on his hands, now he will know my powers and perhaps he will not be so judgmental of me and just leave me alone to get on with my life Helen thought.

Trying to understand what was going on was too much she must concentrate on work and that is what she was meant to be doing and that is what she would get on with. Didn't these people have something better do with their lives perhaps not, perhaps she was giving them the purpose to have a life who knows, Helen found it sad that envious people had to behave in such a manner. Having shingles was the last straw, telling her clients their boundaries so to her children now she would have to say to the major game players they had reach the same boundaries and she would stand for no more.

Her time had come and now her life had begun, she was looking forward to it John on their honeymoon. Their honeymoon started, Helen knew it would be adventuress, fun and fulfilling in every way. He enjoyed making Helen smile, he enjoyed making her happy. John certainly knew how to make an Angel happy, Helen found him so easy, so giving. Every day Helen kept pinching herself was this all a dream, she would soon find out that it was reality.

Each morning he woke her up with a kiss, a kiss here, a kiss there. As he place his lips slowly on her mouth kissing her gently, Helen returned the love, he knew just where to go and just what to do, he did not wait for an ok, touching her breast, slowly Helen moved her body in the signals of enjoyment every moment of the kissing, as he made his way down to the pearl, Helen moaned with sheer pleasure, she moved her body to meet him, John found that part then he began to give her pleasure until she screamed with delight, he then moved himself to a position with Helen watching his every move and manoeuvring sensually towards his penis so hard, ready, standing waiting for her to take him inside.

John knelt before her, placing herself onto him with such ease and delight, she took all of him inside slowly as so to tease, needing to enjoy every minute as they moved together slowly rocking, gently enjoying each other's movements, John found an orgasm Helen joined him and together they were one.

Slowly and gently kissing her lips slowly and gently taking her into his arms. "I love you so much my Angel, my love divine, my love." He now found Helen so easy to love, before when they began their journey she frightened him, he was so in love with her and that fear of getting hurt made love so frightening now Helen made him feel safe in love, so when she spoke he understood that it was the truth.

Helen touched his face and looking into his eyes replying gently to him. "You are the most beautiful person that has ever come into my life." They both were there in each other's arms for a moment chatting about life, love and where they going next. Life would certainly be amazing she was looking forward to the travelling with her books and the travelling with John. All she could see in her future was planes, boats and being in magnificent cars, happy being happy she thought, how could one be so happy with life.

Thinking back to her birthday she was spending time with good friends "John must be a man in a million". Kate said to Helen looking toward Kate, Helen replied, "I do not know why I had to wait until this birthday to be so happy, do not get me wrong I was happy with me and my life, but to feel so contended, so at one with all that is going on around me." Helen laughingly replied. Kate began to remember what Helen always used to say. "Remember Helen you always say to us you signed a contract with the Angels and that is just what you did and you asked to wait until you were sixty five."

"Ok my friend the message has been received well and truly received, thank you." Helen was smiling from ear to ear at the conversation they were having. Looking back to her life, she had come to terms that everywhere she travelled there were mind games and jealousy, so beautiful she was and now to find people and the envy was unbelievable. When was she to be free from all the pain, asking the Angels to now grant her a new home and hopefully it will be soon, very soon her life was in there hands.

Remembering all those month's maybe even years ago, sometimes she felt that what had been promised would never come to her she was supposed to stand tall, too shine with her work. She was good, very good and the recognition of that fact would be good and Helen could feel it slowly coming.

Looking at Kate her smile so bright, does she really now have the ability to intuitively view life, she certainly has grown since their first meeting years before. Kate was still sorting her life out, since her breast cancer scare, she was now living her life to the full and loving life immensely, but working at the UN she still had to find her dream, it was most certainly coming.

Human rights Kate knew it was going to be her road of fulfilment, for now anyway. There were hurdles and an ending of her life as she knew it, then Kate could grow into something special. Special is what she should be. Special is something she would be.

Laura on the other hand had found hers, well even for the moment. Her John was her dream but it had been a long slog, Laura had brought the business into both their lives, she now found their lives were a definite strain, spending time together was not on top of the agenda and there was Billy Blaine he had suddenly moved back on the scene, although it was on a working level Laura knew it was destructive for her too.

Remembering the night they had together, it had been such a connection for her but at the same time losing her father, her special pops, the only man she adored, he died while she was enjoying the pleasures of the flesh and that had been too much too take in too forgive herself it was as if fate had thrown them so close together again for what reason.

Friends, Accepting the Changes

Laura was now slowly becoming bored of the relationship with John he had not satisfied her in a sexual way for a long time, Laura began to look at herself she now had realised that John had not completed her in anyway at all he was slowly becoming so selfish and the time they had together was not at all pleasing, Billy Blaine slowly became interesting again, she was not married so what the hell, she could do what she wanted now as she knew life was short and Helen had taught her to live life to the full.

Helen had taught all the girls a great deal about the spiritual way now and then all of them put it into practice but with Helen it was every minute of the day that she walked that road, the sacrifice she had made to the Angels and Masters before she came back into this world, Helens past lives had brought her here many times before she could count at least six past lives and each time a sacrifice to the Angels this would be the last time as from now any life she would be offered it would be a fun life.

Laura still ached for her father and sometimes the days were hard. Also Laura missed what she had with Billy Blaine the night they spent together was good, interesting, horny and not over, there was something she needed to do, either to open it up as a relationship or it was to close it completely. John was beginning to lose interest in Laura she was working so much she began to shut down their bedroom was just for sleeping he had also removed himself to the blue room for peace and quiet they barely spoke and if they did it was a grunt or a reminder of what should be done, Laura was looking for a little bit more than what she was getting, was she now turning out to be like her mother, cold and calculating in what she wanted, their relationship certainly reminded her of her parents, all that love had gone or was it hiding. Billy Blaine had come into her life at the best time and the worst time.

Laura knew if he made a move she could not resist him she needed that release and she needed it now, carrying on with the project in hand, Laura again her head in work, determination to see this through, she was looking to expand her business abroad so there was a great deal going on in Laura's head, the release of sex would be great if Billy Blaine made a move she would grab him and his sex. When the time was right she would let him go.

With Sarah there was no mistaking that her world had fallen apart and her life was empty, and her son her little boy her Angel had passed to the world of Spirit and Sarah was finding it very hard to live, to move her life forward, she missed him so much and now she was having to spend time coping with her divorce, the passing of her son meant that she felt her life was totally in the hands of someone else, totally non-existent there was a feeling of that she was out of control where her life was concerned, she had found so much before her son had died now in one fell swoop she had lost everything.

As she looks in the mirror Sarah began to view herself as a picture, not liking the painting that she saw in front of her it had lost its lustre, her life would never be the same even though she had mastered the art of sexual persuasion, she was beginning to doubt herself again and her spiritual path in that she was still fighting. Her main colours in the paintings were dull and insignificant.

The man she had found she was beginning to wonder whether he was the right one or not she needed time to think asking for her space to move forward within her life on her own she needed time to heal, he gave her space and moved away from very quickly so as if to release himself from the pain, she had so much to cope with, now was not the right time for Sarah. She let go of love to slip into turmoil, the injustice of it all. When would her life be hers again, when could she make a decision without it being compromised by someone or somebody.

On the other hand Helen was very much enjoying life the back stabbing the bitching from certain people around had taken its toll on her, having shingles meant watching her stress levels every day, so she kept herself very sheltered within. Helen did wonder why the Angels would not move her on, this was before she met her John, she did wonder why the Angels made her life so difficult, surely she had learned all the lessons she needed to learn by now, well on the hard level anyway or was it that the bitching back stabbers were going to be learning their lessons and learning that in life be kind because if you are not it will come back and bite you on the bottom.

Friends, Accepting the Changes

Helen now had asked the Angels to sort all that was around her at the moment and they were, but it was slow she now felt safe in their arms, in their love her life was just beginning to go to another phase. Helen was now living in Spain she had travelled here after losing her son Mark she needed to heal without anybody interfering with her. The stalking followed her, the listening to her phone calls and the hacking of her computer was still there.

It was certainly about time someone realised that they were breaking the law and Helen would have her final say, there seemed to be two lots of people around her telling her what was going on in mind games. To sets of people who were trying to do what they felt was right by her, she felt one was out to play with her life and the other group was keeping her informed as to what they felt and that they were listening too.

Her book now published "Friends, The Journey New Beginnings & Endings" Helen knew that the first and second book would be the books to move her into the life she was meant for, her Life Purpose so to speak, her second book it was being edited and the editor was enjoying the reading of it. An agent she could work with was so important so that life and touring would be fun Kate kept coming to mind.

Her book 'Friends, The Journey, New Beginnings & Endings, and Friends, Accepting The Changes' it was Helen's greatest moment she knew many doors would open, offers would be thick and fast but it had to be the right time and in timing.

Friends, Accepting the Changes

Her second book "Friends, Accepting the Changes" was what all in the Heavenly realms began asking Helen to put together and in this they wanted Helen to make sure each of the Masters and the Archangels were mentioned so that the world would know who they were and she loved it her life was fun and rewarding. Helen looked back to the time her agent was presented to her.

Working on the phone lines, a change of website, there she was up there online in a live situation, people could see her giving out her Consultations, she is a star; a lady had contacted her company asked who she was and wanted to make an offer for her writing.

Coming through to Helen asking her what she was all about, Helen telling her about her books and that they had been published in paperback but also in e-book too. The next day another phone call to say she had ordered books and was now getting her staff to read them, she had already read one and loved it and that she would be in touch.

On the website were her poems and article were there for the world to see. "Friends, The Journey, New Beginnings & Endings, was now handed to a publisher she was on a roll.

John then entered Helen's life and John now very much in Helen's life, the agent had found her and they together had found a publisher. This was it life was now going where it was meant to be. John had asked Helen to move in with him, she was no longer alone the book had been what she needed to show to the world.

Helen had now moved out of her apartment into a new life of joy, happiness and her complete life purpose so much was now opening. "Pinch me, pinch me, pinch me Archangel Michael this is a dream and I am so happy and I now know there is a publisher, and then it is all up to you to take it forward to make it a best seller, I leave it to you, handing it over and please open the journey so that Kate can come with me on my travels, let her see it will be good for her but in her heart of hearts Helen knew Kate would go her own way."

Helen talking to her Archangels and Masters she had done what they had asked and she had done as she was told. Her meditating was a must as she lived her life with the Masters and the Archangels she remembered the time when they called her to go to them, lifting her heart up and Archangel Uriel taking her hand he is one of the wisest, his intellect, practical solutions and creative insight was what Helen was being called for. He smiled as he and both Archangel Gabriel and Archangel Michael stood beside her and taking her to the realms of the Higher Spirit.

They tapped on the great oak door which was the opening the world of the Universe. Helen felt such a peace with such a warmth she looked all around to find so many Heavenly beings, this journey was so wonderful, her inspirations and love, she now was being rewarded for her tine and for her work. As she smiled at her co-workers they all stood up and clapped her presence, there were tears in her eyes she had made it she had gone through the last ten years of pain and suffering from the many who found they needed to play games to get the fulfilment the needed in their lives.

Looking around her she slowly moved towards the Archangels, the Masters and all the Divinity's of The Universe were there all had been called to take part in her glorious moment she knew they were applauding her achievement of the lifetime of pain, BUT she had made it here she was in the highest of the heavenly realms being applauded by the love of the Universe. She was told that she would go through all that she did, looking around her it was certainly worth it.

All the damage of her life being scrutinised by neighbours, police and whoever wanted too, the phones being tapped illegally and her computer the same, wherever she went someone listened and then played it back to her in mind games. Regardless of who it was it was wrong and they knew it but still they carried on as if it were fun to torment. Suing would give her what she wanted and needed.

Looking straight ahead The Holy Spirit stood in front of her, to his left Mother Mary, to his right Jesus, she bowed they came over to take her hands, each kissed her on each cheek, then blessed her. "Our Helen you have been sacrificed, ridiculed, the deceit and the lies all to do with your life path, they have tried hard to ruin your reputation within your work and your personal self, the skeletons have been pulled out of the closet so no more can they say and no more can they do you are free to move ahead.

And we are watching your back until the man we have chosen steps in, we are now going to clear your path, you have worked well for us and now with your path free in a matter of weeks you will then be travelling the road of the 'Speaker of life' your books will speak to the many and that is what we need and of course they will contain everything about life.

We are now taking care of the love that you have been promised, we have handed you over to him, he will take great care of you, as you are here for us, you will speak for us in an earthly manner, so to reach those who do not trust or believe. Go and be happy Helen we will call on you when we need changes in your books, as there are many to write. You must write about life as life itself."

That was now her mission, having been told that many books would be written and that she had to reach not just the changed but the ones she needed to change. They let her walk in front as they followed behind, the sharing of the heavenly table Helen was sitting next to Jesus and Mother Mary to her right was The Holy Spirit as Helen sat down each Master, each Archangel, each Deity came and touched her, their hands blessed her.

Friends, Accepting the Changes

When all the heavenly beings had finished their tasks Helen was then given back to the highest Archangels Uriel, Michael and Gabriel, Helen was now to become The Messenger of the Highest. She had asked for their help and Helen had handed her life to them in doing that she was now was being repaid for her love and understanding of others. The Universe loved her dearly their Angel had come good the rejoicing can begin. Taking her back to the earthly realms Helen felt different, she was a calmer more relaxed lady and happier with herself, nothing would get her down now.

On her return Helen listened to what she was being told by the heavens more now as she knew what her connection with them was and what her life purpose with them together on a path with love and of course enlightenment. She began to meditate and she was told that she must write more. "Helen we need you to make sure all of us here in the heavens, being the Archangels that they are mentioned in your book and also all the Masters too we need you to write about the Heavenly realms of the love we share, each level that all the teachers are on and what happens as you reach the end of your life.

You must mix this with the sex and fun, it will be a great book and we will take over, and make sure it makes it to the top for you, our messenger." Each meditation each time they asked for more, each time she listened to their words.

Helen looked back to the hardship of her town, the main game player and the phone taps had to be stopped. She was told she had to go to church on the coming Sunday 31ˢᵗ October. Waking up to find she had lost a part of her tooth, the dentist she did not need. "Do I have to go to Church I am feeling uncomfortable, not too sure if I want to go now." Needless to say an answer came back quickly and to her amazement she was told. "You are to go to Church we will be with you Helen you are protected from the evil of this man." Archangel Michael said in a calming voice.

She looked to her side, Archangel Michael her protector and Mother Mary her gentle connection would she managed to be ready in time. Walking in the Church, her smile was wide and happy, the ladies at the door looked at her. "I hope this is a sing song service, I need a sing song it lightens the spirit." They both looked at her smiling.

"Yes it is a full service." Helen felt her helpers around her, looking to her left, the person that decided to have her phone tapped one of the main game players the shocked look on his face, to God they seek mercy but still they keep the lies and deceit going, Helen just smiled and made her way to her seat. This was a way for one of the idiots to understand her life.

The service began it was All Saints Day the next day and this was there service it was fitting to Helen also her work, the priest began to talk about how people who work with the Masters and the Angels and how saintly they are and they are not to be judged for their enlightenment they too are Saintly, he told the congregation to take them to their hearts and to enjoy. If you see a person with no food, help them, for in being rich it could be one day it's you that has no food, Helen smiled and kept smiling all that the priest had said related to her and the games that were going on in her life.

The priest then lifted his head from his prayer book and looked to his congregation and said. "Treat other's as you would like to be treated, treat others with love and respect, love thy neighbour and what you give out will be sent back to you, in turning the other cheek, you know you will not be the aggressor for the heavenly beings will be watching and if you do not listen to the Heavenly realms they will teach you very harshly and you will then wake up to find what is to be." He had said the words Helen had wanted to say but couldn't as she was surrounded by idiots.

Helen then took Holy Communion as she was walking forward to take the body of Christ the game player was coming away from taking the body of Christ he could not look into her eyes. Helen smiled a whisper of thank you to her co-workers. The service over, and placing her prayer book on a shelf then turning to take the coffee that was given to her. The arms of the man who had tormented her for the last few years were open wide for her to step in "It's lovely to see you." As he kissed her on both cheeks and went his way.

The Universe had taken over to stop the games all was well or so she thought as it still took many months of sheer nonsense for her to be free. And after them months all the pain had gone all the suffering had now finished or so she thought someone was still taking the law in his own hands.

Her path of the heavenly speaker and her path of the greatest love was being opened by the heavens, the miracle will soon been done, that was the first now to the rest, Helen waited for all that was to come. So much they were showing her, so much was now out in the open. She knew there would be a time for the death of the deceit and lies, but she still had to see her son Mark passed to the world of the Angels and a move to Spain before she was released of all the stupidity around her it took another three years from Marks death to be free of mind games.

It doesn't matter who feels they can play with someone life like this, it not what the heavens wanted or needed. Helen knew their time would come regardless of who it is. The man, yes a gentleman would come forward to her, but what were his plans? She could ask Archangel Uriel to find out and warn her of what her man was planning she needed to be out of the dark now, she needed to be free, she needed to be loved and cared for.

Helen also needed to show love to someone very special to her, her soul mate/twin soul, a man she had met many times over many lives before, this time they would get it right, this time the Angel, Masters, the Heavens were in control. This time it had to be done and when John took that leap of faith and entered her life there were shouts of joyful celebrations, Champagne glasses were at the ready. The lessons we have to learn.

Friends, Accepting the Changes

Helen's book had a way of opening the hearts of the many to the enlightenment of Angels and Masters in a more practical way so to also living in this world and that is what the Heavens wanted. John had found Helen interesting from the start, noticing her from afar, waiting not sure of his moves but then again planning all his moves all the way.

He had kept her waiting even when he joined her life he kept her waiting for a bit longer, making sure, sure that he had found the right one, sure that Helen would except him, his money he hid, his love he tried to hide but found it very difficult to do, he listened too much to others and now began to form his own opinions of Helen.

She had talked enough clients through times like this to know never chase as they soon run the other way and once they have sorted themselves out they will soon make a move, when they do it is because they want to not because they have been forced to.

All this game play was tiring and pointless but men needed to come to terms with what is in front of them before being happy, and he was one of those men. An interesting man with a great sense of purpose she already knew him well and did he know what she had been put through in this small town. But they wanted to know so much, the permission to find out all that was needed he had made Helen's life unbearable even the police watched and played. Such nastiness will come to an end and very soon.

Friends, Accepting the Changes

Helen knew all and was waiting for the time that he would come clean and tell her what had been going on. Would he ever have the strength for that as he would have that fear that she would back away once she knew what he had done, even if he was standing and watching while everything was played out, but he needed to tell her the truth about himself, why did he feel the need to hide his money she did not understand that as Helen was not money grabbing at all.

All she would now concentrate on would be her work and her books. She came back to herself looking outside the window she had reflected all that she needed to. Looking at her books she smiled, what hard work it had been. The books would take Helen across the world teaching as she travelled, all about love, trust, acceptance and life, the travelling had begun and the love was there for the world to see.

The cover was just as she wanted, the table reserved as the friends they were the Champagne that was where she was now celebrating her second book would have to have Champagne too as that's what the friends were.

She remembered the night that Archangels Michael, Gabriel and Uriel came to take her book away too read, she had left it in their hands, after a few days they called on her, they were happy with the book. Timing is the factor now when you are ready there will be a way of publishing that will be shown.

Helen slipped back into the world of the here and now it was good for the soul to return to the past to analyse the pain it makes and appreciate all they have in life. As she looked at John searching through the diary making sure Helen had her free time, just enough for them to enjoy life to the full. Helen was fun and he needed to keep that fun alive, each month John would make sure that they would travel to enjoy life. But she also needed her friends those special moments with her Kate and their champagne Sundays Helen definitely needed her time with Kate.

Reading her book for the first time she looked at the first few chapters and remembered her time in that small town. It would have to be part of her second book what she had gone through. And the continuous idiots that played. Helen loved the river watching the birds she felt so close to the Angels, waiting for them to speak to her through the birds the river was where she made her contact with the Angels this was her time her space, continuously chatting there was so much she needed to understand her journey forward into teaching the world to love and accept what their life's were for.

Birds were Helen's messengers the Angels used to get the birds to tell her what was going on. One was tapping at her French doors and then singing listen Helen your phone is being tapped. Another bird came to the window with a bug in its mouth and kept looking into the window, your apartment is bugged Helen. And another was walking up and down the rails looking he could not see a thing. They are looking in the windows of my computer the games forever games. So too much more freedom and to live a proper life of no games just fun in life she would free herself and allow the heaven to send the karma some people needed and would get for sure. Helen was at last free!

Chapter Two.
The Book the Dream. Working with the Masters.

Helen had reached her goal, her dream, and the life she had always wanted, her achievement was the publishing of her books and there they were on the shelves for her to see. The books were out there in the world, so anybody and everybody in the world in every country could read about Helen and her way of life. Now she needed to connect with the Archangels and Masters much more and on a higher level, each one of them had their purpose, each one of them found that connection with her when she needed them or when they needed her.

"Friends, The Journey, New Beginnings & Endings" the first book, her second book "Friends, Accepting the Changes" these two books would set the stage where she would remain for the rest of her life, her book of poems Ambiance was also on the shelves. Both books of Helen's life were to be best sellers, now too children's books she was being asked to get on with them the illustrations were to be done. Children's books a different outlook and all with the view of opening the children to the world of the Angels.

The new book Helen had started was in its early stages and brought together men and women together in relationships it would be a fun book that people could maybe see their relationships and work on them and some sex which keeps the world ticking and fun with a great deal of laughter. "Hey our Helen how does it feel to be this star, a big aluminous, sparkling, shining star and at least know you deserve it big time." Laura asked while they were sitting drinking a glass of wine, in a place they found interesting by the river. A star and about time, Helen thought. The years of struggle and pain was certainly paying off.

"You are now a Celeb and I think we should celebrate your great success as it has been a long time coming, shall we have a long weekend away together before they want you to do more of the book signing and more of the television appearances for you our starry Rainbow." Kate remarked. "Really looking for a good time, and fun with champagne of course, instead of champagne Sunday we can have champagne weekend."

"Sounds good to me Kate we could make the most of it maybe fly off somewhere with great shopping." Laura spoke at the same time, Champagne and shopping what else is there in life. "Here we go little finger". Laura quickly took hold of Sarah's hand. Now where shall we go, Spain is close and interesting, or Helen do you fancy Italy, when will the second book be on sale, soon I hope."

"February 14th Valentine's Day they are talking about we are only in July so a while yet and my diary has been sorted." Helen slowly handed the book to Kate. "Why do they need to sort your diary Helen, surely John will do that he wants to take over so you have free time." Helen began to smile. "Yes, he has taken over slightly but I do feel it is good otherwise I would be working all the time and I do need time for friends and family you know me Kate, if there is a life to help I will be there." "Ok then where is it to be I do fancy Italy but where can we have good food, wine and be happy, that is not too much to ask is it."

"It seems to be safer in Italy we could do Venice, Rome, Florence or even Sorrento, we can find a good hotel on the that Internet, I think Venice as we can have fun with the Gondolas so is that agreed on, we can dress up and have a good time." Kate would be the one to sort it out she knew what to look for. I do think Italian men are better much more romantic we can have fun but no sex as it is a girlie weekend well that is you Helen and Laura.

As Laura looked up with a cheeky grin her eyes smiling. "I will do what I want and if something tasty is put in front of me then I will grab it with both hands, even one hand as long as I grab it." As the girls looked at each other a loud reply came from them all. "Ok we see, is it a bit like that then eh! But remember we are having a good time not just about you and if you want just sex then perhaps you should not come with us. Kate sternly remarked she certainly knew how to put people in their place it was her way or no way.

Friends, Accepting the Changes

I think we should do two days in Venice then go onto Madrid or Barcelona, Seville for lunch, can we all do that it just means we can have the best of both countries and of their men also. It was agreed on both countries and if Laura and Sarah wanted to leave after Venice they could, Rainbow and Creamy would move onto Madrid, Seville or even Barcelona, they all needed some fun now as life and work had taken over. Helen was thinking more to just Venice and Madrid another time.

Helen's articles were in a magazine so she would be noticed now, and her books on the shelves of the main shops and the e-book stores where they needed to be, and her interviews with the television she knew that would mean intrusion into her life and perhaps that weekend she would be open to that intrusion Helen knew from this day forward she would need protecting. Also that means angelically as well as realistically.

For years Helen had people being intrusive in her life for years and she knew this would be different this time Helen accepted that she with the fame would have people wanted to know what she was all about. Kate well she certainly had gone through a change in the past two years looking for what they called love now instead of the word sex, but Helen knew full well that she had not finished her game of fun as there was more to come before she settled but at the moment it was just friends and fun.

"We do tire of the shagging game don't we Kate, it would be great to have a bit of love with it now and then what do you think to that? Asked Helen tapping Kate on the arm as if to say

Friends, Accepting the Changes

I know just where you are coming from and Helen had found that more in John.

"Yes, you are certainly right there Helen but I do think sometimes that it would be great for a night if he was good but then they also become needy and I have to back off." "Ok have we decided to go to Venice then Madrid or the other two main places what do you fancy we have to have a good time and the trappings of a good time.

Both countries would be good for a five day drinking plus a fun session. Yes, Venice seems to have a good feel about it, all them Italian men to pinch their bottoms but Helen do you think you will be recognized while you are there will that be a problem to you."

"Well I am going to be recognized wherever I go so what the hell, and do we need a bodyguard yes we do, better not Laura might have the notion that he is hers for the taking, that could be a problem as he should be looking after me, he might forget where his loyalties lie but it might be an idea to ask John what he thinks to that.

He will have someone watch us without our permission so it could be better to bring a big man along, perhaps an ex-army policeman figure would be good made of strong stuff with rippling muscles." Helen gave a big sigh as her thinking cap was tightly in place she knew she would have to have a bodyguard and John would want her watched. He was a jealous man. She knew John well and he would have her followed experiences in her past told her that.

Once he knew she was his, he would not let anybody else get too near but not in a controlling factor just protection, Helen was his and he was there to look after her he liked that very much in fact he loved it.

Now Helen had to think of work as her clients were demanding. But then she clicked and said to herself well I am a writer, wealthy, I should put me first I now can work when I want too, it was hard to realise that she was an important lady and with that came fame, with that came intrusion. Some clients were needy and with that Helen had to slowly let go. Letting go was a must as life surely must move for her. But there were clients that were pushing so to setting boundaries otherwise people take liberties.

One such client came to her two years ago but was not willing to work with her so it came to an abrupt end. An OCD problem, Helen not only had to work on that but also bringing her into the world of the Angels would be a test for sure, something she would be doing in her consultations. Emily was a lady who was now forty years old, she was in a marriage but he had a controlling factor which he kept her OCD alive and kicking come to that he liked it just the way it was and with him doing everything controlling her hence she then controlled him in other ways, it was a large circle of hatred not love.

Friends, Accepting the Changes

Their relationship it started well but there were ups and downs, she managed to do a great deal then because something would shake her she then went to pieces and thought she was not getting anywhere. But there were times that Helen could scream as when she had moved her forward within one fell swoop it had all been blown. "Emily what do you want from me I work hard to get you to cook, clean, touch items in the fridge, feed your daughter her milk and because of one thing you create in your mind. We are back to square one you have to work with me as I cannot do it alone." She listened but then again she did not.

Helen being away in Sicily and Emily had made a great big leap as in taking her young daughter to school, which meant she had to go outside into the car and drop her off at school and she done just that and this time with the help of her parents. Helen cannot be in two places at once. Working with Emily was hard because she did not put into practice what Helen wanted her too so the progress was extremely slow but there was progress.

The work came from the Angels so Helen done her best to help change lives a finish was soon to come and Emily either changed or became stuck in a mine field of OCD and hatred. Emily eventually divorced and of course the process of being free in life will help her move forward to find a life of her own. Helen began to ask Archangel Michael how she was to serve them now.

"The book, the dream is where you go you must say to the

world that life is fun and that they are to enjoy and bringing in the positive energies would change the energies of the world there is too much negativity around and you are now on your road to change that and that is why the books had to be good, and it had to be fun with the openings of the Universe. There definitely has to be more of a psychological change in this world for it to generate love, happiness, kindness, respect, trust which will then bring the wealth of forgiveness.

Your next book Helen must be as equal fun and sex. Also learning with the Angels and Masters so Helen your world has just begun, be brave and move swiftly forward, there will be children's books to write too get out your sunglasses and pen to the ready."

Helen remembered the day she met Derek Acora he said the same thing. "Helen you need to have pair of big sunglasses to hide when you want to and a pen just in case you are found." And now that had just started I must go looking for sunglasses Helen thought to herself.

Helen had been asked to write a new book with this book it must come from the Angels with the view of travelling around the world to enjoy and let everybody know about the universal love Helen was to move forward now and help more clients move forward in a more productive way. Loving her work and loving her life in general.

Helen kept in contact with Kate. Soon Helen was going to be

on the television. "Good Morning" wanted an interview then it was onto an afternoon programme and then Helen was also asked to do a programme with Piers Morgan and there were also a few local programmes, leading to radio interviews, Helen was to be a busy lady, she needed her weekend away. So much fun and years of waiting, Helen was asked to travel throughout the war torn and countries that had so much starvation and pain she would visit the children. The Middle East would be an eye opener for her, her heart would be torn.

Helen watched as her room filled with Angels and Masters and the Heavenly realms had now summoned Helen to the table of the Higher Spirit, they needed the world to know what the Heavens meant to each and every one of the Universe, she was told that she must include all the Heavens in her book and how she worked with them, how she was one of the Angels, so her book was to let the world understand what each Heavenly being was there for.

What was she to them a gift to the world, so to the likes of the wonderful Archangels Raguel the friend of God, the Angel of Fairness and Justice he helped Helen when the pain engulfed her, and he helped resolve the situation with all other Divine beings.

She needed you to understand how the Angels can help you in all ways she began to look at Archangel Ariel the Angel that releases Divine magic, and then to Archangel Camael he who sees he is one of the seven truly powerful Angels he stands in the very presence of God.

As she began to stand for the blessing of the Heavens she was touched by Archangel Haniel he was the grace of God, he uncovered all the natural healing he works with potions, powders, and crystals he told Helen that he would bring her the beauty, and beautiful friendships in her life. She knew from now all she would   have was the best friends ever, those who would look at her with great respect and a knowing of who she was and why her journey was so special.

Archangel Metatron stood tall he could reach from heaven to earth, he was one of the two Archangels who were humans before becoming Angels, he is the supreme Angel of Death whom God daily gives his orders as to which souls will be taken that day. He keeps the Akashic records in check which in spiritual terms is The Book of Life he is the chief recorder in Heaven. He will order your death when the time has come he has the power to call time on your life even though you may have other plans.

Archangel Raziel a close worker to the God, he knows the Secrets to The Universe and how it all operates he wrote his book The Book of Angel Raziel. This book was given to Adam and Eve as they were expelled from Eden. Archangel Raziel he has a definitive understanding of the esoteric he will help you open to a higher level of the Psychic, increasing your ability to see, hear, know and feel the Divine guidance he is magic, if you are looking for the way forward in Clairvoyance and Divine

Friends, Accepting the Changes

Magic then you must look to Archangel Raziel.

The last Archangel Sandalphon he came from a mortal he and Archangel Metatron were twins on earth, he will carry your prayers to God the Higher Spirit so that they can be answered. He can if you ask tell you the sex of an unborn child. And all the Archangels are there for you to call whenever you need help to bring whatever you want with life. Never feel frightened and live for the love of yourself and then to whomever you want to bring forward in your life.

But remember you must love who you are first before you can love someone else. She remembered an afternoon lunch with her son Simon and there she was her soon to be for the second time daughter-in-law Anne and granddaughters Olivia and Brooke. Driving to a local pub the Rose and Crown she was to meet them at two thirty as   Helen was parking up then to hear a shout. "Are you supposed to be parking there Nanny it's a double yellow." Brooke was actually doing her bit for the traffic Warden let's hope that is not a career move she makes soon.

"Not too worry Brooke it will give the traffic warden something to do." Helen was smiling such a beautiful girl who Helen had to teach her to open her heart to love and trust she could be cold and wanting it all her way just like her mother, there was not room for compromise. "You're such a naughty nanny come on then let's have some lunch and see what idiots we see." "Always and forever my Angel, always and forever do I have to behave in the pub." Helen replied to the little lady that smiled at her naughtiness.

The table by the window, Helen sat so close to the window with Olivia and Brooke close by. Sausage and mash for us girls, Simon who after three years of no contact with Helen, now had come back as the son she knew. He wanted something small and he was tired and weary through work and decided to order cheese on toast and mayonnaise, so adventuress is our Anne. As they all sat down to lunch Anne decided she did not like the glass of Rioja so Helen had her glass.

"Look everybody this is just like playing chess one move two moves both glasses are mine aren't I the lucky girl then." Looking at Anne's hair and she began to laugh how she managed she to get mayonnaise in her hair she did not know Calamity Jane, Helen immediately thought of the film There's Something about Mary.

"Look at you look at your hair, Olivia cleaned her mother up with Brooke looking straight at Helen. "Nanny, stop laughing you will get us kicked out of here, look this side of the pub is clearing." "Yes, Nanny stop laughing, you will get us kicked out in a minute." Olivia joined in the fun Simon began laughing Helen enjoyed her family she loved the moments of happiness.

"It's the laugh nanny it's the laugh look the pub is clearing." Anne had to say her piece she needed to be part of the family. "Helen the pub is empty now we should take you places just to clear the room so we can have a table." "Well at least I can enjoy myself, not like some of these people life is to be happy, as life is so short." The lunch ended on a friendly, fun and happy moment they all were happy.

Helen slowly began to do what the Angels had asked her to do, to show that she was strong and will not take the rubbish anymore. That is done now moving forward and to forgiving as she went. But the games went on, and on, and on, and on, was there an end to this. But Helen had to let it all go over her head, trying to keep all the rubbish in the dustbin and put the lid on it.

The whirlwind swirled and swirled while she was trying to help her clients, the whirlwind became stronger, and she so remained in the epicentre where it was calm it could not forever there would be an end one day.

She certainly looked forward to that, nasty people, nasty place and how many more lessons should she endure before she was to get the gift from the Heaven, the gift of love. All in the past now, thank goodness but it is good to reflect. To reflect is to clear and move on.

Being asked to stand and do an inspirational speaking day, she would enjoy that as she was an inspiration. Arriving at a place called Southwold such a beautiful place that with all the tourist traffic it was beginning to lose its lustre, there was a fish, and chip shop in the area and Helen noticed the queue was so long, good job fish and chips is not my bag, Helen thought to herself.

Friends, Accepting the Changes

Walking into the main entrance to the hotel, Frank was there to meet her, shaking her hand vigorously. "Helen I believe we have a big problem, we need your help Pat has not arrived and has had to cancel, would you take over, perhaps you could talk about what you do and the Angels I feel it would be a great subject for all to see what you can see, black or are the colours beginning to come through, that is the connection that she needed, just the beginnings of colours and then they would be a connection.

Beside her they would stand one by one, Helen began to have five strong connections on the stage all had a little knowledge of giving messages. But they soon will learn she watched as the connections became stronger. Helen linked into a young lady her name was Sarah. "Can I come to you I need you to feel free as I am being told you are not." She asked her gently, Sarah nodded her head she had not ever had a message before and was not too sure of what might be given.

"You have a Ben in your life but you are not too sure of where you are going. Your Nan is with you and she is telling me that if you need to set him free because you need to be free as when you do he will wake up with a start he will be thinking he has lost you so you must let him go she is finding someone else for you he will make you happy and that is what you need not a man who doesn't know how to satisfy you." Helen finished with a smile and as she finished she went over to Sarah and touch her face, Sarah's eyes were full of tears knew what she had to do.

Friends, Accepting the Changes

An afternoon of work a night of fun, Helen knew that she must get all she needed to do done and finished, the book had now been published and there would be many countries she would begin to travel too. Looking forward to the fun weekend with the girls, when Helen arrived home she took herself into trance and began to astral travel to her Masters to see what was next. Looking around to where she was now, and then where she was going.

Frank was worried about a full conference room and nothing to learn Archangels and Masters were her main tasks and life Helen would tell them all about the experience of the life she lead Helen agreed with the help of Archangel Michael she would do her best with nothing prepared just to shut her eyes and go with it. Walking in she smiled as all who were there smiled at her she had noticed Frank had his hand high beckoning her to come to centre stage.

After a deep breath Helen stepped forward to speak and with a great confidence in which they all enjoyed immensely the men in the audience also stood with applause. "Hello to all of you I am Helen and I'm going to step in, I will teach you what the Archangels and Masters wish me to teach you. First we will start with a song not on a spiritual level but a fun level as we need to raise the energies, choose your song then sing your socks off we want the vibrations to hit the roof. Sing your socks off I will hum to bring you in." They sang an ABBA song Dancing Queen.

Friends, Accepting the Changes

Recording the singing as they were hitting the rooftops, while she was standing in front of these few people she felt quietly confident to the fact that the Angels would look after her, singing at the top of their voices the roof was beginning to lift to the sky, at least fifty people stood and sang the rest slowly join in with the fun.

Slowly the vibration began to change to a lighter, exciting vibration and Helen asked all to close their eyes, they did just that, asking them to say what they could see, one by one Helen asked she needed a person who her Angels must be able to channel well, close your eyes and then back to understand her life.

She wanted to finish her next book as there would be no time soon she would be busy and she needed to focus on a few chapters of the book before the girl's weekend. Meditating everyday brought new visions into her life Helen could see herself travelling afar, talking to children about Angels and singing with the children everybody loved to sing.

Her mind full of the things she would like to do with her journey perhaps even opening a singing school in the much poorer countries so that all could sing and be happy, instruments to play, full of ideas and she wanted the world to have fun with laughter, knowing Helen that she would try her hardest to supply it in bucket loads.

Bringing that forward, the fun and the laughter Helen wanted to teach. Is this why she would be writing children's books to move around the world teaching children her knowledge of the Angels, Helen knew that it really was the Angels and Masters with her soul mate/twin soul that would decide whether the books would be part of her life and she would have to go along with what they said.

Kate rang as always they chatted every day and it seemed that it was always about nothing but everything she was still soul searching her purpose in life and either the moving forward of the breast cancer and she was looking for something to fulfil her completely and the U.N had been in touch but she was still waiting for some kind of answer, Kate wanted to travel far and wide but she also needed a steady home life and that she had not had all her life, but she knew her controlling of men she must now let go, there was a man who Kate liked and as she was trying to change herself and her old believes and patterns,

Kate remarked to the girls while they were having lunch. "I have changed my way of thinking and I am now going to be a good girl and I am not going to do the three minute rule." "How long are you going for now five minutes or even more than that perhaps you should think about one to three months of the waiting until he says the right words or the words you would like to hear so six weeks of waiting for him to realise that he is in love and wants you to be his wife." Laura smiled at Kate as she began to pour a glass of wine. "Well as I am being good I thought I would give it four minute what do you think to that."

As they all laughed each of them lifted their glasses to celebrate, yet another lunch. "Is that being good then, you will have to do better than that Kate with the next one that comes in, take your time and see what happens let him make all the moves not you, show him the feminine you not the controlling you." And to the controlling person was definitely what Kate liked and it was such fun to watch her start.

But it was now Kate's time to come into her own she was a good soul and needed something to get her teeth into she thought many times of Michael and how she was so brutally rape he is behind bars she thought to herself a slight chuckle as she put him there, that was one of her best and worst efforts of her years in law but she felt he got his just desserts, and Kate did not think of the karma that she had now created for herself in doing that said deed and this was not all over not by a long chalk. There had to be a final end to it.

Helen did remark to her about what she had achieved and if only she had let another barrister take the case, the karma would not have been so hard, but Kate brushed it away as it was nothing she had not yet learned what the Angels can do, if you hurt another person out of malice, Helen knew that at some point soon Kate would get heavy payback and she felt it was not that far away as working with the Angels and Masters made Helen think about what she could and could not do.

There are laws in the Spiritual world and when you are an envoy for them you had to work with the laws of Spirit and abide by them a great deal of faiths did not do that being kind and forgiving is part of that process. If you forgive and I mean forgive and the person you are forgiving still behaves like a sick idiot then it is time to move them out of your life and your energies, you have to look after you and protecting yourself.

Archangel Michael spoke to Helen. "Helen you are so beautiful, so calming, I see you have learned so much and now you teach many people how to live a good and a much more rewarding life and here you are embarking on a life that will reward you greatly and to travel the world with your books will change the thoughts and life's of many people all over the world and also if you wanted to open centres for singing then of course that will happen, but you still must have fun as life is fun so get those suitcases packed and go away for your weekend with your friends before you embark on your travels around the world and many sites you will see.

Before her epic journeys as Helen had a tick list for her to travel to the places she wanted to see. Helen was called on to visit the Heavenly Realms her gift was to be their envoy, her souls purpose was to teach, she stayed calm as she thought all in a day's work, it's all in a day's work she said to herself, and then I am called on and the travelling mode kicks in who needs an plane when you can astral travel easily, again she thought all she done was in a day's work. So her calling had come again, what had she done wrong or was it more orders of the day that she had to take on board.

To her surprise not an Archangel in sight she was being fetched by two of the Masters and so proud of that she was Brother David and Mother Mary were at her side, Brother David was a master of enlightenment, Mother Mary a lady of great love and compassion, Mother Mary was now Helen's protector and she was always there when the healing was needed for Helen or for one of her clients.

Helen was an ascendant of Mother Mary and that is why they worked so closely together every day. Travelling to the Heavenly Realms was short but calm, no jet lag here and no air hostess to come along with the drinks either. Just a gentle, calming and releasing energy that felt as if you had been on holiday for a month or more, it has to be enjoyed for the love and healing you will receive Helen loved the meditation and astral travelling. Knocking on the big wooden door and as it opened it creaked.

"Mother Mary the door needs oiling or is it to say we are arriving so that each one can be ready." Helen smiled her soft smile Mother Mary took Helen by the hand and walking her through the open door and into the large hall of which had an array of different candles were situated at every place that could be mentioned.

Friends, Accepting the Changes

As Helen walked in she smiled at all the Masters then looking towards the top table, and there was Jesus next to the Holy Spirit, both were so great in stature both gave so much healing to all. Helen was now going to be introduced to all the Masters as they would be coming into her life in a great way.

El Morya Master of the first ray, the most beautiful blue eyes stood before her, he was connected to the Temple of the will of the Higher Spirit, he connects to all esoteric schools and Abraham is now the Ascended Master El Morya as he took Helen's hand. "I thank you Helen for your great understanding of our world, I look forward to working with you our Helen."

Helen looked to his hands, her hand was small in his she looked into his blue eyes, smiled her joy was so immense, the energy in this room was so tremendously calming, full of love and joy, this would be a journey as he was such a charming master. She began moving around the hall watching all the energy, the glow from the Angels and Masters certainly kept the Heavens warm. Lanto Chohan of the second ray, he was an ancient Chinese Master he developed light in his heart that shone through like a golden ray of sun through his flesh his aura filled her soul.

"He then took Helen's hand nodding his head bowing as he spoke in a gentle manner. "I worked with you many years ago Helen, do you also remember Helen when we healed so many people together and I took you through your divorce but all is soon to be well."

Friends, Accepting the Changes

Speaking in his soft spoken voice he was such a gentle soul, he bent as he kissed her hand. Next to Lanto she saw the beautiful Italian Master he was Paul the Venetian his eyes were to die for, he looked straight through Helen as though he could see all that he needed to he was the Chohan of the third ray, the ray of Love he is easy, light and had started changing all the stiffness of the Heavens it has now become open and reachable to all.

"You have love in your eyes, you have love in your heart, you have love in your mind and you are open to all. We are going to change your world, we will bring your love we will bring the world to you." Helen looked at his eyes they were drawing her in.

She was then taken to the next table Master Serpis Bey stood up to greet her. "Come Helen I am the Chohan of the fourth ray, I hold the temple doors open for you when you visit, I like you are the great teacher and I am the keeper of the white flame." "You have a great way about you and of course you are the keeper of the door of love as Venus is where you ascended from."

It was so interesting to see all these light and wonderful heavenly beings with open hearts and divine guidance. Such a gift and such a privilege for Helen and never to be let go .Helen was watching him why are these men so beautiful their eyes are divine, she smiled they must know what I think she thought. He nodded to her great wisdom she touched his face gently.

Hilarion was next to him and he took both of Helen's hands then placed them together. "In prayer I will help you I am the Chohan of the fifth ray the orange ray the temple of truth is totally where I am connected I connect with you in Truth and Trust."

He held her hands close to his face she touched his face then nodded. Then a women master was the next one to meet she was the humblest of women she reached for Helen the energy was so strong. "How humble have you been, how humble you are Helen   you come with great love." Lady Nada spoke she was the keeper of the sixth ray. Nada means nothing and that is why she is so humble, she is Jesus's twin flame, Helen looked at her. "I hope one day I will Lady Nada aspire to your humility."

"You do and you have we have taken you back to the mountains to think and now you are back here to live and love, we will bring your twin flame we will bring your love do not look for him there is no need, we will bring him to your door."

Helen looking to her left noticed an aura to her delight he was strong, protective and courageous, she felt he would be able to give her the strength to carry on forward with her life and the many tasks the Heavenly world had bestowed on her. She felt that this time of great struggle to find what people wanted and needed to bully her in such a great depth what was it about her that they did not like and what was it about her that they were jealous of.

Friends, Accepting the Changes

Looking at this great energy a turban on his head he was a great teacher he enfolds them in his Cosmic Flame to give them all the strength they need, his name Maha Chohan he was the Chohan of the seventh ray. He draws the energy to supply nature itself, he is the power force and head of the Elemental Kingdom he is the magnet the draws the power from the Sun. He is the Chohan who gives the first breath to the new-born child, also the last breath of every individual before passing to the Heavenly world.

The other Masters stood to be greeted in front of Helen Djwhal Khul stood he is The Tibetan. He is one of the most accessible Master of Shamballa he is the Master of the second ray of love and wisdom taking Helen's hand he squeezed hard and said. "Have Trust and Faith that all will be well we are now moving your life forward into supreme joy, happiness and love to shine." Helen smiled as she knew that she must be strong in whatever they bring forward to her "I do and I am waiting to see it in the earthly world."

Kuthumi he works under a yellow ray and that aura was around so bright and fresh, he gave great love, great wisdom. He was the wise man Balthazar, Shah Jahan and St Francis of Assisi then he works with Archangel Josphiel. Looking at Helen and smiling he knew she was the cheeky one they all talked about.

"Helen I have been listening to all my friend's talk of the cheeky one that is you we feel you have a great understanding of our world." Babaji standing next to him remarked the same he was the immortal master of the Himalayas, the energy in this room was intense healing with such a bright aura, there was such a power with all these Masters with love.

Coming to Melchizedek he was the Master the highest priest of the heavens he held all the secrets of the Universe. And the true history of the planets, of course Jesus was one of the high priests in the Order of Melchizedek. Sanat Kumara he is from Venus he helps humanity from the lighter realms of the world. Each of the Angels, the Archangels and the Masters were now bringing their world into Helen's, they were now certainly going to help her change the awareness, the love of the world, with that she too would become what they wanted and needed to bring forth the changes. So much work Helen needed time to play she would be up for a girl's weekend soon, it would be a definite weekend of fun.

Chapter Three;
Girls Weekend Fun! Fun! Fun!

Here we go and here we are on the way to yet another fantastic, brilliant weekend of fun in which of course had to include Champagne and good food! Helen thought. The night before they were due to fly out to Venice all the four girls were on the phone to each other asking what they needed to take.

They would be going to Madrid in Spain the next weekend away so Kate and Helen will have to get drunk and be insensible the next weekend away they were good at that. Sensible was not what they were about not on the girlie times.

Helen wanted to cram in many insensible days before she was too well known, as there may be too many cameras about she did not need to be photographed playing the idiot, even though the Angels may laugh, most of the humans frowned on such frivolity. "Condoms; pray tell me girls who is taking the condoms then."

Laura needed to know because she was determined to use as many as possible on her trip, unhappy Laura needed to let of a bit of steam so to speak, sex was the only way it seemed that she could let off steam, her home life was not good in the department of John and sex, their relationship was slipping away and they were drifting apart.

John was busy with his past life trying to sort an ex's problems out. Laura felt that she needed something to grab hold of she thought of a nine inch length of pure lust, to say the least. Kate again thought she might go with the flow to see if she gets an offer, it would depend on how tasty he was and if she wanted a quick shag or not, as for Sarah, she was all over the place grieving for her son, grieving for her life and she did not know who or what sex she wanted again she was mixed up failing in life so miserably.

Helen was worried she might go down the road of the undesirable, Sarah needed a weekend away to find herself but now is not the time for any of that, now is the time for fun and if the girls needed to let their hair down with a quick shag in the cupboard then so be it.

Laura had packed enough condoms for the world to use, she was a sensible girl no rubbish would she take home to John, not that he would know as sex with them was non-existent. But of course Helen was trying to get across to her that she should run her life like she said and not always the way Kate wanted it that would be Kate's downfall as she had to learn that people were not the same.

Friends, Accepting the Changes

Different people of course set different values in life. Their life purpose of being here on earth in their lives was completely different to anybody else.

Cases packed and at the airport and walking straight through into the Champagne bar there were a few oysters, sushi and whatever else there was that they had never tried, they would be well on the way to starting their fun weekend in Venice, and John had decided to make sure Helen had a body guard but he was not to spoil their fun and Helen certainly was not to try to behave because he was there.

"That's good Helen he can look after us, does he do any of the other personal duties or is it just body guarding that he is allowed to do, he doesn't shag as well does he it sure would be good if he does as he would save me looking for sex." Laura chirped into the conversation thinking it may save her a lot of time if he did. "NO leave him alone he has a duty to perform and one of them is not shagging you Laura keep your hands off him."

Kate looking into Laura's eyes with a smile and wondering whether Laura would spoil the few days they had pursuing a man. "He should be here in a minute we have got an English bodyguard not Italian never mind, I wonder what he looks like." Helen slowly looked around to see two police officers with a gentleman whose muscles happened to be ripping through his shirt you could feel them move like a stallion as he galloped the fields. "Say no more Helen there he is what a hunk, well girls keep your hands off him if you can.

Mmmm what could I do with him, three or four minutes what the hell." Kate liked the look of him and she began to imagine herself touching his body with the oil she had in her case. Mr Bodyguard please come to me she thought that was going to be his name behind the scenes he came over to them looking the part and to top it all he was smart, tasty and smelling good and he did had muscles to die for.

Rippling all over the place such handsome beauty was walking towards them like a stallion each muscle moved slowly, carefully it was magnificent and he looked as though he knew how to handle anything with everything but he was Helen's and he had a job to do I wonder does he realise what he has let himself in for poor man or lucky man. The beauty of a man who can care and protect and still look and smell the part Helen loved that in a man and a brain that he uses well and at the right time.

He will not be able to party that is against the rules he was there to look after Helen so to looking after her was much in his thoughts as he walked towards them. All four of the women were mouth open and gasping as he arrived to be introduced. "Helen this is Brian he will be with you on your trip and girls leave him alone to do his job, I can see it in your eyes what you would like to do to him but you cannot out of order more than his jobs worth."

Sargent Horricks said with a smile and most certainly a glint in his eye he had certainly picked up on the girls very well. "Ok Sarg but oh what a challenge I fancy a challenge don't you Laura." Kate chuckled at the thought of this poor man having to put up with them fighting and encouraging him to break the rules, would he succumb. This would be definitely a few interesting days to say the least.

"You're terrible Kate he is here to look after me making sure I do not get kidnapped or even worse than that." Helen was looking at Brian, and was thinking out aloud I can see what the girls are on about but keep your hands off Helen you're married. So there he was Brian had joined the fold he was in for a hard time literally.

As the girls continued drinking their champagne and with a few nibbles in front of them, Brian finished loading his gear then to the coffee bar, no alcohol for him he made sure he was in eye of Helen he knew she was safe within the airport.

Kate watching his every move she was a predator Laura was also looking and thinking of touching that firm bottom that is what she liked. "There's certainly was something about a bottom with tight firm buttocks they are always delectable aren't we lucky Helen to have such a gorgeous man in our midst we can go to bed thinking off him, did you bring your vibrator Laura I think there are going to be some noises going on, our floor will sure be a vibrating." Kate looking at Brian as the words began to tumble out of her mouth. She didn't care what she said it just flowed and you had to deal with it.

Friends, Accepting the Changes

"Vibrator Kate you've got to be joking that is not what I want at this moment in time, I am expecting a shag of some sorts so

I brought condoms, Helen I bet you've got your vibrator." Laura slowly began to open her mouth, and then she placed another oyster inside. "My vibrator goes with me everywhere it keeps me out of trouble." Helen watched Laura as the oyster slowly slipped down her throat picking her glass of Champagne up then taking a sip. "You should try it, you might like it maybe it will keep the urges at bay."

"Flight number BA 2043 boarding at gate 22 passengers for this flight, please make your way to the gate." A voice over the loud speaker system, then the girls made a rush of their Champagne and food. "Come on ladies let's go fun to be had we want to make sure we are in our seats and ready for our next bottle of the best Champagne they have on offer for us. Brian come on we are off now the flight is boarding are you in first class too." Kate taking control of the situation as usual, no wonder we called controlling Kate. She knew how to control everything it must be in her nature, here she was Controlling Creamy that's Helen's name for her.

"They began boarding for the flight to Venice and fun to be had with bottles of Champagne and tasty food." Laura picking her bags up, a little bit of airport shopping then moving towards the gate the line of people looked far too long what could they do but excuse themselves to move to the front of the queue. As soon as they were there they were moved swiftly into the plane and into first class, Brian watching Helen all the time watching her back keeping her safe they were all sitting very close.

"Are we having Champagne I am sure there is some sort of food, well I asked for the best caviar etc we are here to live it up. The air hostess started checking their seats, making sure that they were seated properly. "Are you with these ladies sir as I only have four on the Champagne and food list did you also want to sample some of the delights that these ladies are sampling on their journey to Venice, we can make sure you have what you need."

An older very attractive lady and of course she made you feel at home. "No Champagne for Brian, food yes if he would like some I am sure he will like it, it's an experience Brian enjoy it." Helen was looking outside watching as the ground crew manoeuvred them to taxi for take-off there she sat steady waiting for the take-off.

"You might like it Brian a little bit of good tasting, tempting mouth-watering food and little bit of naughty does you good." Laura had started her play for sex and how would he survive the five days of these women. "Bodyguard for our Helen as she needs protecting, Angels protect her and now a bodyguard, she is a lucky girl we all could do with him."

Kate remarked as she settled down to wait until the food was served. Enough said Helen was now taking deep breaths as the cabin crew sat in their positions, they were all set and the hotel they had booked look fabulous to be enjoyed, Helen had chosen well. They were on the runway and racing for take-off and off, they were all on their way.

Champagne for all of them the ladies certainly knew how to spoil themselves, the flight was quick and looking out of the window Venice was insight it looked beautiful. All the girls were ready for a Sauna and Jacuzzi, with the champagne in their system they were enjoying the moment. Brian was booked into the room next to Helen he needed to be close at hand, no good having the room next to Laura or Kate he would not survive, Helen felt safe with Brian about she knew he would put her life first. No more game play, no more rubbish for Helen.

Collecting their baggage to find that they were being taken to the taxi and then onto the Gondola taxi loaded with their luggage as well, two to a Gondola that way it would not sink. Helen was so enthralled it was so amazing, so beautiful. A grand hotel with all that they needed they unpacked and straight to the Sauna for a couple of hours of this, a sleep and then on the town and more Champagne. Laura had already found the man she would have in her bed tonight, once she had said "Goodnight" to the girls she was her own person she could shag the world.

Leaving the hotel on a night of Champagne and fun, Kate kept one eye on what all of them were doing the other on a very young Italian who had caught her eye, tanned, wavy dark hair with dark hazel eyes, she knew that he was her Adonis she could have this one for the night it would only take a night of fun to clear the air. And so to speak the cobwebs at bay but Laura seemed to be the one who was searching. Always searching for something she was no too sure that she would find and when would her time to settle down happen.

Pasta seemed to be the dish of the night as in Italy they would do as the Italians do. "Helen it looks like you are the only one sleeping well tonight, Kate and I have other plans and Sarah well she will have her head on the pillow." Laura definitely had been drinking far too much, also looking as though she had too. Sarah was now beginning to worry Helen as her company was not so good, she had gone into herself but only she would find the solution to the trauma she is having.

"Ok, nobody is taking Brian back then have you all gone off him, or is he just if you get a NO tonight." Helen taking a mouthful of pasta, it was delightful as the fork placed the food on her tongue it just melted. "This pasta is good how many courses are we having it certainly tastes does a bit like heaven it melts as you take a bite and when you swallow it leaves a taste of the sauce." Helen was thinking of going with a little bit more weight on why not a few more pounds will not hurt.

"Only four courses and that to me should not be too bad I'll just have to shag a lot to get rid of the extra calories." "I like the look of Mr Wavy hair he looks hot to me, do you think I should go over and introduce myself he may speak a little bit of

English but after the meet who cares what he speaks as long as he knows what he is doing between the sheets."

Kate staring towards him he looked her way then looked to Helen. "Helen you cannot have him your taken behave yourself it's us the needy ones who should have the fun." Laura beamed as she came out with the words of sheer lust, my goodness she was so drunk. Both Helen and Kate moved themselves nearer to Mr Wavy hair he certainly looked and smelt good. He could see what they were doing, chuckling to himself. Mr Wavy we will call him.

"Hey there Mr Wavy, come over here we are in need of some male company, I do think you will do." Helen and Kate said together as Mr Wavy looked to the women. Brian looking on he did not smile too much he was just watching what was going on around Helen, but then he was there to do a job. Mr Wavy made his way to their table. Dark eyes and firm buttocks, that was enough to be going on with, they sat together and gathered for some drinkies, staring at him with wilful eyes he was certainly scrumptious to look at.

Laura found him very interesting as soon as he opened his mouth and speaking in his Italian accent was enough it was to die for, all the girls sat enthralled with their mouths open. "God, you would not have to anything just speak to us that would be an orgasm in itself." Kate longingly remarked as she watched and listened to his words.

Friends, Accepting the Changes

All four of them took a deep breath as he rolled his Italian in their direction, if only all men could learn a sexy language and then reel it off while in the motions of passion it would be great Kate thought it could be a quiet evening just listening to the sound of Italian being spoken.

"Oh well, enough said girls are we going to keep Mr Wavy with us all night or should we let him go to Laura?" Then Helen's eyes turned to Laura to catch her gaze that was hard to be honest she was mesmerized. "Why me, I think we should all take a vote on that mind you if he is coming with us I want him all night, so at the end he is mine."

"Ok girls let's put the hands up for a yes, down for a no think first this is a man on our fun weekend." All three quickly placed a hand in the air, job done he would be staying the night and ending in Laura's bed isn't she a lucky girl. Whatever next they all shook their heads that was Laura at the moment and there was nothing to be done but smile.

To the next hotel on the Gondola they would travel stopping off just for a glass of "Champagne" at the nearest bar, then to be straight back to the boat and up the river to the fabulous Hotel Emporium a beautiful view, inside chandeliers that were crystal the furniture was Antique and very tasteful the smell of incense filled their nostrils, their senses grew to like the aroma it reminded Helen of a Catholic Church at high mass all we need now is a choir, the choir of Angels and then we would be well in heaven.

Friends, Accepting the Changes

Slowly walking and taking and everything in Mr Wavy hair in his wonderful broken Italian/English accent made their eyes water and their knickers wet. Two huge lounge chairs which were as big as the sofas were before them as they spilt into two each grabbing a chair end then Laura placed Mr Wavy hair completely next to her, Laura wanted to make certain that everybody knew she was not thinking of letting him go tonight. Helen smiled and as they all sat down in their places Helen out of the blue said.

"Do you sense Angelic aura's in here, I do it's so beautiful, so warm there seems to be so many around us, I feel it is the atmosphere it's like a big cathedral, a bishops church so to speak, Helen putting on her teachers hat.

"Champagne man come here please we want a bottle of the best Champagne your finest." Kate lifted her hand into the air as if to summons him to court. "Caio Una Botella de Champagna, grazie bene." Helen was trying to habla in her broken Italian language with a little bit of Spanish it doesn't matter they understand just the word Champagne was enough. "Sie, sie Madam una momenta per favore."

The young waiter answered her with his Italian smile they certainly knew how to charm with a smile. All in hand Kate thought to herself Helen came in handy. Mr Wavy hair was there but Laura had her hands on him, he was hers for the night and she was sure the hell going to enjoy him, she knew condoms were a must here.

Friends, Accepting the Changes

Four glasses, and a beer for handsome here as the girls became merry, Helen turned to Kate. What do you feel about this Kate I am, well I think I am, Kate I am thinking of buying a boat." "What a rowing boat Helen we will not get far with that and not many friends in it either."

Kate again answered Helen in her humorous way, it was either controlling or humorous, no middle ground with Kate. "No, not a rowing boat, not a yacht but a big boat, a squadron 78, actually Kate I thought we could hire a boat and get some horny men to crew it, what do you think it is only a matter of a phone call.

"Helen looking at Kate for the usual smile of naughtiness as they both always had a cheeky glint in their eyes, Kate watching Helen for a moment but the moment seemed an hour as Helen wanted an answer quickly. "Could you do that Helen in such a short time, it could only be you and I on the boat with all those men, top it all Helen you cannot be naughty what a shame I can."

Kate turned around to watch Laura as the words came out of her mouth, she smiled at her then a loud chuckle filled the girls table when they were together it was such fun how Helen loved these times, she knew they were short lived as their friendship was due for a change.

"I have my Architect coming out with some plans so she will be there for lunch, then I will get Brian my bodyguard to drive her to her hotel, you will like her, posh totty but very down to earth." Helen nodding her head as if to say I forgot one more. "Her name is Rose McIntyre but she will let you call her Queenie as that's her nickname." Helen remembered what Queenie had said, she would be pleased to come for a day just to watch the girls at play.

"So is she an HRH like my number plate so will we be fighting over who is the most senior royalty." Kate topping up her glass as if she was on a mission with the HRH number plate Kate though she was most royal. "No Kate you are ok as I am the most senior so let's not get too worried. Helen then placed her head on Kate's shoulder as is she knew what would happen next. "Kate I am thinking of buying a boat."

"What a rowing boat Helen we will not get far with that and not many friends in it either." Kate yet again answered Helen in her humorous mood, Kate was either controlling or humorous, no middle ground with Kate. "No, not a rowing boat Kate, not a yacht but a big boat it's a squadron 78 actually Kate I thought we could hire a boat, get some horny men to crew it, what do you think it is only a matter of a phone call. "Helen looking at Kate for the usual smile of naughtiness as they both always had a glint in their eyes.

All four girls and of course Mr Wavy chinked their glasses. "Here's to fun times and here's to good sex at some point in the next five days." Laura began clutching Mr Wavy's knee her hand slowly stroking his leg, travelling the length of his leg. Mmm I think he is in for a good time she thought to herself when she reached for his crutch. They all laughed to find Laura just did not care who was watching, she was going to screw this man and that was that such a tart we all agreed on she was a definite tart.

To the restaurant for dinner then to doing their own thing Helen and Kate would stay in a room together they needed to do some chatting going on about the book signing, shopping and what to do about nothing. Each ordered something different so that they could sample on another's dinner that needed to be done, the food was extremely delicious, Laura kept a tight hold of her man for the night that is all she needed was a night.

Helen had noticed the changes in Laura, she knew this was needed time from her John, and that they were slowly drifting apart, no talking to one another a recipe for disaster, the food was a delight the wine was exceptional many bottles had past their lips and Brian the bodyguard knew by now what to expect from these ladies.

"Trouble" with a capital T and he would have to keep his wits about him and his main focus was to watch that Helen does not disappear in the night to go out and have more fun. They all began to retire to their bedrooms and this was going to be such an interesting game, Helen left to go to the penthouse suite with Kate. Laura took her Italian Mr Wavy with that she booked a room of their own, laughing and giggling to the lift.

Friends, Accepting the Changes

"Kate do you think, dare we go in with them it may be worth a watch, she would be so annoyed and frustrated that she could only go so far while we were there." Helen turned to Kate with a drunken grin she tipped her head to the side. "No, I think we should catch the later lift, could be a bit steamy in there Helen and there are no men waiting for us upstairs, so let's leave them to it."

"What are you doing Sarah, have you found anything interesting for the night, tonight that is Sarah, there are loads of interesting people for you to choose from both men and women." Helen then took hold of Sarah hand making her feel uncomfortable. "The maid is turning my bed down in my room and I have booked a massage." Sarah answered with an amazing smile, one they had not seen for a long time.

"Good on you, mmm it will help you through the night, did you bring some toys to play with, no don't worry too much information." Kate began to sip the last of the Champagne, the bottle that was downstairs in the lounge Champagne anyway, up to the Penthouse and I am sure there will be a couple of bottles there for the taking.

Waiting outside the lift watching Laura stepping in they all just smiled and then said together. "You're a naughty girl but enjoy we will try not to think of you." Helen, the girls, the laughter hit the roof Helen made the remark. "Can I have the gory for my next book please, it could get someone's juices running hunni and we need the juices running we need for me to stay famous so there has to be more and more books for the world to read Helen and if they are as good as the first we will be laughing all the way to the bank."

Laura watched the faces of her friends as the lift door shut tight hoping that they would not want to join her, she began shutting her eyes she took hold of her Italian Stallion and slowly beginning to manoeuvre him closer to her, his lips felt warm and soft, he did have a tender way about him, then slowly kissing her with more and more intensity he wanted to please her knowing that this would only be for tonight he needed to show her how he could perform, this would be again a night to remember.

Laura most certainly had many nights to remember each man was different, each man was the same and each man pleased her in different ways, tonight was her night she needed this to again to decide what she needed in her life was it John or is there something more adaptable for her on the horizon, she would soon find that out, now to the task in hand.

Screwing this young man senseless was to be an art and she had decided her art skills were definitely one hundred per cent. The lift reached their floor, not an ounce of clothing had been removed, walking calmly to her room.

The key slotted perfectly smoothly into the lock, the door was opened to the room it was slightly messy but did she care no not at all this man was here just for her to satisfy her every need not to clean her room, he sat on her bed as he watched her take one layer off at a time, throwing her clothes to the floor, the last few items she kept on her bra, thong and her stocking they were to be kept on until the last he could take them off with his teeth.

Pushing him back onto the bed he fell back with a jolt then her lips reached his mouth she kissed him with the vigour of a woman who had been without for so long, in sheer desperation she wanted him, he was trembling with excitement, his shirt came off in one tug his body surprised her, taking a deep breath while she began feeling his tanned muscular torso, thinking to herself I hope that the rest of him is just as firm.

Undoing his trousers to see what was hiding she looked in amazement at him there in view she watched as his penis significantly grow and noticing what size he had grown too extremely large, her thoughts were of this was going to be an amazing night. Leaving him naked for just a minute to view what she was about to receive.

He started to sit up taking hold of her and kissing her softly. He being so gentle with her then to slowly taking her thong away to reveal the jewel that he wanted for the night. Slipping down so that he could slip his tongue into her clitoris, finding what he wanted, softly his hands were feeling their way, pushing himself into her feeling the wetness and in her wetness wanting more as she screamed for more, he felt that he could now explode but no not yet, he knew that she wasn't ready this was the fun part and the penetration would be completion.

Laura screamed again with an excitement, the pleasure of his tongue and his hands brought her to a climax once then again and again her orgasms were on free flow, they were flowing from her like a machine gun one after the other, he was rock solid now ready to make his way into this dark, wet, warm and extremely inviting cave.

He lifted her up only then to slowly bring her down onto his firm hardness, he was amazing, could she take all that he was offering then slowly she felt him enter her. Laura in the thralls of passion screamed. "Right there, right there mmm you are there."

God this is good, this is good, this is very, very good pushing his way into her until there was nothing showing he slowly began to play with her clitoris he was inside the wetness, this warm inviting place he loved whoever it was, slowly he moved at the pace she enjoyed if only for a while quickening the pace screaming with delight Laura lost count of her orgasms but then again who's counting it could not get any better than this and this is the first show and this would carry on all night, Laura would be making the most of what was on offer.

Waking in the morning to a man getting dressed and ready to leave was not in Laura's mind, opening her eyes slowly to see the tanned body dressing instead of undressed was not what she wanted. Laura looked at him surprised at his quick getaway she wasn't at all finished with him, there was still a little work that needed to be done. "Where are you going hunni I need you here for an hour just a quick time for me come on we will have a shower."

Laura enticing him with her naked body her advancing years were still good to her the signs of an aging bottom and breasts slowly but surely were beginning to drop but that was no bother, a quick spurt at the gym would make her feel better on that score. In his broken Italian English language he watched her pace the floor and then shook his head in dismay. "No, no I have to go my wife will be waiting."

Wife Laura thought to herself he has a bloody wife, she still did not want to end this situation he should leave when I tell him too not when I am half done a wife she did not need. "Wife, you have a bloody wife ok pack your stuff hunni and off you go I do not need that shit I am here to enjoy."

Marco then left in a hurry his embarrassment was so much in his face. He walked out of the door and Laura slammed it behind him and one thing she did not need was an arsehole and he sure was one of them and yes he was an Italian arsehole to say the least, ok she thought lesson learnt, always the hard way at least she did get a good night of sex before his departure.

Into the bathroom and the shower was welcoming she jumped in and on her own with her vibrator that she would enjoy. Meeting the girls for breakfast in an hour what a story to tell, being mad gave her an extremely high powered orgasm, she had her fix for the moment.

The Hotel Gritti Palace she thought was certainly worth the money, Helen had made sure it was the best Hotel for them there was no scrimping for her anymore as she now had money in abundance and never wanted for anything but she would keep the days of humbleness firmly in her mind because that was a place she would never return to, they had spent their first night at the hotel which actually made life easier, today they all would explore and have some fun.

The hotel was built in the fifteenth century it had been refurbished but to a good taste they had retained its original style and look which was becoming to the energy it felt calm and serene. They would all have their breakfast at the Canal Grande it would be beautiful and a late breakfast as it was now 10.00 am they all met in the lobby. "How was it then Laura, your sexy night with the Italian stallion or shouldn't we ask." Kate gave Laura a hug, she did not seem to have a twinkle in her eyes, normally after good sex you should have a twinkle in your eyes.

They made their way to their table, there were four chairs waiting for them, they were all sitting towards the Canal it was a beautiful. Just watching people go about their day, the Italians loved to chat they were very tactile they had hugs and kisses whenever they met, Helen loved Italy and Helen would be exploring Italy for a new home in the coming months.

Friends, Accepting the Changes

"Champagne for us ladies please and with four glasses, we need some extra nourishment for are walk through Venice and of course the shopping." A lavish breakfast was sure needed just for the stamina for their walking through Venice it was going to be beautiful, and Helen loved beautiful places as her energy embraced the beauty.

Helen made her gesture to the waiter to come over to take their order, she spoke in Italian and her Italian was certainly improving, French and Italian were her goals, Spanish Helen let go years ago as the mind games were played while she was learning, now to breakfast as it was the start of the day a new day.

"Come on then spill the beans how was it Laura you do not look your normal self well come on did he or did he not perform to your liking? Helen gave Laura a wink but Laura still not budging from the face she had. "Fantastic, absolutely bloody fantastic he knew what to do and where to go but in the morning when I was trying to get him into the shower he then told me he had to go home to his wife. Wife was I pissed off or what, wife I do not do wives I was so mad I then threw him out of the door in a hurry."

Laura then taking a sip of Champagne and the glasses they were given were beautiful crystal, none of your standard stuff, they were the best for the best. "Here's to men and their dicks, I in hoping they are not all pricks like this one." Kate then started to remark to all the girls in her London accent. "Common as muck you are Kate yes common as muck, so, so common." Sarah looked at Kate with her posh air about her. "That's our straight and to the point Kate, she knows how to be common when she wants to be and that is the Dagenham girl in her".

Helen loved her Kate she was her best buddy in the world they had some fun times. Remembering the time that she had taken her son Mark to the hospital, blood tests he needed, Mark had been addicted to drugs and now to drink all because of a woman, it broke Helen's heart to see him like he was Mark sat beside her in her car he started to cry his words with his voice trembling. "Mum I have six months to a year to live, I am so scared." Mark was now diagnosed with Hepatitis C common with drinkers or was it the blood transfusion he received the year earlier in hospital when he was so ill.

Mark had kicked the drugs habit years before and found himself a job he quickly sorted his life out then met a girl who was a heavy drinker and his life then began the downward spiral. Helen so wished he had never met this girl she was all of pretence and she hurt him so much. Now he was dying the ex was still having a good time with other men.

Helen's energy hit rock bottom Mark had just taken every single bit, her stomach turned, her mouth was dry another lesson and a heavy one at that what is she going to do she had to work for the Angels to keep herself afloat otherwise they would not connect with her if she was crying all the time. Helen felt angry that he had taken the road of drugs and alcohol abuse and she was going to go through this as well, it was the process of the death she did not want to see, but there was in his death she still could contact him.

Helen was so angry with him for putting her through this when she was so needed by everybody and she had to keep so cool, her private moment would be the tears for her son. Leaving Mark on his doorstep, her tears then became an ocean she could not hold back anymore. When Mark rang her to tell her that he loved her so much and he was so sorry for what he had done to her throughout the years, and her anger came flooding out. "You took me through this twenty years ago and now I am having to live it all over again I am so angry that you are doing this to me.

Let me know when you have had your bloods done and what they are doing next with you, looking at him his skin was yellow his eyes were yellow his liver was now beginning to pack up, all she kept thinking was what was he doing to himself, she could not help because he knew he only had himself to blame but he wasn't strong enough all these hard lessons.

Kate raced to Helen's side to stay the night they stayed together a bottle of wine and enjoying her company. Trying to drown the sorrow of death and only to find in the morning it was still there hard that it is. "Come over to mine at the weekend Helen, we will have fun we will go for a long walk and then some cake and coffee, it will get you away from the home crowd, the so called idiots" Kate asked Helen in a caring way. So Helen did just that as soon as she arrived at Kate's the Champagne was opened, a Jacuzzi then to the next day three hours in the woods.

They walked along the pathway to the woods down came the rain it was so cold and wet but it was fun looking to the road as the cars came them really fast towards them, they were splashing in puddles all these cars.

"Move over here Helen as you could get wet and that's not what we want, we have a long walk ahead of us." Kate was laughing she was watching a car that was speeding down the road. "Look at that there Helen a pothole in the road move over here now." She then remarked as she looked to the length of the road. Splash! The car flew past. Squish! The water flew into the air, and Helen was soaked and it went in her mouth, her face got a soaking, they both fell about laughing.

"Well that's the second, this time last year at your old house was the first and now this, I look forward to next year in your new home in Mundon or could it possibly be somewhere really warm so that I can dry off quickly." She could not stop laughing Helen wiped her face and carried on walking. Finding the way into the woods, Helen's mobile became the navigation system she had hooked it onto the satellite.

Helen and Kate were now acting like a couple of children, jumping in puddles. "How deep is that one, it looks deep too me Kate should I jump in like the Vicar of Dibley to see if it goes over my head I should have wellies on." Helen started to jump as Kate took her hand helping her across the water she was wet enough as it was she did not need wet feet. "You'll find out if you fall in Helen, come on grab my hand I will take you safely across the water." A smiling Kate grabbing Helen's hand so tight just to make sure she did not fall in the stream. "We should have worn wellies we could have jumped in and had a good splash."

Helen was now laughing so loudly, her stomach hurt with all the laughter. "Come on you can be navigator, I will be driver and we will drive around the woods." As Kate pretended to steer the wheel and she was making noises of a car. "Brrrruuummmm". She laughed and Helen with her phone on the satellite working well. "Ok go this way Brrrrruuummmm they were both running and laughing together." Simple fun or was it simpletons more to the point they thought looking at the bluebells in the woods it was a mass of blue, it was so beautiful the smell was of spring.

"Ok we will now be trains come on Helen whoo whoo!! They both started to make the noises of the old stream trains they were a couple of little children playing the fool. "I will be the coalman I will shuffle the coal on the burner, stuiisss cha ka cha." Helen was now making the other noise that a stream trains make they were running through the woods being a steam train.

As they nearer a waterfall they stopped to take in the beauty and the energy, it's so beautiful in here Kate, I am so glad we made the effort. And then a pathway to choose, Helen and the satellite were working well. "Let us be planes now Helen, you follow me as I am the first plane." Helen's stretched her arms out and they both then started making the noises of the plane over head.

"Come on we will both be jets now then Helen eoounn." They were dipping there wings, they were coming to the last part of the woods only to find it was blocked by a log. "Look Helen we are blocked here but not for long we will find a way to get through." Kate was standing with her hands on her hips and so cross looking but not letting a log get in the way of their fun.

"No we are not, we can be horses we can jump that, off you go Kate, neigh, neigh, clip clop, clip clop." Helen noisily enjoyed the moment, Kate joined in with the fun when they left the woods both of them felt light and like a different people Helen felt good.

Back to town, they were freezing and wet with puddles galore. "If only we had our wellies on I love puddle jumping Kate let's go and get cake and coffee." Helen finding that on her way back to Kate's she began to write a poem to her son, the son she knew only had a year or eighteen months before he was taken back to the Angels a hard road lay ahead for him and for Helen to have to watch him slowly fade before her eyes.

Friends, Accepting the Changes

The Son of My Life

The son of my life, the life of my son,
The ending, it has just begun.
To the day he revealed to his despair,
His life was ending, he thought he would share.
"Six months to a year, I have been told.
"I'm frightened mum, I will never grow old.
The tears were falling down his face,
He never wanted to leave this place.

But the Angels have now a ticket given,
The date to be decided, reach for the gin.
My son he was troubled, but so beautiful.
He will find peace, his journey to call.
Hard days lie in wait until the Angels come.
They know to look after him, for he is my son.
Archangel Michael is his caller to the gate.
My father his guide, It's all to fate.

Go now Brendon, listen to them call.
All rushing to help you taking you through it all.
The pain is now gone, I know you love me.
My love goes with you, you are now free.
No more struggle, no more pain for you,
The light it cometh to guide you now through.
Do not be frightened you will see what I see.
Come back for a chat then set yourself free.

Friends, Accepting the Changes

I will not cry for long, as I must let you go.
For with the Angels I want you to grow.
Lift yourself from your bed, into the air.
Climb to those hands, look back if you dare.
It's lovely before you. It's warm to be,
No stress you will have your Spirit is free.
I miss you greatly but my heart will mend.
I will let you go quickly my love I do send.

But low and behold they still keep him here.
More lessons to learn for him I fear.
The crossroads is sure his path to find.
Maybe he does not want to leave his life behind.
She was so sure he would do what he felt.
Living for life, for life to live, his life was dealt.
Hope he soon finds the key to open heaven's door,
As Spirit is true forever, forever more.

Just a few months later my son, his life came to an end.
That journey so hard, in love he left and I did send.
Valentine's Day was the day for Goodbye's
The strength he gave me, the love in his eyes.
He was free from pain, he would soon be well
Soon to be training, a guide for spirit to tell.
My son, my Brendon. Today you are with me.
When fully trained, again to be free.

As Helen finished her tears were falling this is one lesson she
did not want to learn she had so many lessons so much

learning, now to the end of it please. Time for lunch and then to the Hobbit House, lighting the fire, and then to get the Champagne going nibbles and chocolate all goodies to make her feel better. The next day leaving for home a place she hated but the Angels still kept her here.

All these thoughts a million months away but still very much in her mind she thought of her son when she had her quiet time her moments of stillness. And there in her moments of tears he was standing before her. Life can be so wonderful but yet so cruel.

Coming back to the time she is was Venice they were all sitting down to breakfast, Champagne with fruit and cake. "Look girls that waiter's bottom it is so firm, I just want to go over a give it a tweak". Kate was looking for something but what I do not know. "Ok come drink up we have some sightseeing to do I want to go shopping, I thought we would go to Emporio Armani it's on the Calle de Fabbi, San Marco.

And there is a place near there to buy lingerie Calle de Frati, we can do a day of it and then go to Harry's Bar for Champagne cocktails there is one they call Bellini cocktail it's Champagne and peach juice sounds absolutely wonderful to me, shopping and a few of them we can come back have a rest and then get ready for a great night at the restaurant Antico Martini, I booked it last week as it is for the high society which we are this weekend so come on girls lets go party."

They were out in the lobby and not knowing whether to take a

Gondola or walk Sarah who was at her quietest she was obviously deep in thought not only had she lost her son but also her father had passed to the world of the Angels she was finding it hard to deal with it all she needed a good relationship and finding slipping between both sexes wasn't doing her any favours as she seemed to be confusing herself even more but all the girls hoped that their weekend would bring her out of her shell to give her some clarity to life as that should be her focus now.

"Should I go and asked what we should be travelling in to get to this place, as we are going designer shopping I like that, we want the best girls don't we." Sarah said as she walked towards some Italians.

There goes our Sarah trying some of her Italian no doubt. "What happened to are Italian stallion guide then Laura is he worn out he could have come with us today Laura despite the wife at least we could of had an interpreter we need one of them." Kate was poking fun at Laura and she was not too pleased with him. "We'll get by do not worry just smile and they will speak to you in broken English no probs with that and gestures too."

Helen would guarantee that she was beginning to be noticed as her book was now a best seller everywhere they were getting special treatment. Sarah came back all excited she had sorted out the taxi trip. "Ok we can walk or be taken by Gondola or the horse and carriage what do you all want to do." "Let's go by

Gondola we can look at his bottom while he is working away sounds good to me."

All of them picked themselves up and made for the exit waving to the Concierge as they left they knew how to get favours he was all smiles, these ladies he watched wherever, whenever he could they were so interesting. One bottle of Champagne down it was time to shop before they shut for lunch, trying very hard to be ladylike when climbing into the Gondola they set off not too far for the designer shops so that their credit cards would be stung.

This is a time when Helen actually enjoyed spending she had many years of being poor but now the world was her oyster and to enjoy it she will her bodyguard close by her side just behind her she was so special.

The shop they were looking at and needed were full of labels and making their way to the shoes. "I need at least four pairs as I have outfits at home that need shoes, also need handbags to match." Helen was picking up beautiful navy pair of Jimmy Choo shoes. Kate was looking at them then wishing there were a pair in her size.

"They're beautiful just the right size heel for you Helen but a bit expensive too, 700 euros that is a lot of money but they are beautiful smell them they even smell beautiful you have to have them Helen." Kate didn't really care too much about money if it was something she wanted she would have it, it was that simple.

"Yes, that is number one, let's have a look at the Dior ones silver with pink, I have a dress that is black and silver with those shoes I can add a touch of pink that is if I can find a handbag the same." Looking around they did, Kate had bagged herself three pairs of top class shoes Sarah was frightened to spend money as she felt there was no need plenty of shoes in her wardrobe, Laura was sifting through like it was a jumble sale but she did find a pair she liked, smiling around when she placed them on her feet.

"I feel like Cinderella at the ball, look at me where's Prince Charming mind you it will be a bucket and mop for me just like Cinders, woe is me I have to do all the tasks while the girls are having fun."

"Come on Laura who got a shag last night as you know well none of us did only you and a handsome Italian man for you hunni, Kate and I had were left with our teddies Horace and Arthur only cuddle bears nothing else so you have had it good so far but tonight Laura you are out with us and no you are not taking any stallions back to the hotel we are at a well select place and we have to behave somewhat, well in the sex department anyway." Helen nearly fell over herself as she stretched and began to pick up her bags of shoes.

"Ok we are here for another four days so I can play again and that is if you allow me to hunni." Here they were and Laura with her beautiful Cinderella shoes was now off to the bag department to get a match. Kate was checking her bill, they would leave the bill checking to Kate she will know when she is being fiddled.

"Sarah are you coming tonight we can take a Gondola to San Toma and then walk it will be great but we have to be there by nine sharpish as they will let the table go to one of their own people as it is a fall moon do you all want to go to the Piazza San Marco it is so beautiful and the best time to visit is today no clouds just the moon and the stars we can enjoy the Italians and walk around like they do. It is the heart of Venice and a must see when you are here."

Helen had done her research as she wanted to get the best out of this trip also much Champagne was called for. Kate picked up a beautiful red bag and the label said it all Gucci. "Yes, I am having this one it will go with the shoes and the dress I bought in London. Mind you I do need another coloured handbag for my shoes at home so I am going to treat myself today." As they all picked up what they needed it was off to Harry's Bar with Champagne first then some lunch.

Kate opened the door to Harry's Bar they walked in with all eyes were on them, it was as interesting in itself. "Sit yourself down Helen you make the place look untidy, we sure need to be tidy here." Kate said with a massive grin she certainly knew how to be sarcastic. "I am going to have Champagne and cake for my lunch. It will be bellisimo" Helen trying her Italian magic for the girls and enjoying it greatly.

The Italians make good cakes of course all must be tried while we are here Helen thought, the girls would love them. She would go home with a little tummy or a big fat tummy to be precise that was the aim of this break they would certainly be trying all sorts of food. Champagne turned up it looked like it was to die for they would have many of these.

"The menu la tarte por favoure did you hear girls, speaking in the native tongue." Asked Kate, talk about a mixture of languages, Kate certainly knew how to do that. One menu and four cakes on order this would be the tasting and then there was to be another Bellini for each of them placed on the table with the compliments of that gentleman over there. "He looks good enough to eat I might have a go at him if I had loads of Champagne cocktails he could look a lot better than he does at the moment, Mr Champagne Man."

Laura had now named him he was Mr Champagne Man was she going over to do the chatting up or would Laura wait and grab his number for later. There she goes up and at it Laura had reached him, she was about to take his number when he wanted to talk to Helen and made a play for Kate as well, Helen whispered to Kate. "I think he wants three in a bed he should be so lucky Helen." He began to ask Helen about her book and about the sex was it one by experience both Helen and Kate were crying with laughter.

Friends, Accepting the Changes

"What is he like my god do you really think he feels he is God's gift I am sure he does never mind." Kate was surely crying far too much while she was speaking to Helen. So what Laura had done to encourage him over and after five Bellini's it was time to move on and if either Kate or Laura wanted him they are welcome to him that is what Helen thought anyway. She would be returning to the hotel then to sleep. In a couple of hours they would be getting ready for a night out too much all in a day, a great day of fun and laughter to be had. The four friends knew how to have fun.

Long dresses to be worn and they would evening dresses yes they all four of them looked incredibly beautiful Kate and Helen wore a pair of new shoes. "I'm feeling really good tonight Kate I am now where I want to be all those years of struggle and I have finally made it I am famous I am important it still has not sunk in what I am and what I have been through to get here, Creamy lets go and have fun if we do not get to the Piazza San Marco tonight we can go tomorrow it will still be a full moon then." Helen was so humble in her thoughts, no pressure they were on their holidays.

"I tell you what Rainbow we will have a great time we will go with the flow to see where the night takes us I do want to spend some time with the Italians to see how they have fun but we must try and keep Laura beside us not to be taking her knickers off again." They both looked at themselves in the mirror like twins they both came out with the same words. "Looking good we are looking good look at us a couple of horny women." The smiles from both the terrible twins grew bigger by the minute.

They met Sarah and Laura in the lobby Laura had found a Gondola to take them to San Toma the next stop then a short walk to the restaurant Antico Martini. The moment they walked in all heads turned their way mind you they were all stunning. "Your table is ready ladies come this way I have placed you so that you can see everybody that walks in." All four of the girls followed the waiter to their table he must know they are nosey girls.

Their table was in view of all Helen kept smiling she felt like a million dollars. "Look Helen you are being stared at if anyone asks you for your autograph say you are on free time as you could be here forever look at them all." Kate began to look at the wine list this is the most important part of the menu. "Kate do you know what it sure is fun being an Angel." Helen was in her Angelic stance and was looking towards Kate she felt like an Angel, she looked divine what could be more Angelic.

"Actually Helen why not just tell them to fuck off as you know you are on free time and you need that free time." Our Sarah said with an angry smile but we forgave all that she did as her life was one big muddle she needed some guidance and love that is where we all came in to help her on her journey. Helen started to look around the room just to see what the Italians were wearing as she took a glance into the corner she made eye contact with a lady who knew how to dress, who certainly by the looks of who was around her came from good stock she smiled and made her way over to Helen.

She was a definitely a coat hanger for labels looking at Helen she smiled. "Good Evening, I am Maria and you are Helen the author of Friends, The Journey, New Beginnings & Endings may I say it is a brilliant book you have another to come I need to read it a sequel then more books to write and publish."

She held her hand to out to Helen as this was the first time Helen had been recognized in her fame and someone actually walking over to her she found a bit daunting it was different when she was pointed at. The room was beginning to feel rather large and Helen could hear all the chatter around her. Helen stood up and then to take her hand she smiled a beaming smile for her audience which was now becoming excited at the thought of Helen in the restaurant and their presence.

"Yes I have two books ready now to be published one a book of poems and a sequel to the first book, the poems are first I believe it will be published later in the year and my sequel will be published in Valentine's Day next year. It is just as good as the first I hope you enjoy." She looked at the waiter and then turned to Kate. "Let me offer you a bottle of Champagne the best it is wonderful you have come to Venice and I would like to welcome you."

Turning to the waiter Maria nodded just by that nod he knew what Champagne to serve them. A bottle of De Venoge Rose' 1976 arrived at the table as Kate started looking at the wine menu she was surprised to see how expensive it was. "Helen its 600 euros a bottle she obviously liked your book goodness make sure you enjoy every drop of this girls I think I should take you everywhere I go Helen as you could be my opening to a large Champagne waterfall."

Sarah just felt a little out of place the mourning of her son then her divorce was taking its toll on her well-being they were all trying so hard to keep her smiling with great difficulty and what a task for them all. "Come on Sarah you can get drunk tonight we can have to have another bottle after this one has everybody made their choices on a starter and main, Helen has I have we are having fish on both." Kate as normal in control of the life situation and that's our Kate.

As one of the waiters took their order the other made sure their glasses were kept full of the Champagne. "The bubbles are beautiful this Champagne is the bee knees." Laura raised her glass to be followed by all three of them. "Here is too many best sellers of the books too life, fun, good sex and freedom." Laura also smiled making sure she did not spill a drop of Champagne. "Too many best sellers, fun in life and to whoever is in my bed tonight."

Helen and Kate copied each other what was life all about. Sarah raised her glass she smiled and each one of the girls looked into their eyes even though she was broken and said. "Cheers I will drink to that I want to enjoy tonight, I know I must let go." Their evening was full and they were certainly made welcome the laughter from their table was the loudest.

Laura wanted and needed a man any man to be precise and that was the energy she was giving off you could see the determination of the predator as Laura was people watching to see who was free for her to screw. She had John at home what was she playing at but Helen was not going to work she was here to enjoy and would have a word with Laura on their return. They made their way back to the hotel all thoughts were to Piazza San Marco and to the full moon a wondrous sight for them it would be such a breath taking place to be watching the crowds and mingling with them.

Hold onto your purses everybody they managed to find a Gondola it was a different feel altogether at this time of night there was magic in the air and all four of them could feel it. "Helen is it supposed to be spiritual or something or was she just having fun." Kate asked in a loud voice she certainly enjoyed the Champagne, they all hoped to find somewhere that they could have a little drink while being in the Piazza.

They finally reached the Piazza San Marco the crowds were noisy and exciting. "Well it is not that spiritual, it's just fun and let's see if we can find a watering hole then we can walk around to get the feel." Helen was enjoying the moment when the moon was at its brightest and all their eyes were on the clock tower as it was an Astrological Clock for Helen this was so interesting and with the moon shining brightly onto the clock there was a different glow about it.

There was a bar situated very close to the clock so they finished off the night with an Amaretto on the rocks it topped the evening and then to see what was there thought Laura as she was again on the search for the bed partner tonight. "Laura what do you think you are doing you're ours tonight got to keep your legs crossed." Kate starting looking at her with an uncertain glare what was it about her at the moment did she not understand that it was not all about her it was about the friends and enjoying their time together as none of them knew when the next time they would get a chance to do this.

"She's just looking Kate, when you think of it there all Italians well dressed and when they speak to you there is a guarantee your knickers will be wet." Helen squealed with delight at least you know that they will look after you. "Now Helen should we ask what do you mean by that statement have you participated in some Italian delight or is it that what you wish you had of done? Laura started to giggle as she thought of her night of passion.

They all started walking around the edge of the square nodding to all as they passed Kate was continuously looking at Laura each man that came into contact with them she said. "No Laura." They managed to get home without Laura taking anyone back to the hotel then each one of the girls went to their own rooms. With the next day dawning they would have to set out what they were going to do for that day. It would be a Gondola day with stops of Champagne that would be a certainty as all the girls agreed it was called for.

Helen slipped between the clean white Egyptian cotton sheets she felt alone her son Mark she missed so much even though they had their own way of life just before he passed she still had moments when she was on her own that she felt so alone in her grief, the tears began to fall when she remembered the months, the days before he passed, like it was yesterday.

The pain with the anger then to think if only he could get better and to the final passing the anger for her daughter in law who was so hateful and envious of Helen being the centre of attention with the death of Mark he died alone in his bed and was left unnoticed for four days he had been out drinking to celebrate his younger brother Simon's birthday.

Friends, Accepting the Changes

Down the local pub drinking like it was going out of fashion, being found slumped at his own doorstep drunk, his friend put him in his bed and left him there, that night he died alone only the Angels who came to take him back home were with him, at least he was at peace now he had no more pain.

Helen kept feeling someone trying to give her a message she knew the spirit that was trying to reach her but just did not know how to communicate, he was found by his friend four days later dead as cold as ice. The Police were called but they did not bother to find Helen it was his close friends to come and tell a friend of her son Simon and it came to Helen's door in a way she did not want.

Cremating Mark on Valentine's day Helen stood there and read the poem for Mark it was heart breaking and then a month later saying goodbye to Simon as he had been taken over by his wife who did not want him to be by Helen's side anymore it was all about her, all what she wanted and needed, Simon's mother and sister were no part of her life she let them know that she wanted Simon to herself and that is what she got.

Helen had lost two sons in a matter of weeks, leaving Simon to make his own way back to her when the time was right for him but his wife would never be a part of Helen's life again. All she could think of was her son Simon saying that he was so proud of her and the way she stood up in front of everybody and read the poem just for Mark.

She wished Simon was with her when the grieving was hard, where was he when she needed him nowhere to be seen, it was a journey Helen done on her own. Watching Mark changing colour from pink to a yellow was not what Helen felt that she wanted to see.

In her quiet moments she felt him so close to her he had been to see her on his birthday it was a beautiful sight to see his spirit body, it was aglow with a white light he just sat then said "Hello Mum" that is how he always used to greet her. A moment of calmness, she closed her eyes to find that the Angels were there with her protecting her. She drifted and remembered the time that Mark called her saying her was in hospital, that he was not too sure what was going on.

Leaving work behind Helen jumped into the MG and flew to the hospital was this it did all these months of watching him slowly go downhill to a man of nothingness.

Walking into the ward she was taken to the sister's office. Mark has limited time now he wants to see if everybody wants to come to see him friends began to look after him is this Mark's turn around or are the Angels still going to take him back home to spirit and they did, he left her eighteen months later seeing him for the last time lying on a slab looking as though he had just fallen asleep he was at peace finally, Helen was broken but released of his pain.

As Helen settled to sleep Kate was at her door she needed company she needed to chat. "Helen can I come in I need to have some company let's raid the mini bar I am feeling a bit lonely not used to sleeping without you when you are here and around me." "Come on then what is the problem, when do you start the new job soon I hope as you need a focus and it has to be a giving focus for you to understand what life is all about."

Helen opened a bottle of Champagne from the mini bar, she turned around to her delight Kate had now placed herself in her bed on the side she normally sleeps she is so funny. "You have got your side then come on Kate take a glass let's have a chat tell you what Laura's a card she would have found someone else tonight if we had not insisted that she behaved." Helen began to explode into laughter and loudly to her amusement Kate did the same they were beginning to uncontrollably laugh stopping only when they had a stitch in their sides.

"Helen do you think she is unhappy with life as it does say something when you are looking for fulfilment two nights in a trot that spells to me things are not so rosy with her and John."

Friends, Accepting the Changes

Kate exploded into laughter yet again here we go again both of them found the fun they used to have. "Well she certainly needs a good shag to settle her down mind you I wonder if Marco was that as she should have satisfied for a least a day if not two mind you I can remember the time on my own if it was good I needed more so perhaps it was good, what do you think Kate."

Helen then started manoeuvring her way to chinking glasses to say here we are. "Salute." "Well Helen I do not think Laura was happy but you never know perhaps we should let her find another Italian tomorrow night so that she can have a good horny night then she will be really contented."

Kate decide to tell Laura in the morning that she could now have a good night of shagging before they go home in a couple of days that was to be done at breakfast, clear the sexual tension then to get the paper The Daily Mail because it is easier to hold no ink print and it has the gossip we all need that sometimes. The Gondola's were asleep Helen and Kate were now going to catch a sleep before breakfast in four hours and to work out what they would be doing for tomorrow.

Another day, another breakfast all continental that is what they liked. "Did we need the Champagne today or shall we leave it to lunch time we could enjoy just travelling around in the Gondola's popping off at each station to see what was there let's just make it a day of relaxation." Kate was tucking into her

Friends, Accepting the Changes

Croissant not even looking around to see what was going on. Helen looked at Kate and then over to Laura who was then at the door chatting to a very handsome man who was looking rather tasty.

"Kate I think Laura might be a bit busy today it seems she has spotted someone who might be with her today or at least tonight, so let's wait until she comes back then we will decide." Laura looked as though she was certainly enjoying her moment with this man a very well dressed but did not seem to be Italian.

"I do wish she would hurry as I want to find out who he is." Kate was looking at Laura's body language she seemed so sure of herself. "Yes he is I do feel she has already slept with this man she certainly likes him. I have got a feeling it maybe Mr Billy Blaine a man from the past unfinished business here I believe Laura will be for a good time tonight if he is around."

Stepping away from Billy and Laura then returned to the table to let the girls of her plans. "Well you'd never guess ladies I think I am on a promise as I have got my shag tonight Mr Billy Blaine wants me to have dinner with him is that ok with you three as I do need to see if he is willing to have some sort of fun easy going relationship with me until I have sorted my life out with John you know we are struggling a bit and I need to see what this is all about." Laura was now bouncing with delight but the girls were a bit disappointed with her as it was their weekend.

Friends, Accepting the Changes

The Gondola's were waiting for the Champagne Cocktail run. "Onwards and upwards girls let's make a move, we have a Gondola at our pleasure today." Helen grabbed Kate's arm knowing that Sarah and Laura were following behind. "Bye Billy, I may see you later if you are free for me look at him girls it will be worth the shag I tell you I can remember last time it was an all-nighter."

All four of them then said together, Mr Billy Blaine went to look and then just smiled, looking at these girls from the corner of his eyes. He hoped all four women were not around here tonight as much as he was an extremely confident male the thought of these four women together slightly frightened him.

The first stop would be to go to Harry's bar with a few Bellini's, the Bellini's they were becoming so addicted to them, they would move on to visit some of the Palaces then to do a spot of people watching Helen needed to watch the Venetian life, to watch the cosmopolitan way of living. The Canal Grande would be the first trip as the sweeping along the Canal and taking in the sights of the city flowing past the Pink Palace it was so beautiful in the warm sunlight.

Dinner in the evening would be at the Venetian Glitterati, they asked the Concierge to book a table, the restaurant was a hard one to get into, Da Fiore and the menu was to die for they would be looking forward to that, hopefully Laura would come too they could see the dreaded BB was hovering and the girls did not really need all that.

Friends, Accepting the Changes

A man on the prowl like a lion surrounding its prey ready to pounce a man really to pounce is not what was needed at the moment as this was to be a girl weekend it was just horny Laura was at her worst she needed a good shag and that is what she would have regardless of what they wanted of course John who was now in the background, John it seemed was not doing the deed anymore they all looked to Laura she was beaming all over her face Kate thoughts were of fun as much the same as Helen. As Kate smiled towards Helen her question was to Laura.

"Laura when are you meeting the big BB tonight as we have a booking?" Kate said as she was looking to Laura in great anticipation of what she would or maybe wouldn't be doing. "Tell me Kate where are we going then is it a good restaurant? And what if I get asked out for dinner do I say yes or no?"

She then began to wonder what was the right thing to do she was looking forward to a good night of screwing and that certainly was and is a must but it also would be great if she could get some kind of romance going, as she has never found John at all romantic lately. Helen began to feel Laura and her slight distress to see what she should be doing.

"Ok it's going to be sex or friends what a choice I have Laura no pressure sex or friends dinner? Helen immediately spoke to Kate knowing that she would set the rules. "What would you do then Creams as you always set the rules and of course we all have to live by them." Creams that was Kate's nickname it suited her very much sometimes bland and too restrictive not free flowing well not anymore.

"Well to think of it I do not know as I would want to be with all of you but and that is a big but a good shag would be great if you can get it as the old Billy Blaine knows how to please a girl eh!

She then turned to Laura waiting for a reply to both questions that Helen and Kate had asked. "I am going to see how I feel as he may not turn up and I want to be sure that he is there first and go with the flow." Laura had now done the thought process, digested it and worked all through the idea.

"Ok then it is for all of us to be downstairs at eight thirty and we will go from there the table is booked from nine thirty you know it is The Restaurante Du Fiore the food is to die for the waiters are horny need I say more. Oh and by the way it is a much sort after place for the Glitterati. And us being the foreign equivalent we will be going as it normally the place to be I do think we will enjoy girls.

It has one of the best wine cellars in the city we could just get lost in there if you want to and come out slightly drunk."

Helen began giggling it did not take a lot to make her merry just a couple of glasses of Champagne and she was there. Again there was to be a night of fun even though both Helen and Sarah had death's hanging over them. Helen with her son Mark and Sarah with her son and father so they both needed to be sure they were having fun now as they were certainly in the understanding that life was far, far too short.

This life is not a rehearsal it is the real thing and she knew she must make the most of it to get the best this she would have to instil into Sarah one way or another. Helen's thoughts were of her son Mark she remembered the phone calls they had. "Hi, how are you what have you been doing, how's your bloods and is your money sorted?" She knew she was questioning but Helen needed to know what was going on in his life as she could feel every pain.

"Bloods next week mum, I am ok friends are taking me out this weekend so I am being looked after." Mark was sounding cheery well as cheery as he could be. "Are you eating well how much are you drinking and I know you must be drinking as you are finding it hard to let go."

Questions, questions, her questions she needed to ask her life was also in limbo as much as his was she needed to know the time when Mark was being taken to the next life he used to tell her about the spirit's he could see at the corner of his eye, he could see them walking around him, and he knew someone was there with him while he was going through all this soon he would be on another journey to another place.

Helen could feel that the problem with death is that it has a habit of catching you out and it normally is at the most inconvenient moment but then that is life. "I am drinking about four cans a day mum and before you ask yes I am eating well, I weigh eleven and a half stone."

He was now reading her mind they were certainly the questions she was going to ask. "I am praying hard to the Angels as I do not want them to take you to heaven yet, you need to enjoy life and to work with people that are like you Mark when do you think the doctors are taking you into rehab." Helen began her questions again but they were now coming to an end she did not need to know any more than that.

"Soon I hope, I will be in there for two months, I am sorry mum for causing you such pain I love you." She could feel her tears coming to the surface she could hear his sorrow at where he was, she could feel her heart breaking at this time.

"I love you too are you happy really happy I mean?" She asked thinking to herself. I am happy, do not worry about me." Helen had to finish this painful conversation. "Just you be happy Mark please I just want you to be happy it doesn't matter how long you have just be happy."

With the goodbyes and the love sent that was it they had finished their phone call Helen had for moment finished her questioning well for the moment anyway.

The days were now long and the nights were so short. As they were setting off again for the next Gondola they would decide where to go for the Champagne and lunch. Tomorrow there was to be a new addition to the fold, Kate had invited Margaret she was a politician and it would be interesting to find out what she was about. Helen would do the tapping in and then they would see if she could now and then fall in with their way of thinking as she had to be fun, the girls did not want a stick in the mud. Margaret was really interested in Helen's work, Kate had told her all about Helen but she wanted to see for herself and Kate was now looking for a new position in the UN.

Where she was at she was definitely not getting the best out of her life. She needed to grow more and she felt she needed to travel more too as her life was slightly boring and Kate did not like the idea of boredom. The conversation with Margaret would open doors and she knew it she and her contacts would do just that. At least Helen would find out the other side of the political life as they certainly were getting away with murder at the moment. Then a position of power and they thought it was a guarantee to abuse the system.

To the Champagne too much work talk is not too good. "I think we should take a look at Harry's Bar and may I say that I love the Bellini's there. "Ok, let's get today over with we have much fun to cover and I think we should cover that fun and much more because she might not be like us, bit of a toff so I hear and they can be so, so controlling she may even want all the day to go their way, crumbs Kate you will have competition so let's enjoy ladies, enjoy the moment of today as for the tomorrows may be a bit harder unless we can get her round to our way of thinking that is it our way of thinking."

Friends, Accepting the Changes

Helen chuckled to herself she knew Margaret would not be like them. "But." Kate started to come into the conversation knowing what Helen had said would be true. "She will want her own way, we cannot have two controlling people in our company we only need one controlling person and that is me and not everybody is like us we are normal.

There are a great deal of people not normal like us you know that one Helen look at your last home town it took four years to move on and then it was no different how many years to be free again at least six years Helen that is a lot out of your life." Kate pushed Helen gently with that they both laughed and they all knew the past.

"I know nobody is as normal as us and we do not need any more of us in the world there would be too much fun around so to speak we would not get anything done would we Laura when are you meeting Mr BB?" Helen was all smiles it would be great to hear in the morning what the night was like whether he actually came up with the goodies this time or whether the last time was a one off all ears and eyes turned to Laura waiting patiently for an answer.

"Get them eyes off me I am meeting him at 12.00 tonight he is having dinner with a client and then we are meeting for drinks as such then we will see where it all goes, I may have a massive smile tomorrow at least he is not married he is divorced now so he has to change his life."

Friends, Accepting the Changes

"What's the as such then and such is this a new word for sex I want to know more, enlighten us then Laura enlighten us of all the goodies of as such we may go looking for some as such." Kate and Helen both simultaneously asked would Laura answer them well they did not expect her to, she came back with a firm no. "No. I will tell all tomorrow that is if he is any good he might have lost his touch by now who knows, really who knows I do not know.

I am looking forward to it though he was definitely a good screw last time. Could be better this time at least he knows what I like as such." Laura began smiling when she smiled it was good as she could be a bit hot tempered. "There's that as such again we have to find out what this as such is as it could be as such fun." Helen screeched with laughter these were the times she really enjoyed so much.

"Come on then off for Champagne and some lunch, whoo whoo Gondola's are a coming, Gondola's and Champagne or Champagne and Gondola's what the hell all could be fun Champagne is a must or even Champers in the Gondola do you think we can get that then Kate, where do we find the man with the Champagne, bring him on hunni, bring him on as such there's that as such again it seems to be all about as such."

Helen began to gently push Kate with her hand she knew that pushing Kate was dangerous she could come back with a big punch.

Friends, Accepting the Changes

"Helen we could pick up a bottle at the reception and then off to the Gondola that is what we will do them come on who's room should I charge it too?" Laura stood and asked in a mischievous way knowing that it would not be charged to her room. "Let me think Margaret's that will be her first greeting unto the fold our MP unto the fold as such." Kate wanting to see if the MP would except their friendship in a big way or whether she would be too snooty and really did not want to be part of their world.

"Ok, Laura you get it and charge it and then we will see if she takes umbrage then we will pay. As you know that is off course part and parcel to becoming the next into our club." Helen was looking very amused at it all this will be her test of new friendship.

Off Laura went to do her duty collecting the Champagne how would she be able to charge it to a room that the person had not arrived yet well we will see would she be all smiles when she was back all smiles and with a bottle of Champagne more to the point and to have it charged to Margaret's room would be better, fun, and definitely fulfilling.

As they waited moving themselves to the door, Champagne would they get the four glasses or would it be drinking out of the bottle. Four Champagne flutes they needed, then their Champagne then would be ready to enjoy.

They all made their moves to the giant doors at the front Helen looked over her shoulder to find Laura still chatting to the young girl at the reception. "I need your best even better Champagne with four glasses to take out and could you charge it to Margaret Winston she is arriving tomorrow it will be a good present for her." Laura and her chat she convinced the receptionist to give them what they wanted.

"Senora we do not normally do that she is a friend of yours. I will have to ask Mr Franco he will have to agree to this." Off she went to the office coming back ten minutes later all this bother Laura thought to herself and where re these girlfriends when I need them. There again one bottle of Champagne and four glasses came out of the office with the young lady she smiled from ear to ear.

"Now Senora if Ms Margaret has a problem with this we will charge it to your room, room number 268. Sie. Ok." She smiled as she handed all over to Laura the glasses were picnic glasses so they could fit into bags and pockets for the day. "Grazzi, multi grazzi, Ciao.

The girls hiding behind the door laughing at Laura her face was a picture, she was smiling from ear to ear as she walked out. "Come on then Gondolas here we come all we need is a strong man to pop the cork." Laura laughed as she scanned there area for a strong man there were many men around but who would she give the pleasure.
"We will find an Italian stallion, look there are loads standing there men like buses look at all of them there for us, grab a

man Helen, grab a man but watch where you grab that man though not his balls." Kate jumping for joy they were in for a good day. This was certainly a weekend for loads fun and laughter the girls were beginning to like these Italian men they certainly knew the patter, Laura played her games as Helen watched and smiled. They loved their time together it had been a long time since they have had a weekend of fun and more to come.

The Italian men well they were so attentive and all the girls liked that. Moving forward to the Gondola's a man caught Helen's eye he was the most gorgeous looking man she had ever seen. "Let me have the bottle and see if my charm can work on him." Helen looking at Laura to then take the bottle in her hands she was a determined lady and now to have some fun even though she may be happily married she decided men are still there to have fun with Helen and slowly made her move forward tackling this in English would be seductive to say the least.

"Hummm." She cleared her throat it had been a long time since she turned on the charm. "Excuse me, excuse me, could you help me cork my bottle of Champagne as I am having so much trouble trying to pop the cock I mean cork and you look a strong man, you could help me do that little thing." As he turned himself to face her she felt her stomach turned and she was a little hot to say the least he was so horny and it was unbelievable how she felt at this moment. Taking hold of the bottle he then very slowly he took the wrapping off the top of the cork just like he was sexily, slowly undressing her.

Friends, Accepting the Changes

My goodness what could she do with him under the clean white crisp Egyptian cotton sheets. He began to slowly pull and press to release the cork and all this while he was looking straight into Helen's eyes he was certainly making a meal of this she thought to herself he was making love to her while she stood in front of him as he pulled the cork to go "POP" he had an orgasm and so did she standing in front of him she felt so wet, now I can feel what the imagination can do she thought.

"I love the sound of a champagne bottle when it comes to "POP" and then to spurt a little from the top of the bottle." It has sex written all over it. Looking into her eyes Helen just melted she was weak at the knees, wondering what she should say now.

"It does makes you feel that you have come to the moment and a good bottle of Champagne too, may I ask can I join you in a glass it would be my pleasure." My goodness Helen thought what should I do next, she was standing frozen not being able to move anywhere what does she say now. The girls were in a state of shock as this Italian seduced Helen with a bottle of Champagne and they were mouth open and laughing at Helen who was caught up in herself.

She turned to look at the girls standing there smiling they knew Helen had been caught. "Yes come join all four of us, we would enjoy your company very much." He held the bottle firmly. They were only going to find a gondola and sweep the canal's and pop in somewhere for lunch, he could come with them let's

Friends, Accepting the Changes

hope he is loaded as they were certainly not ready to splash the on a man however horny he was.

"My name is Nicolo' Vincenza, I live in Roma I am here to do some work for one week and you with your friends you are here for the Champagne also the Italian men yes how do you like the food it is good for you." His voice his accent was to die for and they would all be totally sexed up all the way around the Canals of Venice. "I am here for chill out time, the fun and the Champagne, if there is a beautiful Italian man for me to look at then so be it we have had such a great time."

She stumbled in saying that just as she arrived amongst her friends. "This gentleman girls is Nicolo' and Nicolo' these are my good friends, Kate, Laura and Sarah." She did actually stutter, nobody had turned her since John, Nicolo knew he was just so horny. "He is going to take us around and some we will find somewhere good for lunch just looking at him will be good, eh girls? Helen started to perk up the girls were winking and laughing at her.

They were helped aboard by Nicolo' he was so attentive, Helen looked at Laura and quietly mentioned to her that he was not there for a fuck. Her face said it all and that glint in her eye said that is just what she would have been willing to do, but he was there to show them around also just for them to look at he was something else.

The sun was hot, the sky the blue of Helen's eyes, there was a beautiful Italian to make the view even better, they were taken down the Canal Grande towards the Canal San De Marco and across the water to San Giorgio Magglore that was the main square and an Italian restaurant that Nicolo' chose he certainly knew where to go. They knew him as soon as his face showed at the door. "Nicolo' how are you, and four beautiful ladies for you and you bring them to us."

The older gentleman who was dressed so divinely he seemed to know just what to say, how to perform and the other waiters just stood and watched the charm. "Nicolo brings to you four English roses we will spoil them and they like Champagne Nicolo." Nicolo' introduced the ladies one by one, Helen looked too Nicolo' she began to speak to him in a commanding voice.

"Nicolo' look here I have an Irish passport not English so you only have three English roses and one Irish Lucky Charm." "Ok three English roses and one beautiful Irish lucky charm and yes you are now the luckiest charm." Such a charmer Helen thought I wish she was old enough to be his mother but what the hell..

Their lunch was a five course banquet with Nicolo' paying for it all he then asked if before we go in the morning in two days he could have breakfast with them all so he could say goodbye take their phone numbers to keep in touch.

Saying goodbye to Nicolo' and finding their way back to their hotel was easy as this Canal they had travelled a bit in their stay in Venice it had been a good trip for them all, tomorrow Margaret would have a day with them that would be so interesting as she was an MP for a constituency in London she would be interesting to find out what was going on in that world of politics.

Morning time, breakfast with Champagne this happened to be the last day of political freedom and Margaret should be here with them, they knew opinions had to be kept to themselves. A loud bounding voice, she walked into the reception area and all the girls noticed her boobs, her low cut blouse when they turned to look at Margaret then at each other a smile to say goodness what have we here.

"Good Morning ladies who charged the Champagne to my room I have put it on expenses it will go through the office as this trip will." Margaret moved in, took her seat she had walked in and then took charge of them all.

"Well ladies what are we doing today I have to chat with my office this afternoon all these tax dodgers we are clamping down." Helen thought there she is putting all on expenses and then worried about tax dodgers. "We are going to be taking a trip around all the canals and dropping off at certain points for a drink and something to eat.

They all could see that this was not going to be a very good day as she was a bit in your face and wanting attention from all who were around her, as to the attention she was getting the girls were not interested in, they all agreed it was going to be a heavy day. They went from bar to bar in all the well-known places they had been too already and also they all had decided that they needed to show Margaret the experience and the different Champagnes they had drunk they wanted Margaret to try before she left for the old world of Houses of Parliament and her meetings.

The day went by quickly the last drink in the restaurant before they all had their chatting time with Nicolo' in the bar, Margaret had left the bar she was leaving at five am and did not want to be chatting any Italian god dam horny man, she just did not know what she was missing.

The bags were packed and ready to leave they were on their way home back to sorting out their lives, waiting for the next weekend of fun it would be in France and a trip to Madrid they would most definitely be without Margaret. The flight was bang on time, Laura was debating whether to shag a young man in the loos she had been such a pain this trip and they all hoped that she could sort her personal life out before the next trip.

Home again they all went their separate ways when they reached the outside of the main Airport terminal. "Have a safe journey all of you and take my love with you." Helen gave all of them a big hug and a kiss. All had their own cars and all went different ways to life, soon to be no more.

Chapter Four; New Addition Margaret!!!

After their day with Margaret in Venice the girls were not sure if she would fit into their bubbly world she had invited them all to the Houses of Parliament also having lunch out in London with her, the arrangements already in place so there seemed to be no going back. They were certainly going to find out what Politics were about. Kate needed to find some answers as she desperately wanted to join the UN in some kind of capacity, Sarah just wanted to look at the art and Helen wanted some knowledge for her new book.

Laura just wanted to see if there were any handsome MP's then how she could take her business abroad was there a tax problem. The girls were back at work now and they were waiting for the plans Margaret had to be set and for her to contact them with the time she was free knowing she was having so many problems in her own life. Her man who was slightly younger than her but he wanted her no matter what he was also in the game of using her.

A builder and not the usual man Margaret would have gone for, his name Jerry he was what Kate called a Jerry boy you would not know where you stood as he would shaft you as soon as you called him up. Kate took an instant dislike to him. Helen just told Kate that it was Margaret's lesson not hers, and she really should keep her opinions to herself.

Friends, Accepting the Changes

They both had fast cars and he was trying to get planning for all sorts of unlikely things to do with building. "Come on Margaret let's see which car gets there first I am sure I will, go on take that challenge." He had a Porsche in black and Margaret a Lamborghini in yellow. The chances are well it depended on the traffic also on the lights and whether he was a gentleman and let her win. They both took to their cars and the starting point was a set of traffic lights.

From red to amber then slowly to green they looked at each other and then pressing the excelorator they both raced off, side by side they kept along the road, when suddenly Jerry pushed his foot down, Margaret did the same they had travelled for at least two miles and with speeds of up to 90 miles per hour then whoosh he disappear trying hard to catch him but to her dismay blue flashing lights appeared behind her.

"Fuck, Fuckerty Fuck. She said to herself not needing this and that this was all she needed, Jerry definitely was a bad influence on her but as she said I love him, Helen was not sure she really did she was sure Margaret just liked the excitement as her job tended to get her down. And the sex was something she held onto. Jerry was not someone she understood he needed to get real.

Would you please step out of the car Mam just for a moment and I want your name, do you know what speed you were travelling along this road, do you understand the speed limit here." The young police officer stared at her, then began to realise who this lady was this was going to be tricky he knew she should have a speeding fine he also knew the consequences of that. "Margaret Henman officer I am so sorry I did not see the signs of the speed limit but I am guilty."

Looking straight into his eyes what was she to do now there were enough problems at work without this being added to them and yes Margaret was being put through the investigation screening for her ongoing expenses she really did not feel the need to be seen law breaking and definitely did not want to be seen getting away with speeding.

There were some onlookers watching her and this police officer, she noticed one of them had a camera he was looking and seemed to be taking pictures. Hell she thought I am screwed if this gets to the House of Commons I would be for it big time.

The police officer started to talk to her about the speed limit in the area she was speeding. "Mam, did you know this is a 40 mile limit this is not a motorway. I am now going to caution you also take your name and number plate down but I will be always watching you. An MP should show an example. So drive safely, no more speeding as I do have your number and I watching you from now on just consider this a warning."

He was straight and firm, so should he be she thought she looked at him with such embarrassment. "Thank you Sir I will remember this day have a good day." She said with a smile the man with the camera just shook his head in surprise he then walked away in disgust at how an MP had just got away with a speeding fine. She knew she deserved it.

Margaret knew it would reach the papers the next day and it did Margaret would have to ride this one and hope it just hides itself eventually. The police officer did not reply to her he just let her go, driving away to another call. Margaret moved away quickly she did not want any more rubbish and needed to see Jerry quickly as she knew he would believe it all to be funny.

Rushing indoors she was fuming and shouting at the top of her voice. "Jerry, Jerry, I have just been stopped by the police and I have a caution, my name taken and a man taking pictures which I know will be in the papers tomorrow, hell I am in the shit. Why didn't you take this problem you are not high profile you must have seen him behind us you're an arse Jerry."

As he walked through to the hallway he was smiling and began to make such an arse of himself, why did she like bad boys. "Eh babe not to worry, at least you got away with it and your here get the dinner on I am starving." "Starving, don't you realise that I will be in the papers tomorrow just by getting away with it all you are the biggest arse I have met in my life."

Walking away from him she smiled to herself; why; oh why do I love a fool, and why do I have someone who cannot understand what I am about hesitating for a moment she then went straight to the kitchen and straight to the bottle of red wine sitting on the side. Two glasses of this and she would feel human again also being with Jerry she was developing a drink problem. But he was a killer in bed and that is what she was so attracted to sad as it was but an addiction to sex was what Margaret had and at least that was a way of kicking stress.

"Good morning Helen I thought I would get a day together so you can come up to London and we will have lunch at the House of Parliament, then we can go to the Champagne bar at St Pancras in Kings Cross, we could then muster over slowly to Launceston in Kensington for dinner or the Babylon that is a roof top restaurant.

There are two more restaurants to try Tipriani in Mayfair, it's an Italian where all the stars hang out you will fit well there Helen there are photographers outside you could be in the papers in the morning, then the late train home there is another restaurant I like Nobu its Japanese and if you wanted to stay in town I could book a hotel for the night."

Margaret so organised and straight and to the point well just like a Politician but was she as devious as a Politician, Helen was longing to find out how in her so logical world would she take to Helen and her Angels. "Ok Margaret I will chat to the girls and see when we can fix a date very soon we are a funny bunch for date fixing as we are all so busy, so be patient."

Helen realising that time was moving on and that she had a client in ten minutes. "Will do I will await your call Helen and by the way Helen I am so interested in your Angels, I look forward to being enlightened by all you have to say." "Ok well that is good I am always worried when someone new pops into our lives and how they will react to me, bye for now speak later."

Helen left the conversation with a smile at least she would not feel uncomfortable with Margaret now she could be understanding to the joys of the heavenly realms, that meant it would not be such a struggle to be in her company. Archangels Michael and Gabriel were standing next to Helen smiling with the glow of heaven.

"Our teacher you are Helen, you are to open the world too love, too understand and start accepting Angels as part of the Universe. People will read your teachings and will also listen to your every word. You are so special to us and you have our protection always and forever."

Helen felt so warm, she was safe with her Angels around as she felt that nobody could harm her as the strength and power they had would keep her safe. With just enough money to keep a roof over her head and food in her tummy she did wonder how could anyone be so envious but they were. It was who she was and what she was, and what she was going to be Helen was an Angel on earth.

But they were testing her to the limit in her beliefs and her strengths seven years she endured she pulled through and cutting out the dead wood of the friends who were not at all what they seemed and with so many admirers understanding her love, her beautiful energy. She soon calmed down and excepted she was so special and would have people on the outskirts of her life that were very envious and that would be a lesson in life for them not her as the old saying goes what you give out you will receive for sure. Helen knew that she was protected Masters, Archangels and Angels all were there wherever she was.

The small rainbows that only she saw were Angels looking down on her, the glow of the aura's, feathers, birds and halo's in the sky all were signs of the heavens looking out for her as they knew she needed them, they pulled their magic together then came to her rescue she had behaved in a way they had wanted her too, Helen had passed the test now to repayment her books working for a magazine and the magic of a beautiful man.

"Kate what day are you free this weekend or can you be free the whole weekend, let me know by tonight as I would like to get this day in London with Margaret sorted as I am so busy travelling soon." Helen laughing down the phone as Kate was grunting and groaning. "What are doing Kate you having sex hunni it certainly sounds good or has the cleaner left you with the work."

Helen needing some answers to the noises that were going on "No Helen I wish I was, I am just exercising and may I tell you it's very hard work, hard work who has decided that we should be fit. I am sure that I am free this weekend so let's sort something out as from then as I am busy, I have now been invited to Washington UN, I am trawling for a good position in a new job I have been head hunted Helen, look at me being head hunted."

Kate was now excitedly chatting, now to the next Helen thought these outings were sometimes hard to get together. "Hi Laura we have this weekend free for London are you ok with that it would be great to get it out of the way as you know Kate and I are really busy the following weeks, I am going to be America storming or putting it all into place and I will not have a free moment after this weekend." "Well then Helen this week it is, do we know the times. I am going on a research journey to Europe finding a place to hang my hat.

I could even try America myself, I do need to expand the business, also John is being troublesome at the moment, but eh! What the hell things will work out I am sure of that Billy Blaine wants to join the business that means I have a great deal of decisions to make at the moment, let me know the times Helen, speak later." Laura her usual self so much to do, so little time to do it in, a couple of days in London shopping and a good restaurant would be fun.

"Ok, sounds good we all seem to be on a new journey but to the ending of special times." The last but not least was our Sarah who was still struggling so much with life Helen was fearful of the phone call to find out what was happening in her life. "Sarah how are you doing, are you free this weekend for

London with our MP we have an invitation for fun." Helen knew that and was asking how she was meant that a big door opening of all the negative things that were happening in her life. The Positive thinking creates a Positive life.

"Well Helen thanks for asking I am not good, I am so lost at the moment I cannot come to terms with losing my son, then my father so soon after each other, there is no support anywhere, still searching for that true love where was it Helen where is my soul mate I yearn so much to be held and understood, who said life was easy.

I am lost at the moment and I could shout help, but this weekend I am free." Sarah a short opening to her sorrowful heart, how they all felt for her and how they just wanted life to be easier but it was something Sarah had to find for herself. "Ok Sarah we will see you Saturday, we will chat soon, before I go to America as I will be out there for a month."

That was it job done Helen now could get ready for her client a client who was so special she too was so close to the Angels and being so close she was being asked to have a special child for them but it was just trying to place the last piece of the jigsaw puzzle in place for completion. She did not want to do that, Helen tried hard to get her to sacrifice her life but she was not too sure whether she really wanted the hassle of working with the Angels.

John came through to Helen's consulting room he loved to

watch and listen to her working. "Angel when your client has gone can we have a special moment as your life is so busy I am feeling as though I need to look in the diary for a free moment for me." John smiling, the eyes were talking Helen thought as she looked at him, walking over to him, touching his beautiful face, his eyes were so beautiful. "John I am all yours after Wendy my client, we can have the next two days of walking and just timeout.

I am in London Saturday but after that all I am doing is getting ready for America, you will be with me some of that time ahhh my hunni I love you." John smiled as Helen looked to the door to Cindy standing waiting to come in. "See you in an hour, a good bottle of wine would be great." Kissing John tenderly Helen carried on with what she was doing.

"Cindy come in and let's question what has been going on you can tell me what has happened and let's see if we can get this situation resolved." Helen took Cindy's coat then pointing her way to the most comfy chair to sit in. "Helen I have had so many Masters and Angels around me and of all of them Archangel Gabriel is now saying the stage is set the show must go on what does it mean?

Cindy sighing as she had been waiting a long time for this all to happen. "Cindy what I am being told is that the stage is set for it all to happen they have the man they need to be your husband and father this is all meant to be you cannot stop it, the man I see that they have chosen is calm, and he knows his job that he has to be kind and protective to you he knows his purpose in life so now he has to make his way forward it will happen you still have to be patient and understand that the heavens are in charge of this you have no choices.

It is as we say fated, destined and all will be fine, but I do see decisions, maybe the child will not be born as it could be too late for all that." Helen smiling she began looking around to find everyone had come for a visit the Archangels and Masters all were nodding at her as if to say you are right, we are in control

"They have put another man in on my path he is to be there if Mr G does not come in. Cindy asking with such worry all I want is for it to be sorted and I can have my life. "What do like about Mr G, does this other man remind you of him, and I also feel you have to allow yourself to move on." Helen quizzed her with an open heart all done with and Cindy had said that the Angels wanted her to have a special child;

Helen was a special child and to become a special adult Louisa was a gift from heaven but Helen kept feeling it was a little bit too late for Cindy was about to have her best relationship ever that is what she had been asking for, years of waiting, The Masters, Archangels, Jesus and Mary were all standing watching Helen as she calmed Cindy then brought an acceptance of what her path in life was.

"Dominic reminds me of my ex-husband and he has so many

traits of him, Genaro reminds me of my dad before he met my mum then settled down." Cindy answering in a calmer voice now was Helen actually getting through. "And if Dominic reminds you of your ex-partner why would you even thinking be going there again even though it's just a reminder, you have done that journey never to do it again. And of course Genaro reminds you of your father; your father was a kind man to you, so tell me why would you go for Dominic and your father changed when he married.

Genaro will change because he will know his role he has to keep his promise Cindy to protect and care for you but you still have to put Genaro on the top shelf and focus on your life and leave all the sorting out to the Heavenly beings. Stop worrying please I always tell clients to go for a man who is kind, gentle, supportive and also extremely protective.

Your life is about to change for the better you must go with it to be free and flow there also must be an acceptance as to what is in front of you also if Mr G does not change and settle then there is another man who will take that role." Helen had the agreement of all who were standing around she knew life, love will certainly calm Cindy down, Helen had learned that working with the Angels she left all to them, in telling what she wanted and needed it was up to them to provide as she was theirs her journey had been hard but in the hard learning she had been given the best in life.

Cindy left with a smile and that is what life is all about still months later still in the same way of life she was blocking everything that was meant to be in her life, Helen could do no more. Helen now returned to John the night just for them was called for as Helen had turned her phone off then the quietness it was so peaceful. The music was Classical Arias she was bathed, smelling beautiful, placing a red smooth as silk dress over her body, also her lingerie was silk and classy but also very sexy she would dress to seduce John they both needed tonight.

That closeness would be a fitting start to a wonderful weekend finding her red high heels slipping them on her feet and standing in front of the mirror she looked so beautiful, even at the age Helen was there was a knowing of the definite beauty she was an interesting lady that is why she creates so much envy.

Taking herself into the Kitchen, picking up her Nigella Lawson cookbook a simple recipe for seduction was called for. A bottle of wine was opened by John he left it on the side to return to the lounge collecting some papers but as soon as John heard Helen in the kitchen he came to find her, moving slowly towards her his arms were welcoming his lips were warm so gentle he was such a gentle lover.

A little bit of Classical Arias made the cooking easy, Helen was swaying to the music her red dress swished and swayed, John came to her side, Helen had placed everything that she needed in the pan, it would cook on its own now, 30 minutes she had before serving, there had to be a chocolate pudding for the tasting, in the arms of her John engulfed her as he turned her around with the sound of the music they waltz together side by side the moment was beautiful, seductively the moment their bodies entwined, the moment he kissed her gently softly with a need to be inside her to be at one with her.

Helen could feel his hardness she could feel his love and how they were so in tune with each other, so at one all they needed now was a coming together in sheer heaven her dress fell to the floor and they were still waltzing with love, the waltz had never been so good opening his shirt to find him so warm so desirable he fell down kissing her gently between her thighs reaching the part she adored his gently tongue bringing her to an orgasm.

Slipping his trousers off his Dior pants fell to the floor he then lifted Helen onto the kitchen side with one gentle push he was in the dark moist cave thrusting gently in a slow rhythmic motion they were both in their moment of passion together, both reaching that time that ecstasy it was something that most people dream of.

With his thrusting slowly becoming faster with more of a sense of purpose to what he wanted to achieve, he kept thrusting until Helen had moaned in an orgasmic cry his hardness then reached an orgasm, the climb, his scream was so passionate, so horny, and so unending their love making was so tender and as they were there, they were one, they were each other together. Looking at Helen that look did not need too many word and speaking softly to her and saying those mortal words of.

Friends, Accepting the Changes

"I love you Helen, you're a beautiful lady I love you so much." Helen touched his face his love for her was so warm, so genuine how could she not adore him. "My Angel of love, I love you big time they were at one again they needed these times to be one again. Their work took over both of their lives, and sometimes making time was essential in any relationship. She listened to what he said.

Dinner, wine, chatting and listening to music was their night only to find the closer they became in their communication it allowed John to kiss Helen he found her so sexy every part of her body was there to be kissed, they slipped onto the carpet she reeled, he kissed her clitoris and finding his way inside her while his hand supporting underneath, touching her again while thrusting hard, thrusting gently, both of them again reaching that climax together.

Both sighed at the point of no return they were there both having to find the love they needed at this time. The pair had an orgasm together in such a gentle sensual way they both fell asleep in each other's arms. While they slept the Angels kept a heavenly watch over them.

Saturday came quickly, all four of the girls met at the station to carry on through to Margaret at the House of Parliament. "Did you bring any identification Helen as you will not get in without it, you have an Irish passport definitely a frisk job for you young lady and I dare say that you may even like it, we will find a delicious young male copper." Kate remarked pulling her passport out of her handbag. "Look me British." "I should be so lucky a frisk job I would get a woman knowing my luck a big butch one and she may enjoy it more than me, look I have my Irish passport, much better than a British one." Helen smiled, looking at the girls as they all waved their passports around so that everybody could see.

Underground travelling, Helen hated that squashed up like sardines feeling it was not very savoury. Soon arriving at their destination safe and sound, Margaret was there to meet them, no frisk was needed to their disappointment and he was an extremely young security man at the main doors.

"Come on girls a quick tour, then small lunch and off to St Pancras I am looking forward to today. "Kate you will be pleased to know that I have found some important information about the UN in Washington, I expect you are going on your legal qualities as your background it is interesting to say the least."

Margaret began to speak so quickly, they were like children all of them had to fall into place it was like joining the local Army. "To you Helen I have gathered together some Politicians that would like to speak to you when you are travelling in America with your book signing, a good bodyguard he looks after the President so he will be sure to keep you safe."

Margaret smiling at Helen, yes she was famous now and how she was enjoying that, it had been a long hard journey, but she had made it.

"I am so looking forward to hearing about Angels Helen and to understanding them and the Angels are so fascinating Helen, I do find it so fascinating and I expect most people find you different and intriguing to say the least but I bet you have had some people envious of you not too your abilities and never mind it's a great learning curb for them." Margaret finished with Helen and then her attention now being directed to Laura slowly taking her hand Laura jumped she was taken aback.

"I have found some businesses for sale in Europe and America you might like to look at if that is what you are thinking of doing, if you want to take more money than normal out there then I can sort that out for you. Sarah there is a good friend of mine who wants some help at her Gallery in London do you fancy some of that." She had at last finished we all could speak now.

"Thanks Margaret for everything on the UN, I have received some information it was sent to me, and it is about me representing and working with children in third world countries so it will be a worthwhile job, I do feel once I have finished with the main interviews I will be fine, so I am leaving Monday for a week and two interviews I should know by Friday what they think so fingers crossed to being in America I know have been head hunted that will make life easier."

Kate commented on her life and what was happening with her

life before anybody else could get a word in Kate like to be in control of her life and everybody else's her life in the past year had not been in her control, to get that control back was a sign that she was now moving on in the right direction.

"That sounds good Kate that would suit you as you can use your empathy." Laura said to Kate as she moved slightly away from Margaret. "But I am still not too sure which way I will go America or Europe as either way it will be a challenge I thrive on that." Laura clapping her hands like a sea lion, she was nutty sometimes. "I will think about the job Margaret, will let you know next week if that is ok."

Sarah wasn't too sure whether she really wanted a job at the moment life was too hard for her but a job would give her focus. "No worries she will not be back in town for another four weeks so you have a while to consider what you want." Margaret knew Sarah was the reserved one not too sure where she stood with her.

Helen just smiled she was looking at all the girls as they received their goodies from Margaret then said. "And I am looking forward to having a chat about my life just to enlighten you a little bit and then the choice is to be yours as there is no pushing here. But you will definitely find it very interesting to say the least and I promise I will not pick up on you at all."

Everybody giggled at Helens comment they knew that would be for certain a first. Helen would keep her glasses off for that

Friends, Accepting the Changes

chat with Margaret.

They all got the whistle stop tour of the interesting areas of the powers in the country and they took in each word of what as so enlightening, this is Mr Cameron office sharing with goodness what's that man's name who joined him. There was a joke every minute, they were laughing all the way to the restaurant.

And a bottle of the finest Champagne and a light lunch, they were all looking around just to see who and what Politician's where in on a Saturday, overtime to say the least and we are all for the overtime it brings the most expensive Champagne to the table, which is what we want to see flow.

"Come on then Margaret how many of these gorgeous chaps have you fucked in the small rooms or your chambers." Kate looking at her straight in the eye awaiting her answer, there must be some shagging done in this place. "Yes this power thing must go to your head sometimes the shagging of the lower workers to keep then under your control, then to again shagging the higher workers just to show them that they cannot control you I may say I love it I might get a job here myself.

Helen kept quiet for the moment she wanted to see what Margaret's reply was, Kate could certainly bring out the worst in people, she did get their backs up sometimes, Helen knew there were at least three young men Margaret had taken into her office also having an affair with one of the top MP's so they knew that Margaret was sure no Angel but she did now have some builder who Helen though was beneath her but it was her choice. Choices we make ourselves some good, some bad. It's far better to allow live to come to you Helen had always lived like that.

They certainly dined very well and to find most of the onlookers were wondering why they were there in such a Political place that was interesting to say the least. Margaret enlightened the girls to her dealings with both the police and her expenses scandal she was certainly going for it. Margaret said it was her man's fault nobody cared about the rubbish she had got away with the speeding anyway.

"Good on you Margaret and I bet that copper was surprised to see you jump out of the car, I am not too sure about that man of yours he seems like a right dick. Laura remarked straight on black and white was Laura you had to be thick skinned when she was around, had losing her father and a bad relationship made her a harder person. Kate also had a thick skin it was her way or no way so if you came in her life and she found that you did not fit in with her then it would be you that would have to change to do so.

Leaving the Houses of Parliament taking the underground yet again to St Pancras for some serious drinking before dinner at 7.00pm they would return home late but not later. Walking into the Champagne Bar there were a few gorgeous looking men, Laura certainly wanted at least one at their table.

Friends, Accepting the Changes

Kate was not bothered at all, she had too much on her mind at this moment and Helen did believe that Sarah was into women again for now anyway they all were so beginning to think there was no hope what should they say to her. Helen well she was well into her John and there was no other that would please her. Margaret was into flirting she and Helen were the well-known women amongst the ladies they knew pictures could be taken and they were watching   all the time for the cameraman.

"A bottle of the best Champagne and some nibbles Henry, and five glasses with that beautiful man over there that is not too much of a tall order is it." Margaret stumbled her words, she laughed she certainly knew him but saying that she did always bring clients here when they had won the game so to speak.

"Margaret, Champagne sie con cinco copas yes but I cannot speak for Vincenzo he is married and he would have to answer to his wife who is now coming out of the wash room." Henry spoke with laughter, women their men and who they want in their lives.

But I could get you Franco he is now available, he would love to keep you happy knowing that Franco was about forty five and Margaret declined the offer they all wanted a handsome muscle bound young man who looked divine. And Franco was not that, to do without that is it and the conversation would be about sex and no sex, how many times would they be in this situation and she conversation had not changed, is this really what women talk about all the time, yes it is.

Friends, Accepting the Changes

Kate watched Helen face as she remarked that her and John had great sex while they cooking, on the worktop fantastic he is so good he knows how to please me, Helen turned herself to Kate. "Well hunni how's your sex life, it have been some time, what we need to do is to find a good man for you." My goodness Helen thought that could be a sore point but what the hell it does not matter.

"My sex life is non-existent, and I expect it to be at least until I go to America and then I will be travelling so I hope he is travelling with me that could be fun." Kate started pushing Helen it was a slightly not amused push that they both understood what was all this about timing, what on earth is this all this about men and their moment.

Laura suddenly took hold of the conversation and remarked about her sex life. "Well mine is good I have old Billy Blaine giving me a look up at least twice a week, there is this young lad in my office that wants to please me he is there for me to play, I could be on the phone to a client and there he is giving me many orgasms. I will have to let him go soon as it is not professional and I know it will get complicated if I do not let him go"

It had to be Laura that took the conversation to the limits. Sarah then shrugged her shoulders as if to say easy come then easy go she really wasn't too interested in this sex business at this moment. "I see this young girl and she is in her twenties she is so besotted with me, I am teaching her, she is teaching me." Thinking to three nights past she began to feel herself become wet as her thoughts were of Bridget as she took off her own clothes and stood there in front of her firm pert small breasts she looked at Sarah starting to play with her own nipples as it was a way she aroused herself, she then her hand between her legs and starting to bring herself to a climax.

Sarah thinking back to what happened next, Bridget slowly walked over to Sarah and taking her clothes off and kissing her nipples until they were hard. Placing her hand between her legs and slowly but surely bringing her to a climax, they both found pleasure for at least an hour so enjoying each other's bodies. Sarah now really wet, sure enough she raced to the toilet to clean herself up. Oh, the pleasures of the body and the pleasures of life itself.

Now Margaret did not have to say a thing about her sex life she was happy he knew how to perform and he knew it well. They were four bottles of Champagne down when Margaret looked at her watch, the time they decided that they should move on and have dinner. "I did book Cipriani we are expected by 9.00 pm so we had better get a move on."

Again they would travel the underground to Mayfair an up market place this is so no drunken behaviour was allowed here we are again when they were out they were either eating or drinking. Then felt the after effects for a few days. The food was to die for and they had decided to share starters as everybody wanted to taste each starter on the menu we will have a mixture of starters in the centre. The wine began flowing, also the sex chat started, Margaret really wanted to understand Helen's work she was so interested.

As the main course reached them Margaret looked straight into Helen's eyes and said. "You help so many people Helen, tell me how does it all work do you have to be a special person you must be so calm and happy." Helen sat looking at Margaret and she began to see the woman for the first time, yes there was a caring side hidden from view she was not that hard-nosed Politician.

"I work in a different way to you I remain calm and let things happen I will always look at what I want first and then once I know what I want I tell the Angels and they will open it up for me, I wait patiently for them to open it up rather than opening it up myself as that way it will sure be true and lesson's to learn it all is a patient game and being me that is what I have to have, patience for my clients and then patience for myself with my life.

Yes, I have had to be trained in my work even though I have seen Angels as a child and I meditate every day and what I see always happens. And yes I feel that I do have an interesting life, I have had more than most in lessons to learn but that is why I am good at what I do." All the girls just looked at Helen then sighed, she was so calm and her energy was beautiful that everybody loved it and it had taken a great deal of hard lesson learning and so much heartache to be the person that she is, a greater and more powerful person she is now, so much more in control of her power, the lessons in life and training had done her proud.

As the evening went on Helen could see her Angels becoming a little anxious at the thought of them all travelling home by train, then one after the other each Angels had assigned themselves to one of the girls, at least Helen would not worry about them getting home as she could see their bodyguards taking up the firm positions to make sure they all arrived home safely an end of a glorious day now to some heavy work for all except Sarah who was carrying her heavy work on her shoulders.

"Bye, bye, bye." They all said and gave a big hug to everyone as they left even the waiter had a hug he must have thought what is going on here. On the underground trains of London they were together and then to their own separate ways saying their goodbyes with a wave to each other, Helen smiled she could see the Angels attach themselves behind each of them so to keeping them safe.

As she turned the corner Archangel Michael came close to protect her on her way he was tall and strong, his power was her power, his love was her love and his divine energy was for sure her divine energy. All in the divine world of the power of love Helen had the privilege to be included in their world. The effect on her life was meaningful and divine living her life in a calm serenity of love and kindness.

But not a walk over as many people seemed to think she was, Helen just allowed the Karma and Fate to bring what is meant to be. And it most certainly did.

Part two; Different Roads.

Chapter Five; Kate, The UN, Her Soul's Journey.

"Helen I have never been so nervous, I have four hours to go the cab is picking me up from here, I am being looked after from the time, I leave here to the time I get backs and it does sounds as if it is an important job that I am being offered in the UN in America, Helen what do you think of the job can you tell me please you with all those heavenly powers I do need you to tell me what I am in for." Kate was finishing the last of her packing it was last minute.

"Helen will I want a few condoms while I am there, I'd better take some just in case I do you never know as I might get lucky." She was totally thinking that she may get lucky, Helen did not want to answer the questions about sex as there was something not right where that was concerned.

Helen knew if she were to tap in she would find out the situation in Washington and she knew Kate did not want anything bad to happen, she still kept thinking about Michael her prosecuting him when she should have kept clear how she regretted it, if he were out of prison he would definitely come looking for her that was scary.

"Well come on Helen what is there to do I think I am going to be safe am I going to meet someone soon." Kate was asking in a stressed way. "Kate you will be fine two interviews the last one will be with a gentleman who you will work with very high up the chain, you will see the apartment you will be living in and it is very spacious, you will have a car diplomatic plates. He will show you what he wants from you there is a great deal of travelling with this job, I do feel that you will find your twin soul on your journey with working at the UN.

You have one new guy and one from the past coming into your life in the next three months, the one from the past, I do not like the feel of him so be careful, you will be in Washington in the job and apartment in the next four weeks and I will be out there so we will meet up to enjoy but you must watch this man from the past Kate he has issue's and an energy that is worrying me keep your wits about you."

Helen was slightly worried about the man from the past the hard energies around it felt revengeful it that was bad news as far as she was concerned, all she could do was warn her and the rest was up to Kate, Helen felt it was Michael but he was in prison, so it was a wait and see game.

"That's a bit scary who is he Helen should I take some condoms as I could do with a good night of sex. But I will enjoy and if I have to move in a month it will be all new things, all new beginnings for me." Kate trying to shut her case up, goodness she was only going for a week, it felt like she was taking clothes for a month.

"Condoms I don't think so you are there to sort the next part of your life, you are there to have some fun not sex. Next time take your condoms you will certainly need them then, I can see lots of sex some brutal my goodness I am seeing too much I hope your man is not an S M freak." Helen began to see some dangerous scenes in front of her not good at all she thought to herself this was certainly bad news but her man was so warm, who was this man she could see the Angels were not giving her all the picture.

"Ha, Ha, Ha. I hope not too I am not into heavy sex, ok Helen well you have a great week sorting out your trip to America, book signing and it's about time too, off you go then Helen our famous Angel." Kate was now looking at the hand luggage, the passport there was so much to think of, so much to do she needed a man beside her so that she did not fall apart well the next eight weeks look good.

Taxi at the door and then they drove off to Heathrow airport, Kate would find some good shopping there also Kate was into people watching and to how people travel, what they wore was fascinated to Kate as some dressed as though they were going out to dinner, other's came to the airport dressed as though they were going to the beach.

Checking in before anybody else Kate wanted to be up front hence making time for the shopping, Kate needed to get to the business class lounge a relaxing drink some Shushi was called for, by that time it would be boarding and sleep, she knew the flight was on time, she felt good about this job it would all fall into place from here. Kate arrived at Washington Airport and was met by two armed men and an official from the Embassy Kate was still very much under the care of the British while she was in Washington.

"Kate I am Frank and I will be guiding you to all your meetings, showing you the finer points of Washington you have a Whitehouse official engagement Thursday evening and a garden party with one popular Senator Hilary Clinton, and she is very interested in meeting you but you actually do have to get through the primaries first, that will take us maybe a couple of days.

You do need to know where you are staying and what you are doing I have booked the finest hotel which is The Four Seasons, you will be made welcome there they love the English, come to think of it the Irish as well. Ok then let's be off, my goodness look you have enough luggage for a month." He was a big chap and nobody would cross him Kate thought to herself, then she has two what seemed like coppers at her mercy let's see how well they do their jobs.

Frank turned to her, smiled he was certainly a force to be reckoned with Kate thought to herself. "Well I might have to change a lot, I certainly do not want to be wearing the same dress that would not do would it, I have to keep up with the fashion you know, they love the English and the Irish that is good I have a friend on a book tour in a month, she is making many television appearances so she will be ok as well but I think she is starting off in New York."

"Ok." Frank said in a firm voice, he was most definitely a bodyguard with credentials. Kate liked him beside her.

"What's her name then Kate is she famous we will see, she must be somewhat famous as she is going to be on the telly." "Yes she is a bit famous but will be very famous soon and her name is Helen Diamond she writes about Angels and such." Kate was beginning to like this man he had something about him he certainly knew how to chat, he never stopped only to let Kate have her say which Kate supposed was good enough.

"I know her yes we have had some conformation about her, she is travelling with a great deal of bodyguards she will need them, if she is not that important lady now she certainly will be by the end of this tour, she has a great deal of functions for charities, there will be a great deal celebrities to meet while she is here, her schedule is mighty full."

Frank opening the door to the car, Kate loved this gentlemanly stuff driving away she could see the traffic also the American way of driving, and she thought to herself she would have to soon be driving amongst this traffic that was something she would have to get used to.

Looking towards the Hotel she arrived to watch as the man at the door raced to her car, Kate was feeling important at this moment everybody helping her get out of the car and into the lobby of the Hotel. Love this Kate thought I am a Celeb, calm down Kate you are off for an interview tomorrow that should be your focus, her room was like an apartment in itself, the mini bar was full that is how she liked it might just have a G & T now she thought. Gin & Tonic coming up and then a long soak in the bath she was tired but excited at the thought of a new job and a new life. What to do, Kate ordered room service as she was tired and in need of bed rest a bottle of their best red would go down well too.

"A bottle of one your finest red wines please, the chicken salad for starter, and beef Wellington main course, plus an ice cream to follow, how long would that be." Asking in a hurried voice as she was waiting for a phone call, not wanting to be disturbed while she was chatting, also she was a strong controlling woman and a need to be in control of any situation.

"Mam it will be about 30 minutes give or take five minutes each way." The young man said on the other end of the phone. "Ok, that sounds good, gives me chance to get all my day sorted tomorrow."

As soon as the phone went down Frank was on the end of the phone. "Hi Kate you are being picked up at eight so gets some shut eye as it could be a long day. I will pick you up with Hank he is your chauffeur so you can use him for everything. He is to be yours while you are here he will be there wherever you go." Frank laughed.

Friends, Accepting the Changes

"Well not so much for everything there are limits for an employee." "I was hoping for a run around but I got a chauffeur instead fantastic he will know all the places to go that is what I like." Kate laughingly remarked to Frank and Frank she thought I bet he is good for a laugh on many a night out.

Sleep, sleep, sleep. That was the order of the night as she was not too sure about the interview but it certainly felt like an extremely powerful job. International Law with the UN would take her across the world she hoped she would be defending children and women as that was in her range of specialties. Kate was flying high as a kite with the energy of a bird ready to take on the world, the nest building had begun.

Buzz, buzz the alarm awoke her, the phone rang it was the alarm call from reception. "Good Morning this is your alarm call Mam are you coming down for breakfast today as you have not told us what you are doing." A bright, happy voice of a young lady not what someone needed early in the morning to be woken up by, that is why she always had an alarm with her well it's done now up she jumped like a child full of high energy.

"Did I order an alarm call but anyway thank you I will be down for breakfast shortly." Kate was surprised by it all did they know what time she wanted to be up. "Mam, Frank from the White House said you would need an alarm call." Again there was that happy voice yet again Kate wondered if all the Americans were this happy in the morning.

Friends, Accepting the Changes

Kate was not the best person in the morning and the sound of a cheery voice reminded her of Helen she was happy all the time, Helen was always smiling whatever was going on. Kate did miss Helen when she was away. Helen always grounded her, her light was something no one could have and no one could. take away.

Up to look out of the window sun shining not a cloud in sight. People were already busy racing around the lights on their cars were bright, and the traffic was beeping at each other this could be a crazy day of driving thank goodness for Hank. Kate had showered, her makeup done it was the precise look, she was out too WOW !

With her intellect, the knowing of the law she knew that she would be a great ambassador for the UN she did wonder who she would be working with. She had her breakfast downstairs with the buzzing crowd then to then walking out like a celebrity. A quick tidy up in her room and now to the lift, there was a new day and a new life beginning for our Kate.

Pressing the button of the lift Kate then began looking at both ends of the corridor, Kate was beginning to wonder why she was so nervous something just was not right, there was an uncomfortable feel to her life at the moment she did not feel safe, what was it that she didn't know but Kate was sure it would cross her path at some point.

Stepping into the lift her eyes looked to the man in the corner, my goodness he is so absolutely gorgeous thinking to herself she could go for the high mile club but not really the right time for that, all she felt was a sudden urge to think of sex, he certainly did make her feel rather horny. He stepped out of her way as she left the lift, then he followed her to the reception desk where Kate left her keys.

"I do not know what time I am back I have meetings all day, thank you for the call but tomorrow I will be ok, even if Frank says otherwise. Kate smiled at her she could now see the cheery voice, a pretty little thing too.

"Ms Kate." A voice from across the room, it startled her he came to be beside her. "I am Hank your chauffeur it is about time we were leaving there is some heavy traffic out there this morning." Hank said with a smile he too was very much the bodyguard. My goodness Kate thought they all have smiles on their faces whatever the time of day it must be an American thing.

In and out of the traffic, thank god she was not driving I hope I get a chauffeur when I work here Kate thought. Arriving at the door to the offices of the UN Kate was quickly shown through to the interview room, scary stuff she opened the door and a long table of men and women all to judge her, also for her to be the judge she thought, oh to be judged.

"Can you sit down here Kate, come on sit down here as we all need to be able to hear you". The man in the grey suit I do hope they all introduce themselves she thought as there were no way she would remember all these names that takes time.

"Ok, I will go through the names as I want you to be able to relate to all of us. I am Bill I will start from top to bottom. Cathy, Jack, Jerry, Martha, Winston, Betty, Paul, George and Maria she is here to take the notes of the meeting. "Frank will be along later to show you what you need to know in the office and in Washington." Bill said to Kate in a very casual manner at least they are human Kate thought.

"Kate could you tell us all about yourself and what you feel you can do with this job, and what your expertise can do to enrich the UN on an international level because you know that you will be travelling for us internationally."

Kate told them all her past dealings with the European Courts where and when she had worked, to what she could offer them, the meeting was a long one it continued until late, food came in and it had been catered for them, they all felt that there was no need for another meeting with Kate, this day was enough.

A long day but as Frank walked in she felt very pleased to see him finally she knew it was all over. "Come on Kate let's show you some of the good places to eat and may I say we have plenty of them here in Washington." He stepped in as though he was in charge well he certainly seemed to be in charge of the situation with Kate.

Friends, Accepting the Changes

"Ok, do I need to freshen up Frank as it has been a long day?" Kate looked at him as if to say please I need a bath I am feeling so tired and grubby. "No, no need for a wash up best we go now and you can meet some of the workers as they eat after work and then go home." Frank took hold of her briefcase, such a controlling man, such a controlling man Kate thought she had left that sort of man behind but then she knew that she too was controlling.

Off she went following him a well turned out restaurant they were heading for. Downtown eating that she loved, the car waited for them and as Hank stepped out to open the door she saw the man again the handsome man that was in the lift and he nodded to her and she smiled as they both went their separate ways.

Then Frank jumped into the car and they sped away and Kate kept watching the man as they pulled away. There was something about him what she did not know what it was but there was definitely something she had seen before had she known him before Kate certainly felt like she had it was indeed a weird feeling.

Arriving a little late to what the rest of the crew had done but she was a in country that they were in control of her movements Kate would never be late in her own country, Kate again met all she needed too, the food was good to brilliant but the company was a little overwhelming and she would have to get used to that.

Friends, Accepting the Changes

Kate had arrived back at the hotel very late and there was not to be an alarm call Frank would be picking her up at 11.00 am so there would be plenty of time to chill, and she did wonder if she would be allowed to jog the streets dare she ask. "Frank how about me jogging tomorrow is that ok with you." Kate asking him politely as though he were her brother, if she needed company would he be able to jog with her.

"That should be ok but I might have to send a copper, one that's out of uniform to protect you Kate the streets are save but you are a stranger to these parts, I have to make sure you are safe." He looked at her sternly and then he took his phone out of his pocket making arrangements for a fit copper to be at the hotel for 8.30 am on the dot. One thing Kate liked is a man to be on time and he was very much on time.

Sleep as soon as her head hit the pillow then her dreams were of the man she met she had seen him twice the third time he would speak she knew that. If only he were here she began to think of him and her vibrator came in handy, it's the need to sometimes satisfying the moment one, two, three, four and more orgasms how could a man compete with that, no man could she fell asleep with Mr Handsome on her mind and in her crutch. It felt very good, very horny she had not felt this horny in months.

The next two days were of Kate with Frank taking a tour around Washington looking at her new apartment and she began to look for furniture for her new apartment her selected stylish furniture and then they also had to be at the office to find out what her role as and who she would be accompany on her journey's around the world, there was a man named Harry who she had not met yet, he would be there when she move to Washington in about three weeks he had a little time to brush up on his knowledge of Kate. Yes Kate was looking forward to her move to Washington America.

The plane journey home was exhausting she was looking forward to seeing Helen and packing her apartment, the amount of junk Kate had collected was immense slowly she was sifting through and found that when she came to the end of the packing she felt her life was truly beginning. As she landed a message came through to Kate, they were finding her wherever she went.

"Hi hunni I hope all went well I am just letting you know to be careful Michael has been freed, he may come looking for you." Helen was beginning to worry now as she saw this man not letting Kate go. Helen reached for her phone she knew she had to tell Kate straight away. "Hello Kate, Helen here how are you are you all sorted Kate are you excited about your new adventure."

Helen waiting to hear how she sealed the deal and what was to go on next. "I am ok the deal has been done I am moving in three weeks and looking forward to it I did met some nice people and saw the gorgeous man I only hope I see him again he was mmmm dishy."

Friends, Accepting the Changes

"What is this all about Michael I do not want that in my life, I really could do without that you know as I am starting a new life now and he is in the past you know Helen, he is not coming back that's quite frightening." Kate begun sounding just a little bit apprehensive about the whole thing but she had brought it to herself.

"I am sure you will be well protected but there is only so much they can do, you have to remember if it is in your life path then you will receive what you are meant too. You are off to America, he will not be allowed there." Helen thought on her feet, well she hoped he would not find his way there. He was a weird man with weird thoughts she needed to be out of the way and soon she would be a new life.

Arriving at the front door she began looking around some of her belongings had been moved that made her feel a little bit uneasy. Checking all around the apartment she began to feel as though she was being watched, she would be glad to get away from here for a few years, she was certain that she was keeping her home for when she returned. Suitcases unpacked her washing in the normal piles, OCD or what she thought.

Running the hot water into her deep bath some Sanctuary bath foam the candles placed all around for her just to relax. Slipping her boots off, her dress unzipped it dropped to the floor and her beautiful lingerie was taken off slowly was she seducing herself, she slipped to the kitchen naked and pouring a glass of red wine then taking it to the bathroom, she was definitely seducing herself.

Looking behind her she did feel as though she was being watched. Mmmm, it certainly felt good sipping the wine then slowly sliding down into the bath to relax her hands touching her body and her fingers finding her most relaxing spot, she calmly manoeuvred her fingers to reach the orgasm she long needed she heard herself breathing, gasping and then a cry of delight, mmm this was the best.

Slowly sipping her wine and just to allow herself soak in her bath full of her own juices as well as the soft silky water and she stayed there in her bath until she was relaxed enough beginning to feel wonderful slipping between the cotton sheets this was so good she thought then falling asleep thinking of Mr Handsome.

Kate's woke with a startled feel she felt vulnerable her naked body on view she felt frightened and unsure of what was going on. There he was Michael had broken into her apartment had he been here all the time watching her until she slept soundly so that he could pounce yet again he had already raped her years ago when she was at University and was this his revenge he should not be out of prison yet.

So he must have escape somehow looking at him she felt vulnerable. He had already taken the sheet away from her body what next she thought and her heart was racing what should she do now. He peered down at her walking forward he came over to her side taking hold of her hand and tied it to the bed, he then walked over to the other side and tied that hand to the bed, Kate was now awake beginning to kick out at him, taking one leg with the rope he tied them apart, she was ready now and Michael was watching and laughing at her intimidating her as much as he could while Kate was wriggling around.

Then Kate began to shout and he then stuffed a cloth and tape over her mouth, he could now do what he wanted, she would be his until he had finished taking his revenge, his bitter sweet revenge. Taking his trousers down and his shirt off leaving just a vest slowly moving close to her he kept saying.

"See this mam it is all for you hard, fierce and look how big it is I am going to fuck every part of you until I think I have paid you back for sending me to prison you fucking whore I will teach you not to play with me." He was touching his penis and then touched Kate between her legs and lifting her bottom, there was such a painful moment as he thrust himself into her again and yet again it was so painful.

"Where are your Angels now Helen where are they to help me." Kate was crying out, she could see nothing but darkness but why me she started to sob those words again and again in her heart. He finished and taking himself away for a moment. He took his vest off he sat on the chair near the bed laughing at what he had done Kate was his until he had finished with her.

"Not so brave now MS Kate the Barrister not at all so powerful now." He began to laugh at her and in his laughter he began to be aroused again, standing tall he showed her his hardness, climbing on top of her he then thrust his way into her until there was a muffled scream is all she could do. Placing Kate on the side of the bed and he violated her.

Kate was screaming there was so much pain and her sobs nobody could hear. The morning came and it was very early he was still there, still he could become hard, this time he would definitely make her pay she was so weak he untied her then turned her over and tied her up again, with that he lifted her bottom and pushed hard into her.

"No no, no. She cried the pain was immense she did not have men near that part of her body let alone being raped. This was to be his ultimate joy for getting Kate to cry out and to take her self-respect away he had then finished, his job done he untied one of her hands and left laughing.

Kate was totally shocked, exhausted and numb she had been repaid. In the distance she could hear sirens what were they she thought. And as she looked up there was Helen looking down at her and there beside her was a paramedic. "We have got you now Kate you are safe, I am so sorry where was I when you needed me I should have been here sooner.

The police have Michael he will be doing time for a lot longer, now my Kate, my poor Kate." Kate stayed in hospital for a week just so she could rest and some tests needed to be done just in-case. How would she cope Helen was watching her change she now was so different, could she now still work in Washington, would she have the strong confident way she always had, Helen would wait a few more days just to watch and see. They sat watching the outside world her inner scars of her body were healing, her mental scars that would take a little longer but at least he was behind bars and faced and longer sentence as he was a danger to the public.

"Kate do you think you will still be going to America are you strong enough?" Helen carefully asked Kate, she was concerned her lifetime job her life purpose now opening the doors, Kate had never been so scared. "Yes I am going and I am now strong enough for this challenge Helen it will take me away from here."

She spent the next ten days packing all she needed then left the rest for Helen to look after and Helen of course held the key. All her belonging were picked up by the furniture removers, being shipped across the water to that big land of promise. And as she turned away from the pain of the apartment she smiled.

"Helen I do not know whether I can live here anymore so I will have to let it go as I have too many bad memories here now, selling then buying something better, more secure sounds good to me." Kate stayed with Helen until the time to leave. Helen watched her as she went towards the plane as it was as if she was watching a part of herself walk away from her she was losing a dear friend and there would be no more midnight chats

Friends, Accepting the Changes

on the phone.

No more meeting for quick lunches, she had gone to a new life and a new man. Her tears began to flow her best mate off around the world but she too was off around the world book signing, television appearances all was happening in her life.

Her lights were to be the famous ones. Kate looked back she could feel her tears falling down her cheeks all the pain she had been through and now she was leaving her Helen behind it was all too much. But she knew that she could now be more empathetic to women and children who suffer the same.

Kate the Angels have made you more open to other's pain so that you can heal them more openly. What a lesson to learn Helen thought as she blew a kiss to her beautiful friend "I will see you in two weeks I have to start in New York first. Have a safe flight Kate, this is a new start let go of the past and remember I love you."

"Love you too Helen, keep them books flowing I want to see loads of them". Kate said waving as she went, wondering if she had the strength to pull this all off. Would she crumble or rise to the best and be in the glory of her work, the Angels would be there for her and they would for her be the protection and the healing.

Chapter Six; Laura the Project, The Moving.

Laura was now beginning to see where her path was taking her since losing her father like she did she knew Billy Blaine was the unfinished business she had to clear, he was the business man that she had spent the night with as her father lay dying and now to start it all up again just to see where it would go was she mad.

Now he wanted to join her business then take it to America also with an opportunity of Europe as well it was now all falling into place and now she was enjoying everything and he did fill her spare time, her John was so preoccupied with a young PA why shouldn't she enjoy herself.

Laura had moved John out of the business as it was affecting her decision making he was always there creating negativity. So now there was a clean run so to speak with sex as well and fantastic sex to call tying all the loose ends up so to speak Laura was on a roll she would make it to become a millionaires through sheer hard work.

Laura come here have a look at the plans this is the final outlay there are a great deal of houses here if we do take them on then we will make a packet it will have to be aimed at the wealthy, as the wealthy always have the money put by."

Friends, Accepting the Changes

Billy turning the plans around so that Laura could take her time looking, that is what she needed to do the taking time to think, she was so excited to have such a good business partner who knew what he was doing but this was Laura's baby not Billy's she was the master mind, she knew he came for the law side of the work and making sure all was above board. They both stood watching the streets of London up high in their ivory tower soon it would be the streets of California.

Then the stretches to Miami it was something else John was not too sure about going with her he would leave her to make the business a success, if they were still together they would be, if not then what the hell. He had lost his momentum in the relationship Laura had been so set on taking the leap of faith changes did not frighten her.

Joseph would be with Laura, they would have a Nanny, he was now three he could have fun with other children that would give Laura the time to open this business, so to make her millions. They both took a step and looked at each other with a smile this was the best path she has ever taken and now too success.

Her thoughts went back to home there both John and Laura were at each other yet again the bickering was far too much for her to handle, it made her feel ill most of the time. But in the next month she would be clearing her belongings from the house and leaving John behind. Joseph was jumping like a Jack in the box around in the garden, would she ever have a second child, has she still enough time for that. "Joseph come here I have some ice-cream you can take it outside if you want." Laura calling through the window she was in the most selected neighbourhood, she was shouting through the window, washer women were her thoughts. Ice-cream she thought, Joseph can have everything.

He came running in his dirty pumps making marks on the floor what should we do with them even when they are little men they make a mess. "Mummy when we go to America do they have my ice-cream like this, can I see Micky Mouse, can I see the Rockets, will we have a big boat." Joseph taking hold of his ice-cream and licking it while he was chatting, her smiles said it all he was such a chatterbox you had to be all ears while he was around.

"We can go where you want but mummy does have to work, my free time will be your time, we will have some fun you are going to meet some nice people you will like them." She took hold of his tiny face and kissed him on his head he was adorable. "I love you my little man even though there are many little muddy pump prints on Mummy's floor." Joseph giggled at her and then raced out into the garden jumping around with his ice-cream.

Looking at the trees he sat watching the birds there was something about little Joseph he had a way about him a certain spiritual way it was as though he knew, he could see and understand, Laura would chat to Helen about him she would know. Mundane chores she hated Laura definitely needed a house keeper and that she would have in America she could not wait for the time of life changes.

As Laura and Billy finished checking the site just finding out its progress for their move completely to America the land had been secured, the piling had already begun, so the footings would be well and truly being put into place when they travelled over they had a month to clear business taxes and shipping.

Sitting back in her chair who would have thought that she was in the position of becoming a millionaire it felt good to be so wanted in business, watching Billy she knew he was a great partner in their business, but would he be the same in love as he liked his freedom, that she could give to a certain point she had to set boundaries.

He turned to her and smiled, sometimes he knew what Laura wanted but he also knew he was here for the kill. "Do you fancy lunch we could go to the Dorchester and have a private lunch in the main suite or perhaps dinner then stay over that sounds better to me it will mean that I can get my luggage organized and shipped today, get them to do a pick up next Monday when I am free, all exciting stuff, there are so many boxes in my little apartment so there is no room for us to get passionate I'm afraid.

I will book a room tonight that seems good to me." Billy Blaine certainly knew how to get his own way in one minute she was having dinner and a good night of sex, it made Laura did wonder how she managed without him. Then she looked into his eyes what was behind them, looking into the soul she thought. "Have I a choice Sir, I will get John to look after my Joseph, I have the excuse of the business, and finishing up and staying in the hotel for the night he will not question."

Laura went to her handbag pulled out her mobile phone and then immediately began to dial John just to let him know she would be busy tonight after work she had brought the deal together, now she was sorting out the move and it was taking a great a deal of her time and energy up, anyway he could have Joseph tonight as he would not see much of him when they had left for the States. John was obliging to her call and agreed to have Joseph.

Miami that is what Laura was looking forward to she had a house there that she was renting until she found one to buy which would take the six months that Laura had allowed for financial reasons. The spare outfit she kept at the office would come in handy tonight as she needed a change of clothes. Next week cannot come soon enough she thought, when they first arrive they were to have a weekend at the Four Seasons Hotel just to settle in and wait for their luggage.

In the upper part of Miami she would be living in a home by the beach only trouble with this part of the world is the continuous hurricanes and whirlwind that she would not look forward to, the season of the hurricanes, she could move home with herself and Joseph further along the coast, two homes one

Friends, Accepting the Changes

in California near the vineyards seemed to be a great idea but she would leave that until the money started to come into her purse. "You're out again oh well I suppose I will have to put up with it as I will not see him much after Tuesday that Billy Blaine seems to take a great deal of your time up and I hope that he is worth the trouble."

John said to Laura in a sarcastic way, little did he know what was going on would they be able to save what they had, would Laura realise that Billy Blaine had not changed that he would have to somewhat for her to except him into her life on a more permanent basis, what was he really after or would John and her patch things up as they went along the next year would be an interesting one, Laura was certainly going to hit the top.

Off to the Dorchester for a change of clothes and to freshen up the body in need and the make up before Billy arrived then the fun would begin. Her room which she would charge to the company, it was to be spacious and comfortable mind you at these prices it should be. Climbing into the shower it felt so good just letting the water cascade all over her.

"What could I do with a shower head she said, no I will wait for Billy it could take the dampeners off the foreplay." Smiling to herself she then turned herself around to find that Billy was standing watching and taking his clothes off slowly one item at a time.

Yes this man turns her on so much he is so sexy, interesting and of course the main ingredient intelligence she loved every part of him, but she was not in love with him she knew that he was such a dangerous man and she knew it would fall to pieces as soon as they reached the beaches of Miami. Enjoy the moment she thought as this would not last long. He stepped into the shower immediately took her in his arms as their lips met they were already at the highest point it's all in the anticipation she thought.

With the water cascading down his back pushed her gently against the glass as she opened her legs he was there the gentleness now had turned to such a wanting of sexual fulfilment he would get and to make sure that Laura reached that point too but not too quickly though this was the starter, the main then the dessert were still on the menu.

It would be a while before they were served. He then thrust into her harder and harder as though there was a purpose to it all they both reached a climax together they fell into each other's arms to let go quickly. Satisfaction guaranteed that was all she needed at this moment it was just the sex and the business.

The Dorchester was one of the best Hotel's in the London their food was delicious staff friendly, the cliental well they were always well turned out. This was one of the girls favourite hotels and the bar area was so relaxing. She did wonder if Miami would have such luxury or such class would be more to the point. Looking around the dining area she could see many important people and a great deal of Middle Eastern people, money was all around her she would be like this soon.

Wishing, hoping and planning she thought it would be better not sing out aloud mind you they all would be in for a treat.

They both plumped for the Rose' and it came from the regions of California it was expensive but that did not matter. "Sir the wine would you like to taste or would the lady likes to taste." The young waiter looked on as Mr Billy Blaine divinely smelt the bouquet then tasted the wine.

Laura looked on and thought to herself you would show off just hurry a drink I need. The wine fitted the part she was in Laura was now allowed to taste. The conversation was about Miami and the part of California that was so relevant to them.

"I do want to see the Everglades, we can go alligators and the old crocodiles hunting, we are not building there are we. I want to go to the Bal Harbour the shopping centre Gucci, Armani, Prada, Dior, Channel Louis Vuitton, Versace, Tiffany, and of course there was Dolce & Gabana all those beautiful designer shops with such a difference.

Then there is The Fall which is a semi open air centre it has waterfalls and tropical vegetarian. Bloomingdales with Macy's and Pottery, there were many shops Laura wanted to walk in and buy. I am so excited just need more money in my pocket to be able to afford it."

Friends, Accepting the Changes

"You have certainly done your homework let's get today over with and then the rest of the week you can pack for the off on Tuesday, you have your packers there already don't you." Billy looking at her like she was like an excited child he wished he had some of that childlike quality she must have got that from Helen as she always has had that quality, most people were jealous of that.

"My packing is done all I now have to do is to settle my banking and all is done so for the next four days I am visiting friends to say goodbye." It was a good time in all their life's they were all getting to that happiness stage. All of them were happy in their work, men and their spiritual road of independence.

Laura made sure that she informed him of her movements they had finished with the office Friday, tomorrow and the weekend catch up to see the good old friends. Then Monday shipping her heavier goods, Tuesday at Heathrow Airport here I come she thought to herself.

Dinner was something, the company was the best the food well there was certainly no complaints there. They now could retreat to their room a bottle of "Champagne" awaited them. And the lift beckoned waiting for the couple near to the lift to take their place as they wanted a free lift.

Laura jumped and a sudden realisation of what was going on, thinking my god I hope my dad's not watching me and the Angels too I would be so embarrassed she thought, do not let that put you off was Helen's voice in her ear, what would my dad think of me having a man in my life I am leaving behind, a man in my life who I am using for business and sex. But then she began thinking to herself do I want more from Billy is this what it is all about or is it just unfinished business. He really fits the part of the husband she really needed. My goodness too much thinking she thought let's get tonight over with, see how the move goes he would more than likely find a newer model in Miami or even California.

Where does that leave her, thoughts going on in her head does she really want the two men in her life perhaps she should settle for a new one altogether. Let me just enjoy tonight dad and I will decide where my life has to be when I am sorted in America as I need this.

The lift was free just the two of them entered as soon as the door shut Billy pounced, he took the strap off her dress down so that he could kiss her breast, he took the top of her dress down kissing she laughed while he was enjoying himself. "Bing." It was their floor then the doors went swoosh, and the doors opened and to their surprise two ladies were tutting away they were not amused.

Laura quickly tidied herself up as she walked along the corridor, the door opened he threw her on the bed her dress thrown to the side all that was left was her panties and with them he teased her kissing around the top of her slim tummy and slowly around to the top of her thighs, he was enjoying the taste of

Friends, Accepting the Changes

her and slowly but surely taking her panties off he entered her as if it was the last shag he would get all year turning her around to sit on him she rode the buck dry. He came she screamed all was done all in a good days work.

The night was of raw sex and after a glass of Champagne they sat talking about work and to her surprise he took hold of her head and forced a situation she really did not want at that moment, she found his sexual approach was always raw and Laura did consider it pushy he obviously gets his own way with women.

Then pushing her head towards him as she knelt in front of him, he pushed himself into her slowly she brought him to a climax Laura certainly knew how to bring a man off with a blow job, her speciality she used to say. He was back to talking business, a glass of bubbly and off they were again this time he was not in control Laura took the upper hand and she made him want.

Making him want her more teasing as she presented herself to him but not allowing him to penetrate until she was ready to take him into her and he would have to completely satisfy her.

Slowly drifting to sleep, what was it that she wanted Billy he would be a good business partner, even a bed partner but there was something missing, how would she address that and when would she address that. She saw an image of her father before her then to her surprise he had come to her in Spirit Laura called him as he came to her side.

"Be careful Laura you are off on a new journey but this man is not for you he will be good for business but not for you I will find the man I want for you."

He left her with a smile a wave she felt that she was so loved so cared for even though he was in spirit. Laura knew that she would have to end this relationship once the business was flowing she knew that would happen within six months of arriving in America, she remembered Helen telling her all what is happening now.

Her bags were packed, the boxes had left on the lorry for shipping, she knew that they would go off today, it was now all happening, an early flight meant being at the airport at the crack of dawn, Billy would not be there for another couple of days. Joseph as usual was jumping around Laura could not keep him quiet, he certainly was a bundle of fun.

"Helen what do I do with him, he is a jack in the box. He is so funny, he watches the birds, he talks to the birds and they sing with him, he is a bit like you Helen." Laura giving Helen a big hug she would miss her, it felt as though all the girls were going their own way in life, but would it ever be the same.

"Yes I knew he would be when he was born he has a massive Angel that protects him, he will start to speak to all sorts soon, you will have to explain or get him to ring me I will be his teacher." Helen picked Joseph up into her arms Joseph gave her a big kiss Helen began hugging him tighter. "I love you Helen." He said with no thought, with no wanting, no selfish gain just pure love and affection.

"I love you too Joseph, I will always be here we will Skype each other, now Joseph be good for mummy and I will see you soon." Helen replied as she let him go. Her tears she held back as this was another friend about to leave her side, all those wonderful times they had. Helen drove Laura to the airport then slowly she began to walk away.

Helen was watching Laura and Joseph they were walking to the lounge before she boarded the plane, Laura turned to wave her goodbyes to Helen, and an immediate thought came into Helen's mind well there goes yet another friend all the meetings for their lunches would stop. Perhaps sometime along the road they would all be brought back together to enjoy their fun times again.

At least Helen would have some time with her in America, Helen would catch up with both Kate and Laura when she too was working and travelling in America, but until then it will be a large gap left by Kate and Laura moving away. A long flight and a tired boy at the end of it all, he was looking out of the window Laura could see the hotels, the apartments and the yachts, thinking that most of them looking rather big and grand.

Friends, Accepting the Changes

Setting down the plane came to a steady halt with Joseph holding her hand Laura stepped out into the big new world of the Property Development game in the parts of Miami America.

Laura would find the energy to strive and become a well-known woman in her own right she would make sure of that and to making it to the top. Kate on her way with the UN and she was travelling to many war torn countries and the rest of the time she was mixing with the best. So now Laura would have to make a name for herself and a positive one at that.

Landing to find that it was extremely hot, she and Joseph would enjoy the next few days. Looking over to the sea and then down to the pool so grand everyone seem so happy and the contentment was to be seen in their faces, also here everyone seemed to be so glad to be alive, all sorts of people lived here many of them were older than the norm but Laura was just enjoying the view, yes it certainly was good to be alive and living here.

The project developing new properties in an area that was so ripe to make money. The moving well Laura was there the hardest journey was done, now she was there to make her millions but also not to lose sight of reality, the material world was fantastic but the spiritual caring world now would open, Laura was sure Helen would visit and do just that that. But now lunch was a must, then some sunshine was on the cards for the rest of the day.

She picked the car up then a cruise down Ocean's Drive, just to show everybody that she was here in America, then to do a bit of people watching. Both Laura and Joseph went onto eat at Le Bonchon du Grove at Coconut Grove the favourite bistro, she would definitely have an outside table, Joseph had his little hat on with lots of cream protecting him and he then played happily with his cars, he did not upset a soul.

Good food with a definite good life for the two of them. Laura was happy with Laura and that's what life is all about to find your own happiness and be happy.

Chapter Seven; Sarah her Lost World

Sarah still lost in the world of grief not knowing where or whom she should turn too, Sarah had lost both the men who were the only connection to the other side of a man the feminine side, her son in a tragic accident and her father died so suddenly, then to fit the lot to make it a three in a row she had divorced her controlling and bullying husband.

Alone and fending for herself was not the deal that she wanted it was hard to say the least, she found that with men she could take them or leave them, with women that they were as insecure and needy much as she was.

So she went between the two and got the best of both worlds she found that in her grief there were a few men that would give her the love and attention that she so needed, the women just needed to be loved as much as she did, what a nightmare she thought.

The days of racing to Helen would soon be over, as Helen was moving on to greater heights, Laura had now moved herself to Miami and Kate was based in Washington and she was beginning to travel the world, Kate seemed to be healing well after that awful incident with Michael coming back on the scene again what a nasty man he was.

Friends, Accepting the Changes

Now all that was left is for Sarah to come to terms with her loss, her life then would move on, but she was finding that extremely difficult and her new found drinking habit and her looking for sex as her comfort was taking up a great part of her life, Sarah of course inside was saying help me I am dying, but few would listen.

"Helen I am in need of some help all that work you done with me has fallen by the wayside, I do keep looking to the time I was in Cyprus and I still keep looking for this unconditional love and now it seems that I am finding only sex what should I do, I need your Angels Helen you can ask them, I find I am in such turmoil to even think of asking them can I come and see you."

Sarah trying too hard to figure out her life, trying to understand what she was looking for, she was such a wonderful artist, her paintings showed the moment, the moment of grief, the moment of happiness she was caught up in one big moment of blunders.

She had two people in her life they both were not what she wanted or needed, but they were there for comfort sex and of course the drink. Martin was a city banker that liked the fast life, very wealthy loving the power of money, he liked Sarah on his arm as she was upper class, pretty and very intelligent.

She could hold her own with him the sex was good, the

conversation was good, but something was missing, in that something which our Sarah thought was greatly important, she was having great sex and a great time, but no connection at all he had this cold way about him, detached with his own insecurities he talked with money, not with his heart he was a man who has been hurt deeply.

"Sarah hunni I am off to dinner now with two important clients would you care to join could you bring an overnight bag to mine, we will leave here at eight." She was daydreaming of some of the better times that they spent together it was always dinner with clients horny sex then home in the morning, Sarah was looking for more than that.

Thinking back to the time when Martin had an extremely wealthy client that came over from America he was in oil and Martin was now investing in another country for him, where and when oil was concerned he knew Martin well, Martin would order him a couple of call girls just to keep him happy. One such time Sarah joined both men for dinner, then back to Mr John Young's hotel for a night cap. She should have stayed away as when she reached the hotel Martin looked at her then quietly said.

"Look after him hunni I have called a girl up to keep him happy but you have the job until she gets here." Martin then turned to John Young spoke in a whisper telling him that Sarah would keep him happy and there would be an expectance of a girl to be at his suite in thirty minutes. Off she went to his bathroom and he then stripped to his underpants while she was watching he did have a cute arse.

Opening some Champagne he poured the two glasses they were full, he disappeared to the bathroom, he was gone for ten minutes. Sarah was beginning to think he had fallen asleep, tapping on the door she asked. "You ok Mr Young should I go I have an appointment in the morning so I do have commitments." He grunted.

"No hunni you stay right where you are I will be out in a minute." She opened the door there he was snorting coke what was she to do now it would not harm surely just once. Moving to the sink there was a line of coke she done her best to do the job right and it hit her straight away.

"Come on girl take them clothes off we can get naughty until the other girl comes." He was already taking Sarah's clothes off for her and he was already groping at her breasts. Laughing as they fell to the floor they crawled to the bed both butt naked, making a move and starting to kiss her breasts, he slowly came down to the top of her and yes they were enjoying each other he looked up and took her to the end of the bed and then sliding into that moist place it was just what he wanted.

It was all he wanted to let the coke and his orgasm hit at the same time, he screamed so loudly Sarah was left with nothing at all but a man on top of her who had selfishly satisfied himself, he was trying all the positions that he could, he was so willing to try anything and everything, placing her over the side of the bed then he came into her from behind, she moaned with pleasure and her orgasm made her scream with such delight, he still kept pumping hard until he finished. In that moment they were together.

Both of them just stayed still for a moment, both had experienced each-other's juices, both were sure they could do this again and yes they did just that. There was a knock on the door, someone was quietly knocking at that and the time was1.30am, the two of them in the bed still had some very heavy energy's left that needed to be expended. Mr John Young casually walked over to the door opening it to reveal a very young girl she must have been 19 years old no more than that.

"Martin sent me to you my time is yours we will get ready for a good time together." She was so forward it was so unbelievable, she wore nothing but a thong and a tee-shirt so not much to playing strip poker thought Sarah.

"Come in, come in sit yourself down have some wine and then go to the bathroom there is a line there for you." John Young began to beckon her in so she would feel safe pointing to the bathroom where the gear was, she did walk with a slight wiggle it was just to get noticed she did not need to get noticed her arse done that trick. She was gone for not more than five minutes and on her return she was wearing a bright red thong and it spoke for itself.

Friends, Accepting the Changes

They sat drinking Champagne chatting about her finding out whether their play would need a condom. She had a bundle of them just in case, Sarah knew that they were off on their journey of sex hard core. John Y kissed both women, one by one. He then moved out of the way so that Sarah could make a move on Freda and yes she was foreign, as their lips met they enjoyed the touch of each other.

As their bodies entwined John Y watching with great anticipation of when he was between the two. Freda kissed every part of Sarah's body she moved herself gently slowly up and down to give Sarah the sex she had never had, Freda certainly knew how to please both men and women.

Her tongue darting around Sarah's clitoris, with the manipulation of her soft hands she began finding her way to that spot she wanted Sarah's G spot, once found she began manoeuvring then having Sarah reeling with pleasure and as she arched her back the motions the intensity of her orgasm was immense.

Sarah was enjoying the moment, John then came over to both of them with himself wrapped in a condom he then selfishly just forced himself into Freda riding her like a horse, she scream with delight as he was inside her, and Sarah kissing her clitoris then Freda finished with an orgasm, John Y came loudly and Sarah waited. They all then returned to the bathroom, a line each to return to the games.

Friends, Accepting the Changes

This time John Y had Freda firmly on him, taking John into her she certainly knew how to give a blow job, Sarah was kissing and caressing Freda from behind, Freda juices flowed directly into Sarah's face an orgasm made, John Y squealed with delight, Sarah of course again just waited.

A drink together, then it was the turn of Sarah, Freda kissed her lips gently and John Y kissed her lips firmly and Freda began to manipulate her clitoris, then John Y kissed and caressed Sarah body, Sarah was gasping with delight, they both laid Sarah on the bed her legs hanging over the side of the bed as Freda began to turn herself around so that Sarah could taste her if she wanted to continuing to kiss with a purpose, while her hands caressed her bottom then kissing and tasting.

Sarah then began to play with Freda, and John Y watched, when his time was ready he came closer to Sarah slipping himself into her wetness, he was slow to begin with, then to thrusting, Sarah enjoying all that was being offered to her, she busted with delight with her juices, in complete satisfaction John Y yet again shared his load.

Hurrying off to the bathroom Laura left the two together, this was the first time she had done anything remotely like this one person at a time was her game. And on her return both JY and Freda were working on each other again Sarah picked up her belonging to leave watching JY pushed himself into Freda's butt, with that Sarah left not too sure of what had happened, she had enjoyed it immensely, never ever she thought to be repeated again she began thinking as Martin was the mastermind in this game she would now have to get rid of him.

Arriving home in tears she did wonder what on earth she was doing what was she thinking of, she wanted a relationship and it had to be a good one at that, there she was screwing whatever was available it had to stop. "Where are you Dad when I need you where are you, I am left here so alone so lonely." She said aloud her tears were bubbling up in her eyes, her heart so broken she needed time now to think more on a basis of what she wanted from life, not what life wanted from her and again her art had been left.

Her moving on had been left, now after the scene she has just had, it had all come to a head, she needed to clarify what it was that she wanted and needed from the Universe that they would be there to bring it to her. Helen was the person she should see, Helen was at the point of her new beginning, the new transformation and in this transformation she would be moved away from all this, she was to make contact now to clear all that was in her life.

To find a way forward and to open new doors for her in both love and work. It was now 6.00 am a cup of coffee in her hand she decided to go for a long jog, then to ring Helen to see if she could fit her in before she left for America, she needed help now not in five weeks, knowing that she would be crawling along the ground by then.

A shower and slipping into her jogging gear, she went to the park where the greenery, the trees would heal her empty heart. Jogging herself into the ground while she was looking to see who was around, thinking to herself, god I had some serious orgasms last night, wow I could become addicted to all this so really that's the end of it, and I had better not do that anymore, she needed to decide what sex she wanted. "Male or female that was most certainly the question, Sarah certainly could not do the two again it was detrimental to her health." She cried and in her crying it was a deep heart wrenching cry.

"Sarah, Sarah, Sarah what are you doing, where are you going, what are you doing, heavens above get a grip of yourself." As she sat on the nearest bench watching the world go by, the different people jogging some were so serious some gave her a smile of joy. "Good Morning." There were some lovely people about but also miserable sons of bitches she thought. Beginning to jog again she felt at ease relaxed, ready to make that important phone call to Helen.

All would be well she thought, all would be well, Helen has that power to make things well. Jogging harder than she had ever jogged before, taking deep breaths, arriving home picking up the paper, there on the front page the death's in Afghanistan, four more of the soldiers had been killed, four more of our boys losing their lives and for what she thought, four more boys who were growing into men.

She would watch their bodies arrive back in their coffins coming through Wotten Bassiet and watching the families come to terms with their loss. Sarah was trying to put her life in order, and looking at the paper she realised that she was so lucky with so much ahead of her.

What was it about death she wondered why was it so final, why did we just have to go and that was it no saying goodbye just off on that journey back to the world of spirit, the journey that the Angels would pick you up and take you, why couldn't they tell you long before you go on that journey that your time would soon be finished so begin to enjoy yourself, death had no boundaries Sarah thought it was ageless.

There were times that Sarah wished that she had been taken rather than her son, he was taken so quickly without Sarah being able to say goodbye. The death of somebody else always brought home the death of someone close to you all that pain was brought back to the surface. Picking the paper up again just to look at their faces made her cry.

Coffee and a shower then she would feel better but how can you come to terms with death, how can someone be taken away, you then have to fill in that gap that has been left by them going back to spirit it certainly was a hard lesson to take and except that they were gone in body, but their spirit was still around. Sarah took comfort knowing that her little boy was still alive but in spirit.

Leaving the apartment she ran for the taxi that would not stop. "Hey there Mr, come on I have an appointment, Dam you come on you bastard". She looked for the next taxi to come along, ten a penny she thought, ten a penny you are Mr taxi, arriving at Helen's late she begged her to stop the pain of death, the pain that killed every part of her body, she ached with the pain, would she ever heal from this curse of death she thought. "Helen will I ever heal from this pain, my life is in a turmoil I am frightened of myself, I am doing things with my body I would never of dreamt of before, I know that I am searching but for what, I am empty."

Looking at Helen for some sort of sympathy, Helen just looked at her as she opened her heart to open her world. Telling Helen about her sexual moments with different people, men, women, where would it all end and even threesomes she had had with Martin's client, she had finished with Martin as he now felt like her pimp to her and who needs a pimp.

"Sarah you have to go through everything that you have done to find out what you want next, if you just curled up and died you would not be in front of me. It would have taken you a lot longer to find what you need in life.

Friends, Accepting the Changes

Now to you Sarah I feel that you have to ask yourself is it a man or women that you desire in your life, you need an artist someone who is as sensitive as you, someone who has an interest in you and what you like to do, is not a controlling person only of himself not you.

But you need to find work and a purpose in life. What is it about your son and your father that you must miss, once you find that out then the man will find you and he will fill that space". Helen started to think about her own father and how John fitted him so well, he cared so much and he was protective of her. Sarah had now decided to look for a sensitive man, not a safe man.

As they both left the house together for lunch they would make sure that there were some beautiful men in front of them as they ate. "We will go man hunting let's see we will go window shopping let's find a cafe with table and chairs sitting outside, we can then man watch. Helen thought to herself all in a good days work my friend, all in a good days work.

"Café solo y café latte por favor." Helen and her broken Spanish comes in handy sometimes but why Spanish well no one knew. "Look at their eyes, then their bums she knew the rest will fall into place."

Pointing at a dark haired man sitting at the corner table he looked smart, intelligent, should she beckon him over or should she just let nature take its course. The nature thing sounds the best, as if you make the play for the man it's not a good thing making it all fit into place is a recipe to disaster as it will sure fall apart.

It is better to let it just happen and come together nobody should be asked to change themselves, it should be done because they want to and not because you want them too.

As to a spiritual coming together in a relationship, that is done by the heavens they are totally in charge you have to except that, but at the end of the journey you would have your twin flame, the man that has been destined to be in your life. Most people have relationships with the same person, a person that has the same pattern as the last one they dated before.

On day you will find it is time to change the patterns of your life that is what we all have to do eventually, even Helen had her fill of idiots before she met John. But now she has a man in front of her who she would never have dreamt of being with. He was so different to the rest, he was his own person he was all that she had wanted but could never get as there was always an idiot that tried to get in.

Helen was so in love there never would there be anybody else he was her twin soul, her one and only they would be together until death. Now Sarah thought that is the sort of person I need in my life, there are not many of them about.

"Watch him over there Sarah he has a way about him, he watches every woman that passes, I have never seen anything like it." As Helen chatted she could see Archangel Michael appeared right beside her what is he here for she thought and what message is he now bringing to her.

"Helen tell Sarah both her Son and father are looking after her now there is a man in France waiting for her she has to find a holiday with an artist course it will bring him to her, he is by the sea with easel and paints, dark hair, dark skin and a French accent, slightly older more refined, that the ones she has been looking at are not for her." Archangel Michael slowed to stop and the continued.

"Tell her Helen we are watching and we all care for her, say that death is part of the path that everyone on earth has to take, we call on them when their lessons have been learned and their pathway has finished." Archangel Michael touched her face then went over to Sarah and blew on her face as Helen watched him, Sarah brushed her hand against her face she had felt the air of his breath.

"Well I never I just felt someone breath on me, Helen what is that all about who is it, you can see them can't you." Sarah watching as Helen smiled and always smiling regardless of whatever happens in her life she smiles.

"Yes Sarah I have Archangel Michael here he has given me a message for you, there is a holiday that takes in the arts as it will open many doors for you it has to be France, there is a man sitting next to the beach he has easel and paints, dark hair French refined, refreshing and not a jerk, he will heal you, you will heal him.

So off to France with you young lady, let's get your life changed for good this time no more seedy sex games take your time with it." Helen was determined to set her friend free as now is the right time for everything to fall into place, Sarah needed clarity.

They left the café' walking home the long way round and Sarah was deciding when to leave for sunny France. Sarah found her way home feeling good about the future, she straight bought a ticket to Nice for the following week and scheduled a course of painting with oils and water painting, there was also an artist sketching course she would go to town with her learning. Helen is good at what she does, if this man turns up then she would have made the right choice.

Collecting all the equipment she needed for her stay, she would be staying at Helen's beautiful home in the middle of a vineyard, she would be happy with that, the sea was not that far away and Sarah also had the joy of the mountains on the Italian borders and to venture into another country if she wanted too.

Her date to start was 11th June at 10.00 am, it would be something she had longed for and this would get her back to nature with a view too nurturing herself physically and mentally with all good food plenty of water also with the joy of the Vino la Helen.

Bags packed enough she would be paying the excess baggage for sure. Looking at herself she had noticed a few lines she was aging with all the drinking, drugs the sex and everything she had been doing, it ages you so much all this drinking, it would be in moderation from now on, she would now just be enjoying the next six weeks as Helen would be in America for a month that would bring her back for the middle of July, a holiday in France for a couple of months before she had the onslaught of the television programming.

It was 6.30 am there was a knock on the door she looked around her apartment just to check that she had packed all she needed. As she opened the door Helen stood there in the doorway with her hands full of brochures she had been looking up all the places she wanted Sarah to visit while she was at Mounta Briava. She loved her Chatauex in France,

"Come on then missy let's get you to the airport. Gatwick was packed, she stayed until the luggage had gone and then again she waved her friend off to another world.

Friends, Accepting the Changes

Marie will meet you with her husband Petre she will look after you and you will be a different person when you return. Enjoy the painting have fun Sarah that is not too much to ask is it, when you meet this man just let him come in slowly." Helen gave her the biggest of hugs as she knew it was all to be an adventure.

"Thank you for this I will ring when I get there, I will watch Sky television to see you on the chat shows. Enjoy yourself Helen and don't make it hard as you have waited years for this day and now it is here for you, all you have to do is smile and crack a few jokes you will be ok."

As Sarah went through security she turned to see Helen with a tear, waving her off had been hard as the memories of all three girls being waved off to pastures new was Helen's theme of the month. Sarah arrived at her destination the weather was so warm, there and Marie was standing with her husband looking the typical French country folk she moved towards them looking straight ahead she did she noticed a handsome man walking towards her, they both looked into each other's eyes and smiled.

Bags in the car this was the first time she had seen the home of Helen's and she was in for a shock to say the least. They were nearing Helen's land she noticed the people of the village waved as she went past, the journey was an interesting from the airport there certainly was a great deal to see Sarah was looking at all the places she wanted to paint, there was a car there for her to run around in it was really going to be a fun six weeks.

The vineyard was massive, the house was so old and so beautiful and inside was contemporary Helen had made something of her wonderful home and whoever done the designing certainly had found out about Helen's personality, now Sarah knew she would enjoy her stay but not too much of the Vino Helen that was Helen's own brand of wine.

Chapter Eight; Helen America Storming

After all the Airport journeys Helen had made in the past few weeks and now it was her turn to pack many bags there were many chat shows and television interviews Helen had been told that there were a great deal of parties and book reviews this was going to be an exciting time. She had been invited to many places on her visit, Helen now looking forward to being shepherded around in the interest of her writing and her life.

There were a few events for her Angel workshops which was good also her Inspirational, Motivational and to the Empowerment of oneself workshops and the Americans were beginning to come away from the old negative ways and that was Helen's speciality to bring changes when people wanted them, they in themselves have to be ready for changes and to set them in place.

Helen certainly was ready for this, many years of struggle, many years of waiting for all of this to happen, John had instigated the moves and then brought it all together, without his help she would still be moving forward a lot slower. John would let her travel to America and then join her in a couple of weeks and when their journey had ended their time in France would be welcomed.

It was the 11.25 am flight to New York, Helen was travelling

Friends, Accepting the Changes

BA Business class, so the journey itself would be enjoyed she would be looked after well. Helen remembered the days of cheap flights and the scrambling like a cattle market, here now it is BA Business Class and well deserved at that, the lounge was comfortable, the drinks were served at a pace that she liked, it was a not wanting a drink to live but enjoying the drink for the taste, Helen certainly had come a long way. Her flight was longer than she had ever been on before but it was calmly done, with being looked after she would certainly recommend BA to everybody.

"Helen we have a gentleman who would like to join you for lunch and we are serving lunch in five minutes there is a spare seat beside you, is that alright with you, we do not want any stalkers do we." Helen began smiling as she commented on what she had said. "You have read the book then it's surprising how many men turn into being stalkers. Yes he may come over but do not let him be a pain as I have a heavy schedule in New York and I do not need my energies disrupted so if I nod then I have had enough of him." She said as she touched the Air Stewardesses hand.

"I loved the book by the way when's the next one out?" She asked as she was handing Helen one of their complimentary glass of Champagne. "Next year Valentine's Day, I am at the moment just reading and finishing, sprucing it up for the public." Helen looked down at her computer as she had begun to write yet another book this one would be very interesting to fit the world she thought a best seller, she had so many choices.

Friends, Accepting the Changes

The Men's Club or Little Boy's Games, there were many titles at the moment going through her head.

Another one was going through her head about men and women in relationships, it would be to the learning and understanding men, their motives, to moving on, then healing, to getting rid of the baggage and to move forward with the completion of oneself and to an understanding of the way to work your life without the trauma of the wrong man and attracting Mr Right but it would be a lighter side of relationships so that women could see themselves and do something about the man that stood in front of them.

The gentleman who came to sit beside her was certainly after her body even at her age did she attract such an energy or was this the be al and end all of a man's brain, he complimented her so much he was totally interested in her books and what she was doing in New York.

"Are you going to be alone in New York as I do have an apartment in Manhattan you could come to have dinner with me, is this just a social visit. How's the books coming along did you make much money out of the first book, what was your price or the second book?"

He was persistent to say the least Helen did not need a stalker in New York. She'd had so many Stalkers in her life. Helen nodded to the Air Stewardess and immediately the man was quickly removed. Let me have some space Helen was thinking out aloud, she found him suffocating what do some men think they are did he really think he was the only man who wanted her company.

As the plane touched down all went quiet the waiting for the wheels to hit the runway and then all of them could breathe again. Thud and there they were on the tarmac safe and sound they had all lived through yet another flight. Helen sat and waited for the Air Stewardess to come forward her entourage were there waiting for her they moved her slowly out of the plane and not wanting anybody pushing and shoving Helen she was a special lady that she was.

"Ok Helen if you would like to come with us now Mr Carrass has rung through to say that they are here to pick you up and I have the pleasure of taking you to him". The air stewardess began to take some of Helen's packages and noticing that Helen had done her shopping in duty free. "Well goodness me you have had some spending spree in duty free, that is one of the perks of my job for me."

Then they both began laughing as they stepped away from the plane. "Are you taking me to arrivals once you show me the way to go I will be ok for sure, well we can only hope I am." Helen was moving fast to the baggage centre many bags to be collected. Young Marcy would not leave her side her job was to make sure Helen was handed over safely.

She was sat watching everybody in the baggage area taking their luggage off the belt, Helen then noticed a rather large gentleman coming her way, he moved beside her, picked up the cases. Smiled and took her by the arm and just moved quickly away. Three suitcases she needed all of them as stored inside were fabulous clothes she had brought with her she had to be the part. He took her quickly through customs and out the other side and into the main exit for everybody to go through.

They were all looking for Mr Mick Carrass a large gentleman and a very well dressed man, then to Helen's surprise to her side another man appeared from nowhere and shouting. "Helen, Helen." He shouted across the arrivals area making everybody there turnaround to see who he was shouting at.

"I am Mick Carrass and I am looking after you while you are here in America. These are your body guards and will spend their time looking after you Helen it's just in case there is a problem."

He pointed to the men who were three times the size of Helen at least she knew that there was protection all around her. She shook Mick's hand and the two men smiled and nodded. "This is Bill and Mark I see you like to go walking, jogging so they are going to have their work cut out and there will be two other men that will protect on a shift work basis.

He was insistent that she followed him to the car, there it was a large Bentley standing there shiny and new waiting for her to step in the door opened and Helen was shuffled inside.

Friends, Accepting the Changes

He began to tell her what was expected of her in her stay in New York, she would be meeting the Mayor also the firemen that were on duty on 9-11. She would also visit Ground Zero to meet some of the people that had lost loved ones Helen would be working then.

The socialites of New York wanted Helen in their company so she had five dates in the week that she was in New York, then three appearances on main time TV. A heavy time ahead Helen thought she did want to see some of the famous sights of New York not all work she hoped.

The Hotel Plaza in 5th Avenue was where Helen's car stopped to all her to walk through to the main entrance like a star she had a suite to herself they certainly knew how to spoil her it was not just a room it was an apartment. She had a theatre booked for her to work in Time Square it had been arranged, it would give the New Yorkers time to see her at full flow.

It would be fun even though she did expect some time wasters and it was planned for charity and the massive amounts for a ticket Psychic Self-Empowerment that was Wednesday at 8.00pm today was Monday and the time was 7.00pm Helen was ready to retreat before being picked up for dinner an hours shut eye would give her time to recharge before she met people at the Restaurant Le Bernarda an expensive Seafood French Restaurant the Chef Eric Rupert would be greeting her that makes it kind of special.

She did not think of where it was or how to get there she left all that to Mick Carrass. She had never been in such a beautiful hotel all expenses paid. There was everything at her finger tips a maid emptying her suitcases for her while she slept and her bath would be ready when she decided you return to the land of the living, remember she must that she was being picked up at 9.00pm.

Her head fell to the pillow and she was asleep in seconds her dreams were vivid the Angels were all around her even when she woke up the Angels were there, Archangel Gabriel then gave her an important message.

This was the new beginning her new start had now begun and Helen was going to be centre stage in life he wanted to make sure she understood what her role and path were it had taken years to get here and she would not let this go. Lots of mind games played by fools who were out to destroy her, she remembered the time of her soul's journey to Spain when she needed to be healed after Mark passing to the heavens.

It was so stalkerish everywhere she went the police followed. Everywhere she lived the phones were tapped and her computer hacked and whatever she wrote or said it was repeated to her in mind games. People need to get a life she thought.

Living in Jerez for the seven months brought out the worst in some of the Spanish people. Every time Helen went jogging she found that she had to put up with being called a bike, to being sold as a bike. When she cried for her Mark with a friend on Skype it was recorded by someone to be repeated by a lottery man. How could he live with himself and she knew the payback would come regardless of confessions in the church. Helen went to the Opera in Cadiz and chose her seat well so that she could see.

But the little man behind her who played and played these silly games, he had the mentality of a prick, and he made his rather large friend seat on the seat right in front of her so that she could see. The Angels were telling her who was behind her she could feel him. Helen could tell many stories.

Staying in the hotel brought other idiots out to play she spoke about sex to a client only to find that a knock on the wall to allow her to listen to an exhibition of sex. Not much good either she thought. To find later these people were following her everywhere she went just to play silly games.

Having nearly ten years of this stupidity it was so childish and after three years of living in Spain and of the police playing games too and two sides in different games one in Spain and one coming over from England. Helen decided she would move back to England and if it carried on that she would deal with it by speaking to the newspaper, a policeman who was senior to the rest and if it came to it the Home Secretary.

Now she had made it even though people tried hard to stop

her. Helen was top of her game with her work and books were now published. So Helen had made it. Now in America and dinner with socialites some very important people wanted to meet her, many books for Helen to sign. As she looked over to her right she saw George Clooney he waved crumbs she thought my goodness here I am. She counted 100 books that she signed a great night.

Jogging in Central Park in the morning to be at lunch with the Mayor at Café' Pierre, Pierre Hotel Five Avenue she had been told the food would be worth it, she found him the most interesting man and the company of the other city dwellers, she met the firemen who were at Ground Zero and the emergency people, it was an interesting day to say the least now to sleep then to jump into the shower and then dinner at The River Café' that's where she was being taken.

The Manhattan skyline was supposed to be tremendously dazzling as the sunsets with the lights of Manhattan coming on what an eventful day she had today. And it was just that an enjoyable evening with new friends wanting to be part of her life.

At 8.00 am sharpish she awoke to find her maid had already made her breakfast she was to be at the Theatre in Time Square for a charity function she would be working as she was there to raise money for a children's charity it would be for two hours she would be up on stage so she needed her strength.

Friends, Accepting the Changes

And it would then be home for a jog and the evening it was a charity function again it was in aid of children and again Helen was expected to give a speech about the protection of children, for the children of the world Helen knew her Angels would be connecting well on this occasion all this work and taking of her time was exhausting but interesting.

The theatre was packed with stars, packed with mega money she felt honoured they had asked her to do a function for them, Helen looked around the room. "Well I can see a great deal of spirits here all with something to say, and some of you are hiding behind masks as what we see is not what you are there is news for you sir about a preparation of a marriage and over to you mam there is a divorce looming and a heavy one."

The Angels had chosen wisely, and had made her pick well, handing over what she needed to, asking the questions she wanted to. Press were only allowed to take pictures at the beginning of the interview, when she was in full flow all picture and articles were not allowed just to save her the embarrassment, if the stars wanted their private lives on show then they could do that.

The Hotel Plaza made her so welcome, there was Champagne waiting for her when she arrived back to her suite and a light lunch was served in her room so that she could relax before the next run of meeting people. A Charity Function she would have her speech ready for that, now too meditate. Her speech written and a great deal she would do on spec, her dress long and flowing of course a designer label expensive but sure would be worth it she noticed that the table she was taken too had many well-known celebrities George Clooney, Michael Douglas, Catherine Zeta Jones some of the top entertainers were sitting all around her.

Helen did not feel out of place nor should she as this was her night, it had been a hard climb but a sure climb at that and here she was waiting for her call they had paid a great deal of money to be with her on this charity evening.

"I would like to present Helen she is going to give us her views on what she wants for this charity and we are truly grateful to you all for participating in are evening thank you, Helen up you come." The speaker was a man unusual but he was defined in his approach. "Good evening and welcome I am so pleased to be here but it has been a heavy schedule and I am enjoying every minute.

As I was that child once, that child of the children's home abuse, the child that did not know where to turn the child that for a while turned into an insecure adult. I have visions of opening a new world for the children that have been left to fend for themselves, the bullying that people do and enjoy doing can be totally unfair and unjust.

I am a person that believes in what you do to other's you it will be done unto you so you will receive back tenfold in this life or the next as karma comes from one life to another so I treat others with great respect and love. I am looking to open centres for children to open their worlds to enjoy and to make something of themselves there will be many courses for these children so that when they leave school, they too can have the power to reach for a University place just by the help we can all give.

It will be a charity but it will work, I will make sure of that and I would love the world to understand the messages of the Angels and Masters they want a peaceful world, they want us to except each other for what we are not for what we have.

Religion and the difference will have to come to terms and except that we all have our own views and beliefs, let's be adaptable to all, learn about life and others for the sake of the children as they are the ones we leave behind when we travel back to the world of Spirit.

I will finish as I started thank you and bless you all for being here." Helen had finished, as she had started making the celebrities she felt were important to her work. She left the stage watching everybody stand to give her the applause she most certainly deserved.

Another good night she thought as she retreated to her room. A television appearance in the morning and one recorded appearance on a chat show, late Friday would be the last appearance on the scene, a function that was being televised to the world. Helen was actually meeting Opara Windfrey while she was in Los Angeles.

After the day's work she was to meet some of the victims of 9.11 that was a day that shook the world and were the Politician's right to do what they have did because so many lives have been lost since the fruit less mission. She had learned not to ask too many questions of other's, they should ask the questions themselves.

The guest appearances on the television programmes turned out to be fun the banter was fantastic and it was not boring Helen was afraid of that she did like a good banter. Her Bentley which drove her around was something else it was the top of the range it did get people noticing for the right reasons too.

Having dinner at Per Se, it had been booked months ahead so not to be disappointed the views of Central Park were grand to say the least a divine place to eat, there was ambiance was something Helen enjoyed. Helen began to chat amongst the people and all of them with something in common, all with a heart so hurt.

Looking for the same confirmation from Helen for that truth that their loved ones were now safe and well in the world of the Angels they all knew losing a loved one was hard now so they have the signs of death. Helen had enjoyed her stay in New York she was off in the morning on the sightseeing trail, of course the shopping she needed to do well and don't we all need to do that at some point.

Friends, Accepting the Changes

Life is all about achieving the goals that you want. All the goals were doing just that at the moment.

Today she was up like a lark to go to Central Park for some serious jogging the amount of food that had past her lips had made that tummy grow so now to reducing it enough to wear a beautiful gown that night, she needed to shop and she wanted to see all the designer shops. Jogging away watching as her bodyguards keeping up as they followed her, they certainly were fit even if they were built like bricks houses, they were still supple.

"How is it that you are so supple Bill you must do a great deal of weight training, do you do any stretching fitness as it certainly looks like it, if only I were single and twenty years younger". Helen kept the banter up as they were great as bodyguards quick to protect he looked at her with a cheeky grin.

"I practice Yoga at the gym, it gives me the stretch I need its ok building muscle but it is no good unless you can move with it. I enjoy it there are both men and women in the class, the women normally out shine us but women have a habit of doing that all the time and you would not have to be 20 years younger you are such an absolutely gorgeous woman". He smiled at her sweetly, now to the serious business of jogging.

Their jog done she would return to her room to do her own Yoga and then to get ready for some shopping, she began listing the best boutiques. "Ok, let's see Madison Avenue there is Valentinos, Giorgio Armarni, Dolce & Gabana, Yves Saint Laurent and Ralph Lauren, I want these shops first and then I think we should go back to Fifth Avenue for Saks, Cartier and Tiffany earrings, rings and everything else she loved it."

She would be fine with that and who said that being Spiritual is being poor as it is not as you can be a Billionaire and be spiritual it's the person inside and of course the Angels certainly did not want anybody struggling no more struggling for Helen she was where she was meant to be.

Her day was full and halfway through it would be lunch at a small restaurant nothing fancy she would decide on the spur of the moment, go with your own feelings to say that it is right normally a spontaneous decision is always the right one just do it and see. Helen and her bodyguards made a move she began thinking to herself how many bags they could carry between them.

Setting off for Madison Avenue the Bentley was ready she certainly felt like a Millionaire herself in which she was now. Clothes upon clothes, shoes upon shoes, handbags upon handbags and jewellery to die for, she was happy it had taken year for this to happen and look at her now she was happy, happy with life and happy with what she had been given at long last.

When she arrived back to the hotel the room was full of

Friends, Accepting the Changes

flowers John had send them all to the hotel all of the bouquet's said. "I love you." Meeting him was her dream meeting him after the nightmare in her life she has never been so happy. Sitting on her bed she cried tears they just fell down her cheeks they were tears of not knowing how it had turned around from nasty, bullying people here's to fame, fortune and the rest.

"Pinch me Mark is this for real I never thought my world change so much and in such a magnificently, wonderful way, I am so happy, happy, happy."

Emptying all the bags to see what she had bought and trying them all on again as she was sightseeing in the morning of Sunday, Monday she would be in Washington DC with Kate and of course work as well but it would be great to see Kate, her clothes all made well, she thought here we are a perfect fit, classic smart gear that she liked to wear.

That evening she would be presented to new people who she would be working with, it would be a function just for them, it was a new designer who was just coming onto the scene of the catwalk and Helen would be at the after party. Dressed to kill she was good at that, then to find the evening was interesting to be introduced to a great deal of people that had read her books and enjoyed them.

And they all wanted the next book they would have soon it was about to hit the shelves in the stores. Book one and book two came out practically together. More books to follow.

Friends, Accepting the Changes

Waking up to the sound of a thud, she jumped as she was startled by the sound. Looking outside she noticed that two cars had crashed and the two occupants were arguing their point, men she thought they think they are the best drivers but they have the most accidents.

Today was the sightseeing day and she was looking forward to it, most of them had agreed on an itinerary. The Empire State Building, Statue of Liberty, Broadway, 42nd Street, a boat ride and a carriage ride through Central park it would be a long day but the Bentley would get them in anywhere, so a long but interesting day.

The views from the Empire State Building would be fantastic so they would leave that until last as there must be a restaurant up there so they could eat at and there was.

Mike Carrass would be showing her the way, what an interesting journey. She loved the view from the Statue of Liberty a very important sight for Americans. She knew that her day was going to be interesting as it gave her a view of the way the Americans live.

The last picture of New York was from the top of the Empire State Building, what a view to be left with. What a great day the carriage ride in Central Park with a cornet of ice-cream in her hand that was a picture in itself, Helen's last day was made most pleasurable by how the Americans had treated her, by the morning she would be off to Washington DC. It was a journey into the hub, the power, and the wealth.

The day began with a jog an early start for a quick run then having breakfast with a dining room too herself Helen loved her own company never to be lonely. Now ready for the next onslaught of her time. Her flight at 12.15 pm thank goodness that it was a short flight to Washington and that she would soon be in her hotel suite again.

One flight was much like the other once you became the traveller the flying becomes so natural. The finest hotel Helen was booked into and again she would walk into the hotel kike a star. It was the Ritz Carlton a five star hotel and with all the five star trimmings.

Helen knew she would enjoy her stay here. It was located on 22 and Main Street and the fitness rooms she was looking forward too and the spar, the main area there was a Restaurant and of course Georgetown she would be travelling there with Kate.

Helen knew that journey would be like old times Helen had a night at the Whitehouse and an extremely long meeting with the UN chief, UN Secretary General Mr Ban Ki-Moon. Helen was on a high and most of all enjoying her stay in America. Some influential people were being presented at the moment.

There was a meeting on some of the policies of the world,

Friends, Accepting the Changes

Helen was staying in Washington for five days only, Tuesday a meeting, Wednesday to the Whitehouse, Thursday a charity function, Friday she was off to Chicago for a couple of days for some book signing and that was that, a very busy schedule, but some fun to be had. Helen landed at Washington Airport and Kate was soon on the phone.

"Helen I am with you tomorrow at the UN building I have loads to tell you. I have met this great man he travels with me, he is wonderful. Good looking, very intelligent I am a lucky girl. I have looked at restaurants, there is Mike's Bar & Crab House this one is on the river and the other is Oceanaire Seafood Room that's on 12th street all are very good we will choose one tonight and one Thursday, the rest of your stay is booked".

Collecting her luggage yet again, I do not think I like this travelling lark much Helen thought. Her bodyguards Bill and Mark had travelled with her and now she was to meet another man at the hotel who would be presenting her to the President, the charity function Kate would be there, Kate would be in charge of the meeting at the UN she was clever like that and she had organised this meeting.

What car will I have today she thought, there it was a Bentley pulled up straight in front of her, it was a black with brown and beige interior Helen slipped into the back seat and sat back as she watched the men take over and protect her, protecting men and about time too, not at all like the idiots she had met over the years, the hotel in which she would be staying in was in sight, The Ritz Carlton looked beautiful, she had been spoilt again.

Just a short trip to the gym, Kate would not be with her until later. Bill then followed her while Mark, was on his phone organising Helen's night, Mark had the same name as Helen's son that had died it's hard to hear names from the past, Mark had organised the dinner tonight just to make sure Helen was safe.

Looking out of the window different places, different people wanted different things from her. She picked up her black handbag which was not too big, she was looking forward to seeing Kate and the chatting about her life here an America and a new man Kate had just met, did she say a name no I do not think so.

The lift made its way to the lobby, there was Kate chatting to Mark, he was making sure the last details were all ok for the dinners out and the meeting with Kate. He definitely was in charge of Helen and she knew it, not a foot wrong, when they said move she moved.

"Helen 'WOW' you are muy importante, Mark has been telling me all about you and what you have been up too. New Yorkers love you have you seen the papers all of them are full of you. Do you remember the days when you sat in that apartment of yours and your life was all about writing, work and wondering when life would open, well here it is open you have made it now, where you should be, look we are going to the river tonight and the next time we will go to 12th street. The car is outside they will wonder what's hit them when we arrive." Kate was excited at Helen's visit she had so much to tell, Kate was like a child at Christmas, taking hold of Helen's hand then holding it tight.

We were together for such a short time there was a lot to do. "Mike's Bar & Crab House coming up." Bill said to the ladies in the Bentley, he knew these women certainly were interesting together they never stopped chatting.

"Let Mark just check they are ready for you, it looks as though there are a few people there and we have to protect from all sides, go and enjoy its clear enough for you to go in." Bill waved at Mark just to say they were on their way. The food was good but not a touch on New York but it had a taste that was divine. Helen and Kate would end up back at the hotel to chat and the sights of Washington DC would be seen in the morning by car.

The morning at 10.00 am Kate would arrive to escort Helen to the UN building here she would go straight into a meeting and their chat would end late in the night, with the stars above shining, now Helen's bed was calling.

The meeting went well he agreed with what Helen wanted to achieve, the children were her love and wanting to protect the poor, wanting to bring changes to those that suffered great pain the children caught up in war was one thing Helen wanted to address, to get the world on her side, they needed to live in peace, with food, clothes and a roof over their heads which was to be substantial not a tent, Helen needed to be there, she needed to help and that did included the small children who she watched day after day on the news, that is all she wanted for the UN to show their power to help change the situation.

Helen mentioned to Kate that she had sent Sarah to France and that she was on an art course. She hoped it would bring someone forward enough so that she could change her life. Kate began to speak to Helen about the man she had come across who is only just speaking to her.

"Yes he was here when I arrived the first time, he was at the UN, I know he is going to travel everywhere with me, I have yet to find out about him but it will not take long when I do he is the man I am going to marry." Kate had now said she had found her man even though Michael had played with her she was still open for love.

The Whitehouse was a country in itself, Helen looking at the lush gardens as she was taken through to the President lounge where he and his wife would meet Helen some time before they were entertained at a function for all the diplomats and staff in the surrounding area of Washington.

Helen found him a calm person considering that he has the most powerful job in the world, he did it was as though it was one of those things, like as if he was a teacher, I wonder what the last one would have been like to meet more of an ego that one, she enjoyed their company it was easy, talking about the world and what Helen was all about, how she herself has been sent to heal and bring peace to the world, a harsh world at that, she felt the need to empower women, making sure that wherever she was in the world her office knew she would have a seminar on bringing self-empowerment to oneself.

They entered the Banquet together as Helen being between the President and his wife. The night of fun was extremely long and exhausting but enjoyable, to finding time to speak to as many people as she could, most of them had read her book so they were interested in all she had to say.

Leaving she was asked to make an effort to come back again as she would be more than welcome. Thursday was another round of Charity functions and chatting to all and everybody that she could in such a short time. She gave messages and read a poem as they were all seated for lunch Helen now found she spoke with authority, with power and with confidence.

Peace

For the peace of love, the peace of War.
Transforming our lives forever more.
To me the love of Peace is to my friend.
Before to find, before to end.
I find in Peace I am in love to be,

Friends, Accepting the Changes

Then to love the Peace you see me free.
Bring the Peace to see, to me.
For in the Peace I love, we love thee.
My Lord, my Master make the powers end.
Bring them together to sculpt and to bend.
For in War we hate, in war we send.
The graves of many, women, children and men.
The freedom of Love is the freedom of Peace.
We bring to the World love that well never cease.

The poem said what she felt and for her there was a loud applause Helen was certainly heaven sent. These wonderful people of America showed how much they respected and loved her for what she was and of course is. Helen's journey ended in Washington DC, with the phone number not only of the Whitehouse but also she had a personal phone to the President and his wife. Also to the personal phone of the head of the UN, if she could contribute to Peace she was an agent from Heaven as the President remarked.

Leaving for Chicago another quick journey in her life, the plane landed this was to be a stopover night, for the next flight for her to arrive in Los Angeles by Sunday, she did wonder what the constant travelling was doing to her energies she was tired, arriving at last Friday afternoon she stayed with the Senator just for Friday and Saturday.

Helen was asked there to look at the damage of a natural

disaster and seeing what the universe could give out when it was angry, also sometimes it was directed at the wrong people.

And just to spend time chilling with a family even though it may have been a very important family it was calming, she needed that at the moment, her energies were draining fast these two days of catch up would do her good. Walking and she would be doing a great deal of meditation to pick up the next two weeks, there were many people being presented to her, looking around the area to see what nature could do, did we really need the wars to cull the population, nature does it naturally for us.

How do people survive such pain, but there they were in front of her smiling and just getting on with life as life itself. Helen had the greatest of respect for people who go through so much and then to pick themselves up and walk onwards to a better life, sometimes better than they had before, some were still unsure of why the traumas had made their lives so messy.

Sunday morning she rose to a beautiful sunrise and a walk around the estate before breakfast was called, she would be away from here by 1.00 pm and then a helicopter journey to the airport, to the next port of call was of course California and it was a dream place, Helen would look to see whether it was worth buying a home somewhere in the area it would have to be a quiet house in the country, not amongst the maddening crowd. Peace is what Helen needed sometimes, and just to go to the hub of the party life when she wanted too.

Again on her journey she was treated like a star, Bill and Mark by her side for every moment they certainly had been well worth the money that would please John and he would be with Helen on this stretch of her journey the public needed to see him with her to see she had a special man and everything good was worth waiting for and to go through such hardship to become one, is very special in itself.

Los Angeles a place in the sun, Helen would be kept away from the rougher parts. Helen was then taken to Hollywood to show her the sets of different films and to meet with the Director of her film of the book. John was at the airport waiting to take her in his arms again they certainly missed each other so much, as she came through customs she could see him waiting with a smile.

Reaching forward he took her into his arms and kissed her gently. "There you are my Angel, I have missed you but it looks as though you have had a busy time of it and made an impression so I am told by those in power."

John would not let go he held her tight, his love, his energy she would have tonight cuddling keeping him close, people did drain her immensely she kissed his cheek and then to his lips. "Come on, let's find the Hotel this is Bill and Mark by the way my protectors, what Hotel are we at then?"

Helen held John's hand very tightly so that she would not get lost and of course John had now joined the protectors so to

Friends, Accepting the Changes

speak. "We are in The Four Season's Beverly Hills it should not take too long to get there, all amenities catered for you Helen you will like this hotel too all these hotels you should become the hotel inspector, actually you might be good at that." John hugged her tightly he did adore her tremendously she was a lady with a difference, a breath of fresh air not like most women.

"I cannot wait to get you into bed Mr John it's been a long time and I need some honey to keep my energies up. We will drop Bill and Mark at the desk, and then run upstairs there is nothing on for us today is there, just telly in bed and room service is called for I do believe." Tapping his bottom just to say she was in charge of this one, not him to be in control.

The bell boy helped with the cases then a maid came in with a view of helping them with the unpacking, could do with her at home she could unpack all my shopping, clothes shopping that is, I would have to go every day to keep her busy Helen thought to herself.

John opened the Champagne and a fantastic bottle of red was opened just to air. That would be joined by the supper they had ordered for later, they needed a drink, soaking in the hot tub and then to make love for a couple of hours sounded good to him. He could manage that with not too much of a problem.

Two restaurants they were going to an Italian, Japanese other than that it would be room service and functions. They were free until Tuesday and then it was manic until Friday. Tuesday was a charity function all the main celebrities would be there, a room full of them, Helen was asked for a poem yet again to read aloud for the celebrities.

Wednesday she would be at the film studios to finalise the makings of her book into a film and the second book would be the sequel, Thursday Helen would be meeting the stars of the film. Friday there was a dinner and social event at her hotel many guests and celebrities would be there.

The maid checked the hot tub for Helen as she watched her carefully put her hand in the water just to make sure the temperature was just right for John and Helen, with clean warm towels they were placed on the side. She left them alone to have the time they needed, John made his way over to Helen starting to kiss the back of her neck then slowly taking her straps of her dress down. He loved the touch of her skin it was so soft, silky, so warm. He felt her shiver as he slowly moved his lips into the nap of her neck.

Gently kissing each part of her as she turned around he felt her warm breath on his face, their lips met, they were locked in the warmth of each other, his kisses were so gentle so warm they were together again. Kissing her around her neck and shoulders, the straps of her dress fell to her side her dress gently fell to the floor her bra he managed to take off in one second.

Helen gently in a seductive way took away his shirt that she loved, slid his arms down through, then to the side. Taking the belt buckle away so that he was open to let her take his trousers slowly down revealing his hardness and her mouth open to receive gasping with pleasure she would bring him to a climax, the fun had now begun.

He gently reared up and with that he came to the finish gently picking her up and kissing her lips she swallowed. Placing her on the bed so that he could say hello to her in a gentle way, this was so much of Helen that he missed. Placing a pillow right underneath her so that he could reach all of her, she would be given the pleasure she gave him.

Slowly kissing around the top of her thighs until he made it into the middle to find her jewel, his soft hands found what they needed to his lips on her jewel, she would have the best orgasm ever he would make sure of that.

Helen moaned with pleasure, to finding herself in that orgasmic moment screaming with delight. This was just the starter, she had the main and the dessert would follow, they had all afternoon, the evening and night to enjoy and satisfying their needs. "Phew !!! I have missed you and I think I should travel with you all the time Helen."

Looking to their hot tub and stepping into the bubbles, the warmth was so relaxing while they were chatting about what they had been doing and who they had met, our Helen was so excited about her past two weeks and she wanted him to know all about everything he had been up too. She excitingly spoke like a child with its first toy, Helen loved him so much he was the best thing that had ever come into her life.

He just watched her hands as they talked, Helen really did not have to say a word, her hands talked for her. Laughing, drinking and food they had ordered something light and it arrived at their hotel room a quiet knock on the door, a startled John jumped out of bed to open the door with a towel wrapped around him, looking at the man on the other side of the door and then he just smiled. What a place to be, what sights they must see. Life can be such fun.

"Do you want me to serve Sir I can set the table ready for dinner". The waiter asked in a moment of embarrassment he stood still trying not to look too far into the room sometimes it is best to keep a low profile. "No, we will manage thank you I could get my wife to do the chores." Quickly John shut the door and the trolley of food he then presented to Helen.

Food in bed was called for and they fed each other piece by piece until they had both finished, slowly they started to play this time John made love to Helen slowly entered that moist dark place with a gentle manoeuvre, bringing himself to her manoeuvring very slowly, and the rhythmic movement she felt his every move.

They both found the energy to keep the pace for a long stretch of time until they both collapsed in a heap of exhausting, satisfaction. Cuddling up they would sleep for a while and then they would order dinner.

It could be a long night these marathons were good after the time away from each other, there was a desperate need to find what they needed in each other again and the slower the better. Tuesday the charity event was to bring her to the eyes of most American people the celebrities of the big screen were there in abundance.

They all began introducing themselves, and slowly showing her that they were interested in her life, Helen sat herself with seven of the most extremely famous people and looked at John as if to say she has now made it, the run of pain she had to get here was really   well worth it. Helen still thought of her time when people played mind games as though she was nothing, now her time was here no more games to be had.

The children's charity fund and the charity for wounded soldiers Helen was sitting very still just watching as one by one they spoke of how their work would change life's one by one they stood while they waited for the next celebrity, each of them made a small speech then left the stage, Helen made her way to centre stage and then she stated to comment on her life.

I have seen Angels and Masters since I was a child now they speak to me about different parts of the world and what we should be doing to help, I as a child there were times when I was alone and vulnerable, if there were to be help in my time I would have had a different journey but not to be. "I have a poem of Peace in which I would like to see in my time and of the child within. Here in my hand I will read it to you."

The Softness of Children

I look in your heart, I find the soul,
I love your softness, the caring the whole.
Keep the child safe, nurture to love.
Arms that hold tight not a fist of a glove.
All battered, all blue did you asked for the pain.
Over and over the tears are in vain.
I look at the child so to the eyes.
So to no love, the compromise.
The heaven's, the love, the touch, the smile.
Can I take you with me if only for a while?
Leave the child, leave them alone now.
The child, the eyes, why, what and how.
I only see the softness of you a child to me.
For a child to be loved is a child that is free.

Moving away from the stage listening as everybody stood and gave Helen an applause, the feeling was that the poem hit home the presenter just looked and smiled, and he imagined the child sitting with her tears flowing down the face of one so young. "Wow what a talent how many of you have dry eyes now, not many I would say, hands up who was moved by the poem." All hands up high.

Friends, Accepting the Changes

That dinner and the millions that they collected, most of them that were there had placed their names for charity runs abroad to raise money, it has been a good day   today Helen thought to herself. And tomorrow the film, making sure in the film her life was true. Being taken to Hollywood by the Bentley was so important. Helen began thinking to herself about the struggles of many years to be where she was at this moment, now to the film of the book that would be something to see.

Stepping into the office of the film set the director came over and shook her hand. "Helen I need to know how you tick, about the spiritual side that my actress needs to know she will have to learn everything about you, so when this film is finished we want it too show every little part of you and your friends it will show the viewers into the world of enlightenment.

That is what you want, that is what we want. We have chosen Meryl Streep to be you she could fit you very well, I have asked her to come along tomorrow we need her to watch your mannerisms as she needs to be you and   also needs to spend time with you, we are filming in a month and we have filled all the character's you will be pleased to know. I did look at the note to see who you and Kate had chosen so we have done our best to fill that image for you both.

Come on I want to show you around, I expect you to be on set at least once every week, I know that you do not live here but it is for you to see that we are doing it right, you and I are in charge.

Friends, Accepting the Changes

It will be a great film, I want what you want I am acting and of course directing I do want your thoughts now and then." Mr George Clooney began to take her to the set, discussion of what each week held and the schedule of the film. It was interesting how they had mapped all the chapters out, who they had picked for each character.

Would Kate be disappointed if she didn't get her Latin lover they had spent a night thinking of who they wanted for each part and it looks like it has now fallen into place, Helen wanted him for the beautiful man who jumped into the pool for Sarah so Kate had to let him go she needed a studious man, not a man for the night it had to be a man forever.

Helen and Kate remembered him in Love Actually he would most definitely fit the part well. Their lunch was a take away, the work load was heavy and Helen wanted to make sure that everything was in its place before she left. Back at the hotel for just a moment before they travelled to Las Vegas for the evening she felt that everything at the moment was a whistle stop and she needed to get her head around it all.

Vegas was respite, she would gamble a bit and enjoy the show that night it was bound to be a spectacular performance and then to fly back to Los Angeles for a luncheon the next day, there were many, many children's charities that Helen was definitely interested in supporting, she would make her choice when all were put in the hat she wanted the one that achieved the most and one that was needing a helping hand, seeing children happy was what Helen was striving for. The helicopter had arrived she only had an hour to pretty herself it would take time to get there, a helipad at the Las Vegas hotel would come in handy, touching down was a dream come true, all these first's she was having and all this fun she was having.

They were taken straight to the roulette tables for an hour, Helen was not the biggest gambler, losing money was not what she was all about, she could remember the days of when her money used to go into other people's hands and now she was in control of her life, gambling it away was not an option, so Helen kept hold very tight of her money.

"Seven red that is the one I will keep too, it's a lucky number for me." Helen looked to John then to the table John placed his bet, now he enjoyed a flutter and the thrill of the winning but who would come off the better. The Roulette table spun around, watching that ball Helen willed it to go into Number seven she would win this.

"Number seven it is, number seven wins, you win madam you win all the chips well done you." The croupier said looking at Helen as she smiled he enjoyed the women winning as they were always so excitable. "Look John, I am the winner, a winner in life, how much have I won." Helen looked at John while she was jumping in her seat.

"Put your bet on Helen let's see how much we can accumulate in an hour." They left the table £10,000 better off, many shoes, bags etc with this money she thought began thinking herself, they managed to find seating while they were dinning also having an array of talent in the show came with magnificent colours, Helen loved to work with colours, paint and colour your life and the world.

Then flying back in the in the early hours of the morning, the luncheon was at 2.00 pm and they would fly straight to the nearest airport and then by helicopter to the lunch, so it was another long day ahead. It was an important lunch with some of the high society, they were the older generation and she was being welcomed into their world, John was with her as she did need his support he was her rock, he needed to become familiar with this fame thing.

They asked Helen when she would be buying a place in California as she had to admit it was a beautiful friendly place but you did need a great deal of money to fit in, of course a little bit of fame also helped. There was to be a presentation of one of her poems that she had written for the previous lunches and the words she wrote with them made sure they were both enjoyed by the crowds.

Leaving California with many friends that she had gained they were leaving this time to go to Miami for a six day stopover meeting Laura for a couple of days would be fun. But again Helen had book signing and a couple of lunches to do so at least 4 days were work, she wanted to see the Spanish side of Miami.

These quick visits were. killing but both her and John had decided they would buy a home in California or Miami when Helen had her return journey for the book, the film she would start to look then. The flight was a little bumpy too many pockets of warm air the Captain said.

"Pockets of warm air John I think he feels that we should all have a go at the rides in Disney as long as we get down safely I do not care, do you   fancy disappearing to the toilet, mile high club Johnny."

 She looked straight into his eyes he had smiling eyes and so practical, strength was a plus to be at Helen's side, as to understand her sense of humour and fun, you   need to be strong.

"Come here you, I still see you have not changed, still the fun girl what am I going to do with you." He pulled Helen close well as close as he could considering there was a seat between them both. Helen's reply was a smart one at that, how could it not be a smart reply. "I take it that is a no then what am I going to do with you."

Laughing at each other they both just held each other tight. Helen looked out of the window as they were coming into Miami, the views were amazing in her travels across America Helen had seen some beautiful sights and she would be back to see more. Jumping here and there took its toll on Helen she needed to sleep and just allow her body to wake when it wanted too.

The trips to America would also coincide with trips around the trip around Italy as her book was on top of the best sellers chart. So her itinerary was becoming rather busy, Sorrento she wanted to visit, it sounded so beautiful, taking in all the spiritual places of India was work for a popular children's charity, China was work for herself and meeting some high profile people looking at the human rights issues there.

Helen wanted to see the culture and to travel to parts of China which had not been touched. Japan was book signing with a little fun and she had always wanted to see a geisha girl. And Australia she had been invited to work so a busy few months, she hoped John was ready for that as she needed him to be there.

Landing safely in Miami Airport Helen lent over and touched John's face and smiled she was beginning to see the life she had been promised all those years ago. Laura was meeting them at the airport Helen would have her bodyguards of course but John was doing the part of the Agent.

They walked through and then past the customs team, the gate to Miami it was hot, humid and that heat hit Helen as soon as she left the baggage belt, the humidity with that it meant curly hair. "Hey Helen over here come on hunni gives us a hug." Laura shouting out, there she was standing with Joseph, they were both pleased to see their friend it had not been long since the last hug but it felt like an age.

"How are you, how's it going out here is it all falling into place. How's that BB is he yours or have you thrown him away." Helen held on to Laura tightly she gave Joseph a kiss in which he was not too sure about. Joseph wanted to walk with John, he felt close to him it was the lack of a father figure, Joseph held John's hand he could do that little job of father figure well even though he would be a grandfather figure.

"Work well that is great and it's all fitting into place, the jigsaw puzzle and yes she had noticed the last pieces were fitting together quite nicely.

We have signed a big deal and are now starting to build houses and we are taking new projects on. BB, well not so great he has found someone new he only comes to me when he feels lonely, so I have knocked it on the head there is one of the Directors we are chatting about work he seems very keen I will see how we go where that is concerned.

BB is only the legal part of the deals I need someone who understands the ways of housing. All good fun here Helen you will love it and the older people living here in Miami certainly love you Helen so do the younger people do also but in a different way and the retired people feel they know you already you are a star here."

Laura and Mark the bodyguard placed the cases into the back

of the car, off they went straight to the Four Seasons, they had a suite there. It would be a day around the pool the morning was to be book signing at Saks. It lasted most of the morning and the queue was long and hard.

"I love your Angels, I now after reading this book have come to be in tune with the Angels, it has changed my life, I talk to them and ask them for guidance you know that have brought real living into it all, that is what is so good about it, it's easy to read and makes sense of life, I bet you are pleased with yourself."

Martha spoke in a broad American accent she looked as though she had lived the test. "What name should I write or shall I just sign love Helen." Helen took hold of the book in her hand and then smiling as she spoke to Martha. "Martha my dad named me so that I fit it well."

"Helen you fit Helen well as it does mean "Light." Martha stretched out taking hold of her book. "I am glad you enjoyed the book and I set out to do just what you have said, so I have achieved my aims and goals I hope the second book you enjoy too."

Leaving Saks to travel for the afternoon into the Spanish part of Miami, as Helen wanted to visit Calle Ocho, Little Havana, she also wanted to see, stop and chat to the Cuban's that lived all over these parts and to see the Eternal Flame to Cubans it was such a significant journey a spiritual one for her there would be many of them in the coming months and then to late a lunch at Versailles Restaurant in which Helen would have seafood her favourite.

At 1.00 pm the next day they arrived for a luncheon again to the speech, the poems, the laughter and she looked to the people there certainly was some money around here and her charities would benefit from the people in Florida and Miami. Helen even met one of her favourite singers Gloria Esterfan that was a joy in itself.

They were off to the Everglade in the morning she was off to see the crocodiles, as it is good to see where her handbags and shoes came from. We buy these things but never think off how where and what happens to get them into our handbags and shoes in the first place.

Leaving the banquet hall she stumbled and found all the Angels were standing in front of her. Ok she thought double bodyguards the heavenly ones had made themselves noticed, the earthly one's were in front of her picking her up, from struggling to fame from rags to riches, from pain to happiness, from hate to love.

She had done the best she could to climb to the top to chat to all about the world of the heavens and what the Angels could do for them she was to be the person that brought the peace.

The crocodiles were racing around when Helen first saw them, well as much as they can race around, they were slow on land but when a prey was in sight their pace soon quickened, all God's creature's came with God's love whatever you were watching them carefully as she still wanted to keep her legs, she bought herself a handbag and shoes to match all made of crocodile skin. "Laura look at the shoes something to die for, handbag to match all good stuff here.

I was going to pick up a sexy crocodile print lingerie, it would have all looked good in the bedroom department I could snap at his middle wicket with my teeth." As they both began to laugh, Laura missed Helen so much but both of them were making new friends. "Too much information Helen I don't want to think of you as a sexy crocodile chasing dick." Thank goodness for the human side of life, Helen liked to work with both spiritual and logical.

Their stay felt as if it had gone very quickly they were already driving back to Miami airport to fly back to London so much to do, it had been a wonderful trip it had opened Helen's eyes up to the world, she had seen the Glitz and the Glamour and the pain of the poor, so now back for a couple of weeks in France, then a quick two day visit to Hollywood.

She was enjoying life and life had changed so much for the better there had to be time for some writing as she wanted to write some children's spiritual books, fun books with teddies, publishing them and perhaps even a film or television was her goal there. Everything now was coming together now very well.

Friends, Accepting the Changes

France was warm, France was the relaxation she needed to clear her energies and write a little have some serious love making with John, Sarah was at the Chateaux, but that was no problem as it was a big mansion they could find places to lose themselves easily. Their plane came to land how many take offs and landings had she done in the past six weeks many came to . mind.

Nice was so beautiful, the journey to Helen's Chateau which was closer to the borders of Italy, Mounta Briava Helen did enjoy travelling through seeing how the different seasons changed the landscape, Italy she was a frequent visitor to Milan, the fashion was so chic there and Helen like the chic classic clothes they made her feel good and feel so special.

They were looking to changing John's place in Spain, all the houses needed updating, France they had only just began to feel it was home, so Spain would be another home and London an apartment in Kensington. America was to find a place for then just for when they were that side of the world and to buy a property in the south of Italy near Sorrento or Sicily.

Their favourite restaurant Alberto's, it was on the border the food was of the local Cuisine and wine from not only their vineyard but also Helen's and John's so they had the pleasure of their own wine at dinner. John had been thinking of putting their wine on the market.

John was waiting for Helen to be that world success that was predicted and then make his move as it would be her fame and the good taste would sell it at the rate he wanted it too, bringing them more time to invest in each other.

John had the vision of moving into France and leaving the hectic, crazy world of England behind and only inviting the people he loved and wanted to keep in his life. But first to Helen's debut then they can sit back and enjoy.

They were both deciding whether to have a house in Italy too as the country and the language they both loved it would have to be further down nearer the south close to the sea, and perhaps an apartment just for something different the world certainly was their oyster, and they knew it. Times and life were better than most.

Sarah met them at Nice airport, she certainly looked better for her few weeks stay in France, Helen looked into her eyes, yes she thought there was a twinkle. She had met her man she knew that much but what had she been up too. A few glasses of wine would soon pull it out of her as soon as the big gates of their drive to the house open Helen was in holiday mode and would open a bottle as soon as she slipped her clothes off to fit the sun's rays and the warmth.

The Châteaux looked lovely, clean and Helen French home carers certainly had looked after it well, it would soon be time to harvest the grapes and she wanted to be there for that it was such a fun time, hopefully she could place it between travelling.

Friends, Accepting the Changes

The doors opened Marie and Petre were standing with their arms open to greet Helen and John. "Helen it is so good to see you, your travel went well."

Marie remarked but it was in her broken English, Helen's French she had certainly worked on the language and found it was totally different to Spanish and Italian she had to think before speaking. But it was getting better. Petre held Helen's hand and then took her bags he was such a gentleman.

"Come on Sarah lets go and change you can update me on your adventures here as you look as though you have been up to some mischief young lady, good mischief at that. Well I would like to see some of your paintings as they must be different now your mood has changed its easier, calmer." Helen grabbed her hand and moved Sarah upstairs both of them changed into long flowing summer dresses with their pool wear underneath, taking a change of clothes downstairs with her it would be a relaxing day.

Lunch was served outside on the patio, the heat of the day was glorious and Helen was dying to hear what Sarah had been up too. "Come on Sarah times up give me all the details even the sordid ones I want to know all about him, have you had sex yet, have you been meditating to bring your Angels closer to you as they will bring your soul mate along.

Come on drink up and spill the beans, John doesn't mind, do you John." Helen looked to John for some kind of approval, did she need it yes as women chat could be so boring. He just smiled then pinched Sarah softly. "I hope it has made you happy whatever." He said softly.

"I expect all the details nothing left to the imagination, I could not stand that." Sarah looked at them both and realised she would have to tell her whole story for them to give their consent for her trip to go further. "Ok, I met him at the airport, he looked straight into my eyes he smiled that was that, I turned, he turned it was one of them moments you get now and then. I left and thought oh well thank you Angels he was certainly worth coming here for even if for a peek."

She took a deep breath a moment of thought, a moment of time to remember. "You have not got time to breathe Sarah, so what happened next." To Helen butting in quickly goodness breathing at this time was done hurriedly. "Ha, Ha, Helen you are terrible, John tell her to be patient. John smiled at Helen, knowing that very word Helen used many, many times to her clients.

"Patience Helen as she has to tell the whole story cannot miss anything out." John started laughing at the girls to find they all started to laugh together one glass of wine and they were in roars of deep laughter, waiting for the rest of the story, it was so good just to chill. And good friends were part of that chilling sometimes there is a need for them.

"Goodness you two, I bet you write this in a book Helen, ok his name Anton, he lives near here and travels for work he is some kind of designer, we are going on a trip to Italy his family live there, he does paint but only for pleasure, he has sold some of his work.

He loved my work, each day he said my work was changing its more subtle and easier to the eye the colours were beautiful and changing as I was changing. He is beautiful Helen just as you said and the second time I met him was down near the sea he was painting just like you said Helen." Sarah took a breath.

"We have had dinner a few times and he has taken me to different places to paint. Yes we have been to bed and not to sleep either he is mmm very good, very surprising and he was generous in his lovemaking I was a happy girl when he had finished I can tell you that, he is back this weekend we are going to see his parents I am totally taken by this guy he has the qualities I am looking for.

So it is a watch this space and I have meditated every day since I have been here and I now have a room full of Angels ready to chat when I start, so thanks to you I am now open to the world of the heavens." Smiling Sarah continued.

I am grateful for that as my work is changing I cannot wait to show you my work, it's Angels and Masters all on a spiritual feel you are going to love them I am taking them to Italy as they are well into Angels and Masters with the Heavenly realms. I will bring them down to show you so that you can choose one for you in your room Helen it would be lovely there or would you like me to paint a special one.

I could do that for you as you have helped me so much, my payback to you for the love you give." The quietness fell as they all digested what had Sarah had enlightened them too. Sarah could paint a whole room, a special meditation healing room for Helen and she would love it.

Each wall would be a different Angelic picture capturing the Masters, Archangels and Angels of each realm how beautiful would that be, Helen would always feel that she was in the world of the heavens and the healing would be something else. Sarah sat   still and she was unusually quiet beginning to think about the night she was invited to Anton's home, he did have a smaller place than Helen and John but it was cosy, he came to the door she was dressed in red, very seductive.

A glass of wine and she went into a relaxed mode, taking her to his studio just for her opinion of his work, they spent thirty minutes there and then made it into the kitchen there was an AGA in the centre to the left of the kitchen, Sarah loved the Aga, the cooking was different it tasted better.

He looked at her and watched her every move, yes she was still very beautiful and the sunshine just tinged the skin enough to make her so attractive. After all the pain the time for happiness had arrived for her she was on cloud nine, she loved everything about him, she loved his home his work his way of life and his beautiful face his facial features were an art piece in itself. Sarah found his bone structure divine.

She found his accent seductively a big, big turn on so Sarah had certainly found a man who could turn her lights on in a big way. What would this man be like in bed she began to think her mind was travelling to that moment she could see it so clearly the Angel had given her that vision.

Mmm she thought let's get dinner finished and onto pudding very quickly. The thought of pudding was making her horny she was feeling well definitely feeling very moist indeed it had been a long time since she felt like this her last sexual experience was not one she really wanted to remember.

It left her doubting her sexual preference even more she would be hoping Anton was the man she could settle with and she did not want to have any kind of sexual relationship with a woman not full time they were a stop gap she needed to move into the right direction.

He cooked like a chef let's see if he makes love like stallion she was certainly looking for that. He had finished cooking and placed everything on the table in front of them both, they fed each other, this was the beginning of a French, Italian lover all my wishes in one man so good, she gave him a kiss placed food in her mouth then gave it to him, he returned the action, it was really getting heated, she was so moist ready for him to enter her but he would still make her wait.

Friends, Accepting the Changes

They left the plates of food where it was then he picked her up she still was a delicate lady, small, fragile he was there to look after her. He placed her on the soft rug, just watching her eyes he began to take her clothes off, each garment was followed by kissing gently over the skin that was left open he gently placed her silk dress on the chair, it felt soft just like her skin.

He saw she had a small pair of panties on and began to kiss them, teasing as he went, she was reeling with total enjoyment of his touch he was soft and sensual, slowly finding her lips, the softness of his lips defined and his motions were from soft and gentle to firm and intense, it was a firmness of the rush of love.

Sarah could feel his hardness as he moved close beside her, his arms holding her very gently but firmly he felt her hands undo his shirt one button at a time slowly taking his shirt away from his body and revealing his tanned chest this was all too much, she began to think what a heavenly body he had and touching him softly as he began to slowly undo his trousers dropping them to the floor, slipping his shoes off at the same time she watched his face change.

He was now beginning to enjoy himself, his fear of women, the fear of her left his face in a moment, kissing him while he was removing his Dior pants and then the Dior creation removed, her face was such a   delighted by what she could see, staring at him she could see he was pleased to know what she was about do.

Friends, Accepting the Changes

Sarah began to move closer her mouth her lips found a way to please him entirely, Sarah enjoying what she was giving to him and Anton was very much enjoying what he was receiving. Sarah watched him while performing his pleasure he made sure he did not orgasm, not just yet he was enjoying the attention too much, gently kissing him.

Enjoying him and he became so aware of the tenseness of this moment was to be there the movements quickened until his climax had been made, she took his juices and for a moment his mind was elsewhere, he found himself in the moment caressing the top of her thighs.

Slowly teasing her clitoris she felt herself coming to a climax, he would back away until he felt that the moment of need to give her an orgasm, she climaxed the feeling of such intense pleasure, and the flowing of the warm juices he captured that love within him kissing her gently.

His heart gave way he felt so overwhelmed by her, her mouth gave him so much pleasure. He was enjoying her so much he slipped himself into her, slowly so slowly and gently he moved inside her very sexually, so sultry and they were at one and the intenseness of both their naked bodies entwining enjoying every moment.

He looked into her eyes as their intenseness was about to come to the moment of explosion as if he needed and wanted to bring them both to a height of extreme pleasure together. They both moaned as they began reaching the place they wanted to be. He slowed to a stop, she stop to look at him, what would happen next this was the time when you knew how a man felt.

If he got up to wash his John Thomas then it would be a thank you very much leave your phone number I will give you a ring if they have the time, or if he had decided to cuddle her, he had enjoyed every minute of the pleasure you had shared and loves your company, there would be many dates after this one, this is just the start.

Anton stayed cuddling her as they fell asleep in each other's arms, a sign of love the love in a true sense, Sarah felt that she had at last found the love she needed and wanted. Chatting to Helen and John she had a smile. Helen and John were chatting away while Sarah was away in her world with Anton the love of her life.

"Where have you been Sarah you were totally gone, you have not been drinking that much was that thought a good one, yes he is in love with you." Helen then began pouring another glass of wine it certainly was a beautiful day. Helen loved seeing her ladies happy, that's part of the journey.

Sitting enjoying the company and the wine, sometimes relaxing in the pool it was just warm enough to enjoy, the bottles were flowing the chat was fun, the food was soon replenished by Marie she was a god send, having a heart of gold, it must have been good to see Helen relax with friends she needed more of this. In time she would get just that.

The weekend came quickly and this would be Helen's chance to see Anton, check him out to make sure he would fit into Sarah's world and to see if Helen could except him into her world. Sarah had started to paint a canvas that was of all the Masters, and Archangels, the Angels, Cherubs and Sprites with all the heavenly beings standing in a soft triumph.

It would be good for Sarah to put her heart and soul into the project to finishing the canvas would be a healing within Sarah herself, to see it placed in Helen's special room, a room full of the heavenly souls the most positive beings ever to be in Helen's life.

Anton stood nervously in front of Helen he had heard so much about her, she took his hand then said. "Anton you are more than welcome to stay anytime, if you are coming into Sarah's life you must look after her otherwise you know that you will have to answer to me." He smiled and squeezed Helen's hand, little did he know what he was taking on and quietly said.

"Thank you for being so open to me thank you for the invite I will do my best to look after her I am taking her for a few days to meet my parents, the family then we will see if they love her as much as I do." Helen moved closer just to touch his face she then whispered to him. "There you go enjoy today Anton enjoy life is far too short."

Friends, Accepting the Changes

They left together, now both John and Helen could have time on their own just to enjoy each other it was the one to one company their bodies enjoying the touch, their love enjoying every moment.

They would find time to walk over the land that they loved, checking to see what they would be doing in the next few months the coordinating was now becoming so rewarding and interesting, the vineyard was coming to be one of the best in the world.

Walking the vineyard they found the grapes were soon ready, they were chatting to the farm manager to see when the grape crushing began and the fiesta time were to happen as they both wanted to be there. "In four weeks we are ready to harvest the grapes and then the process of crushing into wine would take place as we go it will take a few weeks.

The time of the fiesta that is when the grapes have been harvested, in six weeks we will have fiesta time, party time so you must be here." His name Michael he certainly did work hard that in itself was good seeing a man work and enjoying his work too.

"Michael we will be here for the three weeks of harvest we will make sure that into the schedule." A glass of last year's wine, they shook his hand and left for their return to England in a few days and then off to America, Hollywood drop in and check on the film, then a journey to Italy they both wanted to see the spiritual sights. Sarah returned happy from her trek to Italy she had been cleared by the family, all good stuff Helen thought.

So now they would enjoy their time together then to return for the next journey of learning. Sarah had the canvas painting she was doing for Helen and Anton to keep her busy while they were gone, she could stay until she felt she needed to leave, it would be her choice.

There was the hand of friendship when times are hard a friend is there to look after you, to make everything right this was Helen's time to be that special friend, to care to protect, to look after her mind, body and soul to make her the person she should be.

Part Three; Spiritual Journey

Chapter Nine; Italy, The Leaning, The Sights.

The stopover in America a chance to see how the film was coming together, there would be a few months of travelling to see the changes in the production and the director kept her in touch with her every day and now she was going to see some of the film on screen, there had been arrangements made for the girls to be on set so Helen would be meeting both Laura and Kate just to take them to the film set.

The four women were a massive part of the film, actually they were the film, they needed to see if they felt their characters had the right qualities to be them, watching some of the parts of the film and the editing, each time Helen came to see how the film was progressing the girls would be there.

Helen may have written the book but if she had not met the girls the characters would not have been there, originally she wrote the book about herself and finding that it lacked a certain something, it needed an injection of life, sex, fun and laughter. In meeting the girls had allowed Helen to fit it around all four of them and now they needed to be part of the looking on to see how they felt about the characters and the actors and how they were performing in their given character roles.

They all stayed at the same hotel it's great to keep to the same place where they treat you well, getting used to your needs and pitching camp at the hotel and the same suite. Helen was left on her own for the day so that John could search for the home he wanted in to buy in America he wanted to see what was on the market, what was available, Laura brought some details of houses in the Florida area including Miami. John was determined to find a home in America, he had 48 hours to do just that as they were leaving for Italy on Friday.

John knew that he needed to gather all the important information that they needed for them to read while they were travelling and in their quiet moments and Helen left him to it and they could decide while they were travelling where they felt a home would suit them in this part of the world. Italy was their journey for ten days and then going straight to France for harvesting the grapes what a busy life.

The girls watched themselves on set, making comments to the man they have forever swooned about, director George they would call him and when they walked in they were all taken aback to find Mr Clooney sitting there as if he were part of them, and chatting to him was so weird, a bit surreal or something to that effect. Yes, he had practically got the four of them to a tee, all was good.

The hotel had placed them for dinner John, Helen, Kate, Laura with both girls leaving their prospective men behind so that Helen couldn't tap into them they knew her so well regarding her work. Their Supper was at 9.00 pm, Champagne was the order of the day so much to celebrate these days. "Laura has

Friends, Accepting the Changes

BB left you to it now or is there still some controlling with him how's that new man what is his name." Helen asked Laura in a caring way and also trying hard to calm down as the excitement was showing.

Helen looked to the waiter as he placed yet another bottle of Champagne into the bucket of ice this was going to be a good night she thought. "David Brinton to one question and then to the other yes he is still there, he is working hard at the plans and the lay out of the area we have had loads of lunch meetings and he has asked me out for dinner when I get back to Miami, then I reckon we will go places with both work and play, of course he is much more ambitious than any man I have met and he has the most divine house Helen and it's by the water edge, massive I could see myself in that.

John has someone else now and Mr BB is going back to England for a while goodness he is a possessive, obsessive control freak I cannot have that I need more than sex. So David I feel is the one it is weird I have had to move to Miami to meet him, the other side of the world." Laura taking yet another sip of Champagne and too many sips suddenly making her giggly, she certainly did look good.

"Laura what has happened with you Kate, how's that man of yours?" Helen checking all was ok with her girls as they could not call so much with all this travelling was putting a stop to that.

Friends, Accepting the Changes

"Helen he is to die for, he travels with me his name is Robert Jakinsky he has a child, a girl and she is twelve I have met her she is a little diamond really no problem. His wife died five years ago he has a nanny for his daughter and she has just started boarding school so it all fits into place, the school holidays she is always around so if we go away she does come with us and she has her nanny with her, so it fits well for us and we are getting on very well indeed.

We both want the same things it seems we will be looking at working with children in third world countries so very significant. We have a sex life that is fantastic." Kate began to reminisce, her thoughts of the times that they found out what they really wanted.

She walked into Robert's apartment, opening the door to the smell of incense and to Kate's amazement Robert had candles alight everywhere he could find. It was divine noticing the fire and the bottle of champagne resting in the ice-bucket, what was this night all about.

What was in Robert's head Kate was feeling exhilarated and slightly worried about what Robert was planning for their evening, walking around the table was set for the two of them to dine. Kate was ready and would just enjoy.

Oysters for their starter and the plan was becoming clearer by the minute, then to beef steak with soy & spice this was something to be enjoyed. Kate kept her thoughts to herself about the postre which Robert brought forward now it has to be Belgian chocolates, strawberries with cream to enjoy their bodies and the champagne was to lighten their head and let go of the restrains of uncertainty. She was in for a night of sheer sexual pleasure in a loving way, Kate couldn't do hard sex not after Michael and his games, she had to be loved and made love too. Which

h is understandable when you think of the circumstances of Kate's plight but it certainly changed Kate's world and her feelings for others that were in her private life, and her working side was more productive where feelings were concerned.

Robert gently began to feed Kate the chocolates followed by the strawberries they were enjoying the moment. Kate watching as Robert placed the blanket by the fire yes she was in for a good time. Some tantric yoga was the call of the day. They slowly placed themselves in front of each other as they slowly began to undress just a sip of champagne or a chocolate was called for.

Slipping into a top with no bra or panties on it was just a little protection that she felt she needed while they meditated on their bodies they were happy with what they saw. Sometimes an orgasm can be achieved just be visualising and the power of thought. Kate had never done this before. It was empowering, she was not being taken over she was watching Robert enjoy her body.

Looking, visualising meditating in giving one another the greatest of pleasure and to bring a mental orgasm of the flesh. Kate was enjoying the moment as Kate needed to feel safe because Michael had scared her badly. Taking off her top because she began to feel Robert was there for her protection and support he would not harm her and Kate needed to get to that point.

Watching Robert he began to charge like a battery, she could see he was enjoying her. His magic wand was beginning to expand, too want her deeply too enjoy the softness of her body, and then to rush into that dark moist cavern and make Kate complete.

They came closer to the enjoyment of the flesh Robert sitting back with his penis standing tall and significant and Kate wanted to place herself on top of him to slowly enjoy him and bring herself to an orgasm, shifting and making herself open to him, her legs open and inviting him to unpack his bags and come to stay for a while just enough time for them to want more and more.

Her face flushed and her beauty to be seen, her wanting was so obvious that Robert took hold of her waist and brought Kate into position and placing Kate exactly where he wanted her making sure that the position would not do her any harm, slipping and sliding from side to side then up and down.

This would be the most wonderful time for Kate this would set the love making for the future. He pushed his way securely, firmly. Feeling her g-spot as it found his way. Her clitoris was open to manipulation. She was prime and secure within herself and the moment of ecstasy was about to explode. Robert sighed as he his moment arrived, Kate groaned with such delighted as her orgasm came to fruition she was there in her moment she scream Robert joined in as he filled her with his juices.

They were in the delight of each other, their moment spent. Bringing herself back into the room with a jolt and wet panties, Helen noticed Kate looked rather flushed and wondered where had she been in her moment of moments. All in a day's work she thought to herself, life was fun sometimes.

Kate began to speak again. "It's what I have always wanted he is so spiritual and he also has an intuitive feel that I find strange as being with you then with him I am learning so much from you both, I have an Angel with me all the time, I am being drawn to listening to myself more. Listen to me Helen anybody would think I was a Medium."

Well they were all good, that left Helen to do more soul searching in Italy, looking forward to the journey of finding her souls path, wondering what spirit had in store for her what was she going to do and there would be another level to reach for and then she would be fine-tuned to a higher dimension she'd be reaching the highest and then no more learning just living.

Friends, Accepting the Changes

The morning they left America for Italy both of them decided a big breakfast for the journey. At the airport Helen rushed through the channels of security and straight onto the plane. Arriving in the wonderful romantic Italy and Naples International Airport welcomed her with open arms.

Their first port of call was Naples staying the night with the Italians in Naples enjoying the hospitality of the locals and what about the Mafia she did wonder whether they still controlled, the hotel was fantastic in the heart of Naples close to the sea.

They had asked for top floor with a sea view it was to be special, tonight they would be at the Teatro di San Carlo Madame Butterfly was the opera, Helen loved Madame Butterfly. Driving through the Renaissance gate de Porta Capuana this beautiful arch was worth the detour, Helen had asked John to visit the highest point above Naples so that the view across the bay towards Sorrento and Capri towards Mount Vesuvius.

Helen's heart was fall of emotion had she arrived home her heart felt like it had. She was at home with her emotions, settling into the suite that they had been given the champagne in ice ready to be poured the chink of the glasses made Helen feel so happy to be alive there was something about a glass of champagne as they sat looking towards the sea.

The Mediterranean was the most welcoming site. Sorentto and Capri in the distance waiting to be explored, waiting to be enjoyed a breath of fresh air and a deep sigh. Touching John's face he was so beautiful and why did they make her wait so long for such a wonderful man. Smiling back at her he loved her so much could he, should he allowing his hand to stroke her arm, their glasses empty, their glasses always full. Just to sit and enjoy the view and the company of such a beautiful lady. The years and the people who called her such a beautiful lady not a false bone in her body, very much would speak as she found.

Slowly John moved his way towards Helen and their lips met the warmth, the love andthe connection to reach the height of the satisfaction of their love. His hand held her ace as if he never wanted to let go. Taking her blouse off to reveal the beautiful bra kissing her softly, gently as their body's moved with the slow music that was playing in the distance, someone was playing crooners music Frank Sinatra, Dean Martin they could hear it was their background music.

Swaying to the sounds of the best, Helen pulled John towards the bed those clean, crisp sheets were going to be slightly dirty from the love making that was about to go on, falling onto the top of the bed kicking their shoes off and watching them fly. John then removed his trousers revealing the beautiful body of a man getting older but still had something about him. His skin was so soft to the touch Helen loved the softness of his skin.

Rolling around on a king size plus bed, Helen threw her bra just leaving her panties on while they danced on the bed. Watching Helen while she undressed, they both would be experimenting with tantric yoga and sex, there was a determination to keep their love alive and pleasing one another was part of the no sordid stuff as Helen wasn't into that rubbish.

Sitting with their legs entwined around one another moving closer so that they would fit together while the slow motion of them enjoying their body's riding then the waves to the crescendo of the ecstasy of fulfilment, how they loved, how they lived. A short nap and then they would shower and then something small before the opera. Just to sleep was fine.

Recharging before enjoyment, sex was a lift for Helen the warmth of the day and the sounds of Naples made Helen sleep well. Spain where Helen went to heal from the death of Mark was not so good even though her healing she still felt uncomfortable her phone tapped yet again, her computer hacked she was getting so tired of these people.

Spain made her ill even though she was much better. She was tired living there it took her energy away. Perhaps that's what they wanted for her to leave, did they like her well that she did not understand. Police involvement yet again, it was so tiring, she'd had enough of mindless people who wanted to cause damage to her. Italy had a different feel she felt looked after, warm and happy.

She dressed for the occasion as one thing about the Italian's they knew how to dress. Her dress black with silver and silver shoes she was ready to take John's arm and walk like she was in heaven with him. They were a magnificent team, they had learnt to work and play together. A cab to the Teatro and to walk in with the roof open and the breeze cooling them down, now let the fun begin watching, listening and reading the sub-titles just to find out where she was.

Madame Butterfly brought tears to her eyes. They both finished the evening sitting by the port in a wonderful restaurant with just a little something to eat and a night cap to set the night aglow they would sit on the   balcony and watch the moon go down.

Pompeii was beckoning for her to visit the ruins in the town and feel the energies of the people that died. They arrived that day at Pompeii walking through and around the town it was a sight and an overwhelming energy.

Helen taking in the disaster of Italy and feeling, she wanted to start communicating to the spirits that were here in Pompeii, the sun and its energy Helen loved the sun but then again she loved the rain, snow and whatever weather came to her door, Helen just loved life it was as simple as that.

Life is very much about living and very much about living in the moment of time with the view to the future as the future is the aim, the goal and the reckoning with oneself, the achievements one holds over oneself. Helen had achieved her goals many times over and now she was here in Italy where she knew a home would be bought for her and John.

Friends, Accepting the Changes

Helen did notice that her energies were replenishing while she was in Italy the heavens were speaking.

"I love this John, it is so beautiful. Look at Mount Vesuvius it's so real, close your eyes John and feel what happen, feel it as though it is going on now be one of these people I have and then the spirits climb into your body, it is so fantastic. I love that I am so open." Helen was jumping around like a child and this was something she enjoyed so much just communicating with the spirits. Helen began walking forward and then she saw Mark standing next to the old Teatro Grande he was beckoning her over.

"Hello mum, come over here and see what is inside for you, there's something I want you to see and feel." Mark smiled as he walked in front of his mother showing her the way forward as he has done since his death. Helen still felt slightly guilty with his last days but Mark was so protective of her he would have wanted to die on his own and not put Helen through the pain of his last moments.

Walking through to the Teatro Grande and climbing as high as Mark would allow her to and he pointed to a seat that was slightly in the distance there was a red rose just lying there. Helen reached down to pick it up and held it close to her heart, she knew what he was saying to her, and she knew what his heart was telling her. "I love you mum, and this is the rose you left on my coffin, now I am giving it back to you."

Friends, Accepting the Changes

Helen eyes were full of tears Mark had given her back the rose she had given to him as he left her and went behind the curtain before he was cremated that moment in her life came flooding back and her tears were flowing and then Mark cradled her within his soul feeling that warm energy gave Helen that forgiveness for him and what he had put her through with the police and the awful people that did not understand him or her.

Her life now was in his hands and he would make sure Helen reached her goal, Helen was a now a movie star in her own right. Life was now going to be her destiny all those years of people trying to stop her destiny but she had the strength to pull away from the rubbish.

Pompeii had given her something back from heaven and Helen would hold Pompeii in her heart forever, Italy was her home. Thank you Mark, thank you my Angels, my Masters today you have made my heart cry the tears that come to the surface every now and then. I am so happy with this sign. John raced over to Helen. "What's the matter Helen are you ok hunni." He cradled her in his arms she could feel both Mark and John giving her the love that she needed.

Helen for the first time opened her heart up to John and told him what had happened when Mark had died and how she had to work through it all with what was going on around and how the police ridiculed her and her son's death. How people around her played mind games. It all came out through the tears John couldn't believe her pain and took her face in his hands. "You now are so protected by your Mark, your Angels, your Masters and I am here as your main protector and heads will roll for this I can tell you, we will sue. And they did do just that. Helen smiled all the way to the bank.

They sat and held each-other Mark stood and smiled his work now done, he had now created the twin-soul in his mums life waiting for this to happen was an age but there it was in front of him. He would stay with Helen as her guide through her writing and consultations. Soon to be retired from consultations and to continue with her writing that Helen loved so much it was her purpose in life and her life's purpose to allow people, to show people how to enjoy and live from a divine way.

John and Helen walked through the ruins, and they walked through the Temple of Vespasian looking at the wondrous ancient history, life was so wonderful, and very interesting to walk back in time and feel what the life's of others in that time were all about. History interested Helen so much what was it about the time of life where the world came together one of the places Helen wanted to visit was the Middle East.

But there was so much going on there, the world of history was being destroyed by anger and greed. And what would happen to all those spiritual sites that were there for the world to see and understand we needed the spiritual as well as the love science of the understanding the logic in life.

The day in Pompeii was a day to remember for the rest of

Friends, Accepting the Changes

Helen's life, she also remembered the days in Spain all the tapping the phones and hacking her computer for what! In Italy there was no need to do that they liked what they saw and did not need to repeat it to her in mind games. Police and company did get taken to task and Helen won in her own right. Fame was there in her life and those who tried to stop it would receive their Karma. Protection she needed and protection she got.

Leaving the bodies of the people, some small, some large some significant and some just there for the reason. Leaving the energy behind so that they could enjoy their last day for the time being anyway in Naples the romantic city that gave Helen the love of life and the love of John and Mark, that most certainly was a day and what a day our Helen had just witnessed would people believe her.

They left in their Bentley and were driven to their hotel, doors opened wherever they went people just opened them as if Helen had finally reached her goal. Italy was definitely where she would spend most of her days until her return to heaven. Finding a place in Sicily she thought.

An official stopped them as they were in the foyer. "Beonasera Signora, Qual e' il suo lavora?" He asked in a smiley voice. "Sono il Consaltana un Author." Helen replied Italian English. "Il suo nome, scusi." He asked Helen. "Mi chiamo Helen." Helen found herself answering him she did feel that she had done so well. Her Italian, French, Spanish, German and of course English were all used at some point in her life.

Friends, Accepting the Changes

Isn't life so wonderful she thought as this man continued asking both John and her to accompany him to the local Italian Town Hall for a late supper their driver would be shown where to take them to, Helen did feel so special.

The tables were set and they sat closest to the Mayor and his team. They chatted in English and Italian and the food all seven courses of it were delicious and the Italian's most certainly knew how to welcome them to the supper table. All around were the Masters of the heavens they watched as they knew Helen had made it home at last. Spain was where Mark wanted to visit but Italy was Helen's home.

"I am going to soak in the bath John I want to feel free. I am so happy and I need to communicate to my friends in heaven and I can do that in the bath for a while, then you can join me if you like the bathes it is certainly big enough for a few enjoyable moments." A twinkle in her eyes Helen smiled at John and he totally got her. They had such a commutative relationship they just so knew one another it was just like looking in a mirror at themselves. Their driver kept his eyes on the road.

The bath was ready for Helen to slip into just needing that water to cleanse her soul, the candles filled the room the with love of everybody around her and then Helen connected with the heavenly world Archangels and Masters came for a visit and found that it was such a dream of destiny falling into place.

One by one they gave a message to Helen one by one they

smiled and healed her from the past and the envy, jealousy and ridicule. Jesus was the main Master who made the sign of well done our Helen you are at the top of the world in your life and in the heavens. He continued speaking.

"You have shown others that you are strong in love, strong in character, strong with your connections with us, we are your protectors we will deal with the perpetrators of hate." He then came over to touch Helen's head and Helen felt the last change in her spiritual connection she was one with the heavens complete.

They left one by one to leave Helen in her own private soak with love. Pink, red, gold, purple, blue and black filled the room with delight the smell of frankincense filled the bathroom with love and happiness. A knock on the door and John's head peeped around the door his smiled was a pleasure to see.

"A glass of wine M'lady, does one prefer it now while you are relaxing?" John had moved himself completely into the bathroom. "I would love a glass of wine and for you to join me in the bath it's big enough for two."

Two glasses of wine and a man who was completely naked moved and himself around the door and slipped himself into the bath with Helen for a new adventure. "Tomorrow Helen we are off to Sorrento that means ten days of total relaxation and some good food, I know that you would like some facials and a couple of massages so I will organise that you simply relax.

Friends, Accepting the Changes

I think we should buy a new home here, I love it so much."
John enjoying the bubbles in the bath while he chatted to
Helen, sipping the wine which was a Borolo and the laughter
between them was so good just to be listened too.

Snuggling together and the kissing began Helen was becoming
aroused with John's touch he was so gentle, so loving. She was
so relaxed now gone were the days of the mistrust of John
Helen trusted him completely her life was his life, her love was
his love, he moved Helen closer while he found that place that
was inviting him to stay for a while.

The movement was creating the waves of pleasure slipping into
the delight of the energy of Helen, sliding in moving out the
motion was slow to begin with as they positioned themselves
for a tempered manoeuvre, John began to thrust just to find
that orgasm Helen so wanted and needed just to balance her
energy.

Hitting that spot to make the quickening come together Helen
reached her goal of sheer pleasure. Relaxed she was as they
both snuggled together. John wrapped the towel around her
when she stepped out of the bath and then it was cream on and
to sit for a while on the balcony watching the nightlife of
Naples.

Looking over the bay to Sorrento it looks so peaceful and
pointing to Capri Helen said to John. "Look John at the lights
of Capri we were married there and going there will bring back

memories for us, good memories are we going there?"

Asking John while she held his hand against her heart she loved him dearly all these years of waiting had paid off and she knew what she wanted and would not accept anything but what she wanted. John replied in his soft calm voice. "No not this time we are going on a cruise later with all of us girls and boys together I think we could do that and find out just how we all get along."

Magical man that what he was and Helen adored him dearly, she did think 95% of men were complete pricks but John was in the best 5% bracket that is the gentlemen percentage. Why did God make some men so incomplete he should have carried on until they were all gentlemen also why did God make some women incomplete this Helen would not comprehend.

Did God have another pressing engagement that he had to rush to before finishing the completion of humans, 95% completion and perhaps he thought that we could in still our own changes and did he realise to do that you have to except responsibility of the person you are and your faults.

Morning time again and they were off to Sorrento and the Hotel la Favorita. The first stop was to the Palazzo Reale it was so grand and the staircase was to die for. Then stopping off at all of the fountains Helen just closed her eyes and felt the energy of time past, the Italians in their finery were walking around the grounds and not one bikini's to be seen.

Friends, Accepting the Changes

It would have been designer fashion as only the rich would be allowed to attend and the poor would be begging on the streets. The way forward to Sorrento there would be a couple of body guards waiting just for them so they had peace and quiet.

Into the foyer, they were ushered through to the lift the Manager would come to them making sure that they had what they needed. A personal maid took hold of Helen's cases and started unpacking and then placing Helen clothes in the wardrobe, Helen went straight to the terrace just standing on the terrace made her feel free, and in her freedom she was in control of what she wanted regardless of her John's organising.

"We must have a place here John it's so beautiful there is a village around here that we could look for a place it's called Positano and we could just have an apartment in America." Helen sighed with contentment. What would John say to her question, would he give her what she wanted Helen made a wish for a home in Italy.

"Helen let's just settle and then we will take a look in a couple of days I will get in touch with the local agent and see what they have in Positano, anything for you my Angel." John making sure Helen got her wish. They were having a massage and Helen would have an extra facial. Just the relaxation of a holiday, lunch was served on their terrace and then to the spa and relaxation.

Loving the facial and both of them feeling a million dollars as they popped the coke of the champagne and just sitting watching the world go by. The small boats and the liners all sailing into the bay of Naples dropping Anker and moving away, this was most certainly the life and most certainly where Helen could write to her hearts content.

Lovingly John placed his arm around Helen he would slowly bring her close, all this champagne and this was the first time they had stopped. John did wonder whether they could move the business to Italy and just visit France allow the vineyards to be managed and London would be there as a stopover for business with the American apartment that would serve as a visit to films, business, Kate and Laura. Yes he had worked it out Italy was too good to let go. But would Sicily be better for them both.

The night was musky the noise of the fishing boats clanking was something that John and Helen were enjoying, the food sent up for them was succulent and they both were feeding each-other, Helen sitting in her slip and a smidgen of Chanel Mademoiselle she was ready for some love. John in his pants and the aroma of Chanel Homme he was stroking Helen's back and shoulders.

Her slip taken off allowing John to kiss around every part of her body and carrying Helen to the bed he began to kiss her thighs and making his way to the jewel and kissing while stroking her thighs, his hands were doing the talking bringing Helen to her crescendo for him to slip inside her and move his way around her them both in the raptures of the waves of enjoyment and they were both flying to ecstasy and came in and out of the raptures as they both had an orgasm together.

Breakfast and then to visit the Chiesa di San Francesco just the beauty of this special church was something Helen has always loved, she had visited many churches in Spain. Each country she visited a church had to be done. The history, the beauty was there to be seen.

Sorrento Cathedral and the fishing side of Sorrento. It was hot and Helen wanted to dip into the pool but not to sunbathe that needs to be done privately. And they found a villa in Sicily they would view it later.

They would enjoy the Teatro while they were here and to returning home to France, maybe a detour to Hollywood then viewing some property in California, Florida and Miami. It was something they felt had to be done now Helen knew that finding somewhere that it must have a feel to it. What a wonderful journey into life itself.

They were to be in the studio just to get an update of the film, to then view three most amazing properties and back to France, her languages were certainly growing Helen began to master a few. She even knew Cumbrian, her daughter Harri lived there with the girls and her partner, life was good Helen was happy. France was for writing, the grapes would have to wait for Helen she needed free time, some meditation, good sex and great wine.

Marie would have made some French dishes that she loved she was looking out of the window they were arriving on the stretch to the airport, a sigh of relief as they were rushed through only to find a photographer coming over asking just for one picture to say she was in France. "Helen just one picture, how's the trip been how has your book been taken in by the Americans what are your plans while you are here?" He was persistent and insistent that he would get his story, not a thought to Helen.

"Charles, I am here for the harvest and I want complete rest so I would be grateful to be left alone to recharge my batteries and yes my books certainly have been excepted everywhere, I am a happy girl one photo and we are off." Helen gave him the photo she jumped into the car.

Back at the Chateaux the harvest was in full swing, John went straight out to see how the vineyard manager Pierre and finding out how he had been coping with the crops. He settled down to some picking of the grapes and meeting the young French pickers all were happily singing as they worked.

The next two days Helen slept for hours, John done his fair share at the harvest, the whole point of the harvest was to join in, so that when the fiesta's, the celebrations happen you know that you certainly had been in the swing of things as part of the fun. Helen joined in for the last few days eating grapes as she worked and singing with a whistle to the tune of. "Whistle while you work, do, dit do dit do, come on and whistle while you work."

Her singing was all in good taste. Looking around to see show many of the workers had their fingers in their ears, she looked but then quickly put her head down, the humiliation was not part of the plan. When the harvest came to an end Helen would resume the writing.

Sarah had spent so much time with Anton and her painting for Helen was so fantastic, so heavenly and it still wasn't finished yet it gave Helen the gift of the Art world in a beautiful Spiritual painting of the Angels, Archangels, and the millions of other beings in the heavens the universe and the Masters, the Heavens. Sarah would definitely have to do the same in the villa in Sicily she would love that and perhaps Anton could join her in her dreams.

The party had begun and the vines had been stripped now the hard working workers had the time to relax, there would be a great deal of celebrating to do, French bread, French food and the wine from the Vineyard, Helen wanted a good name for the wine as in the New Year they would be marketing it in the shops, could they also have a house with a vine yard in the North of Italy and then perhaps grow the Nebbiolo grape.

They would get some beautiful wines there, yes that was a thought she would hand over to John a manager in both vineyards would give them their freedom and John could make that his business dream, he would love it. Their vineyard in France was close to the Italian border.

The night was young the merriment went on for hours and in the early hours of the morning the revellers went home slightly drunk, the clearing up all could be left until the morning she thought. It had been good they're all happy. Sleeping until late then a heavy breakfast was called for and the day would be spent by the pool.

Helen had toyed over ideas for her books for children and she would now have to concentrate next year on them and her novel it would be an interesting time. She knew the books about the bears would be a success and perhaps a film or a television series. Her second the sequel was now reaching its end and would be published in the New Year her thoughts and her concentration would now be to this book and the bears.

John was returning to England, having to work on a project there. They would be apart for two weeks but the coming together again would be good fun. Now saying goodbye was always sad, Helen needed to work and connect with the Archangels and the Masters, Jesus was so close to her now and she had the added guidance from her son Mark, he was working with her now learning the tricks of the trade so to speak he would let his mum know what was going on around her and where she was to be next on her journey.

Friends, Accepting the Changes

Her next book would be about the coming together of men and women in certain situations, Helen had already started it and what a project, what a life in the timing and how much has she leant in the process of the years that she could put on paper to help the sexes understand one another through their journey's.

The next week she would work and she would also travel to Italy for some heavy duty shopping, Milan would be the choice. With a couple of days at the finest hotel and picking up on the fashion, Helen would travel on her own as Sarah was in love but she did miss the girlie time.

Helen missed Kate and Laura so much and they had planned a trip to France of course Paris and Champagne was on order but that was after Helen's trip to India, China and Japan, that would be a three week long trip. So a weekend with her friends would be more than fun. She was researching her book about men and women there would be a twist which should make people laugh and cry in reading it.

Helen left the Chateau for a while just to go for a long walk and finding herself slowly walking through the vineyards while the branches were bare it seemed a little empty, the end of a season, the end of a life came, and through this ending would become new beginnings in the Spring, Helen was looking forward to the Spring of the next year she would see many parts of her life grow, pacing herself and walking the length and breadth of the vines, Helen could hear a voice that she knew.

"Rainbow, Rainbow, Bows where are you ? Look Rainbow over here it's me Creams I've come for the wine tasting, Bows come on goodness this is such a big Vineyard. Look I am going to stay here where you can see me." Kate or Creams was standing on a bucket just so her best mate could see her. Waving her arms about and Helen, Rainbow or Bows came out of the middle of the vines and ran to her.

"Creams what are you doing here, they have given you a break from the UN then. Look at the vines stripped bare you have missed the hard work." Then hugging one another tightly and walking back to Helen's kitchen, the country kitchen she always dreamt of and finally got it the way she wanted it. "Have you seen my Wine Cellar come on let's look there might be something you fancy down there where are your suitcases and where's your man?"

Helen taking hold of Kate's hand and taking her to the large wine cellar, taking it slowly down the stairs the light switch on they walked in hand in hand to find out what they would be drinking. "Rose' Kate, it's slightly lighter, look Kate we have Champagne here pink as well we could have a few bottles of them today and then decide what to drink tomorrow, how long are you here for?"

Kate looked at all of the bottles weighing each one up for what she thought would have the best taste before looking at the label of the bottle what was she looking for, Creams never did know that it was just a bottle of wine and that was that. Helen wanted a truly exceptional bottle of Champagne for her friend Kate.

"Bows you have some mighty fine wines here, we could stay in here forever couldn't we. Get Marie to send us food, better still Champagne sounds good and I am here for three days so we will have some fun, is there a great coffee and cake shop here?"

Kate taking two bottles in her hand she would have a bit of time to see Helen by herself, looking at Helen she quickly remarked. "How's the books Helen and what have you managed to get finished it must all be coming together now, your life seems to be on the up, celebrity now what does that feel like Helen?"

"The children's books I am going to start to push next year and I am writing about Men and women in a fun and interesting way and the sequel is just coming to the end and will be published in the New Year. Look at me Creams I am famous, how many years has it been, how much crap have I been through.

Look at me I am now there and making my way to the top and by the end of next year I will know whether I have made it, an Oscar would be great but that might be next year come on Creams let's go into the hot tub and relax, Marie will bring some nibbles.

I am writing articles for two magazines so I am busy." They

both changed into comfy clothes and opened the bottle taking it into the hot sunshine and the warm hot tub its sounds weird a warm hot tub but that is what it was. Climbing into the hot tub was divine, Helen put some aromatherapy capsules in so it smell was beautiful and the bubbles were relaxing keeping them cool was the sunshade hat Helen had invested in it was like being in a hot house.

They were sipping their champagne and laughing it was bringing back memories of the times they had when life was such hard work but they had each other it was fun then until a man turned Creamy's head. It was downhill from there, to be rekindled later on their journey's, they were both so connected on a friends Soul-Mate connection.

Marie had made some French snacks and the afternoon was theirs for a catch up. "Marie please I will allow you to have free time this afternoon and I will see you in the morning." Helen said as Marie had not seen Helen on a in her moments with her friends, Helen did wonder what she might think, good food, fine champagne and wines and most of all the company of friends.

"Thank you Madam I will see you in the morning not to early yes?" Marie needed a very quick answer as if these two were having fun the drinks would be flowing heavily. "Yes you go and have some fun see you about 11.00 am, Ciao Marie, we will decide what to cook tomorrow there's no hurry as John is not here to look after only Kate and I and we are easy to feed."

Friends, Accepting the Changes

They both said in sequence together, now they both had the freedom without any ears listening to chat about life and Helen wanted to know everything that Kate had been up to. What was it about keeping up appearances do not let the staff see you plastered as it doesn't look good at all.

With the two glasses full of the best pink champagne Helen and Kate were like a couple of teenagers as they chatted about Kate's new man, it looked as though he was getting good marks to say the least. Kate it looked like she was beginning to fall in love, the sex was good and he even cooked which she thought surprising.

"He cooks Helen he does have lousy taste in furnishing, but I can live with that and we do spend a great deal of time with his only daughter but he seems to be worth the trouble. We are travelling for six months around the world on a UN mission so I will get to know him more, find out his faults and he does seem to adore me, he has never had anyone like me before he says. Sex is fantastic, he really turns me on big time, even gets my boobs to work and that is hard to do.

He knows exactly what I want and gives it to me, only thing is he is a little backward in his places of where he should have sex he likes it in the bedroom only and that could be boring for me so that will have to change I will have to teach him and he is needy and finds it hard to do without me that will have to change too, so not too much wrong but a little that I will have to keep having words until he gets it right."

Kate her normal self, bend for me because I am ok nothing wrong with me here she is so controlling is our Kate.

"Well I am glad to hear he is good in bed as that is important, I expect you have had many words already, does he really know what he is letting himself in for he will have to change and do as he is told but at least he is good in bed Kate and that is what matters. The next day they biked to the local village it would be a joy to see and it was just for Kate so she could enjoy the French life, they sat at the corner café watching the world go by, the different sorts of people how relaxed they were and most of the locals came into the village on their bikes.

They sat and they watched them all, it was fun to see all of them giving them a smile and a wave. "Bonjour Madame's Bonjour." They heard all the time as they stood choosing a table where the greatest of views were the Café' and la Patisserie was the order of the day just sitting enjoying the view, and allowing the drink from the night before disappear.

This was idyllic, seventh heaven so to speak, where Helen had her vineyard in France was beautiful and they would take the long way back and look at the countryside Kate needed to decide where to set up camp in the future, Helen's home eventually would be in France and Italy, she loved the peace and not being mobbed.

As that was beginning to happen elsewhere the price of fame she thought. Spain they had a home in the mountains that was being sold, America soon to be a home nearer to the water and two homes in Italy one in the north and one in the south.

Picking up their bikes they slowly left the village it's a long way home, what made some people so friendly to allow you into their space and what made some people envious with the view of playing mind games not allowing you to even venture into their space, it was something Helen was trying to come to terms with.

Sometimes she felt people were so cruel and unkind, sometimes their envy and jealousy just got in the way of them opening their hearts.

How can people like that be happy with themselves let alone be happy with others and how could Helen ever have someone in her life which were anything like that no she had to choose the best energies to be around her now. They had begun to reach Helen's land stepping off the bikes walking side by side in the sunshine.

"Helen come here can you see look you watch and listen and see how the birds are chatting to us flowing backwards and forwards, I have certainly found the last twenty four hours so relaxing.

I had such a heavy schedule on my return, these few days have given me the strength to carry on." Kate was watching and began carefully listening to the birds some were in hiding some flew right in front of them. The Chateaux in sight and a definite glass of wine was called for. Marie was cooking both lunch and dinner my goodness it smelt good French cooking the aroma in the air, a bottle out of the fridge and opened very quickly a good sparkling 'Pink Champagne' was a blessing for them both. Kate certainly had embraced her spiritual road she was enjoying her work, meeting many people with many problems.

Her private road was just beginning to open on a spiritual journey in itself. What a wonderful sight it was to see a friend coming into their own, that was what is meant by the spiritual way she only had to learn not to be so controlling, to expect so much from people, compassion, empathy and compromise Kate would soon be there, lots of weddings hats upon hats next year, it will be a good year. Helen was now going to have to say a sad goodbye to her friend their time had gone.

"Au revoir Kate, see you soon, Paris in four weeks, Ciao see you in quatre weeks." Broken French was better than none she thought all these languages an absolute pain, why don't we all speak one language and be done with it. Watching Kate as she began to walk towards the security Helen walked away slowly turning her head to see Kate also turning her head yes they were so in tune with each other, she knew when Kate would ring she knew what Kate would be doing and how she felt.

Good friends, happy friends and soul mates they are. Back to the writing before John returned she knew she still had her book the sequel to complete it was such a learning, there were days she just lost herself in her work, she researched before she jotted down then went into full swing head down of course she was strict with herself she had to be she knew she would not go wrong.

John returned looking at him she would spend the afternoon in bed just making sure he was happy, just to see if he missed her as Helen had missed him so much. Sarah would be staying in France for the next two months just to see if Anton wanted more of her than she expected, the painting nearly finished now what would she do, not fall apart Helen hoped but then she thought Sicily Italy was the next work for Sarah.

They chatted for a few minutes, Sarah was now being asked to paint for people in Italy so new doors were opening, she had taken photos of her paintings just to let whoever she met have a view of her work.

So she was now painting on demand which was very lucrative, if she carried on like this she would be able to buy her own little place in France or Italy, Sarah's heart was looking to moving in with Anton by next year it would be interesting and Helen knew it would work she was now finding herself.

Asking Sarah if she would take on the two houses that John and she would be buying in Italy and of course it was a resounding yes. Taking John's hand and slowly guiding him to the bedroom she had an agenda "Come with me John come now let me show you something." She said with a smile her book the sequel finished and the outlay of the children's books were there in her hands and Helen's new novel had been completed, she could write for the next three days before they left but now was their time a little bit of fun was called for.

Helen gently took him by the hand, she placed herself between him and the bed, this was the time for total selflessness he was to be entwined into her body, pulling him closer, kissing him, he reciprocated and slowly undoing one button at a time of her silk blouse, opening herself to him her lingerie was a deep red and black he loved that colour, her hands touch her breasts he then came slowly forward to kiss her gently, placing him on the bed, unzipping her skirt to allow it to fall to the floor, all these moments of seduction.

There she was dressed in only her finest lingerie, her hair was messy she had made sure that it was. Her very, very high heels and stocking matched her smile, looking good she thought to herself, and in her sixties yet still very, very beautiful. Standing in front of John as he reached to touch her panties and stroking her inside leg.

Helen sighed to herself, it was a large sigh of enjoyment as he sat on the edge of the bed and stroking his hair slowly Helen began to kiss him pulling away and dancing for him then bringing herself back in front of him she turned around quickly he then kissed her.

Friends, Accepting the Changes

He found the jewel, her clitoris he began to play brining her to an automatic orgasm in which she enjoyed so much, turning herself around to kneel in front of him, his zip undone to release his hardness, standing tall Helen had to resist the temptation to move herself on top of his firm hardness, instead she placed her lips around his stick of sheer pleasure teasing as her tongue stroked and kissed around this firmness until he could bear no more, with that he came.

Helen had made him her first priority he was her first option of enjoyment, touching her face that touch said it all he did not have to say the words that followed. "I love you Helen, I have surely missed you."

With that she stood up, taking his trousers off, his shirt also was flung to the side, he kissed Helen then they found themselves falling onto the bed he kept her panties on and released her breasts from their constraint, kissing her breasts while he was stroking her between her legs, kissing the top of her thighs her panties still firmly in place.

Helen was crying out the pleasure was too much to bear, whipping her panties to the side, his hands his tongue found where they wanted to go, finding that spot, his tongue began darting across her clitoris, the pleasure was so intense she screamed, and inside a moment she reached her climax, her juices spilled over his hand and face.

Her juices tasted good he thought, they had not finished yet but soon they would be ready just to fall into each other's arms, John moved away from her and she could feel that he had managed to make the hardness rise up to take the pleasure again.

She waited for him, they both came together their kisses were soft and intense then she felt him enter her gently at first to then a thrust as he moved inside further and harder, she felt him reel up, his thrust hard firm together they were both coming to the end of the ecstasy, the end of what was a good love making session as they both reached the crescendo, a final scream of delight then he slowly began to lift himself from her taking her into his arms, what a day, what a man, what an hour.

Thank you Angels for this man you have sent me, I know he certainly comes from you he is the most beautiful person I have ever known, thank you. A gift from the Angels and the Masters a gift of love, a joyful, giving and the most loving, generous person that she knew and he was given to Helen, she had worked hard for this man to be presented to her.

Chapter Ten; India, China, Japan

India, China and Japan Helen had been so looking forward to she was being taken to all the sights that she had always wanted to see. Leaving France Helen had chatted to Hollywood she would see them for two days after her trip, she was so excited about seeing the spiritual side of the countries she was visiting, and the first stopover was India seeing the highlights which was on offer also some of the slums bodyguards were needed here just for her safety.

John was with her throughout the trip. He needed to be protected too. Flying into Delhi International Airport the hustle and bustle so different to France and as soon as she landed her bodyguards came on board two British ex Para's were given to her, trained to kill, trained to protect her and she needed them years ago as living in her town, the town that few were envious and the few that loved her. It would have been great to be protected then more than she was even by the Angels.

Introducing themselves but not by their real names but a name they had picked just in case the worst happened Bob and Ben were in their thirties they were both built like action men. Beginning to look them up and down when Bob remarked. "Are you ok Helen you look as though you are not too sure about something is there a problem we are here to look after you there is no need to worry, so now tell me what's happening in your head?"

Helen just smiled touched his arm as she answered him quietly. "My girlfriends would have been happy to be here with me, look at you both just what the doctor ordered."

The banter and the laughter were heard all around it was true Helen knew the girls would be drooling by the sight of these men. She left the plane with two men side by side her being so small in the middle of them they were not allowing anybody near her. She would try very hard to enjoy this trip even though they were there to protect me she thought.

She was taken to her hotel The Four Seasons and they were book a trip to see the Humayun's Tomb a salute to the Indian soldiers of the British Army and then off to lunch at the President's House, then to get ready for a whistle stop tour of India and off to Jalpur in the morning to visit the Colourful Market.

Just to look at the most colourful clothes and materials it would be the dress designer delight. Would Helen succumb to a bright gown, gold, red and pink she thought, could be good. Then in the afternoon an elephant ride to the Amber Fort.

The Palace of the Winds a beautiful structure in pink, everything was so colourful is this why Indians love to wear colourful clothes she found that the brighter the colour the better she felt, they stayed the night in yet another hotel, the hotels themselves were like palaces, they made you feel

Friends, Accepting the Changes

welcome and comfortable.

In the morning they would be visiting the Bharatpur bird sanctuary and Helen would love it as the birds would speak to her, birds were Angels they and they told her stories.

When the people of the town that played games, and they even went to the lengths of killing a bird and then placed it in front of her on her jogging route, even when Mark had been given six months to live. Helen wrote a poem about him getting a ticket to heaven and two bottles of beer and a ticket were placed where she jogged someone certainly knew her jogging route and she knew pay back would be hard.

The Bird Sanctuary was again full of colourful birds, Helen began thinking that there definitely was a thing with colours here it was so beautiful, she began speaking to the birds and the excitement of seeing her, it was so amazing to see such beautiful colours, she was enlightened so much that she just did not want to leave here as they were all in their glory happy and seeing all that they needed.

Where to next she thought, this was the third day again the spiritual enlightenment was immense, they would stroll around the Taj Mahal very early in the morning the sunrise India was to be seen later as they came away from the Taj Mahal, both John and Helen would be visiting the priest he was Indian and he worked with spirit and the astrological charts. It would be interesting to hear what he said about the two of them what would both their future's hold.

They arrived at the Taj Mahal, the car stopped close to them there was only enough room for the bodyguards to stay close, they gave Helen space to meditate to take the beauty in, she moved over and sat in the place as Princess Diana did on the photo where she looked so lonely the Taj Mahal is the Temple of Love, it was built by the king for his wife who died in childbirth it was to show how much he loved and missed her, a shrine to their love, so for the Princess Diana to sit alone and so lonely was sad and unforgiving of her Prince.

Helen paused for in second to take the ambiance, the sun began to slowly rise and the redness turned to orange, then to yellow. It was so large in the sky and then the night became day and the day was yet another day of the Indian life in which Helen was finding the richness and the poorness, there was no in-between but it seems to be that way all around the world, it's does seem to be the way the world works either poor or rich take your pick but pick well.

Helen thinking for a moment and remembering the days she used to say to her clients make sure if or when you come back you sign the right contract. She took a look back at her own life and all the testing she had while she lived in her home town, and the endless game play, the bullying, even by authority.

She could not believe that such and so many responsible people could behave in such a clear cut way so irresponsible of them and their jobs, but in a way they had met their match in her. She was far too strong for them what were they trying to get her to do by their games, they were they pushing her to the limit to take her own life or to have a breakdown, even when she took time out in Spain it was the same, that little town in England had a great deal to answer for. And all the women who followed the men nobody seemed to have a mind of their own they were all sheep like people for what gain that she never found out, the games just stopped.

Helen spoke to John so quietly. "This is something else look at the sun and it is a bright new day every day is a good day." They stayed close and John placed his arm around Helen to keep her close and safe. They sat for an hour watching and listening to the peace of daybreak and to then the hustle and bustle of the city life.

It began to be busy so quickly and they were hurried on to their next timed appointment which was to visit a priest, the priests of India are highly thought of, they are sacred it is such an open spiritual country, a beautiful country breath taking to say the least. But the corruption and in so many ways and so many people are so poor.

Watching the children begging for their breakfast watching people hurry by on their way leaving nothing but fresh air how they lived frightened her, how can so many have so much and so many have nothing but to beg. The priest watched as they walked in, he stood in delight to Helen's aura, walking over he greeted her and then he placed his hands in a prayer position and bowed his head. Taking hold of her hand with such a gentle smile, he manoeuvred Helen to a small seated stool, sitting listening as he began to talk, he spoke in Indian first then it was translated into English.

The priest in a hand gesture showed Helen that he was giving her the blessing to do her work, to do it in an unusual way. She was to travel and bring peace, she was to work with children, while her powers were to give so many children the strength and she would meet with many, many abused children and to work with the law to help bring the child to some kind of peace, she would be called the Rainbow lady that is how the children of the world knew her they would recognize this lady.

The lady of so many colours, of so much love and of so much wisdom, she had such a beauty from within that children ran to her, they found her warming, restful and Helen found the children beautiful and interesting, and her books of Arthur and Horace were on their journey when published about would bring Helen closer to the children.

The priest called John over, John sat mesmerised by this man he took his hand and then Helen's hand placed them on top of each other's, and his words were short but significant. "You are both like the swans you are a lifetime connection, and a lifetime together you are twin souls made in heaven, Helen you are now on your life's purpose so enjoy from heaven." They left he placed a scared stone in Helen's hand.

Friends, Accepting the Changes

He smiled as he waved them goodbye onto the next country, for yet another whistle stop tour. Both their futures were so bright.

Collecting their belongings they were off to Delhi airport, it was the next journey of learning, a relaxing time lay ahead of them both and they were off to Japan, Helen had said that she wanted to see the sacred gardens, they were thinking of making a Japanese garden in the grounds of the French Chateau or they could now put one in France and one in Italy, and it would just give them the most relaxing area that they needed.

They would transform all their gardens into one it would have all the water features and bridges, many trees and shires with Angels and Buddha's.

They landed at Tokyo, again it was a country that had the extremes of wealth, and her cases and bags were picked up and then they were shuffled through customs into the Diplomat plated cars and they were staying at the Embassy it would be a well-known safe route with police protecting the car.

Their bags were with them, it was straight out to see at least three different gardens. Helen watched as John moved slowly as if he were a praying mantis he was looking to see the creature life that they had in the garden, then he was looking at the house making snap decision of what to do in their Château in France and Villa in Italy.

Friends, Accepting the Changes

"Helen I can see us with the gardens we should build a place like this one so we can have the main doors open to go straight into the garden Helen this could be the best extension off the house. I think it would look kind of wonderful, look how relaxing all these water features are Helen, can you just imagine having sex in these relaxing surroundings." He took her hand with laughter, they both walked around within the relaxing calm of the embodiment of the garden.

"John look it's not what you thinking you are supposed to see the relaxing side not shagging side look at it in the right way as she squeezed his hand she looked to her right there were four masters, the Masters were Mother Mary, Siddhartha the Buddha, White Tara. Babaja, behind them she could see Jesus and Maitraya all the Masters of the Universe, hoping that the world would soon be the peace with freedom, Jesus was smiling at John his comment was so true.

Archangel Michael, Gabriel and Raphael all stood to look at Helen this is what they wanted for her, this would be her perfect peace and tranquillity, the occasional romp called love making would be good Jesus agreed as sex was a part of life as death is.

They would certainly be taking this home with them they left and it was given to the architect to sort a plan for their garden extension in both France and Italy. A beautiful Japanese garden would make the home so relaxing and the energy would be so calm and spiritual.

Friends, Accepting the Changes

The dinner at the Embassy, they were meeting some dignitaries and Helen's wardrobe had to be finest, having packed many casual outfits for her travel to see the poorest parts of the country. The menu was seafood, rice dishes, noodles and sushi a feast of Japan.

Helen was looking forward to her day in the countryside and to visit as many shrines as possible and they would be visiting one of the orphanages Helen had the infinity of an Angel she wanted to make all children enjoy life. The morning came and Helen stood looking out of the window wanting to see the sunrise and the sunset but they would have to be in a Japanese garden to enjoy it completely.

With her Angels and Masters all gathered around her in peace and love, Helen would choose the last night getting John to make sure the bodyguards found a place for her to go.

They were off to an Imperial shrine then there were four more shrines to see. The   Sinai, Bachman, Enjoin and Semen, Helen knew that was a helicopter journey to make, she made sure that she would visit them all, the need for the spiritual input for her growth was something Helen always looked at, even though her consultations with people were slowing down.

Helen still needed to focus on her connection with the Masters and the Archangels they were her work in other ways, she loved her life with them, forever chatting, forever there.

Friends, Accepting the Changes

They were off to an orphanage in the outskirts of Tokyo and that too would be a long helicopter journey as it was safer and so quick. Each shrine was so different she found them interesting the history, the surroundings were so clean.

The last shrine was a journey through the wild side of Japan the scenery was so out of this world, it was untouched no harm from man well not yet anyway, man had spoilt the world in some places and in doing this the opening of different lands, they have spoilt the beauty of the land for progression.

The helicopter hovered over this land so beautiful, the snap of the camera she took so many pictures. Not realising how beautiful the world was, this certainly was Helen's journey of the soul, a journey of the love, what fun she had being an Angel a hard path when people do not believe, the sceptics tried hard to drag her down, but Jesus and so many others kept her heart strong.

The orphanage was a different matter pushing open the doors Helen walked into the gloom and she was so much taken aback by the children how they were subdued, the unhappiness was painful. She would spend time here talking, she needed to know how they were all feeling, touching them too making them feel more like children was what Helen was here to do.

"They all look so sad John, children are supposed to laugh and jump around. There are no smiles here could we start some singing classes, can we put that into place." Helen spoke softly to John a very understanding man he was and he could see her compassion. They were having such a great experience with life and now they both really loved their lives at the moment and that's what life is all about.

Gently taking his hand then John beckoned one of the men over to question them in English about Helen's request. He called someone else over then asked them about Helen's request, there were a huddle of men chatting amongst themselves someone must know how to get things started. With Helen walking over to the children and being watched all the time by their keepers Helen sat amongst them all and began singing some children's songs all in English.

They understood what she was singing and then started to copy her. She sang the first verse, then as she sang it again a small girl started to mimic her and she started to sing, softly at first but then louder each time they started singing the song and then the other children just a few words to begin with started singing, she knew it would all come.

They all sang and sang, their smiles were growing and they were clapping their hands, yes she thought there would be some sort of singing lessons here in this orphanage and once Helen had put it into place here in this one she would carry it on through to all the other orphanages in the rest of the country it would be well worth while. The Rainbow Lady had done it again, the smiles of the children they were singing as she left and waving her goodbye.

he would be back just to make sure all that she wanted had been put into place, and Helen wanted to see different children, most of these children had lost their parents that does not mean to say that the children should be so unhappy, the wonders of the world through a child's eyes. Leaving in a better mood, she voiced what she wanted to the official, now it was all to do with them, they would have to sort it and quickly children needed to be smiling.

The next day they were off to the relaxing hot springs, all of them were in need of some healing, Helen had been talking to the two bodyguards about healing and the enlightenment of what her work was all about and her connections to Angels and Masters.

They travelled to Ryokon staying overnight just to soak up the minerals of the springs the water was warm with the healing powers it meant that Helen could give just that little bit more a journey by car an hour long journey at that and yes the scenery was special the mountains in view so very green and lush, they arrived the next morning and Helen had booked a massage with a facial.

She would have the hot spring first so that she had the minerals stay in her body, a two hour bath then a facial and massage, small snacks during the day and by night she feasted on a buffet of the delights Chinese and Japanese traditional food and staying in her robe to keep all the oils and the minerals in her body, sleeping that night was a dream. They left with a small token and the owners asked Helen with her entourage to come back to this beautiful place and enjoy their country also the baths.

Helen remarked looking as though she had relaxed more than was expected a drunken relaxation. "I have had the most wonderful time here in Japan. Both Mr John and I have enjoyed the time we have had here to relax in your baths, it has been a dream come true, the wonders of Japan, thank you."

The car pulled up very close to the pavement to pick them up, so much of a rush now they were off to the airport, they were due in an hour to fly into China, Helen wanted to see wild China and was not too sure about the other side of China.

The killing of babies and the poorer regions, so Helen would be careful of where she chose to go in these couple of days and then it would be onto Tibet the places of spiritual interest especially the holy side of Tibet was beckoning. They also fitted into their schedule to see migrating birds and then to touch the Himalayas, and the river estuaries most of all to see family life the old way then to walk the great China wall so there was a great deal to do.

Helen was looking forward to it all but she was a little unsure of the politics in China. She would have to be very careful about what she said there. They were landing again it was the hustle of a country that was growing fast beyond belief. They seemed to be determined to be a significant country of the world. They awoke to find that their plans had been sorted before they had a chance to say yes or no, their first stop would be the highest peaks of the mountains they would cheat the climb to the top being seated in a helicopter.

They landed gently with the rota blades still moving when the door opened the draft from the rota blades blew Helen to the side, John reached out to grab her it was freezing. Kitted out in warm clothing they all began to walk for a while not losing sight of the helicopter.

Helen could feel the buzz of why people feel the need to climb and conquer. On the way back they flew over untamed territory, it was so beautiful and man had not been here to spoil it, untouched, the only hope was that man would stay well away to keep this beauty alive. "Look John paddy fields can the pilot go down lower I want to see the age of these people John."

Helen having to ask for permission to get closer and doing so she found that there were mainly children and women in these fields all of them looked up at the big bird staring at them. They slowly flew to the estuaries watching the birds, the magnificent colours of each bird all of them were making themselves known they all spoke to Helen, fun and exciting this was a special journey for Helen and John was enjoying it too..

A picnic they were having there sitting amongst the birds, their food was brought from the hotel and it was good to sit in nature with the birds and chatting with their guides to find out just how they really lived. "Most people here are working hard for very little money, they were very poor. We always control all that we do our children are getting a better education now so they will have better jobs. As the sun set they flew back to the Hotel, dinner and bed.

At 6.00 am the alarm rang and they were up like the larks walking along the wall would take most of the day, an interesting but a long gruelling day. The sense of the day was to have lots to eat, her energies would deplete quickly with the walk, and her iPhone on and the ear phones plugged into her ears she was happy. The walk was long and tiring but refreshing and a sense of achievement, the company was good and the banter was amazing, that is what she knew she needed, there was banter between themselves and all the men.

Every stop they made there was a fluid intake and laughter, in the entourage were twenty five fun people, it made the journey of learning fun, all the walk was done for charity and they would be collecting their winnings when they had finished the long journey, her protection was not only the bodyguards, but also two police officers who joined her.

The charity would get a bit out of this, Helen had gathered the sponsors before she travelled, with her book she knew billionaires were happy to give all Helen had to do was walk the wall and walk the wall she did.

The scenery tremendous what a lucky lady she was and of

course she knew it, they neared the end and a crowd of people waited for Helen, the pen handy as autographs had to be signed. She was happy to give, feet tired some of them had blisters, silly shoes they were wearing, some were just plain tired, Helen kept herself fit which made the walk easier, she done what she needed to do and then went back to the hotel for relaxation.

Her supper was to be with a Chinese family an altogether upper class family just to see what their customs were, Helen was looking forward to that. Helen then arrived at the hotel and being met by the receptionist. "Ms Helen I have a phone call for you it's a charity for children she said that she wants you to call her back as soon as possible. I have her number." She was such a small delicate young lady, so pretty in her own way very polite, Helen liked that in young people well she liked that in anybody. Manners weren't too much to ask for in this day and age.

Reaching the house of one of the wealthiest men in China, this was a side of China Helen wanted to see, she had made it in life and wanted to surround herself with lots of interesting people, wealthy does come on the interesting level, as there is always a story, he had invited a few grand people along.

Helen's need to be with the children and the suffering and to find changes she could bring to the table and of course to the other end of the scale with the wealthier the hope of converting them into her way of thinking and getting what she wanted, she needed them to give some of their money for a worthy cause and that's what all this was all about and a great friendship would come of it.

The home was on one level massive to say the least, each room led to another, each room had its own character and style, there were many rooms to check out and they came to the area that Mr Wingling casually entertained and yes the room was big enough for a wedding and had red in the décor it was fascinating to see the beautiful way that his home was decorated, the colours were pastel in some rooms and bright in others.

Mix match but so calming and energising and each room greeted by each of the guests, they sat down to eat proper Chinese food it was an interesting evening and of Helen managed to open the eyes of the majority of the diners to give her agent a call and the donations to charity came fast and bountiful.

They were back late to the hotel and the schedule for the next three days in Tibet it was to be a Soul's journey to Tibet a place that is spiritually mystical and a natural beauty, the sacred land of monasteries with monks in crimson robes, the mountains were so white and soaring.

Day one flying in on a private jet to where they were going staying in a small place near Tashi Lhunpo Monastery, the Dali Lama founded this Monastery, Helen wanted to experience how he felt on a meditation time, it would mean she could feel and be him, their spirits would entwine for a spiritual learning for

Friends, Accepting the Changes

Helen.

Of course he would tell her what lay ahead in her future and he would bring some healing to her heart, she still missed her son Mark so much, but in heaven he had learned to grow and he had learned to work with Helen on a mediumship level, he was clever and showed her everything she needed to know.

Mark in his last months had gone downhill so much and someone had pinched his phone so Helen and Mark never had the contact they should have done in his last few months. Helen knew that was a set up as she was going through her own trauma with her neighbours and the police for no reason at all, squeaky clean she was what was it all about.

The neighbours were playing mind games and the police joined in. The so called friends next to the pub The Crown on the river's edge were all laughing while playing and making her life hell. The tapping of her phones and hacking her computer came from Mr and Mrs O'Kell and their friends who were along the river. The West Quay was a place of torment the numbers before Helen's number 17 and the numbers after Helen's from 19 onwards were laughing at Helen's expense.

Helen' car was being tampered with someone had pulled the tube from the pump so it damaged Helen's engine, Mr Handbag was pulling wire out so it cost Helen a great deal of money. But pay back comes in many ways. And that pain followed her through to moving in with Simon as the phones kept being cut so her pay was short. Moving in with Simon was painful as within a month Mark had died and Helen hadn't been able to see him. The police did not want to know they were happy that he had died as they did show her that in mind games.

A bike she was called only because they had set her up with Barry and the stalker. Sad that the police seemed to have the mentality of a law for themselves and a law for others, moving to her daughters the police came too and the mind games carried on.

Her phone was tapped and her computer was hacked and they had begun to listen to her life there must have been a bug in the apartment in Wivenhoe, her sons Simon's house and then her daughter Harri's house.

Moving to Spain to heal she found the same rubbish going on the phone, and the computer and her life was being listened to. This had all started from Mr Bollery and Barry the people that set Helen up. Helen did have the police investigate the situation and investigate the police themselves. To sue for what they had done to her and she won the compensation for the lies, deceit and game play.

Living in Jerez Helen had the lottery man playing back what was going on in her life, the taxi man with the white teeth was laughing. And her life again was the subject of ridicule by the English and Spanish. The mind games of her being a bike because of Barry. And again they kept showing her that they were then selling her off to the next lot of men as a bike to see if they could get into her knickers. It was like playground mentality, children playing games.

Moving to another area of the Costa del Sol the same rubbish was going on there must be something mental with these men and women. They were all were to be sued starting from the beginning Mr Bollery, Barry and Mr & Mrs O'Kell were the first people Helen had investigated to bring them to court because what they had done was criminal.

Each hairdresser played, each nail technician the same games and every neighbour showed Helen that she was still being listened too and Helen's last place to live in Spain was a small community close to the mountains, it was the beauty of Spain but the idiots of Spain who of course where the neighbours and they smiled and played while they were listening to her life.

The police were still playing mind games thinking that they could get away with it. How much more did they have to put her through, what was the envy, fear and hate that was going on.

But enough was enough and Helen then took the hairdresser to task. She has been abusing Helen by picking and picking of course there was someone pulling her strings because she never had the brain to do what she was doing a sheep that she was like most of them. Her party Helen watched as she still played and then she was drinking heavily. The next bar Helen came too she quietly asked her. "What do you think of me?" Betty answered.

"Well you do not allow your life to flow and let men to stroke your leg to have sex with them." Helen was taken aback by such a statement and what envy did she have. "And I do go with the flow with my life and tell me why I should have sex with men for the sake of it. You have picked and picked and picked on me and calling me a bike on fb what's more I am quite happy with my life thank you, how many men have you slept with?"

Helen asked slightly annoyed at her. Betty then gave her answer with a smile and a great smugness about her. "Fifty men I have had sex with but my husband doesn't know that, you know they touch you and then you just fall into the sex."

Helen then became very annoyed and answered her. "And you have the cheek to call me a bike you need to look at yourself as I am an Angel to you." With that she left her crying and Helen had now changed the ball game and would not be taking any rubbish from anybody. Now she would start the process of payback and payback would be nine years of sheer hell.

The phones and computer was still being tampered with and her life still being listened too for them to repeat, time to be strong and time to sue. Helen would definitely be a millionaire by the time she had finished. Yes, no money worries would be so good. And it did so much happen. Helen left Spain and moved herself back closer to Harri, close to York was her next journey and she found her adventures taking her to Italy and that's where John came in and her destiny was in front of her, no man from the past would be in her future. She was back to her day in China she had come back to the here and now.

That was the call of the first day just to walk around the monastery to take tea with the monks to meditate and take prayers for the first day, she needed to give to her Angels and this was her way of doing this. They placed Helen in her own silent room for an hour for prayer and meditation.

It was the most exhilarating time, she felt that all who lived in the heavens had joined her on earth, and then into her little world of meditation, they had now told her she was on her road of her life's purpose, she was the breath of fresh air that was needed around the world.

Her life's purpose was to write, to help children and not just in her own country but also in the rest of the world she would be known as The Rainbow Lady all her books must have the Rainbow on the front, so that people would know it was her that wrote it. She now would have joy coming into her life, joy and happiness in such abundance.

Her visions for herself were true she would meet some unhappy children that she would have to place her love deeply into their lives but to be careful of her own heart for it will be so open to love all the children that cross her path and that each child in their own pain would be hard to bare.

Friends, Accepting the Changes

She would have to love and protect not only the children that she came into contact with, but also her own heart that was so big and open. The meditation done, she would be collected then taken to the prayer hall to begin her prayers with the monks before their eating time. Jose his name this was an easier name for her monk and Jose collected Helen then taking her through the most sacred way to the epicentre of the monastery, the hub of ground control.

Here Helen did feel was where all prayers were answered the most religious set they are. The master of the monks then called her over to him, he wanted Helen to be at his side for prayers, she was such a great   teacher and he was such a great teacher, learning from each other.

Helen's energies blessed with such powers and blessed with such qualities. What love she had for each person who crossed her path, the time she gave to everyone that crossed her path Helen the Angel. Prayers were at the hands of her Angels and their Buddha's they would come together in harmony.

After prayers was the feasting not like she had been used to, very small but there was wine not enough to get drunk on but enough to make her feel good with the laughter and the chat, the energies in this place were divine, they all finished the feast of the Heavens, all had been harvested, all had been hand grown by the monks, all had been carefully chosen for Helen.

Friends, Accepting the Changes

They wished her well in her journeys on this earth, they wished her well in her love and happiness forever in her life and then they wished her well in her writing. The night was full of visits from the heavens she woke to feel that she had walked miles, travelling on a level of the auras in astral travel. Breakfast was large, thinking of the day ahead and perhaps not eating for a while.

The next journey of Tibet which was the natural scenery of the turquoise waters of Yamdrok Tso Lake, could they swim here or would it be too cold, their guide was pleasant enough and smiled when Helen asked to swim in the water, she would paddle.

Then to the helicopter to the Mt Everest Base Camp, the views were stunning and all God's interesting points of the world were there to be enjoyed. They would trek here as far as they were allowed, walking around the Monastery Rongbuk and staying overnight in Shegar. In the morning they were going to depart for England to the next schedule.

The monastery was calm and beautiful and the views from Mt Everest were stunning no wonder people wanted to get to the top not only for the challenge but for the beauty and the striking views of the mountains, how many had died in their own search of self. It is Tibet that makes one go into the soul searching of the heart, soul, the self, the one of life, to be found in your heart.

So many have been here, the few have met their Angels then

taken back to spirit. It was their time, their moment, they had finished their own journey's now they were off to be yet again the part of spirit. Life is precious, life is to be enjoyed, as death has no boundaries, it comes when you least expect it.

Helen left Tibet and all the countries she had visited with a greater sense of what her life's purpose should be, she was a happy lady at long last, not just in her material world, but her learning ways of the Universe. Job done for Helen, back to England catching up with her bestest friends and her publishers, John had arranged business meetings so it was a long week of endless meetings. France was to rest for a week or so.

In Hollywood the film was really coming along and Helen was looking forward to sitting through the parts that had been filmed and edited, the progress had been good. Property viewing they both decided that were going to take their time to search for their home, John wanted a mooring and a sense of freedom to find that they would be searching for a long time it had to be right for them both. Their next trip was France, Paris Reims and Champagne the girls were looking forward to that.

Heathrow was busy people rushing around finding their place to go and a security scare kept Helen in her plane waiting for her freedom, after waiting two hours she was set free, arriving home her agent rang to say that the charity that she would be working for had left the details of where Helen would be visiting with her next journey with them and that she would be taking a film crew with her to let the world see their work as

Helen was the right candidate for the job it certainly would bring more money to the charity and more recognition, the children would benefit in the end.

Resting for a while before returning to visit her daughter, her much loved granddaughter's and her son, Helen wanted to get away to France to sleep, as sleep was eluding her, trying to do the research for her new book, finding it hard as she was travelling far too much she needed space and time to meditate to connect which would bring the inspiration to her book.

Helen was very much in demand which was what she wanted and needed all those years of nearly being there and now she was there she had decided that she must enjoy for her own wellbeing. A visit to the children in hospital in London, some of them were so poorly. "Helen come and chat to Caroline she has only a little time left we try to make her as comfortable as possible." Penny took hold of Helen's arm ferrying her to Caroline.

"Caroline how cute are you how old are you hunni?" Helen asked her in such a sensitive tone. "I am five years old my birthday is soon I think and then I will be six." Caroline said in such a sweet angelic voice. Her mother Janet smiled, Helen could see in her eyes the sadness her soul was there to see, the pain of losing a child and one so sweet how could the heavens take such a beautiful child back, Caroline had not had a life did she really ask for all this and such a short life too.

She was so small and delicate. "Well Caroline you have a lovely birthday, I will find a beautiful cake for you what would you like." Helen looked to her mother and asked her gently. "Can I do this for you and please take my mobile number please let me know what else there is that you want and need I will make sure you have it, I wish in my heart of hearts that I could ask God to spare this angel and to allow her to stay here, but if he wants her for a purpose then he will take her."

Helen comforted Caroline's mother as Caroline touched Helen's arm. "I like fairies can I have a fairy cake?" Looking into Helen's eyes Helen noticed that her eyes were so bright and her soul was still very much alive. Helen felt that her time wasn't over yet and would have a few words with the heavens on her return home, her own room that Sarah had been painting would give her the energy she needed for the meditation. I wonder she thought can they allow Caroline to stay she would find out soon.

A week at home, John was looking at the garden just figuring out where and when to put the Japanese garden into place, the landscape gardener had made an appointment for a visit and John would make sure the plans were done before they left for America Hollywood and the film, they had achieved a great deal she was pleased with all that had been done.

An apartment in Miami next to the water, getting it all set to buy next time, also a boat to go with it was on order that is what they needed at this time and this moment was just the quietness of the water, not the noise and the frenzy of Los

Angeles, she could have holidays in Miami, in Los Angeles she would have to have face lifts and Botox that Helen was not up for. She loved the facials and all the treatments.

Two days in America then flying back to France for a week's rest that is what she did a week of nothing, slight research for her next two books. Arriving back in France was a sigh of relief, wine, good food, good sex and sleep were the call of the week and that is just what she did. Calls from Italy the villa in Sicily was ready to sign on the dotted line and for Helen and John to make some changes and they would be looking at a place near Milan perhaps near the lakes that would be another adventure.

Chapter Eleven;
France, Paris, Reims & Champagne..

This was going to be a week of fun with the girls and then to top it all off they would lunch in Madrid. There was going to be some heavy shopping and a great deal of champagne drunk for this journey the champagne tasting was what Helen and Kate wanted to do and the views of France were spectacular. Shopping in Paris why not isn't that what most people would love to do so here they would be doing just that.

The Japanese conservatory house was now complete listening to the soft sensual music and relaxing into the furniture which was made for comfort and of course Helen had to have the features of meditation, Buddha's had been placed all around and some Angels that Helen had situated around the garden it was a place of peace, calm and tranquillity, the garden would be finished so that she could enjoy it for at least two weeks anyway, before she flew off to have some fun with the girls.

Sitting watching the men working and with their shirts off she sat nodding at the Angels as they were coming and going she could see and feel them. Each of the pieces in the garden fitted well Helen smiled they will be finished in the next few days she fell sound asleep watching the men work, as in sleep visions came to her she could see the children in the Middle East something would soon have to be done there, she felt a need to sort something significant and yes it would just open and Kate could be part of all that, it's just was not right at the moment.

She awoke to find her room full of Angels, her garden finished and the men were packing up ready to go all looked so beautiful now this would be happening in the two homes Helen would secure in Italy, her life was good, love was good and she was so happy all that pain she had to endure and now to find that her destiny was there for her.

All those people who tried hard to stop her life were now getting their pay back in Karma, prison for some, a loss for others and Helen came out of it very well indeed hence the new homes in Italy she was a happy lady.

Helen walked around as though she was already in heaven, if heaven was like this I would book a ticket now she thought. Finished at last just the fiddly things to do she would leave them to that but it was so good she sat next to the flowing fountain and made her wishes, the wishes for the dreams to come true.

"I am going to have a wash in the springs they had even managed to make it look as though it were a Japanese spring it was so magically beautiful they had done so well, she was so relaxed and ready for her journey.

Picking up the phone hoping she would catch at least one of her friends in, they were slightly drifting apart and Helen didn't like that, all very busy and all needing time out. "Kate, hey it's great to hear your voice look about Madrid and lunch I thought

Friends, Accepting the Changes

I would hire a private jet to get us there I could be the Pilot for the flight there and we can have a pilot for our return to France.

You can call me Captain Rainbow I think it could be fun Creams what do you think?" Helen was being serious and waiting for some kind of reaction into what Kate felt about it all. "Rainbow, now we cannot have a drunken Pilot you would be called slightly tipsy Captain Rainbow, as you know the highlight of our flying is to enjoy the day and ourselves, you would be the sober one and that is not fair.

I agree and think we should hire a jet for a day and go to Madrid for lunch then get a Pilot to fly us back after lunch as you would have been drinking that sounds good to me."

Kate knew she was right about what Helen was trying to do she had her pilot's licence and wanted to impress, Helen worked hard enough and she needed her time out drinking of Champagne "Ok yes we agree, we could go to Madrid or Seville for lunch hire plane with a Pilot and I can do one journey he could do the other.

Does anyone want a membership form for the high mile club we could choose a handsome pilot, Laura could do or is she happy, I think everybody is loved up such a shame, I have so many membership forms here with no one to give them to." Helen answered and she excitingly suggested what she thought.

Kate remembering the days of creeping into the toilets with

boyfriend in tow, having sex that really was not allowed but had to be done. Pierre was a man that Kate could remember he was so beautiful, dark hair, dark eyes and a body to die for a toy boy no doubt, he was fifteen years younger and she met him a few months after dropping her husband like a brick a man she did not talk about.

Holidaying in France he chatted to her near where she was staying then a meal and a few dates, they both wanted to fly to Paris and a plane was the best option so a plane it was, he paid as he came from wealth. Sitting near the toilets was ideal and as they took off they had thirty minutes before they landed again.

Kate rushed to the toilet he followed, for two people to be in such a small place was just a bit of a squeeze, but her panties came off and the kissing went on he was slipping his trousers down, pushing her against the flat part of the wall, stretching herself open for his hardness he was erect and standing tall slipping inside her, a push and she gasped as he was bigger than most men, moving gently to the movements of her body as she had to take all of him into her, they both were reeling in each other's pleasure he pushed harder until the orgasm screamed from her, to find he soon after he followed.

Meanwhile as all this was going on a knock on the door. "Hello, are you ok in there you have ten minutes until landing." The gay steward tapping at the door, they would now have to look him in the eye as they made their way to their seats, leaving the loo Kate but a brave face on and smiled as she open the door to walk down the aisle.

He looked at her and smiled, she sat down then Pierre made his way down the aisle with a smile, sitting himself next to Kate. "Would you two like a drink or a freshener, it's slightly cramp in there but you managed." He smiled the gay steward knew exactly what went on but slightly discreet about it all. "Yes thank you we have managed and a bottle of water will do." Kate looked him in the eye as if to say no bother.

"We aim to please on this flight water will be here in a one second enjoy." He stretched for the water and left them alone they landed. Memories Kate thought I wonder if Helen and John would be up for the High Fly Club, he was a gentleman and he also knew Helen had this exciting energy about her, a lady who was different from the normal women a breath of fresh air.

Coming back into the room the phone call with Helen she had been in dream land. "Are you with me Kate you've gone quiet what are you doing at the other end, Helen was interested in her thoughts. "I was just remembering a time in a plane loo with Pierre and how good it had been. Kate replied.

Helen chirped quickly. "By the way Creams I now have my Japanese conservatory all finished with my Japanese Garden, it is really relaxing, I even have the hot springs like we had in Japan, they send the minerals by FedEx, see healthy living with FedEx wait until you see it you will love it. I am going to do it in Italy too. Ok so we will meet in London St Pancras Champagne bar and then take the train to Paris.

We can do Paris, Reims and Champagne tasting with some good meals, spas, massage and facials. Sarah is coming I think anyway as her and Anton are pretty heavy at the moment. I have persuaded her to come, told her she needs to have some fun with us, we could have three weddings in a few months of each other I like weddings and new hats for everyone." Helen chuckled down the phone she was looking forward to seeing her friends again timeout was needed.

John was taking a trip to Miami to settle the house, the furnishings had to be what Helen wanted, the papers were all signed and John was picking the keys and meeting a designer for some changes that he and Helen had agreed on. Make sure it was ready for Helen as she would be waiting to see the films progress.

The Japanese feel certainly did have its healing qualities, just by stepping into the hot spring and with the water cascading down was heaven in itself and to sit in the warmth and comfort of the garden was Helen's delight she would meditate even fall asleep at the same time.

The books she wanted to get to the goal she had set and she had been strict and then making herself achieve that. It was the day before flying into Gatwick, making sure she had her licence for the flight to Madrid. Life was so good and she was so happy. This would be a good trip for the girls, a trip to the past.

Packing many shoes for this trip just in case, mind you she began to think I will take two pairs and buy three more new pairs that sounded better. Lingerie to die for, clothes for all occasions, she was classy and it showed in her dress sense. Cases packed ready, the morning was upon her, she was ready to go, breakfast with John, he was making sure she was looked after for the journey, the time came for John was to drive her to the airport. Leaving her to the security staff he kissed her gently.

"Helen now have you organised protection as you will need that protection." He asked knowing she had not but he already had it in hand. "No I am with my friends and I need a break with them with no one watching me or what I am doing." Helen looked into his eyes knowing what he would say next. "Ok Helen but you do need someone there for your safety I will organise it just one bodyguard for you. It's for me to protect, you are famous remember you need protecting from good and the bad people."

He let Helen go, watching her as the French Policeman walked with her chatting away, all she needed was a special man to travel everywhere with her, John would find that man, he would be sent to Gatwick airport ready for Helen when she landed, walking through customs a Policeman from the Met was to meet her, he would be on Helen's protection duties they could afford that now.

Friends, Accepting the Changes

He rang a good friend who then managed to reach a high ranking Policeman. "Jeffery I need a retired army personal now working with the police for protection duties that we can employ full time, can you see if you can get that man, and please have him meet Helen at Gatwick in two hours let me know, he will be travelling with her to France and Madrid an then he has to work with us."

John eagerly wanting the job done Helen must not be in a crowd of people with no protection. "John I have just the man leave it with me I will get him to contact you in five minutes."

Jeffery placed the phone down back in its slot and then doing what was needed of him, he had found just the right person for the job. John was waiting for that call as he did worry about Helen with her travelling alone even though she was with friends she was still very much alone.

'Brrring' the phone rang and John quickly picking it up had he found just the man. "Hello John I have been told to ring you I am Steven, I am an ex SAS Para trained and now work under the protection field with the Police." Steven began telling John about his past, his qualifications and the recommendations he had collected, he had sent his portfolio to John and while John was chatting he was looking on the Internet.

"You look impressive, I feel as though you are just the man to protect Helen, she is having a break with her friends so you will have to step aside sometimes so she can have fun, I do not need to know what she is doing it will be between you and Helen when you are travelling with her will you meet her at Gatwick I will get a photo of her to her, get yourself a rail ticket on the Euro Express to Paris.

I will transfer money to your bank account then we will set up a contract with a money order for your monthly pay but I need you there with Helen for the next six days then come back to France with her we will set you up with us." John had done just what he wanted and Helen would just have to go along with it.

"Consider it done John I will let you know when I have found her then leave it at that, I will take my instructions from Helen but whatever she says I will remain with her and be the protection she needs." Steven had now been employed on a protection level for Helen she would never be on her own again.

Sarah standing at her side she and was a bit miffed at the police officer. "What the hell Helen at least we have a nice young copper to look at and we will be safe well you will be." Thinking about what she had said they would have a bottle of what is called Champagne at the Champagne bar at St Pancras and then again on the train not Helen's normal Champagne but it would do.

Looking out of the window London Gatwick was in view and the girls would meet her there and of course John had now employed a Policeman to protect her. Standing there waiting for Helen yes he looked good as long as he had a quiet tongue she did not mind.

She would have to tell the girls not to touch, there she was with a bump and the landing was successful, waiting seems an age for the doors to open, it will be great when she has her own Jet on standby, that was her dream none of this being ferried around like an animal.

Walking into the arrivals there they were her friends Kate and Laura and close to them but standing on his own was Steven Helen's copper Helen walked over to him and introduced herself to him then walking with him to meet her friends. "Kate, Laura I have missed you, I have achieved so much since the last time we all were together it's unbelievable but we will chat about that, has someone got the Champagne on ice."

Turning to Steven with a nice bright smile she said. "And this is my copper Steven he is with us for the duration of our playtime." Helen turned around to look at the girls and they were smiling girls all had given him a sweet smile as if to say you just do not know what you're in for.

"Steven you are joining us I hope you can keep yourself from joining in the fun." Kate knew what she was saying all of them knowing Kate of course she began looking at him and weighing him up. "I am a professional man so I will be watching Helen making sure she is safe."

He looked at all of them bent down and picked his bag up to follow. "Ok check the bags in then we will go straight through to the Champagne bar and some sushi and shopping." Laura was in form she was out to have a good time and she wanted to know just whose turn was it to screw that would be interesting or is it just the flirting that would be going on are all of them so much in love.

They were giggling through the security Helen was searched. "Always me I must have the face that says touch me up and being famous too I think it's the passport it's no good having an Irish one." Helen would have to change the passport or walk through another way.

Steven followed like an Angel he was in for the ride of his life how would he keep a straight face that would be interesting. The train was on time for a change they took their seats and Steven sat behind Helen. The normal bottle was ordered with food this time she was happy our Helen happy to be with her friends, happy to be on her way to a fun six days it would be great just have some idle chat it had been a long time.

Helen was so happy with life the contentment showed in her face a long journey from the age of six and to the last ten years of nasty tormenting people who followed like sheep and played mind games and the police allowed it to happen even to the point of joining in the games, even though it was all illegal shutting off that memory.

The day that Mr O'Kell let Helen know that they had formed The Men's Club and she found out later after getting through the trauma of losing her home, her son Mark and her son Simon through his wife and the years of healing in Spain to her torment The Men's Club followed her continuing the torment of tapping her phone, hacking her computer and intruding in her life, she made sure the people that were part of the torment from the beginning to end had their payback.

Games after games, listening to her phone calls or texts and playing them back in mind games. It was as though Helen was behind a mirror with everybody that was around her was viewing into her life, was this what Wivenhoe, Mile End in Colchester, Brampton Cumbria, and then also Jerez, Calahonda and Mijas in Spain was all about or did the police feel Helen was fair game because she was single, a medium, a grieving mother and so vulnerable.

Well not anymore. Fame beckoned! Fame was here. So she sued receiving more money than she had ever had before, it was in the millions and that is more than Helen deserved. She could retire now and just do what she wanted that is what life is all about. Here we are today all smiles and her perpetrators behind bars and receiving their Karma. Life was all about treating people how you want to be treated. Helen returned to her friends and a fun time to be had.

The train was boozy and they were treated like royalty in first class, and even to being taken through to their car very quickly. As they streamed away some people looked as if they knew who they were seeing, some pointed is this all the price of fame she thought and yes sometimes good but to be in a goldfish bowl is not so good.

They were off to Paris centre for a few days and then onto Reims and Champagne tasting. They would have a Bentley at their service for their journeying around Paris even when they were on the trip down the Seine it would be there waiting at the end to take then to their next port of call.

"Ok everybody has to say how they are going with their men then we will banter with all the men here." Helen turned to Sarah first she knew Sarah had fallen in love big time but she wanted to hear how it was going. "Anton has asked me to marry him and to live in Italy, his family are pleased with his choice guess what we are to be married in September as the fall is supposed to be cooler for them, so that is one wedding this year." Sarah was full of the joys of spring and it was great to see.

"Well done this one will make you happy you can paint and he will sell them." Helen clapped loudly like a seal and Kate joined in, both Laura and Kate then said. "That calls for a drink I think let's see Champagne here please." And yes there was another bottle that had been ordered for them all. "Me here well my lovely man has asked me to move in with him at his apartment I am moving in when we get back she suddenly put her left hand out, I have a ring but we are not getting married yet."

Friends, Accepting the Changes

Kate did look so happy she certainly had changed since moving to America, yet another celebration to be had but no wedding that would be too much.

"And now to me I am now in the process of becoming a business partner to David Brinton he has asked me can we take it further so we are looking to buy a property together he is ready for marriage but no ring yet. We are getting engaged when we move in our new house. So yet another wedding, we have chosen a wedding on a ship out at sea so get your sea legs on." Well that was the three of them sorted Helen could now sleep peacefully, their spiritual roads had been opened.

Kate's man who she had only just named was about to come up trumps as well, his name Robert Jakinsky he was a great success as a business man and now he was giving his time to the UN, opening projects helping them run smoothly that he could use his business sense in and he was good, Helen had a feeling that Kate did not know just how much Jeffery was worth. But now there were no worries left for Kate on her friendship front.

They had arrived at Paris main line slowly they began to embark for the drive to their Hotel and Helen had booked five star and such a wonderful hotel for them to spend two nights at the L'Hotel du Collectionneur, Arc de Triomphe. What was called for in Paris they had all agreed to the shopping part and then onto a little bit of sightseeing and then they would be going onto Reims.

Friends, Accepting the Changes

They all had their own room Helen had pushed the boat out and she had reserved a suite for herself and it was so well deserved for Helen she was the lady who work all the hours for her Angels and Masters, with all the cheques in her bank account that she had asked for. A millionaire she was. Placing her case and her computer on the bed she fell back onto the bed just to shut her eyes for a moment this was the life.

Helen's mobile rang; "Hi Helen I thought we could go out for tea and have dinner late today around nine and start all the shopping and sightseeing tomorrow what do you feel Helen." Kate taking charge yet again had said with authority.

"I am hungry and it would be nice to have high tea with cut sandwiches and cake, have you spoken to the Laura and Sarah and are they both in agreement with all this Kate if they are then give me fifteen minute to freshen up s'il vous plait." Helen answered her with broken French; Helen was learning French and Italian as it would come in handy with her journeys through France and Italy.

Off to the Ritz for afternoon tea this was on Helen's list it would be special, this is Paris and they would be on the look out to see who was who having tea with them. Helen found her little black dress with the accessories of red would bring Christmas cheer to all.

The Bentley waited for them at the front slipping out of the doors and into the car muy importante they all were and now to eat those wonderful sandwiches and cake and of course they would have a glass of champagne it would only be the best for the best.

The door of the Bentley was opened for them and the door to the Ritz was opened for them to reach their destination of L'Espadon. They were shown to their table and straight away the bottle of pink champagne was opened for their delight. "Cheers, and Salute' to us."

Helen held her glass high for all to chink with as their laughter filled the air and it was loud but friendly. "Helen what are we doing first tomorrow I thought we should do the shopping bit and then lunch and then some more shopping then the sights the next day. When are we off to Madrid so you can fly us Captain." Kate was questioning the time they had together.

"We can shop until we drop tomorrow and take a cruise down the Seine Friday and we are off to Madrid Saturday for lunch and Sunday we are off to Reims until Wednesday where we will fly back to Heathrow. I do have an appointment with my publisher so that's our stay in France done." Helen had the diary done in a jiffy.

The cake stand and the sandwich stand were brought to them and then placed on their table, a share of two sandwich stands and two cake stands, dinner would be late. "Look Helen tiny sandwiches salmon here, these are wonderful. Taste one you will love them. Watch Helen's little finger as she eats." Laura started smiling at the lady and her little finger that stood high. "Look at these beautiful cakes Kate, Sarah have you tried one. They are so divine." Helen handed a cake to Sarah. "Pour the tea Kate you can be mother one pot is Assam the other Earl Grey, divine people so divine." Ladies that take tea they were today, anything that ladies do they done it, and enjoyed the process of their heady fun. Fun, fun and yet more fun. Life was good when life was positive, just keep a positive flow and watch life fall into place.

Chitter, chatter for nearly two hours watching who was coming and going, a smile and a wave Helen got now and then. This was fame at is best not intrusive but kind and appreciative of Helen's space. She needed her own space and time for fun. Steven stood at the door of the Ritz just watching Helen every minute just in case somebody was too friendly he would be there like a shot just one person crossed the boundaries.

Those divine sandwiches were gone in a moment and the petite cakes had been so scrumptious they all had loved the Ritz in Paris there first stop.

Back to their hotel and a rest and then dinner at nine thirty. "Sleep that's what I will be doing for the next two hours please just call me at eight and then I will get ready for nine fifteen." Helen looked at Kate as they both walked into the foyer of The L'Hotel du Collectionneur. Kate smiled and replied with a great sense of urgency. "I am to bed with my vibrator for an hour and then sleep, no sex so I have to create it myself."

Friends, Accepting the Changes

"Too much information missy Kate keep that to yourself, see you later." Their beds waited for whatever they used them for. Helen did wonder how all of them would do here alone and without their sexual comforts, but then again apparently Kate had brought her own device.

They all would be wearing long designer dresses to impress was the purpose and impress they did. All walked into the Restaurant Pur for the evening of French and also European food with the atmosphere that made them feel welcome lots of French speaking people here Helen thought she was deep in catching some of the French and to understanding what she had taken time to learn and it was such a sexy language.

Helen wore black with gold which suited her so much. Kate went for red. Laura choose a silver our and Sarah wore gold that was the first dress event of the holiday. They would be shopping for more dresses while in Paris. Their table was close to the window so they could see the lights and the restaurant for the evening.

One after the other they walked in like models to glide and not strut. Placing one foot to glide to the other a slight wiggle and then to have the waiter move their chairs one by one for them to sit and enjoy. "Kate shall we have a decent champagne throughout the night or also have a French red a bottle of Bordeaux what do you feel Creams I will go with you."

Helen asked how they felt Kate and Helen enjoyed their

Friends, Accepting the Changes

champagne and the wine they could both remembered a few nights that bottles were tossed one after the other. It would be a shame not to enjoy what France had on offer while they were in Paris.

Looking at the menu Helen remarked. "No snails tonight Creams I am going to go for a light starter with beef and truffle sauce to follow and chocolate for pudding." "Me too Rainbow I think that looks like a positive move." Sarah and Laura looked at the menu and chose something different but that was it a night to enjoy.

The champagne came with an aperitif a little something to get the palette open to all the tastes that were going to be presented to these ladies that dine. Warm French bread arrived at their table Helen was in dreamland and enjoying every minute of the dining. The champagne a bottle of Krug it would serve the starter with the Bordeaux for the main and then they would choose a glass of a special drink it would have to be a brandy with coffee.

Sorted for this evening a day to remember yet another day they were listening to the piano being played was memorable and they resisted the urge to sing. Helen and Kate were miming the words to the song that was enough to be going on with.

The morning came and croissants for breakfast made the French way, French coffee and a buffet to enjoy. Today they were shopping in Paris and dropping in for lunch at Restaurant

Epicure just French food would suit them today. The Bentley arrived to take them to the rye du Faubourg-St-Honore' and avenue Montaigne all they needed was the cards.

They would shop until they drop. Shopping in the Avenues des Champs-Elysees' would be for the Chanel, Cartier, Giorgio Armani, Prada and even Versace all designer labels here that would suit them, Helen was looking for dresses and found some they were elegant, beautiful and she found shoes to match, a box full of make-up and creams and that was it, lingerie was bought so special for the special lovers that they all had.

Their car arrived and it took them to Epicure with the bags as they wanted to look at their goodies that they had in the bags. "What do you think Helen look how beautiful these shoes are, I now have lingerie to match so sexy." Laura showing everybody what she had bought. Helen remarked in a surprised voice.

"Ok, is this all you are wearing have you bought a dress Laura?" "Yes but I wanted to show you these first." They were all laughing while they ordered their wine and food. More shopping and then back to their hotel to get ready for dinner at Le 114 Fauborg this was a high quality Parisian food again it was a night to be enjoyed.

Long dresses called for Helen arrived in black and pink even to the point of classy pink and black shoes. Looking divine, Kate dress in cream and black, Laura in blue and Sarah in brown it was a fashion show, still they glided to the table and two waiters came along to make sure they were seated.

What to have tonight champagne yes and it would be a Mercier that would be brought to them. Then they would decide what to do. A wonderful night with great food and the music again Helen had to watch that she didn't sing out in front of everybody.

They were up early breakfast and a drive to the cruise along the Seine and stopping for lunch near the Eiffel Tower. The cruise was to take in Notre Dame and then all the historical sites view from the cruise boat they would only embark for the Eiffel Tower. The lift to the top and then to view Paris which was so wonderful.

Lunch close by and then continue the relaxing cruise down the river Seine their car would pick them up at the end of the cruise. Dinner was going to be A L'endroit again they would dress and the colour had yet to decided, this was the life and they all needed these long weekends.

Helen in blue, Kate in green, Sarah in black and Laura in pink so beautiful that's for sure, the holiday had brought the glow to their faces that they needed it was good to meet friends and have a great time. It brought them back together again so when they returned to their men they would be happy and glowing and if a man loves his woman then he wants to see her happy not stressed not sure about life.

Friends, Accepting the Changes

It was the morning of Saturday and they would be taking a flight to Madrid for lunch, they had reservations for a restaurant that had been recommended La Capilla de la Bolsa it was central in Madrid the dinning there was meant to be wonderful and to be told it was an unforgettable dining experience, the atmosphere was supposed to be divine.

They were delighted to be given a reservation at such short notice, they must know of Helen.

So Helen slowed her drinking down to a stop, she did want to fly her friends to Madrid. A light breakfast as they all were waiting nervously, Steven watched as the Bentley arrived in stepped the girls making themselves comfortable. They had Spanish Pilot and he was waiting for them at Paris airport, the Jet was one that Helen wanted to try as she was in the mood to buy one it had ten seats and it was very smart.

They were taken through security quickly as the Jet was ready to go, Jose' was very young, very smart and yes very beautiful and he was theirs for the day.

He made Helen feel comfortable as she sat in the Captains seat she smiled gingerly while the girls sat waiting for the take-off. Now Helen was checking the system of checking the flight log, it was all systems go. Sitting back the three of them Kate, Laura and Sarah were nervous, Helen well she was just plain excited.

Flying her girls for one hour to Madrid airport she was again showing them her skills and they were ready for take-off, Helen began to speak into the speaker letting the ladies know she was in charge of the jet.

"This is your Captain speaking I would like to introduce myself I am Captain Helen would you please make sure your seat belts are fastened and adjusted properly we are now ready for the take-off." Kate remarked to Laura as they both sat seat belts tight, awaiting the take-off of this wonderful jet trip to Madrid. "Ok well here we go say a little pray that we will get there safe."

They both laughed as they asked the Angels to keep them safe. Starting to run the runway they lifted into the sky, and Helen felt the exhalation of being up with the birds as high as they were allowed.

She swayed then curved and made her way to Madrid, a fantastic lunch awaited them. The mountains came into view as they were nearing their destination. "Look there's the airport Laura this is the tricky bit will we get down." Kate pointed outside as she could see the runway to her relief they had not got lost up there near heaven. "Kate I must say I cannot believe you do not trust our Helen I knew she would keep us safe."

Laura replied with a smile as the Jet touched down a great sigh of relief they landed on time, now to a private car in the private Jet area. The Jet stopped still. "This is your Captain Helen we are now in Madrid, I hope you enjoyed the journey as much as I did." Helen spoke with a smile in her voice as she knew the girls were just a little bit apprehensive about the flight but their Captain did good.

Helen went through to her passengers with a big grin. "Well ladies did you enjoy the flight we hope you were looked after."

She turned to Kate knowing she was apprehensive of Helen being their Pilot Kate just stuck two thumbs up. They were on a role Madrid had great shops too so it was a yes to the designer goods and there would be bags and shoes.

Arriving in time at the restaurant and they were on time their private car picked them up from the airport no going through the normal channels this time Helen's bodyguard Steven came into his own, he knew a few people there and they were now seated to wait for their dining experience. The food was divine well worth the money the Spanish waiters had a thing about the girls she knew they were having a wager to see who could be their waiter.

There was so much banter going on while they were there, making the most of the time with her friends. Helen began to banter with the waiters asking them to bring certain wines through so that they could taste and if it was not to their liking they would change the bottle. What restaurant would do that, ordering lunch which was a typical Spanish lunch enjoying the parading down the main street and with a bit of retail therapy the ladies loved their day in Madrid.

Friends, Accepting the Changes

Carlos flew them back to Paris airport where their car met them at the airport and took them onto Reims and then onto their hotel Chateau d`Etoges this was for three nights of sheer bliss, they had booked at La spa du Chateau and the massage was "Fleurs de Bach" for the three days that they were there and the restaurant would serve Gourmet French Cuisine and fine Champagnes all for their enjoyment this was a place to relax. They would be going out to view a few vineyards and then to taste the different Champagnes it was a delight to them all.

Leaving their clothes in their rooms they had collected quite a few shopping bags since they had arrived in France. Helen and Kate were now on a run of champagne tasty this was something they had dreamt of for many years. For lunch and to find that their day the next day had been organised to go to Epernay in the morning both Kate and Helen were ready for this journey into the world of sipping champagne.

There were so many different choices for them to make. They would take bottles home. Lunch was a light pate and fish cook in a French style with herbs and garlic. Having booked the spa for when they came back from champagne tasting much to look forward too.

Up to the gym early and then off they were going to Epernay Helen wanted to see what was on offer. The sole reason to visit Epernay was to borrow into the chalky caves and to taste the champagne Epernay was an undistinguished town that lived of the profits of the champagne.

Friends, Accepting the Changes

They walked through the doors and smelt the champagne this was going to be a good day. Straight to the caves and the tasting began. They walked around picking and choosing the champagne to taste with a view to buy. Sitting down to the tasting the champagne had the girls in screams the seductive bubbles gave them the thoughts of the love they wanted and would be receiving on their return home.

"Look girls we should have a seductive photo taken with us and the champagne." Helen remarked. Kate got the girls together and each one had a bottle of champagne in their hands making love to a bottle the laughter and tears began to tear through them. They were so funny together. "The Vibrators will be at the ready when we return the Chateau." Kate shouted out for the world to hear.

A bottle of Moet & Chandon, Mercier, Krug, Pommery, Veuve, Clicquot and Carnard Duchene each it was to be enjoyed at home just to see what they felt was the best for them. The Avenue de Champagne was the best journey they'd had in a long time, this was it.

They all had enjoyed their day learning about the makings of the champagne that they all loved. Very tipsy to say the least Kate began to slur her words. "Rainbow I think we should go and stay in the spa for a couple of hours just allowing all the champagne to pass through our bodies very gently".

Helen just laughed at her she knew her Creams well. "We have a massage and facial booked so we had better calm down a bit on the champers and just have a late lunch to soak up what we have drunk." They left the champagne behind the order had gone in for their champagne to be delivered. They slipped back into the car and a detour for lunch that was left to the driver he knew the place so well and he would make sure they were ok. The views were spectacular Helen loved good views.

A robe around them as they stepped into the Jacuzzi so relaxing France was a delight. Each country had its qualities each country had the downfalls of sordidness. But they girls enjoyed their time. Helen was called to have her facial and massage. Then to her surprise she had bagged herself a young French man for the massage.

"Helen if you ask him nicely he may just be glad to give you more than you would expect from him, an orgasm may be on offer". Kate squeezed Helen's knee smiling with delight. "I hope I have a sexy speaking French man you can do what I want". Helen shook her head. "What are you like Missy Kate have you brought your vibrator for the massage too".

Helen came out of her room looking relaxed from her massage with rosy cheeks as if he had satisfied every part she needed to be satisfied. Looking towards Kate she did wonder what was going on in her head. Did she, didn't she Helen would just keep her guessing that rosy glow may make her think about what she has been up too.

Friends, Accepting the Changes

"Helen, well how was it. I may order him next time look at your face I want that glow." Kate asked with the urgency about her questioning. She knew that she wanted and needed a decent orgasm. "Kate will you just take a look at my face and then look into my eyes and tell me what you feel about my state of play."

Helen let Kate wonder what had gone on if she wanted her masseuse she would have to order him and find out. "I am going to book him for my session next time I want some of what you have just had".

"It's not all about the sex Kate it's the way her moves and makes you happy." Laura said as she came from her massage room with a glass of water in her hand. "I feel so good this is fantastic I want to book this tomorrow." They agreed to swap masseuses just so they all could get the feel of Helen's young French man.

And Kate was such a jealous person she had to have what was good for everyone. Tomorrow was another day and it would bring some fine things to them all.

They were off to Reims and to visit the old parts of this ancient city. It was squashed in the war but now look at it. Breakfast early and to them find the place for lunch. The Bentley had arrived for them all to climb into this was the life both Kate and Helen thought how would they survive the work after all that they had done here.

Friends, Accepting the Changes

They were still the same old fun, lunch and dinner girls. "Stepping out with my babies, the French and love were on the plate. Look at us and come what may be Champagne and fun at the gate." Kate was singing away and all of the girls joined in the fun. They loved their own company all of them had found their life's.

They arrived at the Cathedral Notre-Dame. It has stood on the site 401, the present building was begun in1211. There were some wonderful things to see. The smiling Angel is situated above the left (north) portal, this enigmatic Angel with unfurled wings is the celebrated of many that grace the building, the gallery of Kings which is at west harmoniously decorated with over 2,300 statues it is the most notable feature at Reims.

There are fifty six stone effigies of French Kings form the gallery of the Kings. The Apse gallery is crowned by mythological beasts. The glass windows were beautiful each telling its own story, it was a grand day in a grand place. Their lunch was to be at the Le Parc les Crayeres it would be expensive but most enjoyable.

Then to lunch this was going to be a definite posh lunch and the girls deserved a push the boat out lunch. They would all have champagne in the Brasserie then to lunch with further bottles of the champagne this was expensive but worth it. The menu was so divinely interesting and choices for them all and would anyone succumb to the snails.

Kate wanted to taste the truffle sauce with the prime steak.

Friends, Accepting the Changes

Helen had already placed her order for the steak with trufee sauce, she loved trufee sauce as the French say, it had a deep richness the tastes of food she loved.

The starter of course had to be French pate you couldn't do better than that, they would be dinning on five course there was a fish dish the local fish for the second dish, then to the prime steak which ended up everyone was having the same and a chocolate pudding it had to be champagne being in such a beautiful place would bring that through.

Trois Chocolat Tarte de Champagne was for pudding. Each plate was placed in front of them and it tasted divine, the steak was so rich in the sauce they all just kept saying. "Delicious Helen and so wonderful it is most certainly like being seduced by French food".

One after the other they felt that were being seduced by a Frenchman. When they came to the pudding they just sighed as it was brought to the table and of course another bottle of champagne was put into the fresh ice, and they would certainly be coming back to France and perhaps a week here would be good. Also other parts of France needed to be explored.

Helen placed her glass into the middle of the table and the words just flowed. "To my beautiful friends we have come so far, here's to the cruise and the men being with us this time, please be at one with your-selves and enjoy the time in the Mediterranean I will be me as always, Salute my friends Cheers."

Friends, Accepting the Changes

"Cheers Helen, here's too many, many good times in the company of ourselves and our men".

Kate was enjoying this break and did wonder how the men would get on with the cruise, would they all bond as the girls did need to shop. They would be flying to Nice and getting the rather large private cruise ship and of too Cannes, then onto Monaco for a few days shopping, then to the islands of Sardinia and Capri for a rest and the enjoyment of the sun flying back from Naples until they meet again.

They had such a wonderful time in Reims and they did look at the package that they could have here if they came back to La Parc Les Crayeres. They were now travelling back for a spa workout the massage and out of the four of the ladies who would have the wonderful Frenchman today.

Then the morning would be another massage and just time to relax in the surroundings and then to pack for the travelling home they decide to train it again as they could get more through customs.

Kate had the wonderful Frenchman giving her a full body massage. Their day in Reims was wonderful so enjoyable and only two days left to just relax before returning home, this was going to be spent in the spa with facials, massages and whatever else they could have. Lunch with champagne, dinner with champagne they would be champagne out. Life was good, life was wonderful and life was grand. Helen couldn't ask for more than this.

Chapter Twelve; Cruising, Capri, Sicily, Monaco, Nice, Marseilles, St Tropez and Cannes.

This was to be a journey of friends and the start was where they would all meet and that was Nice Cotes D'Azur airport they all agreed that it was of course the closest to the private cruise boat. This would be a cruise for them all to remember and Helen wanted to see how the men were with all of them being together.

Also she would watch to see whether they could they do a holiday together again and weddings to see if there were any and when they would all be organising the day. There were the three ladies to be married Helen had already done the deed and had her John in her arms.

"Helen we will get to the airport before you, there will be a car to meet us and take us to the harbour". Kate was chatting loudly down the phone to Helen. "Yes Charles is meeting you, now he is French and quite the charmer. It's a good job you have Jeffery with you otherwise he wouldn't be safe with you ladies."

Helen replied in a soft voice to calm the situation down she thought to her-self as Kate was excitable with the view of all of them having fun on the boat together.

Friends, Accepting the Changes

This was the first of many holidays they would plan together they all needed to bond as couples. How would it all end with at least two weeks together and at least these ladies would get some serious shopping time and perhaps the men could play golf or something similar to that something to do with balls anyway.

Helen was deep in thought to how the heavens had brought them together at a dinner club and still they were together but independently apart, that's the way life should be as it was the best way to love friends and to set them free to enjoy.

This would be a great adventure for them all. How they would spend the time getting to know each-others partners how Helen would pick up on these men and watch how they behaved with her friends, she would see the long life partnership that they were all falling into the joys of being open to Helen and her gift.

How would it all work that was the joy of friends bringing their loved ones into the process of a deep and meaningful way of loving and laughing. Nice Cotes D'Azur Airport was busy and that made Helen slightly nervous at being recognised she wasn't sure of all the attention and wanting to keep it all very simple not being asked for this then asked for that.

They all came off different planes from different areas. Miami, Milan, Washington and of course Helen flew in from Sicily her and John had been visiting friends and looking for a villa just to add to the places they had.

They were meeting in the executive lounge Helen was there first and then seeing Kate with Robert, they were walking close together always a good sign, Kate then noticed Helen smiling and then she waved. "There she is Robert, look over there there's Helen come on we can have a glass of wine before the others get here, it will break the ice."

Kate took hold of Robert's hand and she then quickened her step until she had her arms around Helen. "I have missed you, this is Robert and he has so been looking forward to meeting you Helen." Kate said in introducing her man. "Come on Kate we can have a glass of champagne before the rowdy lot get here." Helen took hold of Kate and left the boys to introduce and find out about each-other they did not want awkward moments here they would just allow it to happen they were Helen's words.

A bottle of Moet would do the job and a few nibbles, Helen and Kate chatted about all that was going on, Kate and Robert had moved in together in an apartment in the central area of Washington and now building a life as one, and also working very hard indeed. Both Kate and Helen turned around to hear the men laughing, well they had hit it off. "Good Kate they have both come together quite nicely, we can relaxed." Helen smiled while she was watching both John and Robert.

Friends, Accepting the Changes

Helen was watching everybody come and go while chatting to Kate then watching the screen for the flights of Sarah and Laura with their respective spouses. There was a wedding to arrange while they were all on this holiday Sarah is the one to marry this year she knew that and then Kate and Laura the following year. So there was a great deal to organise with her friends for the future.

There they were one after the other Sarah and Laura's planes were landing. Collecting their baggage and off to meet the friends of a lifetime. You know that we have friends for a moment, friends that on agendas they try to disrupt the flow of your life those you get rid of as soon as you feel that, friends for a season of where you are in your life at any given time.

And of course those friends that are there no matter what and that you can pick up the phone after months of nothing and it's just the same as before, the always and forever friends that see you for who you are.

Laura and David helping each-other along with their suitcases, yes Helen thought at last a match and it would be Laura that made the noises where sex was concerned she knew that, he wouldn't worry about anybody while she was enjoying.

Sarah and Anton hand in hand with a smile all the way, these two are a match made from heaven that was for certain Anton would look after Sarah at last Helen had her troop together, nobody feeling alone within a group that was what she always wanted.

Hugs and cuddles then introductions and they were then moved along and into two Bentleys to travel to Le Port de Nice they had an eight berth boat to take them on their cruise. Dropping off the luggage and then a quick refresh and onto Restaurant La Boudoir 10 Rue Chauvain in Nice, they knew this would be a divine way of eating Helen had already checked out the menu.

The door was opened for them and as they walked in the décor was very smart and very interesting with beautiful colours of black, grey and pink it had a French feel for sure.

"Bonsoir." The young man ushered them into the restaurant and taking them to their table. The restaurant was full of chatting diners all in French. The group de Helen all had some knowledge of French so they didn't feel out of place. The first thing was to order was the wine and then they would all order dishes to taste.

A bottle of white wine was for their starter and they ordered a bottle of Chablis from the region of Bourgogne it would give the pallet a clean beginning. And for the main a rich red Haute Cotes de Nuits it would suit the meat they were going to order and for dessert they ordered a bottle of Moscato yes it was Italian but it would suit the desserts as we know most people love a good dessert.

Friends, Accepting the Changes

They were all ordering their food and the Entrees were of Foie gras mi-cuit confit figueset oigoins, Carpaccio St Jaques aux agrumes, Tartare de truite saumonee aux bais degoji, Salade de Burrata accomagnee so don caviar de Trufee. It all looked so yummy, and wonderful French food, with it all being so divinely cooked.

The Plat were again very tasty French food had a definite richness about it Filet de Boeuf rossiniles, Tagliata de Boeuf auxgirolles, Marcaronnis a la creme de Trufee blanche et copeanx de Trufee, Raviolis de sonbressa de facon Thai.

Rich and tasty wonderful food that all would enjoy and the chatter between them would bring the company together in the way all would enjoy the trip of many trips, the boat was a big enough for space for them all.

Dessert was a joy in itself it's the ending of something good. Mousseaux specules crunch emulsion Nutella glace vanilla sucre petillant, Crème de Mascarpone compote de Framboises Fraises Crumble, Moelleux au Chocolat cœur fondant Nutella, the last dessert Tiramisu aux fruits rouges.

The lunch was made so easy and welcoming and the laughter was infectious as one laughed so the other did and so on. Speaking in English and French so that the locals or whoever was there in the restaurant could understand the merriment of the group de cruise la France e Italy. Leaving with laughter they decided that just a little walk around Nice as they ventured to the boat in Le Port.

A conference between them and then they all had decided to visit the Musee d'Art Moderne et d'Art Contemporain and of course the Cathedrale-Ste-Reparate in Nice and then they would walk to La Port via the Promenade des Anglais and along the seafront watching the different bodies that ventured to the beach.

Helen did wonder why people worry about stripping off when the views are amazing all different sizes amazing to say the least, do what you want and enjoy. They would walk through the Tunnel of Freedom Helen enjoyed that as she was remembering the time in England then in Spain where people who thought they were in control of her life but they weren't their silly games would and were repaid.

The Police in both England and Spain who felt to torment her was all in a game. It's so it funny how people become sheep so quickly when one person says do this, do that. Do they feel that they are so big to do that never mind, children may play games but adults get their payback and it came with a heavy blow.

Her life was being listened to and privacy Helen held dear to her heart. Privacy she did not have. It has now turned around she was in her own power, her own love and didn't react to silly games.

Nice and the colours were so interesting beautiful the interesting walk through the tunnel and along the seafront brought them to La Port and the large vessel that was to be their home for the next ten days cruising the waters of the Mediterranean around France and Italy.

Stepping onto the boat they sat and watched the Captain manoeuvre their boat out of La Port de Nice, Laura and David had disappeared to their room. Helen thought sex was the purpose she didn't care and would sure satisfy her needs whatever.

They left La Port de Nice watching the buildings disappear in the distance and a bottle of champagne was opened to celebrate the beginnings of a journey that the friends would take together before the friends went their own separate ways, life was good.

Meanwhile Laura was in the shower with David was getting to grips with his penis and enjoying the feel and touch he was giving her. Washing and caressing each-other with the soft soap David's hands were soft and caring easily delivering the sexual tension Laura found hard to resist.

David was already ready for her hard as could be waiting for the permission to enter Laura and that tunnel of freedom of their own. Feeling, touching and Laura began to climax not too quickly this was to be enjoyed for the pleasure, sex for Laura took the tensions away so that she could think.

Friends, Accepting the Changes

Turning Laura around his kisses so gentle but yet so firm, placing Laura against the glass wall of the shower he put one of her legs around his back and then he slipped his penis gently at first but then to thrust with a purpose to an ending, they both grunted and moaned with delight as they went through the sexual adventures on the boat, thrusting with an ending of them both enjoying an orgasm in true fashion of erotica.

They had loved every part of the scene. A moment of tender love and then they both dressed and resumed their time with their friends.

"Where have you been we have left the port and now are on our way to Monaco, a glass of champagne?" Kate smiled as Laura looked her way and Laura knowing that Kate knew exactly where she had been. They did all fit so well. Just sitting and sipping champagne watching as slowly the boat began moving towards Monaco they would be there for the next day and spend some time looking around.

The night was beautiful to be at sea and the stars in full they would have a full moon time while they were cruising it is so relaxing, so healing.

The night was becoming late and they all started to find their rooms for sleep and pleasure, who would keep who awake with the pleasure of each-other Kate wondered. It would be a quiet one for most of them as the sea did bring out the noises of a moving beds, their rooms did have some privacy of being sound proof. But there would certainly be some movement on the boat.

The morning came one by one they all came to the dining room and selected their breakfast, they had their own chef on board so even out at sea there was wonderful food to be tasted. Sitting on deck with breakfast in hand they all enjoyed the views of them slowly being taken to Monaco, in the distance they could see the hills and the buildings rising above the water. Here they would just relax during the day.

They would be popping off after breakfast to visit the beautiful Palace Princier the Monaco-Ville is the seat of government it sits on the site of the thirteenth Century Palais Princie. Then it was onto the Fort Antonie and the views then they would walk to the neo-Romaneque Cathedrale.

A coffee and a French tarte which was very similar to a crois-sant, Helen wanted to visit the beautiful place the Jardin Exotique it was supposed to be the best garden in Europe and had a huge range of tropical and also subtropical plants that they could see and maybe want to add to their garden. Here everything was so beautiful, so French, it was so magnificent and Helen loved it all.

They were all enjoying Monaco and it was very rich in money and culture.

Friends, Accepting the Changes

Back to the boat and to lunch a prepared lunch of light fish and salad. A bottle of wine opened with plenty of water on the table. The afternoon was of sunbathing just to get a healthy glow that's all that was needed in this instance. They all left the deck for late afternoon a sleep and a cuddle were needed.

They were not going to have drunken behaviour yet. It was getting to know and enjoy. Helen snuggled into John feeling safe and warm. A long wait for this man but he was well worth the wait and the people who tried hard to stop him from entering Helen's world.

The snuggling then produced a loving, caring and fulfilling sexual interaction. John began to carefully move Helen kissing her gently, her face, her neck slowly moving down her body to her most erotic part the fulfilment of her it began to begin the nourishment of Helen wanting but not pushing for him to satisfy her at all he just wanted to make her happy in everything. Helen would never be sad again.

Nobody would touch her. He gently entered her as they both fell together in the motions of the sea gently rocking with a delightful ease of sex so gentle, so beautiful. Sex can be and is so different. The loving caring sex and of course the just plain don't give a toss what happens sex.

They arrived at an orgasm and just lay and just chatted about what they were going to do and how everybody had easily come together as friends. Sleep and snuggle, their bed was so big so they could sleep soundly on their own.

Arriving on deck they all had dressed the part the men in dinner suits looking divine and the women in long dresses looking really spectacular princes and princesses or kings and queens it depends how you want to feel on the night. It would be the grand dinner at a family run restaurant and then to the casino to play. How much to spend and who would be the winner.

What would you allow yourself to throw away for the night yes that would be fun Helen would throw caution to the wind and gamble some of her well earned money away hoping for a win and the exhilaration of a gamble don't get addicted. It would be the while night to enjoy.

They stepped ashore as they were lucky enough to berth for the night and set off again in the morning for Cap Ferrat. Now the drive in the Limo to the restaurant La Maontgolfiere Henri Geraci 16 Rue Basse it was just a jump from the Prince's Palace rue basse was the ideal spot for a Gourmet dinner, it was tucked away in the old town on top of the rock of Monaco, and the restaurant salmon pink was a colourful and picturesque place and it was a pedestrian street so a small walk which gave them change to show their finery.

They had the best area of the restaurant the table with a view of everybody in the restaurant.

Friends, Accepting the Changes

Menus in front of them and they would be dinning fit for them all. Wine was ordered and they would be drinking Chateauneuf du Pape Domaine du vieux telegraphe "La Cran" 2009 a snip at 130 euros. Their menu was the best for the best it was a holiday of expense and enjoyment. Entrees Maki de fois gras.

Fine de Claire Marenne Oleron Oysters Cream of ceps from Cevennes, the Plats were the first course of was Roasted Sea-bass from Cap Corsica Duck fois gras, Blanquette of Farmer Veal and Scallops, Dessert, we love dessert that's what it's all about as now the Chefs to put the boat out where desserts are concerned.

The Desserts were of Soft Pumpkin Cake Chocoquicoule, Green Chartreuse Iced Parfait, Moelleux au Chocolat Grand Crie Creme d'Infusion de Menta, Souffle Chaud au Grand Marnier. They all loved their food and their wine all were very much on a connection where that was concerned.

A wonderful restaurant that if they were ever in the area again it would be a definite must to return, six bottles of wine expensive but tasty. The laughter between them was infectious they all gave out and took all the banter that what friends were all about. "How much is there in the kitty to spend dear Helen in the Casino?" Kate asked knowing Helen hatted gambling.

"I have a budget a few thousands and that will be that Kate I will be finding somewhere else to enjoy." Helen touched Kate on the arm just to let Kate know to be careful.

Friends, Accepting the Changes

The limo then drove the streets of Monaco to the Grand Casino Monaco flags were flying in front of the famous and glamourous place made for the wealthy Billionaires. Marble columns the Palace like buildings has and does stage Opera's, Ballet's and Concerts it was such a shame that there was nothing to see while they were they it would have been better than the gambling.

Walking into the lobby there was a statue of King Louis XIV horse and there was a touch for good luck just in-case one of them were the luck of the evening.

The chips were bought and the tables were ready to be played. "Kate should we walk around together, I am not too sure how this all works." Helen was out of her comfort zone being in the Casino. It was something she would have to deal with in a client and it did make her feel uncomfortable.

Where should she go, what should she play. "John where should I go, I really do not want to play poker, what about the wheels you know with the ball that goes round and round." Helen was showing her naïve her John just smiled.

"Let me take you Helen I think that European Roulette would suit you girls and then just play it by ear, how does that feel for you Kate, I will take you and Helen there, Robert is going to take a look at the American Roulette and then come back to us." John took hold of the two ladies and motioned them to the private Roulette tables.

"Sarah, Laura what are you doing, I know David and Anton are going with Robert. If we spread out we may win." His smile was bright.

"We are all going together John you go with David, Robert and the lovely Anton." Sarah winked. "And of course the lovely David too Sarah actually you men you are all lovely." Laura winked as she took hold of Helen and Kate. Off they were going to those black and red Roulette tables.

Who was going to be the winner! Chips out and on the tables Helen felt a twinge in her tummy was it now that she was going to win she felt something was going to happen. An hour later they were about to leave and Helen said. "I am going to do one more and then I am calling it quits." Her number she was about to place her chips on was the seven black.

Watching and waiting, she placed her chips down. "Number seven black." Helen said looking into his eyes as he threw the ball and they were all watching the ball going round and round waiting for the ball to settle on the number it wanted too.

"Come on then my number seven, come on my Angels." Helen whispered under her breath. Round and round, then slower and slower, it was coming to the end of its journey, should she cover her eyes and wish, she did just that and heard the shout of. "And number seven black it is."

Friends, Accepting the Changes

Helen looked up and he was smiling. "You have won madam, well done." All the chips were Helen's and there were thousands. How much have I won she wondered. "Thank you so much, where do I cash the chips in?" Helen asked the wonderful young man he had such a bright smile. "Go outside to the cash boxes they will add it all for you and either give you the money or a bank transfer or cheque it's up to you.

" It was in euros so Helen could put the money into her Italian bank on a transfer and when they arrived in Sicily she could sort it to put the money abroad so she didn't pay any taxes. What fun she thought how much have I won.

The cashing lady kept smiling at her. "You have won a great deal here madam. Look someone has been putting in chips of 500.000euros at a time. So my calculations you have won 5,000,000,000 euros how do you want this to be given to you, I can transfer it into your account tonight on a quick transfer and you should get it by late morning tomorrow.

I will give you a receipt for it all. You have a French account?" The young lady asked. "Yes transfer it into my French account then I can transfer it where I want to tomorrow when I receive it." Helen gave her details over and the money was there within two hours.

Leaving the Casino with a smile everybody had won something big or small. It had been a good night. They would walk along the promenade and then the limo would take them to their boat. The night was still young and they would open a bottle of the best champagne to celebrate their wonderful day. Helen done the asking and paying for six bottles of Moet & Chandon Grand Vintage Champagne and six bottles were taken to their car while they walked around promenade while the men caught them up.

"Helen won, well we all won but Helen won 5,000,000,000 euros wow John what do you say, we are going to celebrate the night away." Kate hugged Helen then John, then Robert, Laura, Sarah, Anton and David she was on a high. "And we have six bottles of Moet & Chandon Grand Vintage 2002."

Kate was so excited. They all stepped into the limo to be taken to their boat. Laughing aloud and placing the bottles into the fridge waiting to be drunk later, and champagne flute into the freezer just for a few moments while they all put snuggles on.

Make up off and clean then each one of the girls put on their summer onesies and up on deck the men had the champagne flutes and one bottle about to be popped and then to party in style and they were totally vintage. The champagne cork popped like a dream, yes the girls did love that sound. "Here's to the winning of millions and the happiness, a wonderful holiday with special friends." Helen raised her glass for all to connect and celebrate.

Sitting and laughing looking at the surroundings that they were in to afford such time with good friends and never to worry about money ever again. Their glasses filled again and this time just to smile, relax and laugh at what was around and the jokes the men were coming out with. They all had such wonderful men in their lives and they were so much adored. Adorable men how wonderful and they did fit into the world of laughter and fun.

Sex and sleep that was the order of the night slowly, gently and the best was yet to come. The morning was to be a slow cruise to the Peninsula Cap Ferrat, the Captain would sail off as soon as he knew everyone was settled and beginning to sleep. It was already 4.00am. Sleep would come fast for everybody, there were to be more exciting times as they journeyed the holiday of France and Italy.

Feeling the motions of the water allowing them to move slowly along and into the sea it didn't take too long for them to reach Cap Ferrat the anchor and the smell of a hearty breakfast being cooked. Porridge and a cooked breakfast French style, coming from Monaco to such a beautiful serene place, once breakfast had settled and they could jump ship and view this bay.

They found many villas of great wealth and the views from the top of Beaulieu lies where the cap joins the mainland just to sit and watch while the men found the lunch venue to be simple so that they can have dinner on their boat and just relax. Walking around would bring the women together looking for some shops to buy expensive but special items.

Friends, Accepting the Changes

They really hadn't had a shopping spree yet Monaco was a small item as it really isn't the place to shop far too expensive. It was a place to enjoy eating and gambling with a view to watch, people watching.

So little shops and some fine foods to be had, lunch was a family restaurant and something small but divine. French cuisine and they just shared with drinking water for the ladies the men a beer. Yes a good relaxing day and down to the sea. Bodies everywhere and they were so enjoying the people watching it was so interesting.

Their speedboat was waiting to take then to their boat. A relaxing day and a relaxing evening for them too, the chef has been busy cooking all day for them he was special.

They had their laughter together and the champagne under the stars looking to the moon that was soon to be full for them. The sea was calm and the glow of the moon on the sea was spectacular. The movement of their boat woke Helen up. "It's only 7.00am John and we are off to Cannes I am going to enjoy seeing the places that the stars go to.

John I do hope we have a lunch booked somewhere special or will it be dinner and lunch here on the boat, how should we spend the day in Cannes, and I am feeling amorous do you, will you, can we." Helen whispering in John's ear snuggling close while caressing his body, his movements showed that he was enjoying her touch.

Snuggling, caressing and kissing him so that he woke up gently and then replicated her embrace. Slowly Helen took herself under the cover. If this didn't wake him nothing would a movement of his hips as his hardness stood without his eyes being open. She took him very gently into her mouth and began to make him understand what it was that she wanted.

Slowly she got him to the point of an orgasm when she pulled away to the sound of. "Helen what are you doing down there, I thought I was going to wake up with a smile, come here and let me please you." John began pulling Helen out of the bed covers slowly bringing her up and on top of him as they both went into the passion to achieve the set goal.

It was a heavy session as after the first, there was another and again in the shower he pulled Helen in and kissed every part of her body before entering and satisfying her with as many orgasms as she could have.

Cannes loomed in the distance as they both were drinking coffee on the deck. The rest of the crew began to join them one by one. Breakfast and then they would dock before going on a tour of Cannes and lunch would be on their boat something light to eat and dinner was a dressy time and a great restaurant in St Tropez.

The film festival was the place they were looking for it needed to be experienced while they were in Cannes. Stepping onto dry land and walking along the promenade people watching, the different sizes, the no care attitude was there in fall. The love of oneself and how to do that, and not care what anybody thought about your body it took some sort of confidence to do what they are doing.

They travelled to the old town and onto the slopes of Mount Chevalier, there in front of them on parts of the old city wall could be seen and on Place de la Castre which is dominated by the Notre-Damede l'Esperance all the tourists places they quickly visited.

Restaurant Aux P'tits Anges 4 rue Marceau was their place for lunch. Helen loved looking at the menu and trying to work out the French. Languages do come in handy. It was a divine restaurant the décor was of pink and mauve it was very smart.

The menu was a dream so succulent. Speaking out aloud Helen ordered her Entrée. "La foie Gras Mi-cuit Cylindre Macaron et Chutney de Chataigne à la Vanille, home made duck foie gras in macaron chutney.

La Sole Desarette en Fillet Bonillon Reduit de gambas au Kaffir Legumes Sautes, roasted deboned Sole reduced King Prawn Sauce and sautée Vegetable. All good so far Helen thought. The dessert was a chocolat delight. Now to the eating and enjoying the wine was chosen by John and Robert they both had an acquired taste for wine.

Friends, Accepting the Changes

This certainly was a holiday of divine restaurants with food to die for, wine to cherish and love to enjoy.

Back to the boat and sailing to St Tropez it wouldn't take too long. They would just enjoy the sun and the champagne. The view as they arrived was breath taking it was so colourful and quaint taking into consideration that it was a tourist attractions they had been to it was nice to see something off the old France not developed too much. Here they would have dinner and sail again to Marseilles.

La Vague d'Or was the restaurant that was attached to the hotel it used to be called La Pinede. Dinner in dinner suits a dressy time. Their table booked, it was dusk and they chose a table that had a view of the sea the lights in the distance as they were slowly beginning to shine one after the other. A table for eight and it would be a set menu. It was An Epicurean Adventure and they had chosen five courses (acts) for the price of 325 euros a snip of a price. Helen's winnings in Monaco gave them the money to splash out and enjoy.

Wine was being paired with the food by the head waiter, it was all too divine. They were certainly being spoilt here. They view as the dusk became night was amazing, the finished the night with the coffee, chocolat e brandy just to soak the energy. And the chatter was mainly French, Sarah and Anton had decided this would be the night that Anton asked for Sarah's hand in marriage. So our Sarah left St Tropez with a rock of her own shinning on her finger.

Friends, Accepting the Changes

Back at the boat the champagne was open and the celebrating had begun. The boat set sailing for Marseilles for breakfast they will certainly need a heavy breakfast as the celebrating would and did carry on until they docked into Marseilles harbour and it was named "The Gateway to the Orient" the entrance to the harbour of Marseilles was like a picture an old picture.

They would walk to the old harbour which was seized by the romans and became the gateway to the west for most oriental trade. It was like walking into that time a picture of France. Musee des Docks, Romains and the Musee d'Histore de Marseilles they were now venturing into.

They had a late breakfast/lunch at La Table a Deniz 63 rue Sainte it was again a family run restaurant French Cuisine of course as this was the last restaurant in France as they would be sailing onto Capri and Sicily. They all would now relax and enjoy the cruising.

They pulled the anchor up and then sailed away into the sea watching the lights of Marseilles' disappear in the distance it was a poignant moment as they were leaving France for Italy. The lights became dark and they retired to bed all snuggled up and excitingly waiting for the morning as they would be nearing the harbour Marina Grande stay there for a few days to enjoy the exploring of Capri.

Marina Grande was in view it was the main port for Capri all the ferries from Naples came here and other ports came to his part of the Tyrrhenian coastline. There was an array of very colourful houses overlooked the harbour, the rainbow colours made Helen smile. Helen was the colour of the rainbow and also wearing what colour she wanted.

She remembered the time when men played games with colours pink for one man, red for another, blue for another, then black and white and keeping to neutral colours as white was all the colours in an open sense and black was all the colours in a hidden sense could she keep these idiots off her back. The world and its idiots thank goodness she had John now, no game playing with him.

Coming into port was wonderful it was so warm and everybody on the cruise agreed that they loved the Italian people they were friendly to the English. Food with good wine was called for and the Italians knew how to dine in style. Capri had the beauty and reputation as a sybaritic paradise it is nearly eclipsed by the notoriety as a tourist trap.

However this view is unmarred by the throng. And it was also the home of the Emperors, seat of monasteries and a place of exile, the future of Capri changed in the 19th century and then the German expatriates discovered its charms. It doesn't seem to have a low season farmers run little hotels and fishermen rent pleasure boats. Capri enjoys its well-deserved reputation as the 'The Garden of Eden'. They would all enjoy Capri.

Friends, Accepting the Changes

They disembarked and found a café' for coffee and an Italian cake. The Italian made some wonderful cakes and remembering the time that Helen had in Sicily enjoying the wonderful cakes with her friends. Now she was back in Italy to enjoy the scenery and the food. Sarah and Anton were in each-others pockets holding hand no one being able to separate them.

Sarah looked towards Kate and Helen questioning their smiles. "You two look like Cheshire cats what's up with you two. Anton and I will be going back to the boat after lunch for a nap." Sarah began smiling herself she was so happy yes it was at last good to see.

Kate answered in her normal was straight and to the point. "Sarah how lovely it is to see you in love and getting married soon. Helen my friend are we going to be visiting your church while we are here as I feel we should do a little bit of memory jolting don't you?" Kate looked toward Helen questioning her was always prevalent as Helen could see all having the gift she had.

"I am sure that we are going to the highest point of Capri we can drive around and see everything we want and then we will go off to Marina Piccola Kate as there is a beautiful restaurant there Restaurante Da Tonino via Denlecala." Helen always looking to the best she enjoyed good food and of course especially decent wine she wasn't a drinker she just enjoyed the taste of a good wine.

Friends, Accepting the Changes

Their night here in the main port was off looking for what they wanted, buying and enjoying the local food. The morning would be to explore inland and get to the point of the views across and towards Naples they were also going to see Capri's second town Anacapri it was a tourist's view of the island.

Kate and Helen watch Sarah slip away while they all were enjoying lunch near the water. Laura noticed what they were doing and quickly questioned where they were going. "Sarah hunni are to off to get a room, do you want some sex and we are in the way when we are all on the boat." Sarah just waved and carried on walking she wasn't going to get into the sex of the group.

Climbing on board both Sarah and Anton were safely in their room just opening a bottle of wine so that they could enjoy the view out of the port hole. "It's such a beautiful island Anton I find it so relaxing." She jumped into the shower and washed all that she needed satisfying. Her under regions were clean.

Slipping beside Anton as he too disappeared to the bathroom expecting some good sex slipping into the bed the top sheet flung away to reveal the clean crisp sheet to allow their bodies to enjoy the moment.

Anton now allowing himself to enjoy Sarah's body kisses her breasts and beginning to enjoy every part he could get to and her breast stood tall, and her nibbles erect with pleasure. He moved lower and lower until he had Sarah reeling with pleasure how he knew what she wanted and needed the pleasure was all hers for the taking. Receive she did.

Her back arched to accept more of what he was offering. He then slipped into her like she was waiting for this moment, the warm moist place felt his penis enter and as he did he just stopped for a moment before he began to enjoy her and Sarah felted his moments were of pleasure divine pleasure his motions were slow and then too quicken as they both came to an orgasm together, slowing of the gentle motions.

Sarah had waited for this. She kept her noise to the minimum normally not to annoy the other passengers but today she expressed her emotions and yes she enjoyed every minute of it.

They enjoyed their dinner at Restaurante Terrazza Brunella on via Tragana24. Helen ordered for her Antipasta she choose Salmone affumicato con semi di papavero her Prima Piatti Helen ordered Ravioli de Farro con cozze e fiori di zucca and the courses were numerous, Secondi Piatti Salmone el vapore con patate el profumo zafferano con Asparagi all' agro, to the Dessert was of a Selezione di dolci della casa (per due) so John joined her in Dessert.

And an Italian red many bottles too enjoy. Then the day became night and the night became morning as they were sailing to Marina Piccola and Anacapri stopping off at the Grotto Azzurraor or known as the Blue Grotto.

Friends, Accepting the Changes

They had arrived at the blue grotto and jumping into the small boats the men took them through the cave bathed in indecent blue light, it was so healing, so beautiful. Helen then imagined the blue engulfing her body and took herself into a meditation. The colour streamed through the light divine. They came out feeling sorelaxed and happy.

Tonight they would be dinning at the Restaurante De Tonino via Denlecala 15 in the Marina Piccola. Nicely placed the views were beautiful, they ordered everything they needed and each dish came so well presented and also tasted like heaven. If this was heaven they all said we should stay here and it also felt so much like the paradise they were expecting to find in this beautiful island. Happy people they all were.

There were Chocolates for dessert and this was Helen's idea of heaven anyway. Enjoying their time in Marina Piccola sitting until the restaurant shut their doors the ambiance was so refreshing and so relaxing, the Italian food came with the Italian experience and hospitality that they give.

Leaving for a brief stay in Ischia just to stop at thermal springs and the therapeutic mud baths, the volcanic mixtures is believed to be the most radioactive in Europe and is good for a variety of health treatment it would be good for Helen's knee as being knocked over by a van it had damaged her knee, she knew when she needed help as the bone ached.

Friends, Accepting the Changes

They would venture to Poseidon and enjoy the thermal pools and the mud baths were good for the skin. Coming away from there meant that they had the most wonderful skin and relaxed.

Their last journey was to Sicily and only to Palermo as time was moving on and they all needed to return to work. Helen and John had found an apartment in Palermo they would stay there and visit the Opera house to watch Carmen, and then onto one of the best restaurant in town.

Helen was introduced to it year before. In Via Trepani The Restaunte Regine was the best and the doors were closed so feeling safe was on top of the list. Would Helen ever see her Italian friends again, should she make the effort to see her Italian friends again that she would decide and bring it forward when she felt like a trip on her own.

Sicily is the most beautiful island and is worth a visit. Helen found her friends were accommodating to her needs she had enjoyed her trip with Kate, Laura and Sarah, they also connected well with each-others partners which was the best. John, Robert, David and Anton had all got the thumbs up from all the girls. Also looking forward to Sarah and Anton marriage later in the year it was a joy in itself at last she would be happy.

Laura moved in with her David and their business grew for them to become the millionaires they so wanted, Kate and Robert enjoyed each-other and eventually married they worked well together joining a charity and giving the expertise they had.

Friends, Accepting the Changes

Helen and John grew and enjoyed life wherever their home was. Helen wrote so many books and came away from the pressures of being a psychic medium she still had her connections for herself and her writing.

Chapter Thirteen
The Fun, The Learning, The Love and The Peace

The contract that Helen had signed with the Angels and Masters was in her mind, and being pushed by the Angels to earth to fulfill that contract she had signed, Helen from fighting for her life when she was born really did not want all them lessons, yes maybe Helen had asked for a challenging path but she was sure that she hadn't asked for a hard road, in those lessons Helen knew she needed to grow.

Looking back at her whole life of learning, the fun Helen had in her years of being herself, the love she received with her children, grandchildren and her friends. The Peace she has now found with her Angels, looking back to the years as a child with the knowing she was there for a great purpose, she was left at the doors of a children's home to find that the bullying from then continued throughout her life until she stopped it.

The Matron had an envy of a small girl who was so special, could she see the child that sat reading in the corner, the child forever on her own, the child that smiled even though she was being hit, being abused, this child would not fight back, she stayed so calm, a child from heaven, did she know the child was a heavenly Angel.

She knew this little girl had something that she could not

control that she did not like at all, she had a knowing, a peace, trying to knock it out of her would do no good, it would serve no purpose, this child had a purpose and that was to love she was the love of The Rainbow Lady, her life's purpose, the peaceful dove.

Even to the fact of the first husband and the envy still there in his sisters and mother, Helen worked through that and left when she knew there was nothing to recapture, having her three children Mark, Simon and Harri which taught her the love and to show her how to love unconditionally.

The second husband, who was the hardest lesson for her to come to terms with, he spent his money on drink, then spending Helen's money too, never again would she keep a man, the envy of the mother, the ex-wife and the step daughters and Helen was again learning about the hate in life, to find that in the greatest envy of her and the way she was.

Her second husband wanted Helen for the class and a girlfriend for him that Helen would not put up with, so beginning her book was his move out of the door, the Angels had finally taken him out of her life as he just would not leave.

Helen handed Roger over to the young police woman there was not a tear but a smile of delight as she began her new life. Her twin soul to come, her learning of life was a lesson to learn and it amounted to the heaviest lesson in life that she had to endure. The men and women of a town who could not understand and really did not want to understand, the love, the peace, the power, the fun, the Angels they mocked, listening to Helen telling her Granddaughter that birds are Angels, a lesson to learn, her life was so full of her lessons, she had been sent to Wivenhoe to show them her power and they abused her.

Colchester too and again Cumbria then to find Jerez, Calahonda and Mijas Spain the same games and the men and women who loved to play, it was a great lesson for them to learn and soon their lessons would begin.

Her life was now no more lessons, her life was now full of peace and her purpose in life has now begun. Helen has moved on to all good lessons, the lessons of life, the lessons of love and the heart that is always open to love, Helen thought to herself What Fun I am an Angel, The Friends all had come to the acceptance of life move on and they all had their own life's now but they would enjoy holidays together and an occasional weekend of fun.

So to the fun in life, that is what we are all here to have, she learned that when she was alone in her life she was to make it fun with the Angels, learning, working and resting, when she had her friends around her they found that Helen is sometimes open, and sometimes closed.

Three books published Friends, The Journey, New beginnings & Endings. The sequel Friends, The Acceptance of Changes and Ambiance a book of poems Helen was now an accomplished Author she was happy.

She learned in her later years that fun is a great part of life and the biggest part so she enjoyed. Her friends she had been given from the universe to enjoy brought fun to her life, with the pain came laughter it was to find the whole solution of she could not give a shit, her clients she instilled empowerment and for them to see life as a method of growth.

Having fun was part of it, you start by learning to love life to the full, to have fun is not to be heavily drunk, you can have fun and laughter, remember fun means that addictive substance doesn't have to be used.

Addiction is no fun at all. She had learned that by her son Mark the addiction of alcohol and watching him pass was the hardest lesson to learn, the grieve which she was going through while the games were being played, mind games can be mentally destroying to a weak person but Helen was and is strong in mind, body and soul, with the police watching even joining in the mind games.

For what, why and there were many questions to be answered, she was totally shocked by it all her sons wife who controlled, but no more having decided to be free from rubbish, as life was so dammed short to put up with shit.

The love of oneself is the love of others, when we learn to love ourselves and to love what we see. To look into the mirror and like what you find is the greatest love of all. And once we have achieved that, then we can move on to the greatest love a Twin Soul in life is to be the love forever more, a love divine, a love that is mine, it comes from the heavens, they hand out the Twin Souls.

Helen had found all the love she needed she would not have to worry about leaving this behind and Helen's greatest moto is To Receive is to Give and this is the greatest lesson in love, enjoy the love of receiving, as receiving is a joy for the giver and the lesson for you to be loved and protected.

The peace is to find that there in the heavens are the heavenly laws, written in the Rainbows, in Clouds, in Birds, they speak as they find, watch and listen, the Birds, the Rainbows are Angels themselves will tell you what is happening in your world, when there is no rain to be seen or felt and a Rainbow is to say that the Angels are watching over you and will keep you safe. The Clouds also talk in picture look to see what they say and a Feather is an Angel.

The pictures in the sky, most people watch as they travel by, and not a thought to the other side of the world, take a moment to sit, take a moment to look, take a moment to watch as the Heavenly world that looks at you and talks to you. So to see what life brings in a whole life, the lessons to learn, the fun of life, in life we have fun.

All the love that is given from the universe is to set you free, all the love you give is the love to be free. The peace is in finding a world in love, trust, faith and patience. In finding the peace within, is to find the peace of the world and Helen knew she was there to bring peace to the children who were lost in their own little worlds, teach the children for they will teach the world to always love and to be understanding.

Helen knew whatever she said people would listen and do what is needed of them. An inspiration to all, the strength of her lessons, she thought she would not be able to reach her heights because of mindless games but the Universe, the Heavens secured her life in the looking back and her life is to look forward to the now, the moment and now to the future of love and joy in all that she done. A breath of fresh air that she was, Helen in her life's purpose now beginning, her joy was heaven sent forever.

Chapter Fourteen
Angels, Masters, The Divine Love.

To the Masters; the highest order next to God, The Seraphim the highest order of Angels close to God, that shine so bright as they are pure light, The Cherubim's; are cupids the second highest order to God, they are Pure Love. The Thrones; are the bridge between the material and the spiritual they are God's fairness and justice. The Dominions; are the overseers, the managers of the Angels all are according to God's will.

The Virtues; too whom they all govern the Universe, the moon, the sun, the stars and all the other planets in the Universe. Powers; the peaceful warriors and to the lower energies of the world they purify. Principalities; these Angels ensure God's will of peace to all on earth. Archangels; are the humankind overseers their specialty's each represents an aspect of God. Guardian; Angels, all of us have a personal Guardian Angel which walks with us from birth to death.

The Angels and Masters are there to help us with our life's don't question are they there open your heart to the love of the universe and the universe will return their love to you. As Helen came to finish her book in the comfort and peace of Spain she knew that in her finding the last chapter it would have to take her up there in the astral traveling and back to the heavens to meet the higher powers who have helped her throughout her life and then to the completion of her book, complete, then to find another book they wanted, they never stopped asking for more, this one would be challenging and researching and we all like a challenge.

She was writing to find not only Archangel Michael standing watching but Archangel Gabriel entered the room as well, the room soon became full of the heavenly beings, she watched as one by one they bowed then stood in front of her the work she had done for them, the pain she taken for them, her new work now beginning, the years of patience had brought her to the place she was in.

Helen felt humbled by the presence of the Masters and all the powers of the heavens, her room then tuned into heaven itself, normally she would be called to them, this time they made the journey to visit her, how she felt blessed at that purpose and love. Mother Mary came to her she smiled as she touched Helen's hand, she felt so soft.

Whispering to her she said. "Helen you now know your life's purpose but in your hard work you will also have the love from the man we have given you and the love from us.

We still have many books for you to write and many journeys for you to take but in your visions of the world, the future you will be loved for who and what you are as well as what you do. Helen you now have your peace, you now have your own love.

Friends, Accepting the Changes

Go and be happy, we are grateful for all your work that you have given for us, we will always be here." Stepping aside Mother Mary was nodding with a smile, Helen knew then that was where she came from, she was Mother Mary and was now doing the work she did not fulfill in her time.

Jesus was looking towards the door it was closed, but as they all looked to the door it opened, the heavens had made all what she needed come to her, she was the strength, the power, the peace and the love this mass of glowing aura's, all the colours of the rainbows, it was so immense it filled the whole room with heavenly love.

Helen looked around at all the spiritual beings that were there the Archangels, and Masters, there seem to be so many beings in one small room. The figure moved closer, she felt the aura its power moved with a glow slowly as a glide the figure stood beside her.

"You are the chosen one you are the peacemaker for us I am your follower our words will be heard in many countries far and wide. Helen you are the Ambassador of Heaven, take the word of peace, look after the children you blessed our Helen you are the truth and love."

As he came to a stop beside Helen she knew straight away she had just spoken to the higher spirit, he stood close to her, his aura healed every part of her, all the pain of life was gone in a second, all his love had engulfed her, the heavenly realms rejoiced in such glory. Helen was part of the heavens, the universe, she had been given unlimited powers to go forth and use them in all ways. As they all waved then disappeared one by one she felt they had left heaven behind in her room, to Helen this was the power of the love of life. She watched and sat in amazement as she had been chosen to win the world with love and peace.

Finishing the last page of the book, Helen now felt that in her writing achievements she was there to help others. To win such love, the love of the world and in closing the final chapter, it was closing a part of her life she would now be sent around the world to help with the peace of the children and the peace of women.

The pain of each child she would take on as her own, the pain of each woman she would make stronger she would empower in an inspirational way. This was it and keeping her feet firmly on the ground Helen felt that she had won the moon, sun and stars.

All look to the love in your hearts, the love that sets you free from pain, the love that lets you grow over and over again. The love within the world that now has to shine with peace and love from the divine. Bring to you my Angels, bring to you the peace of the love, of life that I have within your heart, open it to me and make us all grow together in the divine light of the heavens.

And May Peace always be with you, may love stay in your heart always and forever. Take care Helen xxxx

23023139R00245

Printed in Great Britain
by Amazon